Spinella
NORTH KINGSTOWN FREE LIBRARY
P9-DJU-652
30073003767226

Unstrung

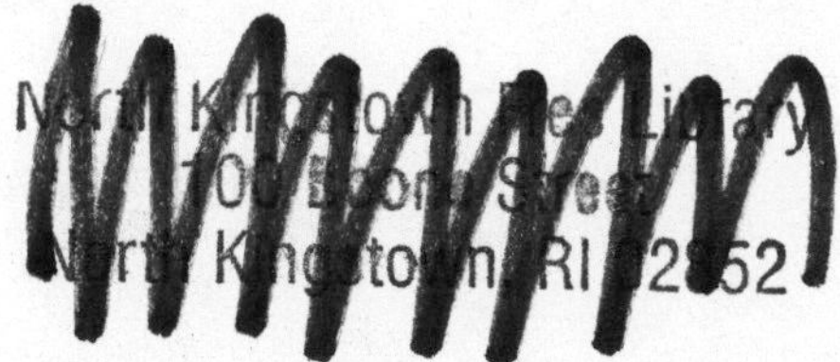
North Kingstown Free Library
North Kingstown, RI

OTHER TITLES BY LAURA SPINELLA

Ghost Gifts

Perfect Timing

Beautiful Disaster

Writing as L. J. Wilson, the Clairmont series

Ruby Ink

The Mission

Unstrung

LAURA SPINELLA

This is a work of fiction. Names, characters, organizations, places, events, and incidents are either products of the author's imagination or are used fictitiously.

Published by Montlake Romance, Seattle

www.apub.com

ISBN-13: 9781503937352
ISBN-10: 1503937356

Cover design by Adil Dara

Printed in the United States of America

This novel is dedicated to Melisa Marian Holmes.
For showing Southern hospitality to the Yankee girl,
whistling the theme to the Andy Griffith Show after
hours, and having endless "conversations that matter,"
especially the ones that inspired this book.

LWS

CHAPTER ONE

Suffolk County Court

Boston, Massachusetts

Olivia

Sasha nudges me. Not only am I to move my head—propped on ink-stained fingers—I'm to stand. Following her lead, I rise and squint at the judge, a dour-looking man cloaked in black. He moves with condemning authority. My hazy gaze registers pilgrim.

Burn the witch!

It reverberates across three hundred years and into this modern-day courtroom. A baritone voice announces Judge Nicholson. Gravity dominates and I begin a slow sink into the chair. Sasha grabs my arm. "No, no . . . no, Liv. Don't sit." I've never noticed the grating tone of Sasha's voice—a woefully out-of-tune E string. Slapping my hands on the table, I thrust upward. Good thing the fingers are insured. I jerk my arm from Sasha's grip. I need legal counsel, not corporeal support. I can stand on my own two feet. I've been doing so for forty-six years. The judge hammers his gavel like a blacksmith on steroids. Mercy would be a direct hit to the head.

"Could you please not do that?" I ask.

"Pardon?" His eyes match all his narrowness.

"The gavel—must you? I'm erect. What more do you want?"

"Miss Pease," he says, addressing my best friend, who at the moment is dressed as my attorney. "The Starbucks your client frequents may not have opened yet, but even at this early hour she continues to test the law." He glances at some papers. "Disturbing the peace, possession of a dangerous weapon, malicious destruction of property, and resisting arrest. It will pale compared to the charges she's already facing, but if she likes, I have no issue holding her in contempt as well."

"Absolutely not, Your Honor. Our apologies to the court. Mrs. Van Doren has had an incredibly upsetting night."

"Pffft . . ." I breathe, stealing a backward glance at Rob, who is the lone spectator in the galley. "The only incredibly upsetting part is that I didn't smash the taillights on his Porsche before the cops showed up."

Sasha juts an elbow into my side. "Liv, shut up." The remnants of a half-dozen gin martinis slosh about my stomach. I press the back of my hand to my mouth and nod; speaking isn't an option.

"Mrs. Van Doren, are you going to be . . ." the judge asks. I nod more fervently. He points to the baritone bailiff. Like a knight in shining armor, he whisks a metal trash can from across the room to under my nose. The retching echoes as it would in any hollow castle. "Get her some water, please."

A different courtroom worker delivers a water-filled paper cup. I sip a mouthful and grasp the bailiff's arm as he attempts to retract the trash can. Rinsing, I spit into the receptacle. "What?" I say to the bailiff, who looks at me as though I've spit on Lady Justice. "Like it's not already a trash can full of vomit?" He backs away. I turn toward Sasha and spin back to the bailiff. "Thank you." I have manners, they just have so very little to do with my life.

"Miss Pease, can your client proceed in a civil manner? Or perhaps spending the remainder of the weekend in lockup would give her perspective."

"No, Judge Nicholson. Again, our apologies."

I lean into Sasha and whisper, "Is his name really Jack Nicholson?" Another jab comes via Sasha's elbow. She's *so* going to hear about that later. "Right. I'm good," I volunteer. I want this over with. I take a cleansing breath and state my case: "Yes. I absolutely beat the shit out of my husband's Porsche with a baseball bat."

A *looks could kill* glare darts from me to Rob. One arm is slung over the chair beside him, his fingers tapping as a rhythmic unit. Fascinating—visible nerves from my cool-to-the-core husband.

"Liv," Sasha repeats. "Just don't say anything." Her flawlessly aligned teeth are tightly gritted. I peer hard at the near ventriloquist feat. I should probably take a hint and be her cooperative puppet.

It's not in me.

"I'm sorry," I announce to her and Judge Nicholson. "I didn't realize we were questioning the part about me bashing the Porsche with a Louisville Slugger."

Honestly, by the time the cops showed up, I doubt a junkyard compactor could have done a better job. I'm nothing if not thorough.

The judge looks curiously from me to Sasha. "Were we, Miss Pease? Going to debate Mrs. Van Doren's actions on the evening of September 8?"

Sasha sighs and closes her eyes. "No, but . . ." she continues, rallying the war cry that makes her a hell of a best friend, "there are extreme extenuating circumstances. Unbeknownst to Mrs. Van Doren, Mr. Van Doren used her family home in Wellesley, entrusted to her by her late father, for collateral. With the failure of Mr. Van Doren's latest business venture, it means she'll lose the home. And her mother—"

My mother . . . Now we're getting somewhere. Although Eugenia Klein is, by far, the lesser mitigating fact linked to this evening.

"Is counsel under the impression I was being anything but sarcastic? Have the rules of law changed? Is it your assumption that I'm going to entertain 'extenuating circumstances'"—the judge places air quotes around the phrase—"during an arraignment?"

"No, Your Honor," Sasha says with a demureness I would never tack to her. Yet she's so willing to rush to my aid. If they recast Wonder Woman, she'd get the part hands down.

I turn toward her. "Why the fuck aren't there more women superheroes? That's just wrong."

"Liv," she says again, her jaw as stiff as cut glass.

The judge ignores me. "As it stands," he says, "I'm certain Mrs. Van Doren will regale the court thoroughly on her appointed date." His practiced gaze shifts to me. "The beauty of the weighty wheels of justice, ma'am. It gives you time to rehearse and craft." He slips glasses to the end of a nose so pointed I'm thinking about woodpeckers. Maybe Jack Nicholson cast as a woodpecker. Judge Nicholson reads from desktop papers. "Ergo, by the appointed date, I'm sure the defendant will have counsel convinced she was arrested while holding a Q-tip, not a baseball bat. Certainly not while assaulting a $90,000 vehicle, aggravating circumstance by demanding that the responding officers . . ." The judge clears his throat. "Let me read directly from the report . . . The alleged perpetrator said, *'Super. You brought guns. What's the going rate for shooting asshole husbands? And do you take credit cards?'*"

My head clears as the visuals crystalize. If someone was documenting Olivia Klein Van Doren bad behaviors, this might make the top ten. I chew on a thumbnail. Sasha sighs again.

"Miss Pease, I suggest you come at this with your plea-bargain tools honed and ready. Based on Mrs. Van Doren's in-court behavior, I'm inclined to go with the DA's charges. Since the Porsche is only registered in her husband's name, those charges include malicious destruction of property, disturbing the peace, and so on . . ." Judge Nicholson speaks to the Huckleberry Finn DA seated next to us. He hasn't uttered a word and continues to scribble on a legal pad. No doubt he's comparing the charges with fresh-from-law-school crib notes. "Does the State wish to add anything else?"

"No, Your Honor. I mean yes."

I roll my eyes.

"The State is willing to set bail at $25,000."

"Your Honor, Mrs. Van Doren is a respect—well, a longtime resident of the Back Bay community." Sasha yanks the lapels of her stylish suit. She's remarkably put together for the crack of dawn. I rub my hands over the thighs of dirty slacks while trying to hold a torn pocket in place. I'm guessing public vomiting and my appearance don't scream *Back Bay resident*, an elite edge of Boston brownstones that most people pass by to daydream about. "Aside from her prominent, permanent address," Sasha says, "Mrs. Van Doren is a professional violinist. She's an extremely gifted musician." I sling back my neck, wishing Sasha hadn't brought that up. Apparently she thinks it's a plus. Maybe it is; it's hard to tell. My relationship with music—well, it's in worse shape than the Porsche. Sasha goes on, "Clearly, this was a singular . . . uh, unusual, private domestic issue that unfortunately turned public."

Is she nuts? I never realized what a cool liar Sasha is. In the past year, *domestic issues* have become more of a staple than a quart of milk in our brownstone. Yet, Sasha continues to spew accolades.

"Her professional commitments alone guarantee that Mrs. Van Doren should be released on her own recognizance." That part's true. Thanks to my husband, I'm not in a position to abandon a stable income. I glance at Rob. The judge raises his hand, and Sasha immediately ceases and desists.

"Olivia Van Doren . . ." But as he reads from some papers, his narrow look widens. He smiles. "You're Olivia Klein, violinist with the New England Symphony?"

On the other hand, when thrust into the spotlight . . . "Yes, Your Honor." I'm not a household name. But in the right circle, I have rock-star status. Apparently Judge Nicholson knows the circle. I run my fingers through my hair, prepared to gracefully accept inbound compliments. Or as gracefully as one can with drying vomit on the ends.

He sits up taller, as if suddenly in the presence of greatness. "I'm a tremendous connoisseur of the arts—music, art, the ballet." I nod in solidarity—as if violinists spend off-hours scouring museums and dining on . . . well, *air* with ballerinas. "If I'd only had the skill to . . ." He clenches silent what are surely pained words about never progressing beyond third-chair, high-school-musician status. His gaze returns to me. "I'm afraid my only talent is listening, an acute appreciation for the fine arts. Music in particular."

I never would have guessed . . .

"My wife, Conchetta, and I have been season ticket holders to the New England Symphony for more than twenty years."

I smile admiringly. "Is that right?" What are the odds? A judge who covets symphony tickets more than box seats at Fenway Park. Perhaps he'd like an upgrade to the gallery balcony? A glance at Sasha says I shouldn't make the offer.

His expression changes, and he points his gavel at me. "But the reason I know your name is because I saw it in *Musical Notes.*" I nod at Judge Nicholson's reference to the highbrow, online journal that covers New England's finer musical offerings. Orchestra mates subscribe. I avoid. He taps his gavel lightly, as if recalling specifics—perhaps a review of the ensemble recital given at the governor's mansion last spring. Even I admit it was a stellar moment. But from the obvious knot of anger that is his face, I'd say we're not recalling the same *fine arts* experience. "The article, it was about the Sotheby's auction of your Amati violin."

Shit. The gig at the governor's mansion would have been a much cleaner talking point. "Uh, that's correct, Your Honor." Quickly, I craft strategy. This can play to my advantage, maybe get the charges dropped. "How impressive that you noticed," I say, coaxing tears. Sasha twists toward me; her face contorts to a confounded look. "I'm afraid the sale of the Amati was a cruel necessity. Before tonight, that incident was my husband's only financial catastrophe. It came as quite a shock to me. And the Amati, as painful a sacrifice as it was—"

"If I recollect from the article, the instrument was a gift from your father on your sixteenth birthday. Is that right?"

"Yes. It is." I sniff at his photographic memory, which prods a vague recall of the article. I didn't actually read it. Sasha summarized the story when it ran: a dozen intense bidders, the vintage Amati going for a cool $600K. It was $50K over what I'd anticipated. I paid off Rob's debt and bought a case of Cristal with some of the surplus. As for the rest—I did what I always do with extra dividends. But that's not the story Judge Nicholson needs to hear right now. "Years ago, in light of my gift, in hopes that I'd attend the Boston Conservatory . . . well, *Daddy* only wanted me to have the very best. He treasured the Amati—almost as much as me." I briefly close my eyes, forcing down a slight surge of vomit.

"But the article, it said you didn't graduate from the Conservatory."

"Uh . . . no," I admit. "It wasn't a good fit. I transferred to the Manhattan School of Music."

Satisfied with the mention of the Conservatory's rival school, he looks back at the paperwork. His constricted gaze shoots back up. "And so you earned your degree in music there, at the Manhattan School of Music?" My mouth gapes at his anticipative outcome. The judge shuffles in his high seat. "I see. Not a good fit either. Is that correct, Mrs. Van Doren?"

I note that I am no longer Olivia Klein, New England Symphony violinist. "Uh, not quite. Again, not the right atmosphere for me." He waits. "But after that I was accepted into UNC School of the Arts. It's in Winston-Salem . . . North Carolina." I say this assuming he cannot recognize culture beyond Connecticut. "UNC, it's an excellent program too."

"From which you finally graduated."

"No. Not exactly." My teeth are clenched. The demand to know pisses me off. In fact, any mention of North Carolina pisses me off. I shake my head, which now throbs from the fresh smack of ancient history.

Sasha comes to my aid. "Your Honor, is this really relevant to Mrs. Van Doren's current circumstance?"

Judge Nicholson stares as if I'm being arraigned for homicide. His tiny eyes cut to Sasha. "You're not without a point, counselor."

"Just to add . . ." I say.

"Don't add anything," Sasha hisses.

Too late. "Since Your Honor is such a connoisseur of the arts, I'm sure you appreciate the challenge involved in earning a chair as a violinist with a major symphony." He nods, apparently aware of the grueling three-day ordeal, whereby symphony applicants are listened to via blind audition—you're not even allowed to wear shoes, which might indicate gender, onto the partitioned stage. About two in two hundred violinists make the last round of cuts. Only one is awarded the coveted available chair. "Just so you know, I earned my place with the symphony sans degree, on my first audition."

"Personal history speaks to your talent." He looks between the papers on his desk and me. "As well as your inability to follow the law, which you may wish to note is not a suggestion."

Judge Nicholson removes his glasses and taps them on the desk. "Your counsel is correct, Mrs. Van Doren. While irrelevant to this proceeding, I just happened to recall the article about the sale of the Amati. Such a coveted, beautiful instrument. It made an impression on me."

Excellent. A chance to regain his sympathies. "I was under a great deal of duress at the time." I glance back at Rob. He does his best to avoid eye contact, inspecting cracks in the courtroom ceiling. "It nearly crushed me, parting with the Amati—a sacred piece of musical history." A breath shudders from my belly as I swipe at a tear. "Then tonight, when I learned that my husband lost my family home to—"

Judge Nicholson holds up his hand. "The reason I recall the article, Mrs. Van Doren, is your quote in *Musical Notes*."

"Was I quoted?" I glance at Sasha, whose head has bowed, her delicate cheeks ballooning with air.

"Yes. Something to the effect of 'I told my husband to take it . . . sell it . . . burn it . . . whatever.' Said you 'never wanted the damn thing in the first place.'" My fragile smile crumbles like Rob's latest investment deal. The judge continues. "While I'm surely paraphrasing, it's the type of callous remark that sticks in the craw of a true music lover. But by all means, I'm a fair man." He leans back in his high leather chair, brushing his hand through courtroom air. "Tell me if *Musical Notes* fabricated a slanderous remark for the sake of sensational content."

I dip toward Sasha and whisper, "Am I, like, under oath here or anything?" She doesn't reply, rubbing two fingers across her forehead.

"I, uh . . . It's not that simple, Judge. You don't—"

Sasha interrupts. "Your Honor, my client is here for an arraignment based on the incident stemming from the evening of September 8, not—with all due respect—to have her character judged."

He holds up a hand. "It pains me to say it, Miss Pease, but you are correct." Sasha relaxes a bit, though it hardly stops him from sharing his opinion. "However, this is my courtroom." He smiles. "Aside from your client's careless disregard for an instrument that is a revered piece of art, her admitted conduct this evening proves her character could benefit from a modicum of judgment, perhaps some advice." He looks directly at me. "When you return here, Mrs. Van Doren, know that overprivileged attitudes won't be tolerated. Not the kind that takes for granted a God-given gift or callously sells a coveted Amati like it's a garage sale fiddle."

The word *fiddle* sinks into my ears, triggering a full-blown eruption of ancient history. *"Come on, Livy . . . Grab your fiddle and play me something fun . . ."* I close my eyes; the smell of Kentucky Clear is sudden and strong, so is Sam's voice.

Judge Nicholson interjects; the visuals vanish like dying fireflies.

"Clearly you were an overindulged child, who grew into an entitled adult. One who sees it as acceptable to destroy property like a common hoodlum, blaming others for her behavior." He pauses to offer Rob a sympathetic glance. "May I suggest some serious introspection before returning here? Perhaps an anger management class. Work past whatever it is in life that has turned you into, exactly . . ." He looks me up and down. *"This."*

That's it. I won't be judged. Not by a man who is the most abhorrent garden-variety elitist snob—an *admitted* talentless wannabe. "You know what?" I take a formidable step toward the judge. The bailiff takes one too. "Go fuck yourself, Jack Nicholson. Parting with a hunk of wood that came with more strings attached to it than an entire violin section has nothing to do with how awful I turned out." It's said with more clarity than anything I've uttered so far. But as I lunge forward, the stiff arm of the bailiff impedes any progress. "Superior, presumptive jerk!" I say, flailing about. The next thing I know, I am physically subdued and cuffs are clamped around my wrists. I don't look at Rob or Sasha as two bailiffs usher me out of the courtroom. But I do glance back, speaking to anyone who is listening. "You don't have the first clue why I turned out exactly like this."

CHAPTER TWO

Olivia

Something like a day and a half later, I wake up in my own bed. Rob's side is empty. I don't know if he's slept in it. I don't particularly care. He's probably out trying to glue his Porsche back together, maybe collecting the parts in a bucket off Newbury Street. Yesterday was Sunday and today isn't a rehearsal day. That's a good thing—though I am curious if my brush with the law has made its way back to New England Symphony brass, and I don't mean the horn section.

On the nightstand are two Excedrin and a glass of water. I see Remorseful Rob has been to my bedside, if not between the sheets. I shovel in the pills and gulp the water, which dribbles down my chin. I face-plant into the pillow, screaming bloody murder and kicking my feet like the spoiled child Judge Nicholson sent to a timeout. Mercifully, it had been a cell for one and I only had to use the toilet to pee. The food was inedible, making it easier to convince myself the whole thing was some trendy fast. By the time Sasha picked me up, I was hungry, dirty, and doubly pissed off. I specifically requested that she come instead of Rob. I wasn't ready for that showdown. I'm still not.

On the ride home and during a night in my own bed, I decided Judge Nicholson was right: I didn't give a fuck about the Amati. Technically, I sold it to save Rob's ass. Realistically, parting with it gave me perverse pleasure and a financial boon—money that could be put to better use. On the other end of that scale, surely the sale of the Amati left my father and the revered craftsman Nicolò Amati spinning in their graves. I never wanted the violin or the ability to play it like one of Nicolò's seventeenth-century apprentice virtuosos. Similar to Nicolò Amati, my parents had no son to inherit a stunning musical gift. Well, that's a lie. They have a son, my brother, Phillip. But luckily for Phillip he doesn't possess my father or Amati's ear for music—which is to say, in so many ways, he might as well not exist. It's a slight exaggeration, but not meritless. At the very least, Phillip's parental disappointments—abandoning life here to live abroad and his sexual orientation—can be swept under the rug. My transgressions are far more glaring.

Propped up on my elbows, I flex my delicate digits. When you tell people you're a violinist they immediately stare at your hands. Permanently ribbed fingertips show on the underside of mine; they are the dents most rarely seen. I reach for the phone and call Sasha. I hear, "Hey, Liv," and the Spice Girls in the background—Sasha's been on a nineties music binge.

She's in her car, en route. The peppy tune clashes with her voice, which sounds tense. Sasha informs me that while I paced a seven-by-ten box of introspection, she was schmoozing with the Peter Pan ADA. It's probably not something she planned on fitting into her Sunday. She says she'll fill me in when she gets here and hangs up. It's my hope she and Pete have been snorting serious fairy dust, reaching a plea bargain largely slanted in my favor.

Before getting out of bed, the clock radio catches my eye. In brightly bolded blue are the numbers—9-11. The annual date would cause anyone to look twice. For me, it evokes a frame of reference that surely differs from any other human being. I shake it off and pull on loose loungewear, ambling toward the first floor.

I love this house—one of the few tangible things I'd say that about. My address, the décor, would make you believe I'm into *stuff*—gratified by possessions. I'm honestly not a *stuff* person. I shop because it's Sasha's hobby, because Rob *is* gratified by possessions. As I descend the creaky but well-preserved steps, a twinge of sympathy nudges at me. If Rob needed collateral, I get why he put the Wellesley house at risk. If he'd used our brownstone, I would have taken the bat to his head. The Wellesley house was a twisted, if not careless, compromise.

Inside my music room—a small, sunny space that was once the front parlor—are pages of sheet music, among them *The Planets*, Gustav Holst's seven-movement orchestral suite. It was written between 1914 and 1916. As a child, the facts were drilled into me. Ironically, the music connects to the Wellesley Klein home. The story goes that it was the private setting for the American debut of the English composer's masterpiece. Holst and a few fellow musicians debuted the suite during a dinner party given by my great-great-aunt . . . or was it a distant cousin? Anyway, I've known the complex piece and the story about how it connects to the house my entire life. At the time, the stately property was owned by the American clique of Kleins. Closer relatives, including my grandfather, would not emigrate from Germany for another thirty years.

"Mars, the Bringer of War," sits on my music stand. How appropriate. Holst's suite is slated for the symphony's fall-winter schedule, and the first movement boasts a couple of rough sections that even Amati would have to practice. My current violin, an eighteenth century Guarneri, eyes me from across the room. I like it well enough with its darker sound, deeper tone. While the Amati looked smart in here, I never felt the jaw-rattling reverence Judge Nicholson or Gustav Holst would, certainly not my father.

No matter my reasons for parting with the Amati, my father would have only been appalled. Not surprised, but appalled. I pick up the Guarneri and pluck at a few strings. I'm a formidable musician, but my real talent is dodging my past. The violin is good for some things, and I aim for a quick fix. Snatching up the lesser instrument and bow, I fly into a furious attack of *The Planets*. I can detect a difference between the sound this instrument makes and the celebrated Amati. But frankly I'm good enough not to allow it to matter much. Only music purists, people like Mary Alice Porter, my symphony stand mate, would notice. She would have taken my father's side and nearly did pass out when she learned I auctioned off the Amati.

My bowing intensifies. It's not the music that soothes me, more the drowning of memories. Like a deep ocean, it swallows all disappointments—the ones connected to my father, and others that are not. I close my eyes and the past sinks to the bottom, where it belongs.

At first I don't hear the doorbell. I assume it's been buzzing a while because whoever is out there is leaning on it like a drunk on a wall. I put down the violin and head for the entry. While most brownstones have been converted into condos, ours was vertically divided into just two units, making it a rare single family gem—also a better example of Rob's financial prowess. It's too soon for Sasha, who said something about having to drop legal papers off to Nick Zowzer, her chief rival at McCluskey, Reingold & Schwab, and the largest thorn in her side. She loathes him; another hobby is casting him in every bad lawyer joke: "Hey, Zowz, do you know what would happen if a lawyer like you took Viagra? You'd get taller!"

In the foyer, my socked feet shuffle to a halt. I can make out the glob of a figure through the opaque glass. It's not Sasha. Not even close. I do an abrupt about-face, scurrying toward the stairs.

"Olivia!" I halt, my head drooping forward. "Do not even think about it. If I must, putting a potted plant through this glass is not beyond my resources—or mood."

I pivot on the herringbone hardwoods. Returning to the door, I repeat the mental prayer I do every time she turns up. *Dear God, please do not behold my future . . .* I flip the bolt and swing open the door. And every time, God answers with a belly laugh. Before me stands an aged looking-glass image. My mother's hair, while shorter, is chemically preserved to the same sable brown as mine, an oval face with bone structure that looks surgically tweaked. When I was a girl, she liked to show me off to her friends. Proof that her nose and chin come by her naturally. Her once full lips have collapsed like a puffed pastry into fine layered lines—years of cigarettes before cigarettes were no longer fashionable. We used to stand at exactly the same height, so I know that in my early sixties my five-foot-five frame will begin to shrink. Our similar glares have a volume all their own. Right now, hers is on full blast.

"What brings you here, Mom?" I ask cautiously. "Early for you on a Monday, isn't it?"

She glides by me and into the living room. As always, I check to make certain her feet are touching the floor—there is a presence to Eugenia Klein that defies human form. She pauses to twist a lampshade so its seam doesn't show. "I'll get right to the point," she says, turning. "Yesterday, I played bridge with Marjorie Levinson."

"Ah. And did you run right over here to tell me you actually bid a grand slam and made it! Are they sending you to a Vegas tournament?" She narrows her eyes. My mother would rather take a bus to Pittsburgh than go to Las Vegas under any circumstance.

"Hardly. I understand you had an interesting weekend, Olivia." I pin my hands behind my back and take a glancing inventory of the hardwoods. I neither confirm nor deny this. I need to know exactly what she knows. "According to Marjorie, it was quite the scene. Outrageous comportment I haven't witnessed from you in ages—certainly not since your years at UNCSA."

I bristle at the mention of the dedicated school for the arts. Like Judge Nicholson, her conclusion sparks my indignation. But unlike the judge, I've been sparring with her for a while now—four-plus decades. I stay on point. "So you've come to hear about my weekend firsthand."

Her stare is stoic. "I didn't assume you stormed over here to let me know that Marjorie Levinson is spreading vicious rumors about me."

"If only it were a remote possibility." She cocks her head in the opposite direction of mine. "Marjorie can be cutting, but she's not a liar. Can I tell you what a thrill it was yesterday? To be sitting with Gail Shumer, Bitsy Devine, a few other of my closest friends, when Marjorie—who I did beat handily—pounced at the precise moment to ask if my daughter 'had been released from prison yet.'"

My smug expression folds. "And how did she know—"

"Seems Marjorie is chummy with Conchetta Nicholson. They serve together on the Gardner Museum board. Now," she says, pointing a rose-colored nail at me, "I realize you don't know Conchetta. But I heard you met her husband, Judge Nicholson. I believe he was working at the time." She smiles so wide my jaw aches. "Apparently, you offered a few choice words to the judge. But, of course, this is only a morsel of Marjorie's tale. The kind a mother would likely endure at a support group meeting. A setting where the parents of out-of-control, rebellious teenagers come to commiserate. Tell me, Olivia, after all these years, am I still that parent?"

"I don't know what you heard, but—"

"Oh, by all means, let me recap." She takes two steps away from the corrected lampshade and toward me. I back up. I haven't backed up from her in twenty years. "According to Marjorie, you threw a drunken tantrum in the middle of Newbury Street, beating your husband's Porsche to a pulp with a baseball bat." I open my mouth and she holds up a hand. "Then after resisting arrest and a myriad of charges, you appeared before Judge Nicholson and suggested to him, by way of an expletive that I won't repeat, to go fornicate with himself." Her tone shifts from mockery to outright anger. "How close am I?"

"Close," I admit. "Did Marjorie bring a transcript, or was this all from memory?"

My mother's gaze delivers glancing blows off the objects in my music room. I suspect she was hoping I'd say Marjorie was exaggerating. That the whole incident really amounted to a few unpaid parking tickets. She clears her throat. "I see. Tell me, Olivia, are you on drugs?"

I narrow my eyes. "What?"

"Drugs. I understand it's not unheard of—people from well-to-do backgrounds can be just as susceptible as those from a lower socioeconomic status. In fact, I suppose once you've succumbed it might even be easier. You have means—inherited money from your grandfather that you do God knows what with, surplus from the auction of the Amati."

"I'd never—"

"Did Rob find out? Was that it?"

"Mom, I'm not on . . . How could you even . . ." My hand slams against my forehead as I turn toward the music room. While blurting out what instigated Friday night's episode would be exquisitely ironic, I don't. Telling my mother that Rob's put her beloved Wellesley home on the chopping block isn't an option. I don't have enough facts, and, frankly, I believe Rob should be on hand to take his share of the blame. I squeeze my eyes shut. Wait. Doesn't he deserve all the blame? I whip back around. "No, Mom, I'm not on drugs. Would you like me to pee in a cup for you?"

"Then explain it, Olivia. Explain what could have possibly happened to incite such disgraceful conduct." She glides through the foyer, and I backpedal until I am pinned against the antique secretary in the music room. "What could have possibly occurred to make you revert to behavior that I haven't had to endure since . . . well, since before you married Rob."

"Why don't you ask Rob?"

"Fine. Is he here?"

"Not at the moment."

"Then I should assume some sort of marital discourse started it?"

"You could say that."

"I did say that," she seethes. "Would you say it? I realize sharing your personal life is not something you do. That leaves my imagination. I know Rob well, but I know you better."

"So no matter what started the whole thing, the downward spiral of the evening is surely more my fault than Rob's?"

"He's not the one who spent the weekend incarcerated. Other than the Porsche, Rob wasn't even part of the story I heard from Marjorie. But you were, Olivia, like you always are—right at the epicenter of trouble. Everything from running away from home when you were sixteen, through your tumultuous, endless college years. Dismissals from one music program to the next. Treating your gift like a burden—an extra appendage you'd like severed." I attempt to speak, but nothing short of shoving the lampshade down her throat would stop her. "When you abandoned school in North Carolina, I'd hoped some time away, with your brother, would settle you down. Foolish me. Upon returning, you continued to ignore your music education and chose to job hop. Such an impressive list." She smiles warmly and rolls her eyes toward the coffered ceiling. "Let's see—waitress, ticket taker at the USS *Constitution*, beer wench at the Sam Adams brewery and . . . Oh, what was my favorite?" She looks me up and down. "Right. Working as a dog-walker-slash-pet-sitter in the Commonwealth Ave, Beacon Hill areas. It was quite gratifying, knowing I had someone to recommend when Tallulah Carson needed a reliable pooper scooper for her Pomeranian."

"And the nasty little bastard bit me, if it makes you feel any better."

"Not entirely, but good to know. My point is that nothing in your life settled down until Rob showed up."

"Not even the part when I made your dreams come true and won a symphony chair on a whim of an audition?"

"Whim?" she says, raising a brow. "More like retribution. Winning the chair before your father died would have been a bit more on point. You know what it would have meant to him." My chin tips upward; I view the timing as purely coincidental. She prattles on. "While I shared in his expectation, the hope for your talent, playing in the symphony was truly his dream, not mine."

"I'm aware, Mom. I'm so very well aware."

CHAPTER THREE

Olivia

The doorbell interrupts the mother-daughter standoff going on in my music room. I dart around her, hoping it's the FedEx guy. Maybe he's delivering another life. While no such fantasy awaits me, my one-woman cavalry does.

Sasha passes by, her nymph-like frame weighed down by a bulging leather tote, a large hobo handbag, and a coffee tray clutched in her hands. I don't warn her about my other visitor. There isn't time. She is moving at a swift Sasha clip. "Sorry. My stop at Zowz's took longer than expected." As she moves I swear there is a hint of aftershave, maybe cigarettes. "The lazy fuck thought *I* filed his motion to delay, and—

"Christ!" Sasha gasps as she makes an automatic turn into the music room. "Eugenia. How . . . *nice* to see you. I wasn't expecting—"

"Obviously not. Lovely to see you . . ."

"Sasha," I supply, coming around the corner.

"Of course." My mother touches her fingertips to her forehead, recovering. "And what a colorful, expletive-filled entrance, dear . . .

Almost as striking as the contrast between your snowy white blouse and skin tone."

Sasha smiles tersely at me and the backhanded biracial compliment. But after a decade of this snide behavior, Sasha is impervious. She moves along, more focused on explaining her Monday morning presence. "I, uh . . . sometimes I stop by, bring Olivia coffee . . . the paper." She raises a cardboard tray as if it's evidence. Her tote slips from her shoulder and falls onto her crooked arm. "If I'd known you were here, Eugenia, I would have brought three coffees." I brush alongside Sasha, removing the leather bag as I go. Inside are several legal-looking envelopes and today's edition of the *Boston Ledger*. I place the tote on the sofa.

"Interesting," my mother says. "You have such a busy job at your legal practice, yet you have time for a social call on a Monday morning."

"The brownstone is really right on my way and . . ."

"Please," she says. "Don't perjure yourself on my daughter's behalf. Clearly I've heard all the explanation I'm going to for now." She checks a delicate diamond-trimmed watch—a treasured gift from my father when tiny-face watches and enduring marriages were *en vogue*. "As it is, I have a salon appointment." Our gazes clash as she passes by me. "Perhaps I'll get lucky. Perhaps ShiJu has a relative who's not in the manicure business. Do Asians work in the Suffolk County correctional system?" She tips her head at the two of us. "It may be my only way of getting the rest of the story."

The door slams and she is gone. "How much does she know?" Sasha asks.

"Nothing about her house. Only enough to place blame—everything that happened from Friday night forward is my fault. Certainly it has nothing to do with her precious Rob."

Sasha takes off her coat and holds out a cup of coffee: black, two packets of sugar substitute. It is one of the zillion things Sasha knows about me. There is only one she doesn't.

I wait for her to say something cutting about my mother. She's silent. "Uh, Sash. This is the part where you berate my mother for insulting you and throwing me under the bus."

"Your mother's no picnic, Liv. I'm sure that was . . . *unpleasant*."

I take a step back. "But she's not incorrect?"

"Well . . ." she says carefully. "She'll be pissed at Rob when she finds out about the house. But—"

"But what?"

"Just stating facts. Rob's not the one who spent the weekend in jail or the one facing charges that could come with real jail time."

"Seriously, Sasha? You're going to take the judge's side and my mother's?"

She swings her coffee cup toward the door. "I'm just saying, I don't usually deliver the paper, and I'm not here to socialize, am I?"

"No, I suppose not." I sip the coffee, which burns my tongue. "Thank you, Sash. If I didn't say it when I called . . . *from jail* . . . or after jail."

"No problem." She looks past my head. "I take it Rob's not here?"

"No." I look from the newspaper tucked in her tote to Sasha's face. "Why?"

"Because, despite your mother, it's too quiet." True. If Rob were home she'd hear him on his cell phone, pacing while wheeling and dealing. "I was marginally concerned for his safety," she says. "You know I draw the line at helping you hide a body, right?"

"He was gone when I got up. But how long can you stay? I'm sure that showdown will make the highlight reel for this year."

"Liv, I get that this is Rob's second major money screwup. But do yourself a favor and take it down a notch."

I am silent. It's not my mother's dig, but it translates the same: Rob has caused trouble, whereas I am the textbook diagram for trouble. I'm not surprised. Sasha loves me, but she *likes* Rob. Everyone does—he's easy on the eyes and clever, so quick with the right words. No one ever notices the double-talk. We've been married six years. It took the first four to hone my Rob-listening skills. By our fifth anniversary, and right after a memorable trip to Italy, Rob hit his first financial skid. It's what led to the auction of the Amati, causing the initial crack in our marriage. Not so much because it happened, but because he withheld the monetary particulars right up until my American Express card was declined—it was during a birthday luncheon for Sasha, where I was supposed to pick up the tab. I shake my head at the not-so-distant memory. "My guess is Rob's working the phones from behind his barricaded office door. But the office space is only a rental. His investors can't repossess it. He'll turn back up. He always does."

"You'll work it out, Liv. You always do."

Until this past year, that would have been a true statement. We take a seat on the sofa, the tote bag in between us. Sasha reaches and squeezes my hand. If it were anyone else, I'd withdraw. But Sasha and I connect on the unspoken, sometimes inexplicable level that best friends often do. I sigh; she talks. "Despite current circumstance, and at the risk of agreeing with your mother, you and Rob are good for one another." She smiles. "Together you're like a violin."

I glance at the Guarneri, which I left sitting on top of the secretary. Everything else in the brownstone is *Rob urban chic*, an *Architectural Digest* wet dream. This room and the Guarneri are pure eighteenth century. "Tell me you're not going to compare us to a cliché involving a Stradivarius?"

Sasha can't help herself. She's a natural fixer-upper. If she were an HGTV producer, instead of a lawyer, she would have parlayed me into a blockbuster series years ago.

"After I stopped at Zowz's, I was thinking, Rob's the bow, you're the strings. It's not a bad thing. Yes. Sometimes it makes a god-awful noise. And then other times . . ."

"Say we make beautiful music and you'll go out of this house." I point dramatically toward the door. "Lately, the best we can do is a decent capriccio." Sasha furrows her brow; I explain. "A short composition, known for its fanciful, improvisational qualities."

"Oh." I know as little about the law as Sasha knows about music. It's our balance; we are each other's missing notes. "Anyway, about Rob," she says. "I knew from the moment *I* kissed him that he was *your* prince." She smiles at the mention of a favorite story, the kind that never wears out at dinner parties: Rob and I met as a result of their blind date.

What makes an even better dinner party story, however, is the way Sasha and I met, also a date. Ten years ago, Sasha and I were paired by a popular Boston-based dating website—before the internet was quite so savvy. The site was big on things like whether or not you preferred loud parties or quiet evenings, if you were into casual sex or had strong Christian values. They wanted to know if you liked to dine out or cook for your partner. What they sorely lacked was a proofreader. Somehow, on the cyber paperwork, between our personal profiles and a mutually-agreed-upon meet up for drinks, "Olivia" turned into "Oliver." By the time Sasha and I realized we were each other's date, we were onto a second drink and sincerely hoping no man disrupted our evening. As we exchanged phone numbers and made a lunch date for the following week, our biggest disappointment was heterosexuality. As far as the dating website goes, we both left five-star reviews, claiming ourselves a success story.

At the moment, I'm not as certain the same can be said for Rob and me, and I scoff at Sasha's *prince* remark. "Ha! Make that a prince who just sold the family castle out from under me."

"Rob will fix it. So keep that in mind when he shows up with roses and a willingness to meet you halfway." I huff at the predictability of my future.

"I'm just saying, despite this latest incident, Rob is there for you." She draws the cup to her mouth but stops. "It's more than can be said for some of the men who have come . . . *and gone* from your life.

Given the circumstance, historical perspective isn't the worst thing to consider."

And sometimes a best friend can know too much and not quite enough. Sasha's referring to my life long before she existed. Sam Nash was my first husband. He comes after the runaway incidents and prior to the years of hourly-wage jobs. He's part of my North Carolina days, or more accurately, he was the nucleus. It was long before he achieved his baseball legend status. Sam's subsequent fame is the part of the story that makes the marriage memorable—at least to everyone but me. Back then, he was just a boy from the South, both of us mixed up and rebellious. It's a tale I've shared in pieces, mostly on drunken New Year's Eves.

With that timely reminder, we've now touched on all the things that caused me to rupture a vein in front of the judge. However, the fact that Sasha has alluded to my first husband tells me how concerned she is that Rob and I may not fully recover from this wild ride.

As noted, she's a Rob fan, though their blind date ended a little differently than Sasha's and mine. When the two of them arrived at the obligatory good-night kiss, with Rob's tongue in her mouth, she withdrew—as Sasha likes to tell it—saying, "Damn. You are a really good kisser. But I've been thinking all night . . . I've got a friend you should meet."

I assume it was a litmus test on Sasha's part. Setting me up on a date with a poor kisser wasn't worth the risk. She still likes to joke, "Thank God I didn't sleep with Rob for shits and giggles. It might have been a deal breaker."

You think?

Their personalities are like oil and oil—determined minds and bodies (both are fitness freaks) and driven to the core, but perhaps more importantly, Rob and Sasha are equally willing to love the DNA experiment that is Olivia Klein, something that's worked out on most days.

Sasha's fingers tap the top of her leather tote. It's code for *"I'm weighing my words."* "Liv, I get that Rob is far from perfect. But I did warn you that—"

"Don't say it!" In response, Sasha purses her lips tight. "This is not my fault. Not by any stretch of the imagination. Certainly not because I added Rob's name to the Wellesley house deed."

When we first married, Sasha warned that adding Rob's name to the deed on a house, bequeathed solely to me, wasn't a great idea. My father left Phillip an equivalent sum in trust. But being as Phillip ran away to New Zealand nearly three decades ago, the house and our mother became my responsibility. My mother was to live there until she, too, expired. Then the house would be mine, to do with as I pleased. I had big plans for it—Rob knew that. He knows every detail. But adding his name to the deed allowed my husband to jeopardize the house via his most recent murky business venture.

I attempt to qualify. "When your shiny new husband gives you a Boston brownstone as a wedding gift . . . Well, my gesture seemed reciprocal." Sasha looks unconvinced. "Listen, I didn't get married—not for real—until I was almost forty. Aside from you, long-term relationships are not my strong suit. I was just trying to play nice."

"And it was a nice gesture, Liv. Just not a great business decision, as the past seventy-two hours has proven." She sips her coffee. "So let me ask: Are you going to tell your mother? Or, if need be, are you just giving her change of address cards for Christmas?"

I hurl myself into the cushion of the sofa. "No. I'll leave the house explanation to Rob."

"I can't disagree. Eugenia will take it better coming from him." Sasha also sinks into the sofa and bats her honey-copper eyes at me. "Doesn't she still own a condo in Boca Raton?"

"She does. But in her social circle, summering in Florida would be tantamount to moving to a Southie flat with a window air conditioner.

With my luck, Rob—in his own magnanimous gesture—will invite my mother to move in with us." I leap from the sofa.

"Where are you going?"

"I don't know what I was thinking. Destroying Rob's Porsche doesn't solve a thing. I should torch the brownstone, collect the insurance."

"Olivia!" she calls in a shrill tone that smacks of my mother.

In the pocket-door entry I spin back around. I glance up, then down. The pristine foyer shows off a stunning coffered ceiling and high-shine herringbone hardwoods. I could never set a match to it. "It may be easier just to give her the brownstone."

"Because my selfish side insists I need the small pockets of sanity you possess, I won't dismiss it as an option." She narrows her eyes at me. "I remember your father. I know your mother. I do feel for anyone who actually had to live with them."

"Doesn't excuse anything," I concede. "But it explains a few things, doesn't it?"

Sasha smiles. "Give Rob a chance to come up with a plan. In the meantime, we have something more immediate to discuss. While you were enjoying your stay at Suffolk's day care for the wayward, I hammered out a plea deal with the ADA."

I stride cautiously back into the music room. "And what did Justin Bieber offer, because right now, factoring in my mother, six months to a year in a seven-by-ten room isn't sounding so bad."

"Don't joke, Liv. I may have avoided jail time and a record, but who knows how the New England Symphony front office will take to the news. They may not find infamy all that appealing."

"No, probably not." I cock my chin toward the newspaper sticking out of Sasha's bag. "Did I make the papers?"

She pulls out the neatly folded edition of the *Boston Ledger*. "Sorry to say you did. It's buried enough, page twelve police blotter. And it refers to you as Olivia Van Doren. Maybe no one will notice." I cringe at the odds. "If you're lucky, the symphony front office will only read three pages in, to their full-color ad touting the fall schedule."

"If we're lucky."

"The good news is the ADA is amenable to community service. Of course Rob won't press charges for the damage to the Porsche. I mean, I don't know that for a fact, but I assume he . . ." I widen my eyes at her question. "Right. He wouldn't dare. Before your court appearance, that would have left us with disturbing the peace, resisting arrest, and the weapons possession . . . If it were just that, I'd have gotten our ADA down to twenty hours. As it is . . ."

"As it is, what? I didn't do anything else." I run fingers through my hair, squeezing hard.

"Liv, you told Judge Nicholson to go fuck himself."

"Yes, but I spent the night in jail for it."

"He didn't see it as sufficient comeuppance. He viewed your remark as that of a rude, spoiled, privileged woman who needs a lesson in decorum." She raises her hands in an *at a loss* gesture. "Real Housewives of Boston?"

"Me? Maybe he has me confused with my mother—or her housekeeper. I don't even know where we keep the vacuum."

"Liv, you're not your mother. But you do have a tendency to . . . display token abruptness at inopportune moments?"

"What eloquent code for I'm a bitch."

"Code it however you like. But this time, I'm afraid it wasn't the waiter who brought you a vodka martini when you ordered gin, or the man who sat in your first-class airline seat—it was a Municipal Court judge who has the authority to punish your behavior as he sees fit, within the confines of the law."

"Meaning?"

"Instead of twenty easy hours of community service, he's advised the ADA to accept no fewer than a hundred. He was agreeable to taking your symphony schedule into consideration."

"One . . ."

"Hundred," Sasha repeats. Her gaze glances over me and my sudden shake-and-stir life.

Three days ago, I sat down to a sixth-anniversary dinner celebration at David's Bistro and a perfectly made gin martini. I was preparing for my seventh season with the symphony. It's an enviable gig, despite my bad-blood history with music. I get it. Rob and I . . . Granted, we've slipped into a marriage valley during this past year. That said, I know how good the peaks were. As for my mother, she was sequestered behind the walls of her Wellesley fortress. In my own way, I was managing—which isn't something I could always claim. I know a lot of that has to do with Rob. But because I tell a judge to "fuck off" for not understanding anything about me, I'm to be punished for that?

I wonder if karma has finally bitten me square in the ass.

Sasha pulls what I assume is the plea agreement from her tote, along with a list of possible community service options. I see she's redlined the ones to which I'd be completely opposed. It's more than half. Her phone rings. She says she has to take the call and strolls off toward the dining room. Even at five feet two, sporting a waistline that means I can always find her at the size-four rack in Ann Taylor, Sasha is the poster girl for empowered women.

I brush my hand over loose loungewear and disheveled appearance. I struggle internally—the good and bad that is me. In some ways I've tried to do better. I sink back onto the sofa. In most ways I've failed miserably. But as Sasha noted, as Rob is also aware, the deck has always been stacked against me.

When I was four and Phillip six, it was concluded that he possessed my mother's near tin ear and I my father's profound gift—the same gift that belonged to our grandfather. Phillip had no idea how fortunate he was. Many things are inherent, or so I have learned, including reckless behavior. At twenty-three Asa Klein, my father, succumbed to his eccentricities, a careless act that abruptly ended his dream of being a violin virtuoso. My inborn talent became his second chance. Expectation mounted, year after year, a weight so heavy Atlas would have dropped it, muttering, "Fuck this." The never-ending practice and rehearsals, the vetting to find the right instructor (few ever were), recitals, auditions, competitions, the swirling vat of endless anticipation. In almost every way, I was not his daughter but merely a conduit, albeit a faulty one.

So many years later and I still recall, clearly, his incensed frustration at my dismissal from the Boston Conservatory: "Come collect your daughter, Professor Klein. Brilliant as she is, Olivia doesn't possess the discipline of even a Salvation Army musician." And that was the cornerstone of our relationship, my value hinging on the outcome of his gift, reproduced in another human being.

As my mother notes with regularity, my father did not live to see it come to fruition. As he lay dying of cancer, he asked me to play at his bedside. In her delirium, my mother insisted it was the least I could do. She sat perched on the other side of the bed. Rob sat quietly, almost invisibly, in a chair. As I emoted Korngold's Violin Concerto over his withering body, he drew shallower and shallower breaths. I prayed as I played, *For Christ's sake, would you take a last one . . .* Being as he was Jewish, I'd forgotten Christ was not involved in Asa Klein's impending exit, which may have been another reason he found the strength to lift his head and say, "Olivia, you're rushing it. I'm certain it's marked moderato . . ."

Sitting on my sofa, I put aside the plea agreement and pick up the newspaper. Its pages crinkle in my hand. My life has been lived, not with precision, but through the mist of a rolling fog. Emerging from each opaque patch, I am amazed by where I'm standing. Sometimes I wonder where I'll be standing at fifty—assuming I'm upright. I look between the community service options and newspaper. *What after-the-fact, bright light will this moment produce, Liv?* Perhaps it's best to let a neutral, wiser Sasha choose my poison. I need a diversion—something weightier than my own fate. I open today's edition of the *Boston Ledger*.

I'm not interested in the police blotter or seeing my name in print. God and my father know I couldn't care less about the symphony advertisement. I peer toward Sasha, who's deep in conversation with a real client—someone she'll bill an exorbitant fee to for her time and professional services. It's the September 11 edition of the *Ledger*; there are a couple of smaller stories that relate to the reverent and ominous date. They've dwindled in recent years—large exposés turning into tinier respectful mentions. Four pages in and I find what I'm looking for: Shep Stewart's annual column dedicated to the children of 9-11 victims.

Shep chronicles the lives of six children who lost a parent that day, all with ties to the Boston area. Their stories are compelling; one in particular mesmerizes me. Overall, the column is a sobering distraction, and today I need it like air. I scan the first five updates, names that have become familiar over the years. I skim bits and pieces of the lives of children who are now, for the most part, adults.

I turn the page and read the last entry—Theo McAdams. It's the one I'm looking for. Theo was ten when his father died in the North Tower. His mother, Claire—a publishing executive turned stay-at-home mother—has provided the narration to Theo's life. Theo is also a musician—a fascinating fact that resonates. I run my fingers over this year's picture. At twenty-six, Theo has lost all semblance of his boyhood self, a glimmer of which was visible last year. This image depicts a man with wavy brown hair and an oval face. The photos are black and white, so I've wondered about the color of his eyes.

I think Theo was read to a lot. This idea may have more to do with his mother's publishing past, rather than something one can glean from a photo. But I like the premise, so I pretend it's true. In addition to his musical prowess, Theo's mother has talked about her son as if he's been running for class president these past fifteen years. But photos of Theo are equally telling—a familiarity in his face that penetrates. I straighten my spine and catch a glimpse of myself in an adjacent mirror, guessing this is what a less benevolent, musically gifted child looks like. I raise an eyebrow at my reflection—a wide forehead, bangs to hide the fact. My mother's tiny nose makes my mouth too big for my face; I also see cutting blue eyes that were my father's. Fine lines are slowly overshadowing all of me, visible from the width of a room. On second thought, maybe I just look like I spent the weekend in jail.

Like every year, Claire touts Theo's genuineness and giving nature. It comes off as slightly gooey, and some years I've wanted her to share the story where Theo got caught shoplifting at Newbury Comics or smoking pot with his friends. Maybe in 2008 he wanted to quit piano lessons. If those things happened, Claire never goes there. Sometimes I don't think it's triumph over tragedy that Theo's mother wants to convey, but for the world to know that her son is a good and productive human being. I'd imagine lots of parents would like an annual report like that in their newspaper.

While Theo went to Cornell on an athletic scholarship, he ended up with a degree in music—his choice, according to Claire. Last year's article regaled his fresh-from-college job as the orchestra/band leader at Weston High School. It's one of a few Massachusetts communities where the public education system could pass for private. Claire has often noted the inbred talent that made Theo a star athlete, but she takes extra pride in his decision to pursue music. "Wouldn't Asa Klein be ever so envious . . ." I murmur.

As a distant observer, I've wondered if Theo's choices would have differed had his father lived. I know from Shep's stories that before becoming a financial analyst for one of the brokerages so hard hit on September 11, Theo's father was a star running back in college—so surely sports mattered to him.

I continue to read but grow increasingly alarmed by the rest of Theo's update. Last year's story said Theo was engaged—a girl named India Church. This year there is no mention of a fiancée. The story goes on to say that Theo chose to leave his cushy Boston suburb teaching position.

"That's not terribly smart," I say. "I'd think overseeing the casual music education of rich kids would be a no-brainer job with summers off." I sigh, kind of sorry I didn't think of it. My head shakes at the mere notion of children and me. But for sweet-faced Theo, what could have been the most taxing issue? "*Please excuse Buffy for missing her French horn lesson. The family ski trip to Italy just cluttered the calendar.*"

I widen my eyes as Shep further enlightens his readers. Theo has accepted a position at Braemore. Braemore rolls off the tongue with the connotation of the private school Weston High isn't. But I've seen headlines, heard local news reports. I know about this school. Braemore is a last stop for kids put out by standard Boston public schools. Behavioral issues run the gamut—delinquents with criminal records, drugs, others who are just DNA time bombs waiting to explode. (I'm allowed to say that. I am one.) Braemore isn't like other schools from lower-income neighborhoods. It's a holding cell for future unrest and violence. Boston Public Schools can't figure out what to do with these kids; I'm not sure why Theo should.

"Oh, for God's sake." I grimace. "What are you thinking? This isn't *Mr. Holland's Opus*—no one's going to yell *'cut'* when someone pulls a gun!" I'm angry and frustrated. It's not the uplifting story Shep Stewart promises each year. It's not the distracting story I need on this topsy-turvy morning. I run my hand around the back of my neck. Little hairs are standing on end. I may not know Theo up close, but I know musicians—they are not wired for environments like Braemore. I get up and head for my desk. I need to put the story out of mind, which means getting it out of my sight.

A small pewter box shaped like what else—a violin case—sits on the desk and from it I retrieve a key. It unlocks the bottom right drawer of the antique desk. Inside are all Shep Stewart's 9-11 stories. Under a mess of sheet music is a pair of scissors. With three large snips, I cut out this year's article. I'm about to file away Theo McAdams and his story when Sasha turns back up.

"What are you doing?" I look up, staring at her like an out-of-place fermata mark, the newspaper clipping clutched in my hand. "After my client call, the ADA beeped in," Sasha says. "We need to accept the plea or not by five o'clock today."

"Or what?" I say. "It's pistols at dawn on the Freedom Trail?"

She picks up the paper listing community service tasks. "Nothing so dramatic, but you are going to have to pick something, Liv. Soup kitchen, Mass Pike litter removal . . ." Sasha looks back at the list. "Wait. Here's one. There's a green area near a historic cemetery that's being refurbished. It's some cleanup work, painting—you wouldn't have to deal with the public, just the project supervisor, other perps assigned the detail."

"What kind of *perps*?"

"Don't know. The location won't limit offenders, not like a playground. Could be anything from robbery to assault to sex offenders."

"Great," I say, blowing out a breath.

Sasha's expression shifts to concern. "Right. Not that one. Don't worry. We'll find something else."

I shake my head. "It's fine. I'll do it. I mean, I did the crime, right?" I scratch a hand through my hair. "It's probably about where I belong anyway."

"What's that you're holding?" She cocks her chin at the news clipping.

"I, um . . . nothing." I shuffle right and sway my hip into the desk drawer, shutting it.

"What are you hiding, Liv? Let me see." Her gaze drifts to the sofa, spying the hole in the newspaper. "Starting a scrapbook of your criminal offenses?" I shake my head. "Or did you want the symphony advertisement as a keepsake?" I'd cop to that, but Sasha is too savvy. Rob might buy it—not Sasha. She crosses her arms, her sleek suit looking courtroom ready. "Come on, Liv. What did you take from the paper?"

"A half-off coupon for Lord & Taylor. I thought I might spruce up this year's black." Black, of course, is our staple performance wardrobe. "I may need the discount."

"Mmm . . . you'd wear last year's black before you'd ever bother to clip a coupon."

I cling tighter to the Shep Stewart article. I prefer my interest remains private. I don't parade mawkish emotion—no self-respecting Klein does. But being as I've been caught, emotion steers my next thought. An idea occurs to me; it's totally out of character, though it fits smartly into the context of this conversation. I hold out Shep's story. "I saw this in the paper. This boy . . . *man*," I say. "A teacher, Theo McAdams. He took a job at Braemore. Do you know the place?"

Sasha's looks befuddled, taking the clipping from me. "I've defended a few students from Braemore—required pro bono work. Braemore is badass, filled with worse-ass kids." She looks at me. "But what does it have to do with you?" She scans the article and her crafted eyebrows rise as she reads Theo's story. "Huh. Sad. The 9-11 connection and all . . . But, wow. I give him credit. I usually ask for a cop to be within ten feet while making a case for a Braemore perp. Accepting a gig as the music teacher takes balls." She looks from the article to me. "But I still don't get it. What does it have to do with you?"

"I was thinking . . ." I say slowly, because now I am. "Do you suppose the judge would let me volunteer at Braemore—assist this McAdams teacher to fulfill my community service? It would be a better use of skills than green space beautification."

Sasha cranes her neck forward, eyes narrowing. "Liv, am I unaware of a blow to your head from the other night?" I shrink back at the remark—which honestly makes more sense than the suggestion I've made. "You're joking, right? I can't fathom you doing cleanup work in a green space with pedestrian perps, never mind going inside Boston's most violent school."

"It could be that Judge Nicholson is right. My attitude needs adjusting. Maybe it's time I acted more like Phillip and my grandfather—they're big givers."

"Yes, but you're hardly—"

"Think about it, Sash. I might not have Phillip's résumé when it comes to charitable causes, or my grandfather's penchant for philanthropic ventures, but I do have his gift for music. If I skip over my father, it's not such a bad lens. I could do more with music than dress up in black and parade in front of audiences that my mother would consider her peers."

"Let's not go overboard here. I agree that the judge set down a harsher-than-necessary sentence for mouthing off. But that doesn't mean you have to plunge into some dangerous, life-changing experience."

"I'm not doing that."

"Then how else do you explain a suggestion that's the modern-day equivalent to volunteering with the militia and facing Redcoats?"

"I'm not . . . And it isn't. I just thought this McAdams kid could use some help. Musically, we have something in common. And I do have a sharable talent, Sasha."

"Right. A talent that you barely tolerate to earn a living. Why would you suddenly—"

"I'm just asking if you think it's feasible. That's all."

Sasha looks skeptically at the article. "Feasible . . . yes. But *crazy* might be a saner description."

CHAPTER FOUR

Five Months Earlier

Boston, Massachusetts

Theo

Rain pummels the windows of a Ruth's Chris Steak House. It is pouring like the heavens are crying—a phrase Theo's mother often used after his father died. On a wall of glass, water spreads into vague scattered tributaries. Foreboding presses into Theo's gut. India arrived, soaked to the skin, and he's waiting for her to return from the ladies' room. He stares into the gloomy night and heavenly tears. He will never look at rain and not be reminded of loss. It can make weather difficult, and sometimes Theo considers moving to the desert.

After the turmoil of the past few days, Theo wishes he and India had moved to the desert a year ago. If they lived in the desert, India would not work for Take Me to Church Catering or have been at a caterers' convention in New York. If Arizona or the Sahara were home, his fiancée might have gotten sunburn on Monday or found some variety of arachnids in their bathroom tub. But she wouldn't have run into an old boyfriend and agreed to a friendly drink. She wouldn't have kissed him, which is what India confessed to Theo that same night. If they lived in the desert, a half-dozen phone conversations would not have followed, the ones in which India's words went from being mortified by her actions to uncertainty about the two of them.

A waiter delivers drinks. India follows, her damp red hair glistening under what is supposed to be ambient lighting. Theo is surprised she insisted on meeting here, a carnivore's paradise. India is a vegetarian, and a Ruth's Chris Steak House is not their style. But it's midway between their apartment and the train station, and Theo guesses India is anxious to talk face-to-face.

She sits and smiles, then doesn't, her fair face paler than usual. It's an odd look for India, whose smile is the thing Theo notices more than her wavy red hair. "I ordered you a glass of wine." Theo points to the Cabernet as if she cannot see it. He's more nervous than he was on their first date. It sticks out because Theo is not a nervous person. This and countless other things are the effect of India—her airy upbeat laugh that sounds like music and her ability to keep track of the everyday things he cannot, like his phone, which he has misplaced again. All of it sets India apart from any girl he's ever known.

"Thanks." She reaches for the wine. The Cabernet sloshes about the glass like a rough sea. India puts the glass down. "I don't think I can drink this." Her hazel gaze is trained on her finger. She spins her engagement ring in antsy edgy whirl. Theo wanted to take the ring back to the jeweler for resizing. India insisted it was fine. "Theo," she says abruptly. "A lot's happened in the past few days."

"Really, just one thing," he states. But the gravity of the circumstance weighs down on him, more so than during their phone conversations. It feels as if the roof of the Ruth's Chris Steak House may give way. But the sensation is not linked to what India has done—though this hardly thrills him—it's trepidation about what she's going to say. Yet

Theo stands his ground; he is the injured party. "If you want me to tell you it's okay that you kissed another man, I can't do that. It stings . . . like hell."

Her dewy eyes shine brighter than her hair. "I'm sorry, Theo—so sorry. I never expected to run into Tom. I certainly never intended to have two martinis, kiss him in public, or run headlong into . . ."

India's words peter out. Theo closes his eyes, willing the heinous vision away. "Who, uh . . . I'd like to know, who kissed who? It might help me understand."

"Tom—he kissed me." Theo is relieved, but the feeling is short-lived. "But I . . ."

"You didn't pull away or slap his face?"

"No," she says, wiping a trembling, freckled hand across her nose. "I didn't. I mean, I didn't think it was a wonderful thing. For a tipsy second it only felt I'd fallen into a memory, like the whole thing was a bizarre dream."

"Did he want you to go home with him?" This is the easiest way Theo can think to ask if the old boyfriend suggested he and India have sex. She was having sex with Tom when she and Theo met, so it's not as if India's never been attracted to another man. Theo just liked it far better when the other man was him. He shakes his head and tries to clear his mind. India broke up with Tom before she and Theo had a second date, almost the second she realized "having coffee with Theo" *was* a first date. She is an honorable person. "Never mind," he says before she can answer. "Of course that's what he wanted." Theo imagines lots of men would like to have sex with India—she's confident and pretty in that uncommon redheaded way. "But you didn't consider it." She shakes her head slightly. Theo feels he's on his way to fixing this. "You made a mistake, India. And you did tell me right away. You didn't lie or keep it from me. It's not the end of the world. We can recover from it." Theo draws a Coors Light bottle to his lips and downs a long mouthful.

"Theo, I don't think we can."

With the bottle to his mouth, Theo considers how useless one beer is if trying to get drunk.

"It might not be the end of the world. But what happened . . . It says a lot about . . . *me*."

Like all tragic events, the next moments move in slow motion. Theo lowers the beer bottle, and India slips the ring off her finger. Tears run down her sweet face, rivaling the rain on the window. She says something about choosing the restaurant because she can easily get a cab back to the train station. India's returning to her parents' house on Long Island tonight. She will not come back to their apartment. There's more talk, but India cannot be persuaded. In the end, she leaves a shaken Theo inside the restaurant. India is swallowed by the dark and rain while Theo ponders loss and the rarity of precipitation in the Sahara Desert.

◆ ◆ ◆

Present Day

Theo glances in the dresser mirror. He takes in his tallish frame and pressed Brooks Brothers slacks, starched dress shirt, and tweed sports jacket with ivy-league patches on the sleeves. His naturally wavy brown hair is secured with a dab of gel. He should have shaved. "What the fuck am I doing? Add a pipe and Braemore students will probably shove it . . ."

He quickly changes into black jeans and a wrinkled button down that could use a trip through the wash. He keeps the jacket. It reeks of intellectualism, but it is also a vintage item that belonged to his father. Theo has filled out enough that the jacket is finally a perfect fit. It's one of a handful of mementoes he possesses. He would like David McAdams as close as possible today—his first day as Braemore's music teacher. He decides not to shave. The scruff may present a harder image. He might need it. Theo remembers to purge his wallet. It's part of the helpful hints tip sheet he was given upon accepting the job at Braemore. Rule one: Do not wear jewelry. Even costume jewelry is discouraged. This is an easy one. Theo's not a jewelry kind of guy. Jewelry is too easy to misplace. But he does open the shoebox-size cedar box that sits on his dresser—another keepsake of his father's. Before storing his credit cards inside (another handy tip), Theo looks reverently through the box's contents.

Inside is India's engagement ring, a perfect emerald-cut diamond in an antique platinum setting. While it's been months, it only takes a glance at the ring for everything to rush to the surface. When Theo played lacrosse, he was once hit square in the chest by a ball, which was traveling at about forty miles per hour. It felt like a locomotive slamming into him. Compared to India's departure, the lacrosse ball now feels like the tickle of a feather. He still cannot believe she gave up on them so easily. His breath shudders. But their breakup is still fairly fresh and this is to be expected. It's one reason Theo took the job at Braemore; he's intent on making changes in his life, finding a new one. It's the rational thing to do.

Theo closes the ring box and focuses on the other chattels kept inside. There's a fraternity pin from Cornell and a never-thought-about high school class ring. Theo keeps this ring because throwing it away seems wasteful. That and he's somewhat amazed he hasn't lost it. At the bottom of the red corduroy-lined box is his father's driver's license.

His father's last birthday was September 10, 2001. Ten-year-old Theo gave him a new wallet. While transferring personal items that evening, the driver's license was mistakenly left out of the billfold. Two weeks after September 11, Theo found it between the cushions of their living room sofa. At first he thought they should bury the license—it was all they had left. His mother, in her grief and wisdom, insisted otherwise. Of course she was right. It wasn't until years later that the irony struck Theo: his father's ability to board a flight, which did land safely, sans driver's license. Regardless, fate had followed, right into his father's early-morning meeting in the North Tower.

Theo removes his own driver's license and holds it next to his father's. Only here are the names identical: Theodore David McAdams. His father went by his middle name to avoid confusion with Theo's grandfather: Theodore David McAdams the first. No one was ever "Ted" or "Teddy" in the McAdams lineage. Theo feels privileged to be a part of the McAdams family. He likes to think he sees himself in the plastic preserved image of his father, whose blue eyes pierce through, even in the tiny photo—a strong man with solid values and a well-timed sense of humor. David McAdams was also a hell of a running back. Lacrosse was Theo's athletic addiction, though music is his passion.

His father had witnessed a glimmer of who Theo would become at the age of four—stringing rubber bands to the knobs of dresser drawers and plucking at them, beating the bottoms of pots to a level that required earplugs. But David McAdams never got to see Theo's gift come to fruition. They are even on that score. Theo never saw his father play football, not live anyway, and he thanks God for the videos his mother kept along with more personal footage—baby Theo in a carrier coming in the front door of their Newton home. It was the start of a brand-new year, a new everything for the McAdamses, who had waited so long for a son.

There is footage of Theo celebrating his first birthday, as well as his eighth. In the video, he and his father are lying on the den floor. They are building a Lego tower. The footage captures a teetering structure that finally gives way to the shortcomings of amateur architecture. Theo and his father plop on the floor laughing while trying not to roll over the scattered Legos. So when Theo thinks of towers falling that is the image he tries to keep at the forefront of his mind. He tucks his license back in his wallet and puts the rest of the items in the cedar box with the red corduroy lining before leaving his apartment.

Music classes start one week later than required classes at Braemore. During his forty hours of summer training, Theo was instructed on how to best succeed as a teacher in a challenging educational environment. It was explained that very little at Braemore works like Weston High, where he was previously employed. For one, there's an entire team of police officers dedicated to the building. For as much as Braemore wishes to educate and mentor, they are realistic about the danger roaming the halls of its weary institution. Principal Giroux, a well-educated man whose presence is daunting from every angle, explained it to Theo. "Park your ideological aspirations at the curb, son, and hope it still has tires at the end of the day. If you manage to get through to one kid before you hit burnout, consider your career here a success." The average tenure for teachers at Braemore is a year and a half. The average stay for students who don't drop out is six years in a four-year institution. It's clear why the students retain the upper hand.

Theo has taken the T and arrives a half hour later at Braemore. At the front entrance, Theo shows the on-duty officer his driver's license, which matches his name on a pre-approved list. He's given an ID on a lanyard and told not to remove it for any reason, even at gunpoint. He's unsure if the man is joking. Theo is granted access to the circa-1940s building and hears a lock tumble behind him that sounds a lot like a prison cell. He wonders if the students feel the same way. The officer instructs him to check in at the office. Two boys with no facial hair, who still look older than Theo, lean against graffiti-covered lockers. Theo offers a friendly smile, though his heart is racing. The boys don't immediately respond, but then one does. He gives Theo the finger before turning his back.

Maybe this isn't the best idea Theo's ever had. In his deep determination to prove life will go on without India, perhaps he's made too large of a leap. It could be that what he should have done was chase India to Long Island. Theo wonders if she is still living there. Her parents own Take Me to Church Catering, and India ran the small Boston leg of the business. Catering's not India's dream—but neither, as it turns out, is Theo. Maybe all along he misjudged India's uncertainties—or the fact that she had any. Yet he cannot make a real argument for indecisiveness. While he's endlessly replayed their breakup, he's also considered the months leading up to it. There were no hints of ambivalence. When India left for the convention, her parting words were about how much she loved her fiancé. A thing like love, it isn't a sweater or an iPhone. You can't just lose it on the streets of New York, between a convention center and Booktini—some trendy Midtown bistro. Yet this seems to have been the case. Theo is frustrated by all of it. He's only concluded that the India he fell in love with is not the India who left him, though he suspects he's still in love with both.

He saw her once, briefly, after the Ruth's Chris Steak House fiasco. India returned to Boston a week later with a U-Haul and her sister, Helen. Together they claimed her bulkier possessions. His emotions ran the gamut that day: stunned to hurt to angry. It was similar, yet so very different, from what Theo experienced when his father died. He allowed anger to rule the U-Haul day, and he ended up telling India to go if that is what she truly wanted—a life apart. Theo left the apartment while she and Helen packed. On foot, Theo circled Boston for hours until his feet blistered and he was sure India was gone.

The memory puts Theo in a foul mood, which turns out to be a good thing. He's quick to note that Braemore students carry the same blueprint of emotion. While they're not likely to take shit off anybody, neither is Theo. He mentally thanks India for his current attitude. Inside the music room, he peruses the sad stockpile of instruments, gum-laden chairs, and ancient music stands. Students wander aimlessly into the room. They look Theo over with clear intent: *"How fast can we intimidate this lily-white asshole out of a job?"*

Not as fast as they think. In his most commanding voice, Theo instructs them to settle down. To his surprise, to a point, they do.

It doesn't go as badly as anticipated. Yes. They are tough and they are unruly. But they are not unmotivated. Sure, there are three linebacker-size boys, who look like men, seated in the back row of risers. They completely ignore him. Conversely, Theo does not try to engage them. For today, it appears to be an amicable arrangement. One thing at a time. There are only twelve students in the class—music appreciation. Unlike math or English, music is a voluntary elective. Theo takes this as a plus; they must have some desire to be there. He doesn't try anything flashy or too out of the box, like bringing up Mozart or early-twentieth-century modernism in music. Instead he asks what they want to accomplish while they're there.

A girl with long blond hair continuously twirls a tendril around her index finger. She eyes him up and down. "Before I came in here," she says, "I thought it might be an easy hour to kill until they unlock the doors at three. You know?" She cracks her gum. "Now I'm kind of wondering what you're doing after three? I'd give you a blow job behind that bass drum for the hell of it." Theo manages zero reaction, as if she's offered to wipe down the dry erase boards. She's rattled the control he's mustered; catcalls and complementary remarks fill the room. Theo's face grows warm. He considers sending her to Principal Giroux's office, but he doesn't want this to be the topic of his first student-teacher run-in. He needs to handle it.

Theo glances at the girl, who smiles at the discomfort she's created, or at her offer—he's unsure which. Realistically, the girl's suggestion isn't his first encounter with sexual overtures from students. In his previous teaching job at Weston High, a couple of girls made inappropriate remarks, though none were as direct as the blond. After a second girl at Weston came onto him, Theo asked his fiancée to accompany him to a few school functions. It sent a corrective message. That wouldn't be an option here. He'd never bring India to Braemore—with her eye-catching smile and sweet figure. Then Theo remembers he no longer has a fiancée to invite. He ignores the blond and moves on.

As he suspects, it's music that allows him to shove a foot through the door and start a semi-civil conversation. Theo sits on top of the desk and asks for iPod examples of what they are into musically. It is totally rap oriented—Drake, something called Wiz Khalifa, White Iverson, and a more violent Eazy-E are among the most popular. It's offensive and crude and hardly anything a young man with a background in classical music can appreciate. But they can, and that is of use to Theo. He allows them to educate him, at least for today. Theo suspects developing a rapport is paramount to taking the target off his back.

There is another music appreciation class after lunch. Only nine students show up to that one. Five minutes in and an African American boy remarks, "This is fucking bullshit, man. What I need some cracker who ain't never set foot in Dorchester to tell me my shit. Fuck yo ass—"

He knocks over a chair, which gives Theo more of a start than the blond girl did. He leaves the room, and Theo is admittedly glad he is gone. The boy is particularly angry, and while all Braemore students had to pass through a metal detector, Theo imagines there's more than one way to obtain a weapon on the inside. Things quiet down after this incident, and later that day, students are invited to sign up for band and orchestra. Theo is encouraged when eleven students add their names to the list.

When the day ends and Theo heads for the T, he thinks it's gone about as well as can be expected. No one pulled a knife on him or took a swing—the offer of sexual services was the only one. There was a fistfight between two girls in the hall, but he wisely left that to the officers on duty.

Theo is still unsure if Braemore is the right decision. Taking a job like this should be about altruism and desire to help change a life. Selfishness bubbles; the life Theo most wants to change is his own. By the time he arrives at his apartment, Theo has reasoned it out this way:

maybe he can accomplish both things—help the students at Braemore and help himself. That wouldn't be too awful. Maybe it will work out. Maybe Theo will forget India. It could be that she was right, and they would have been a mistake. A quick check of his cell phone supports this idea. There's no message from India. He wonders how long it will be until he stops looking at his phone, anticipating a missed call from her. However, there is a message from a phone number Theo doesn't recognize.

He opens the apartment door. The smell of home cooking wraps around him like a blanket. In the kitchen Theo finds a pot of homemade spaghetti sauce simmering on the stove. There's a note.

I'm not interfering. I'm not intruding on your adult decisions. I'm only making sure you have dinner. There's garlic cheesy bread in the oven. That and could you please call your mother so I know you've made it through the day unscathed?

His mother has been heartbroken for Theo since India left him. She worries like any good mother would. When he announced his job at Braemore, Theo could almost see Claire grit her teeth to keep from yelling, "*Like hell you will!*" That was if she ever cursed at him or raised her voice. She's always shown remarkable restraint. Even so, Theo almost turned down the job because of her. He can't imagine being the thing that causes his mother more pain or unhappiness.

Like Theo, she's moved on from the tragedy of September 11. But his mother has never moved beyond the loss of her husband. Theo finds this perplexing in that his mother is an attractive woman and a lively conversationalist. Yet in all these years, she has not pursued a relationship beyond one or two dates. Although, this is not to say his mother is lonely—she works in a freelance capacity with her old New York publishing house and sits on the board of several charitable organizations. She has many friends. However, Theo also knows that he has been Claire's priority.

Theo sniffs the air inside his apartment. It smells of love and Parmesan cheese. He's poised to dial the phone, calling to thank his mother and assure her that he's in one piece—it's not something that could always be said in the McAdamses' house. But Theo chooses to listen to the odd message first.

"Hi. My name is Sasha Pease. I'm an attorney. Your name and number were given to me by Principal Giroux at Braemore. I have an, um . . . an *unusual circumstance* . . . I have a client with a profound musical gift. She, uh . . . she's not a teacher. She's a . . . Well, she would like to volunteer with your classroom work at Braemore. She . . . It's like this . . . Maybe you should give me a call back and I can explain the details."

CHAPTER FIVE

Olivia

At seven, Rob comes through the door of the brownstone. In his arms are the roses Sasha predicted—two dozen, at least, and white. A formal peace offering. I'm stretched out on the sofa, covered in a cashmere throw, reading a book. Well, I'm staring at a book—something about ghosts, or gifts and ghosts. *Absurd.* It doesn't matter; I haven't absorbed a word. The wide entry to the living room frames Rob, his dark hair styled to its usual coiffed state. If metrosexual were still a popular term, Rob would be the definition; perhaps he was the inception. He looks like a cologne ad—the cardboard kind that falls from a magazine as you sit on the toilet, flipping through.

I shut the book and place it on the coffee table. My hand hovers near a weighty glass-and-pewter cigarette lighter—not that anyone smokes. I saw it in an antique shop and thought it would go perfectly with the brownstone. A wry smile edges onto my face as Rob takes a step back. I pick up my wineglass. A dry red slides down my throat. I tilt my head at my husband. "Rough commute, hon? City bus or did you walk?" Rob loathes public transportation.

"I took a cab," he says.

I'm hardly surprised.

"Liv, are we going to discuss this—calmly?"

Calmly as I can, I reply, "The Wellesley house? The money—or I should say what it's worth. You understand how much worse this is than last time? You get it, right?"

"Believe me, Liv. I get the potential fallout of this. What it means."

"Do you?" Calmness slips. I shake my head; I'm still not ready for the larger *what's at stake* issue. I spy the plea bargain agreement, also sitting on the coffee table. "Well, at least your transgressions won't be documented within the Suffolk County court system. Apparently, reparation for my . . . reaction will require more than a weekend in jail and complimentary balcony seats." I put down the glass and poke at the papers. "Not to make excuses, but I wasn't thinking too clearly while I was swinging that bat."

"You were drunk."

"And you wouldn't have been?"

He bobs his head up and down, a nonverbal agreement. "Actually, in court, I was surprised you so clearly recalled the details. Usually when you've had that much to drink you tend to forget."

"Perhaps it reflects the severity of the incident—yours, not mine."

He nods. "What, um . . . what reparation?"

"One hundred community service hours to be served, by me, in amends for my smart mouth." I smile broadly. "Apparently a gavel and power decreed by the state of Massachusetts makes Judge Nicholson an expert on the inner workings of Olivia Klein Van Doren."

"Huh," Rob says, perplexed. "I have the better part of a decade under my belt, and I'm not sure I could explain you."

"Flattery will get you nowhere." He walks farther into the room. "Neither will the roses."

“A hundred hours—geez, that sucks. Sasha couldn’t . . .”

“No, I’m afraid the community service hours are mine to keep. Although Sasha is working on a . . . She’s attempting to negotiate an *environment* more suited to my skill set.”

“Damn. Is Harvard offering a class in the lasting effects of sarcasm on the human psyche? You being the control substance, of course.” The attempt at humor falls flat. He smiles—a dazzling effort that also misses. He quickly sobers. “What, uh . . . what does that mean, ‘an environment more suited to your skill set’?”

“It means if my idea pans out, I won’t have to pick up trash off Storrow Drive—a fact that can only work in your favor.” I am reminded, again, of the catalyst for the whole outrageous circumstance. “So you’ve come bearing roses. That’s the easy part, Rob. Go ahead. Enlighten me. Explain how the Wellesley house ended up a hostage in your latest venture?” Casting the cashmere throw aside, I lurch off the sofa. I eye the roses that rest in his arms. He looks like the master of ceremonies in a beauty contest, about to crown the winner. It seems like a job Rob would handle deftly. Since I would have been eliminated during the congeniality portion of the contest, I brush past and take refuge in the music room.

On the desk is the Shep Stewart clipping from today’s *Boston Ledger*. Rob’s actions, while upsetting, have created the most unlikely possibility: *I’m going to serve time in Theo McAdams’s classroom* . . . This has gone too far—further than smashing a Porsche with a bat. A smarter Olivia would cancel the Braemore idea before it spins out of control and . . .

A plea from Rob disrupts burgeoning wisdom.

“Liv,” he says, coming up behind me. “I’m working several angles to save the house. Look, I know what it means to you—or what its value means in the future. Believe me; the value of the house means as much to me.” I turn, rolling my eyes at him. “If you want the nitty-gritty details we can go over everything. It’s quite amusing when you hear the whole story . . .” My mouth gapes at the notion. “Okay, so *amusing* isn't going to fly here, but it really was an oversight. I'd forgotten . . . Or I didn't realize the house was part of the collateral package I'd put together for my share of a golf course deal in Vero Beach. The deal was tabled about six months ago—the land got tied up in some legal snafu when a local Indian tribe tried to claim the property, and—"

"*Indians*. You're going to blame this on Native Americans?" I retreat back to the living room. "I don't want to hear it, Rob! Just fix it!" I fold my arms and turn. "I don't have another Amati to sell!"

"I will. And, I swear, you won't lose the house. If all else fails, I'll raise alternative capital. The house as a future asset will be safe. But there's every chance the local tribe's claim won't pan out, and your mother—"

"Yes. My mother. Another great point. Wait until Eugenia Klein finds out you lost the roof over her head—the home she's lived in since running away from hers more than fifty years ago. All the security she's ever known, Rob. Security that was entrusted to me! Yes. That'll go over just swell."

He looks at the herringbone parquet and to me. "Geez, I'd forgotten that part."

I soften at his sheepish glance. "Well, it's not like we regale the story every Christmas Eve." I breathe deep and close my eyes. My mother is from the South—a stark white, pretentious, upper-class 1960s South. Eugenia Strathmore met my father while he was on tour with the Indiana University orchestra. It was before he mangled his hand, while he still planned on a future as a professional violinist. Regardless, a well-bred girl, fresh from her society debut, was not supposed to fall for a Jew from the North, not even a rich one. Since her family all but cut her off, the Wellesley house has been her refuge. Dying in it, I'm sure, is a nonnegotiable plan. "Do you know my mother showed up here this morning?"

"As a matter of fact, I do."

"She knows about me and jail but—" My flailing arm halts midway. "You do?"

"Yes. I talked to Eugenia. Do you really think I expected you to explain the Wellesley house issue? I told her a good bit of what's happened. She was . . . *surprised.* When she said she'd be in the city tonight having dinner with friends, I thought it best to explain the rest in person. I asked her to come by."

Before I can react, the doorbell rings. For a moment, I think Rob has stowed my mother on the front porch. I move toward the door, eyes narrowing. "And you think this will remotely help you how?"

I open the door and my mother glides through. Surely she's furious, having learned what set off the tirade, which led to my incarceration and her public humiliation. She approaches the living room with the decorum of a high-ranking diplomat. It's the civility shown after your piss-poor country has accidentally blown something up in hers. "Rob."

I note that the greeting lacks its usual *favorite son-in-law* warmth.

"Genie," he says.

He is the only person who gets away with this nickname, a privilege that is not lost on me. Not even my father called her anything less than Eugenia. She's changed her clothes—a different dark suit, complemented by fresh blood-red nail polish. The world has gone casual, everything from airline travel to what you might wear to a finer restaurant. Eugenia Klein is determined to keep up appearances for the rest of us. She will be the one properly dressed when either hell freezes over or the masses see the error of their ways. "I assume you're still working on rectifying the unfortunate situation we spoke about earlier."

"I am, Genie. It's going to take a little time. But I swear, I'll fix it. You needn't worry."

She smiles and I blanch at their unlikely comradery. Anger is not something she wants to feel for *her Rob*.

"I have confidence, Rob. Of course, I'm hardly thrilled by the news, but I trust you'll repair the situation."

"Even so," he says. "I thought you'd like to know the particulars, how the house got caught up in it in the first place, and what I plan to do to resolve—"

She waves a liver-spotted manicured hand at him. Something is missing; I can't place it. "Heavens no," she says. "I've no desire to listen to dry business dealings. That's your specialty." She does shoot him a fine-point look. "Just remedy things so we don't need to speak of it again. Can you do that, Rob?"

He nods dutifully. "Already in the works—promise."

"Good."

So if you're not here to play twenty questions with Rob . . .

My mother comes toward me. "I accepted Rob's invitation this evening because I want to speak with you, Olivia—again."

"Me? Why? Did I only imagine our mother-daughter tête-à-tête this morning?"

"When we chatted, you left out details." She points to Rob. "Now that I'm in possession of those facts . . ." Her gaze ticks back to my husband. "Would you be a dear and fix me a Manhattan? Maybe see if you have that wonderful organic cheese Olivia sometimes buys. I didn't care for my dinner. It's difficult to find a restaurant that can craft a proper meal nowadays—everything's about atmosphere. Seems the day's events have left me lightheaded."

The prod to leave registers and Rob exits toward the kitchen, saying something about putting the roses in a vase. My mother waits until we hear the squeak of the swinging door. She motions toward the music room. With her smartly painted fingertips, she grips my upper arm with a strength you might not expect from a seventy-five-year-old woman. She closes the pocket doors behind us. "What?" I hiss, wondering if the news has caused a plaster crack in her well-preserved comportment.

I know what the Wellesley house means to her. She lost her husband; the property is her tangible connection. It's as though we are sharing the same thought when a flicker of emotion sparks on her face.

Damn if I don't feel one in return. "Mom, I know what the house means to you. I know this came as a shock, what Rob did—"

"Yes. What Rob did." She opens her eyes so wide the wrinkles around them vanish. "Not his best moment. But it would have been helpful if you could have mentioned as much earlier today."

I'm stifled; perhaps she's come to apologize. "At the time, I didn't have the finer details. Without Rob here to explain, especially explain how he plans to fix it . . ." I graze my hand through the air between us. "But maybe now you understand why I behaved like I did the other night, why things spiraled out of control."

"Actually, Olivia, not in the least."

"You do understand he's all but gambled away your home." She remains stone-faced. "To Indians! Your coveted Wellesley house?"

"Naturally I'm upset about the house. I'm irritated with Rob. And while I don't deal with financial matters, I'm not an idiot. But one has to choose their battles." She looks me up and down. "If I have to expend energy on a cause . . . Rob's transgression can be perceived as an honest mistake. Highly regrettable but honest."

"Are you serious?"

"He'll rectify it. Rob isn't my point in coming back here this evening," she says. "You are. I've been thinking about it since he called. The way you handled the situation—instead of trying to be a partner to your husband in a time of need, you chose to beat his vehicle into a pile of junkyard metal. Out of the two . . . *events*, I find it to be the more troubling aspect."

I take a short turn around the room. "Oh my God. You are serious."

"And you should be too." Her face falls to a fantastic level of soberness. "How far do you plan on pushing him?"

I need a drink. Fortunately, the music room also comes with a small but well-stocked bar cart. I grab a bottle of gin and pour, downing a mouthful like tap water. I do not offer my mother a drink—let Rob get it.

"I've been witness to your calamitous folly in the past. I know what you're capable of if you feel provoked. Tell me. What mother—aside from Jane Fonda's—enjoys hearing about her daughter's vigilante behavior?"

"Oh, for Christ's sake, Mom, get an analogy from this century, would you?" Secretly, I think my mother has always been fascinated by Jane, her acts of applaudable dissidence. Marrying my father was Eugenia Strathmore's single act of dissent in an, otherwise, all too obvious woman.

"Forget Jane. Forget your crimes. I'm far more concerned about what you'll do next. When consumed by emotion, Olivia, you don't possess the clearest head. I came here to offer a warning."

"A warning?"

"Yes. A warning. Marriage is difficult. I appreciate that Rob is not perfect, but you'd better take a good hard look at your own imperfections—you've been fighting them for a while now." The observation draws a stinging breath from me. "That man appears to love you unconditionally."

I hate it when she refers to Rob as *that man*. It makes me feel like he's more her business than mine.

"I thought it quite lucky when he turned up in your life, particularly so past your prime."

Sadly, I don't even flinch at her circa-1940s remark about my expired sell-by date.

My mother looks toward the closed pocket doors. "Rob was second in his class at Princeton. He possesses a Juris Doctor, even if he chooses not practice. He's never even been divorced! He comes from a widely respected family—albeit New Yorkers." She pauses, drawing closer to me and her point. "Add to the fact that *this* husband hasn't responded to trying circumstances with outrageous behavior. He's certainly not the kind of man who would shirk his responsibility by—"

"You're not seriously going to compare Rob to . . ." I can't believe it. No. Wait. I can absolutely believe what she's about to say. She's going to parlay Rob's current mistakes into an opportunity to point out my past ones. I put down the drink and fold my arms. "Don't do it, Mom. Don't you dare say the words *Sam Nash*, or use *now* to rehash history so old it couldn't possibly matter to anyone beyond the Clinton administration."

"History, Olivia, is what we learn from. And currently, I find yours extremely relevant. As I said, at the moment, Rob's not standing in his best light." She shifts her bony shoulders. "Even so, it might be worth focusing on what he hasn't done. Rob's not a coward, Olivia. He faces his responsibilities. I would think coming to me, confessing this *issue*, is a fine example of that."

"Here we go," I mutter.

"Rob didn't sneak off, marrying you without giving a thought to me or your father. As it is, look how long it took you to find someone compatible with your personality."

I roll my eyes, guessing pre-Rob she had my future laid out. After she was dead, I'd take up residence in the Wellesley house, fill it with cats, engraving the word *spinster* on the 1905 plaque marking the front entry. "Or it could be that I simply didn't want to get married until I met Rob." I take a large sip of my drink. "Even Jane would cheer me on there."

"Mmm . . . And why is it you were so anti-marriage? For heaven's sake, who would have thought I'd select from the wedding registry at Bloomingdale's for Phillip and his husband before you!" She says it aloud, but it's a tense whisper, demonstrating that she acknowledges but does not approve of her son's life.

I smile at the rub—her gay son with zero proclivity for music, a manly buff surfer dude from head to toe. Tell me the gods weren't in on that one.

She continues to ramble. "Was your distaste for marriage about independence or dedication to your career?" My face grows warm as she points out modern, commendable reasons for not being fixated on a significant other. Then she hits the nail on the head—or into my hand. "No, not you, Olivia. Your aversion to marriage was all about the colossal disaster of your first marital go-round. Does that make more sense?"

History rolls in, repeating like Beethoven's *Moonlight Sonata*—irritating endless measures. "Look, if you're going to start in with—" I sigh. She is. She's also blocking the exit.

"Rob didn't get you pregnant at twenty. Then, like your first husband, do nothing but breathe a sigh of relief after getting into a horrific accident. The result of which could have killed you and did end the life of your—"

"Don't be dramatic because it suddenly suits you, Mom. The accident didn't come close to killing me. I had a two-inch cut on my forehead and seat-belt burn."

"Regardless, the accident did end a pregnancy that was not part of Sam Nash's plans."

"Or yours," I reply.

"Perhaps. But it wasn't your father's reaction or mine that sent you into an emotional tailspin. You couldn't handle it when Sam Nash left. I'm merely attempting to head off a repeat—"

"Sam didn't leave me." It's how I prefer to see it. "I told him to go. There wasn't any reason for him to stay."

"Regardless, I told you from the moment I laid eyes on him he was nothing but low-life trouble."

"You mean from the moment you decided he was nothing but what you and your family would have labeled white trash, worse than the kike you married."

"Olivia!"

Her fair eyes go so wide I believe they may dislodge from her head. It's an epithet taken from one of a few arguments I was privy to in my youth, a handful of twisted visits my mother, Phillip, and I made to Atlanta's Cascade Heights, or as I eventually called it, Cascade Whites.

"I'll blame that remark on an example of your reckless state of mind."

"I'm sure you'll blame it on whatever you want," I mumble, sipping the gin.

"This situation and all those years ago, it's a reminder of how erratic your behavior can be. Because of Sam Nash, you didn't finish school. You were so distraught you sought refuge with your brother."

I snicker. "And you think that had any more to do with Sam than it did you and Dad?"

"I recognize the signs, Olivia. I'm just trying to ward off—"

I thrust my hand up like a stop sign. "Shut up. Just shut up, Mother. The situation with Rob couldn't be more removed from the one with Sam."

"Precisely. Two different men. That's progress and not so far from my point. While the past few days don't prove it, you're also not the same chaotic young woman you were back then. Granted, I've learned to live with the impulsiveness that drives you—I accept that where artistry like yours exists, there are bound to be eccentricities."

Finally, she gives me an opening. "You mean like Dad and his own disastrous escapades?" The double standards are endless.

"Do not compare, Olivia. Do not bring your father's misfortune into this."

I pick up the glass, firm in my grip, recalling my father's badly mangled hand and what artistic eccentricities cost him. It's too bad he just couldn't have cut off an ear. It would have saved us both a lot of trouble. I cheer the glass at her. "Fine, Mom. Is there an end to this lecture anytime soon? I do have symphony rehearsal tomorrow."

"With pleasure. Despite what Rob has done," she says, assigning him a modicum of blame, "do not allow impetuous tendencies to drive a permanent wedge between you. Don't do anything irrevocable. Rob has only encouraged your gift."

I frown. "Maybe so, but I didn't hear him screaming 'Stop!' when I auctioned the Amati."

Her matching expression inverts. "As if Rob had any real influence in the matter." She holds up a hand, precious gems wrapped around her fingers. They highlight her bare wrist.

I see what's missing. "Where's your watch?"

"My—" She dead stops and glances at her wrinkled wrist.

Her wrist hasn't been watch-less in thirty years; it's like her nose is missing. "Why aren't you wearing it?"

She appears confused, examining her bare wrist as if it belongs to someone else. Her gaze hardens, looking into mine. "Do not change the subject. Rob remains one of a few moments of clarity in your life. Don't make your response to this the glaring takeaway. The thing that haunts us all years from now."

I stride to the secretary. With my back to her, I run my hand over Shep Stewart's 9-11 article. I down a burning last gulp of gin. Turning back, I hear tapping rise from the pocket doors.

"Uh, ladies?" Rob slides one side open. It's a small room, and from the entry my glassy gaze meets his. "Your drink, Genie." He holds it out, though his eyes never leave mine. "We didn't have any cheese. Liv, what, um . . . what's going on in here?"

"Nothing," I say, gripping tight to the empty glass. "Mother's just come by to remind me that life can result in even more precarious choices than beating the shit out of a Porsche with a baseball bat."

CHAPTER SIX

Olivia

Later that night we are in bed. I've sought refuge in a different book. Ten pages in and I can't relate to this story either. Moody women's fiction—emotionally charged prose with characters on a deep introspective journey. Fuck that. Catharsis isn't always the answer. Why can't the story ever be about fitting comfortably—or not—into what you're handed? In my case it might be my own skin or a house in Wellesley. *Journeys* don't interest me. At least not as they are reflected in moody women's fiction.

Rob closes his laptop and puts it aside; I close the book. Both overhead lights are on. Simultaneously turning them off seems like what should happen here. During the past year, turning things off has become more customary than talking them out. By the time Rob confessed that the previous investment deal had gone wrong—the one that caused me to forfeit the Amati—*grave financial peril* was not an exaggeration.

While Rob went on to recover his investment business, the fallout has taken a toll on us. Perhaps this is because I have always equated Rob to stability, and I was shaken by the idea that I could be living on a fault line. Since then, arguments have escalated. Ironically, most have little to do with money, or they did until last Friday night.

My knees are tucked to my chest, and Rob reaches over, his hand resting on one. I don't pull away, though I wonder if my mother has affected my compliance. I run the Rob pluses through my mind. Despite or aside from money, Rob is steady; he is present. He gets me. In turn, I get that this is no easy task. His fingers squeeze my knee, and I place my hand over his, like I'm trying to recapture the moment, maybe a feeling.

"I really am sorry, Liv. But I've made good headway—called in a few cash-heavy favors. Like I said, I'll fix it." I retract my hold, and he removes his hand, scrubbing it over his face. "I didn't imagine Eugenia would come here to call you on the carpet."

"Your ability to underestimate one another is fascinating."

"What did she say that had you so upset? I knew better than to push it when she was here."

"If you're worried that she's thinking of stepping down from her presidency of the Rob Van Doren fan club, you needn't be."

"I wasn't thinking that at all. I was wondering what she said to you . . . about you. I'm not blind, Liv. I'm not entirely sure why I get a pass on Eugenia Klein scrutiny, but I know how hard she can be on a person."

"You get a pass because . . ." A swell rises in my throat; an attempt to swallow may be life threatening. "Eugenia just did what she always does—unearths the past, thinking it will ward off future mistakes."

"Whose past?"

"Mine. More specifically my Sam Nash era."

He nods. We rarely speak of it; it was so brief. I think Rob sometimes forgets he's husband number two.

"And ancient history factors into this how?"

"She wanted to remind me about stone casting and houses made of glass. While short-lived, Sam Nash did manage to bring out the worst in me."

He twists in my direction. "Worse than beating up a Porsche?"

"The Porsche incident, while admittedly not smart, expressed a lot of anger. Sam was more of a slow burn."

"What made him so different?"

I shift in the bed. My first husband is the last subject I anticipated discussing tonight. "A lot of things. Because of Sam . . . *us*, I chose to leave school, instead of being tossed out, like the Conservatory and MSM." He cinches his waxed eyebrows. "Manhattan School of Music," I clarify. He nods. "Sam gets the blame for that, and my mother isn't completely wrong. I did run away to Phillip. When I came back . . . Well, when I came back I was probably in a worse place than when I left." I clear my throat; Rob remains quiet. "I might not have cared for what she said tonight, but I can see how she got there." I turn on the local news; the volume is low.

"Okay, I understand that your first marriage was tumultuous . . . the car wreck, the miscarriage, but what does it have to do with us years later?"

"Nothing," I say. "It was more about bad choices, the places I end up when threatened or hurt—acting out in regrettable ways."

"With him or with me?"

I glance at Rob. Sometimes I wish he weren't quite so clever. "You, of course. I told you, Eugenia didn't come to here to disenfranchise herself from your fan club. She came for the booster committee meeting."

Satisfied that he was not the cad in the conversation with my mother, Rob lets it go. I do not take thoughts of Sam Nash one step further; I even turn up the TV volume to signal, if anything, the topic is boring me. In truth, another word might undo a dam of well-guarded emotion.

Rob takes the remote from my hand. He turns the volume up more. "Liv . . . are you seeing this?" He nudges my arm.

I focus. A reporter is talking about a group of middle-grade kids from Boston Public Schools. They're posed in front of Faneuil

Hall—with instruments. They've won a local contest. I tip my chin upward and listen. It's newsworthy because these kids are from lower-income schools. They've been brought together by a sizable anonymous endowment. The kind inherited money and surplus from the sale of a coveted Amati violin might buy, providing them with quality instruments and private lessons. If they win the next round, they'll go on to the district competition. "Well, bully for them," I murmur.

"I won't start, but you know what I want to say. Your mother could benefit from an earful of what, precisely, you have accomplished. She should know about a daughter who is responsible for something more than poor choices. She should know whose money—"

"Stop," I say softly, touching his leg. "It's not going to happen . . . ever." I grab the remote, listen for a few more seconds before shutting off the television. I serve up a corner-eyed glare. "Do it and I'll only move down the list. After the Porsche, that'd be your laptop, LeCoultre watch . . . maybe your Concept2 rowing machine. Did the bat go with the tow truck to the junkyard?" Rob shakes his head, unsure if he should laugh or hide his possessions, but surely weighing my threat. "Proving myself to her isn't the point. It's not the reason I . . ." I reach over, touching his knee. "It's not the reason *we* did it."

He's quiet for a moment. "Honestly, Liv? It's not your mother's perceptions or just opportunities for those kids I hoped we'd alter with the endowment." Rob snaps off the light on his side of the bed. "I hoped it might change how you see yourself." He punches his pillow and slides beneath the covers.

I turn off my light but pick up the iPad. Like this morning, I want to escape today. I click on the online version of the *Boston Ledger*. It's a quieter distraction as I read about the five other 9-11 children that are part of Shep Stewart's annual update, perusing them reverently.

Andrea Wakefield was barely a toddler when her father perished that day. She's just started her senior year of high school in New Hampshire. Her mother and new husband moved there when she remarried. Andrea and her two half brothers are posed on the front porch of their handsome country house. I don't anticipate any sense of loss in Andrea's expression—and I don't see one. She appears to be a well-adjusted young lady. She wants to be a social worker or a fashion designer. I envy her freedom of choice.

The story is almost the same for Stacy Roche, who was three when her father died on Flight 77, the plane that hit the Pentagon. The article says she's starting her sophomore year at Ball State University. She wants to join the Peace Corps—a dream inspired by the tragic start of her life.

There's a cursory mention of Joaquin Perez. His father, a Southie native, was a chef in the restaurant of the South Tower of the World Trade Center. Last year Shep reported that Joaquin had relocated to Canada. He no longer wanted to be a part of the chronicle. Learning this about Joaquin upsets me greatly. One will leave, and soon they'll all go, including Theo. I'll never know how his life turns out.

The other updates continue. Tara DeMarco Randall and a memoriam mention of Andrew Vaughn. He became a firefighter, like his father, who was training with NYC firefighters on that fateful day. Doubly tragic, Andrew died in the line of duty two years ago. This hasn't stopped Shep from keeping vigil, starting over with the Andrew's son and daughter, a family that continues to spin in a never-ending cycle of grief.

I finish reading and close out the *Ledger* webpage, placing the iPad on the nightstand. It doesn't compare to their lives, but it's been a nerve-racking few days. I hug my knees tight, wanting to squeeze into a tiny, unnoticeable ball—like dust. My mother's not wrong. The girl who made bad choices, acted out, isn't so different from the woman in bed with the tucked-tight knees. I'm still making bad decisions, everything from music to memories of Sam Nash. I know I am. Today's community hours' choice is only one more example. As if to confirm as much, the iPad lights up—a telltale glow of light. It's an e-mail from Sasha. Subject line: *Braemore and McAdams are a go. You start ASAP.*

CHAPTER SEVEN

Six Months Earlier

Newport Beach, California

Sam

"Sorry to keep you waiting, Sam." Bogey makes his way from the doorway of his office to a high-back leather chair. For every time Sam has sat there in the past year, it's seemed like a mile walk. At first Sam thought it was Bogey's age, the elderly oncologist having to take his time. In subsequent visits, his slackened pace seemed to imply more bad news. Sam would count the steps. It normally takes nine to get from the door to his chair. Today it takes eleven.

That can't be good.

Sam stiffens his chin and prepares for another punch. He is unsure if his frail frame can do the same. "What's the word, Bogey?" The need for small talk passed long ago. As he's about to answer, there's knock on the office door. It's Maura, his office assistant. Bogey's wife is on the phone. Sam points, insisting he take the call. He knows Dr. Bogart's wife has been as ill as Sam. While he is anxious, he is not without compassion. He leans back in the chair and tries to relax.

When Sam was initially diagnosed with myeloid leukemia, he spent most of the appointment not reeling from the news, but asking how someone had the balls to deliver it. Dr. Elias Bogart—Bogey to Sam—eventually confided that it was the most bizarre reaction he'd ever witnessed. Sam Nash asked every question but the ones that mattered. In different ways, both men were stunned.

"Sam," Bogey said that day, "I'm sorry to tell you that our initial findings were conclusive. The bloodwork and further bone marrow testing was positive. The prognosis of myeloid leukemia on its own can be dicey. But my ultimate goal for you is remission. I'm going to do everything I can to help you."

Sam slapped his back against the chair opposite Dr. Bogart. "How . . . how can you just sit across from someone and say that—like it's fucking going to rain or you decided you're out of here today because you want an earlier tee time in the California sun?"

Sam always viewed himself as a straightforward man. But this was beyond his comprehension.

That day, Dr. Bogart didn't reply directly, not to Sam's question. He only ran his fingers through the wispy white hairs on his head and added a grimacing nod. "I've put together some literature on your diagnosis. Naturally, we'll discuss treatment options at length. But I want to be clear about what we're facing in terms of—"

"Now?" Sam said, dumbfounded. "I can't be sick *now*. I've just accepted a coaching position with Cal State. I was planning on—"

"I understand, Sam. Absorbing a difficult diagnosis is hard. And unfortunately, timing is one of those things we can't control."

Timing. Aside from a multimillion-dollar fast ball, timing never was Sam's forte. The future wasn't something he dwelled on. In fact, Sam prided himself on his *live in the moment* attitude. There'd been some fatigue, bruises that wouldn't heal, a couple of odd fevers—nothing that said, *"Hey, dude. You're dying."* Sam brushed it off as too much booze and middle age, maybe the idea of real employment at this point in his life. He hadn't done that since . . . Well, ever. A successful career in major league baseball had ended a few years before, leaving Sam with more money than most people dreamed of. What Sam lacked was purpose. He'd decided a coaching job wouldn't be the worst thing. Just as Sam accepted a sweet position at Cal State Fullerton, his life turned upside down. The pre-employment physical, the bloodwork, it was all routine—until it wasn't.

After receiving Bogey's initial diagnosis, Sam went home and tossed the paperwork, which seemed like a death sentence, onto the hall table—a dumping ground for all the shit Sam didn't want to deal with. But eventually he had to pay the electric bill and car insurance and open investment statements to see how long his money was going to last. Sam never imagined looking at the sum and saying, "I probably won't need the interest . . ." Five days and four shots of tequila later, Sam found courage to read through Dr. Bogart's options and assessment.

Because he wasn't a complete idiot and maybe the future was something he wanted to see, treatment began immediately. As Sam suspected, it wasn't the dying part that bothered him so much. It was avoiding dying that proved incredibly intrusive. He was stunned by how fast chemotherapy swallowed his existence. It was the only course of treatment without a viable bone marrow donor.

Sam never relied much on his *family*—a poor noun for the Bulls Gap, Tennessee, squalor and trailer in which he was raised. Regardless, his father was dead, his mother never a factor. Sam did have a few cousins who volunteered to be tested, though Dr. Bogart insisted they wouldn't be a match. He was, of course, correct. Siblings were the most likely candidates for a match, and Sam did have a brother. But if Sam Nash lived life like one big day at an amusement park, Tate was the guy who never got off the ride. Sam hadn't seen his brother in eight years.

The last time he did, it was at their father's funeral. The two brothers ended up in a blood-soaked fistfight.

After the brawl and a trip to the ER to fix Tate's nose, which Sam had broken, his brother returned to Texas. From there, time and a window for apologies passed. One brother had no use for the other—not until Sam did. Along with aggressive phases of chemo treatment, Sam went looking for Tate. He hired a private detective, Rex Simmons, who tracked him to La Vernia, Texas. But like a thief on the run, Tate had taken his DNA and potentially lifesaving bone marrow and disappeared. He left behind a common-law wife and possibly a two-year-old daughter. It sounded like the kind of thing a Nash boy would get himself into and out of by changing his address. Wherever Tate went after Texas, it was a lottery ticket question with Sam holding the losing stub. Randstad, the drilling company Tate worked for, sent his last paycheck to a post office box in Bellingham, Washington. The PI tracked the lead, hitting a dead end after learning no one had picked up the mail from there in over a year. It seemed as if Tate Nash simply vaporized. "Damn," Sam said to the last of Rex's bad news, which was months ago. "Dead end probably equals a dead man. That's, um . . . that's a bitch."

Sitting in the renowned oncologist's office now, Sam mentally reviews recent months and the completed phases of chemotherapy treatment. In addition to this, the National Marrow Donor Program remains a hopeful avenue if need be. He hangs on to the backup fact, particularly since he has no idea what Bogey will report today. It is an ongoing effort to self-comfort. Sam has a foreboding sense that today's news is not good. As an ace closing pitcher for the Los Angeles Angels—Anaheim Angels during his glory days—Sam guesses he had his turn at good fortune. He has money, fame, and a World Series ring. Though lately he only thinks of the ring in terms of whether they should bury it on him or off him. He's tried to stay positive, the lowest point coming when his old agent called to tell him there was a chance he'd make it into the baseball Hall of Fame on next year's round of balloting. Sam suspects it will be a moving posthumous acceptance.

As Bogey ends the call and adjusts himself in his chair, Sam finds himself mirroring the doctor's gestures. A wildly deep breath rattles through the chest of the usually sedate doctor. His head starts to shake, almost erratically. Sam wonders if Dr. Bogart's heart is thrumming like a jackhammer. Sam's is. Could be the prognosis has turned imminent. Instead of hope, there may be only half an inning left. Today Sam is there to get the results of extensive bone marrow tests and new bloodwork. Internally, Sam senses the innate wind up of being on the mound, the gut feel of knowing he's about to put one right down the middle of the plate.

"Sam, I . . ." The doctor blinks widely.

"You know me, Bogey. Just say it." Sam wants it over with. He grasps at ways to remain in control of his destiny. Maybe he will go from here to a pawn shop and trade his own memorabilia for a .45 automatic.

Dr. Bogart removes his glasses and brushes a knuckle past his eye. He opens a folder. This takes all of .04 seconds, but it feels like an oration of *War and Peace*. "This is amazing," the doctor says. "While it's not unheard of, it is rare to see numbers respond like this . . . Quite something."

Jesus, maybe he is already dead, and this is some kind of after-life penance. On longer nights, Sam has considered how much penance he has coming his way—the people he owes an apology to, one live-wire violinist in particular. Crunching his fingers into his thighs, Sam feels just enough pressure to ensure live nerve endings.

"It's, um . . . it's fantastic, Sam. Every test came back better than anything we expected. The bloodwork, the bone marrow biopsies—your white count is within the perfectly normal range, 7.0. I am so very glad to report that your initial remission is holding steady."

For a moment Sam thinks he will pass out. He tells himself to breathe. The batter has, somehow, miraculously, missed a shitty pitch.

The ball smacks with a life-jarring thud into the catcher's mitt. Sam steadies himself, thinking this is the brain compensating for horrific news. But looking at the unlikely smile on Dr. Bogart's face, Sam guesses he's heard right. "I . . . How can that be? You said the success rate was . . . That bone marrow donor would be . . . You said I should be prepared."

"All medicine is an educated guess, Sam. We talked about that. While the odds were not in your favor, you beat them. You've achieved remission. It's extremely encouraging."

Dr. Bogart continues on, about further monitoring, reiterating the meaning of remission. Sam hears him, but he doesn't want to think about it. Not this second. All Sam wants to think about is the fact that he's going to live.

After unhooking the canvas top on the Jeep, Sam drives home. The sun is shining on his peach-fuzz head. It's the first time he's ever removed the ball cap outside his house. Sam has always believed in luck. But now he wonders if he believes in God. This seems like too much luck for one man. For the first time in ages, he doesn't walk into his luxury condo wondering how many more times he will do so under his own steam. He has gone as far as projecting leaving in a body bag, almost feeling the bump of the gurney over the front door's threshold. Instead, he is thinking about maybe selling the condo and buying a house—one with a thirty-year mortgage, just for kicks. The stack of unopened bills and investment statements looks like fine reading material; he will deal with them later. Sam takes a turn around the granite-clad kitchen with its stainless-steel appliances and sunny golf course view. He bought the condo a few years ago because . . . Because he had to live somewhere.

After a live-in relationship with Charlene, things ended and Sam moved out. She wanted stability, marriage, maybe a dog. He wanted to keep the party going for as long as he could. Charlene came by, called a few times while he was sick. He thought it was nice of her. Now Sam can't remember if he thanked her. He should do that—tell her the good news. She'd want to know. She'll be nearly as thrilled as him.

Inside his condo, Sam takes the steps two at a time to his bedroom. That morning he dragged himself downstairs like a dying man, thinking he barely had the energy to lift a coffee mug. Dr. Bogart explained this has more do with the lingering side effects of the last treatment phase. In time, Bogey insists, Sam will be feeling more like his old self.

Catching a glance in the bedroom mirror, he looks forward to life getting back to normal. During the past six or seven months, Sam found he didn't necessarily know the man in the reflection. After a while, he avoided looking. Now he strips off his T-shirt. The mirror's image further reminds Sam of his reversal of fortune. His once muscular physique has withered like a dying tree limb. He is thin and pale and hairless—a disturbing contrast to the Sam Nash photos and plaques that hang on the wall of his condo—a parting homage to the Angels ace closer. He can still hear the announcer. "Now pitching, number forty-four, Sam Nash . . ."

His career with the Angels was a wild ride, and Sam enjoyed every minute of it. During his illness, Sam tried to come to terms with unresolved issues: his father's death, his glory days, his own demise—or maybe it was the incredible mistakes he made with Livy. Which thing did he have the most trouble getting his head around? He still doesn't know the answer. Mostly, Sam is stunned that he'll have a chance to think about it.

He might have a future, a second career in coaching if he wants it. Of course, the Cal State job is long gone. Gazing at the memorabilia and photos on his bedroom wall—a good-looking guy who had it all—Sam reconsiders the idea. Surely there are other coaching positions out there. But before he gets too far ahead, Sam looks back to the mirror. There is something to be said for posterity. He picks up his cell phone and aims it at his gaunt reflection. The device clicks, capturing the startling image of what no longer is a dying man.

Charlene lives only three miles away, in a town house Sam bought her as a birthday gift one year. Her car is in the driveway and Sam assumes she is home. His luck continues. She could have been in Japan or Orlando today. Charlene is a catalog model turned flight attendant.

Before leaving his condo, Sam traded his T-shirt for a long-sleeved button-down, one he'd recently purchased in a smaller size. He thought they might bury him in it. Now it's just a shirt with a better fit, enhancing the Sam Nash that was fading from view.

He rings the doorbell. He hasn't been to Charlene's town house in two years. Even so, it is odd to ring the doorbell. It occurs to him that he doesn't know if Charlene is dating someone or maybe living with someone else. The couple of times she visited, Sam didn't ask. Or he didn't remember what she said if he did ask. He feels uncomfortable and glances back at the driveway. There's only her car, so it's likely that no matter her relationship status she is home alone. He doesn't have another second to think about it as the door opens.

"Sam." Her fair eyes pulse wide. "What are you doing here?"

For a moment, the question flummoxes him. Since they broke up, he has seen Charlene four times. First to collect the big-screen TV he couldn't take upon exiting her town house, having camped out in a Residence Inn until closing on the condo. The second time he ran into her in the frozen food aisle in Trader Joe's. Her cart was filled with all the healthy junk she used to force on him—organic everything, fresh fruit, the various ingredients required to make some god-awful green shit she would pour into a glass every morning. The other two times Sam saw Charlene he was sick, lying on his sofa with his head over a bucket. He is prodded by the imagery and reason for his visit. "I wanted to tell you my good news." She looks curiously at him and holds the door wider. He goes inside. The interior hasn't changed; maybe a new sofa or paint. He doesn't remember.

"I'm getting ready to leave. I have a flight at one." He sees her tidy luggage packed and sitting near the door.

He shoves his hands in his pockets, suddenly aware of the lack of gesture—she doesn't offer a hug or even a *"How are you?"* "I just came from the hospital. I got some really great news. Against all odds, the chemo worked, Charl. Doc says I'm in full remission. I'm going to live!"

She nods deeply. "That's wonderful, Sam. I'm happy for you."

"Yeah, it was pretty grim for a while—I mean, it looked like I was in the permanent checkout line. At first, Bogey—that's Dr. Bogart, he tried to be positive, but I knew the odds weren't great. It was, um . . . working the available options," Sam says, recalling the diplomatic way Dr. Bogart phrased things. They stare at one another and silence grows awkward—more the feeling of telling someone you were ill rather than the astounding news of a recovery. "Anyway . . ." Sam says, clearing his throat. "I wanted to tell you. I thought you'd want to know. Thank you," he says quickly, "if I didn't say it those times you came by."

"You're welcome." Charlene folds her arms across her blue airline blouse. "But the first time, I only came by to get the key you never returned. That's when you told me you were sick." Sam nods. He doesn't exactly remember it that way. "The second time, I admit, I felt guilty, or maybe like I owed you." She gestures around the generous gift of square footage. "I came by . . . Well, I knew you didn't have anybody else. I couldn't imagine anything sadder than having to fight that kind of fight or worse . . ." Charlene purses her pink lips.

"Worse what?"

She runs a hand through her blond hair. He remembers the antsy tic. Charlene did that when they fought; she did it the day she told Sam she wanted him to move out. "Worse than dying alone," she answers. Sam tugs on the ball cap, though he doesn't remove it. Charlene is being dramatic. That was part of the problem. She was always making a big deal of shit. Sam wasn't alone. He's kept in touch with a handful of guys from back in the day. Sure. He hasn't exactly been in a social mood lately. Hell, he was kind of busy trying to save his own life. But Charlene is wrong about him being alone. Sam was the charmer on the outpatient list at Hoag Hospital—uber-friendly with every nurse on staff, not to mention a guy he met while in treatment. He had some sort of cancer and was a huge fan of Sam's. The guy even worked his chemo schedule so they came in at the same time. Then, just as they were forging a friendship, the guy died.

"Is that all?" she asks.

"Uh . . . I guess. Geez, Charl . . . I thought you'd be happier for me. We were together for three years."

"Yes. But it's been over for more than two. And if you want to know the truth, they were three of the hardest years of my life."

"Wow," Sam says, his eyes drawing wide. "Where the hell did that come from?"

Her expression turns a little squirrelly. "From you—mostly." She sighs and examines the carpet beneath their feet. Then she looks right at him. "What were you expecting, Sam? Yes. You were always a fun guy—the life of the party. The problem was the party never ended. I spent three years putting up with your come-and-go friends, glory days, and poker nights that lasted into the next day. Of course, it was nothing compared to your inability to accept everyday responsibility. That included everything from your laundry to paying your car insurance."

"Wait a second. If I recall, everyday life was something you also wanted to avoid. Sure, you had free flights to just about anywhere. But if I remember, I was the one paying for the fun in the sun . . . or the spur-of-the-moment trip to Vegas or the Kentucky Derby. 'Sam, I've always wanted to go to Monaco—live Grace Kelly's life for just a weekend.' Who the fuck do you think funded all that, Charlene?"

"You did." She coughs up the answer like it's been a bitter pill, stuck in her throat for the past five years. "I'm not saying I wasn't an enabler. It worked while it worked. I'll always be grateful for the town house," she says, glancing around her home. "But I did offer it back to you. And I don't think a desire for normalcy, maybe even kids, was such a crazy, off-the-wall idea."

"Seriously, Charl? You seemed to have a damn good time globe-trotting with me. That's what I remember."

"Of course it is, Sam. I understand that it's just me who remembers *us* getting pregnant and your reaction—something like the IRS was moving in to do a lifetime audit."

Sam swallows. He hasn't forgotten that part. He just doesn't dwell on it. It all happened so fast, more like a blip on the radar screen of their relationship. "It wasn't my fault, Charl."

"No, it wasn't," she admits. "It was more about your words afterward. They kind of stick with a person. 'Hell, Charl . . . we can get that dog now, if you want.'"

In hindsight, Sam's remark does strike him as thoughtless. On the other hand . . . "The only conversation we ever had about kids was that neither of us was interested in any. I'm not sure why *not* changing my mind makes me a prick?"

"You've got me there," she says. "And if I was the one who changed, so be it. Look, I'm not going to stand here and rehash history so old that I've forgotten your birthday. We were fun. When the fun ran out, you couldn't deal with any alternative. Things got ugly, and I asked you to leave."

Sam's never thought about it quite like that. What he recalls about Charlene and the downside of things is someone yelling at him to pick his shit up off the floor or demanding to know why he and his poker buddies couldn't use a few fucking coasters. Sam veers his glance toward the dining table. A number of overlapping rings are visible. Charlene is rambling now, more reasons about why they broke up—none of it, in

Sam's mind, has anything to do with a baby that was a two-second fact, or Charlene being so upset by his reaction. The truth is, when he thinks of a circumstance like a miscarriage, it's not Charlene's pregnancy and loss that comes to mind.

"Yes," she says. "I felt sorry for you when I found out you were ill—it's called human emotion, Sam. I don't know, maybe your illness was a good thing. Maybe it will give you some perspective about life and the tremendous way you've managed to waste yours so far."

Was she always so angry and bitter? Time has changed Charlene. And waste his life? Sam strongly disagrees—he has a World Series ring and the memories to prove it.

She grabs the handle to her suitcase. "I have to go . . . and so do you." She walks out the front door and he follows. At the edge of the walkway, she turns. Tears cloud her blue eyes. "When we met, most of the things about you dazzled me, I won't lie. And our breakup wasn't all your fault. But the way you're wired, there's something missing. It's not the Tinman and his heart—you have a fantastic capacity to love. It's more like a ring around it that won't let a damn soul get too close. I tried to find a way in, to fix it. I don't think it's fixable. So if you're *not* going to die, my advice would be figure out how you can do a better job at living."

CHAPTER EIGHT

Boston, Massachusetts

Olivia

Sasha removes her sunglasses—her eyes never fail to attract attention, even mine. Their amber hue reminds me of the actors who wore contact lenses in those famous vampire movies. Had a casting director passed her on the street, she would have been hired on the spot—part destiny and part luck. Despite Sasha's choice of significant others, which includes me and Jeremy Detweiler, she lives that sort of charmed life. The breeze blows back her hair, enhancing the camera-ready shot. Sasha looks from the passing crowds to me. She hasn't said so, but she's tagged along to the Starbucks near Braemore to ensure I keep up my end of the bargain. Today is my first day as a music educator assistant.

"So, how are things with Rob?" she asks. "Is he still sleeping on the sofa or the futon in his man cave? However it is you two handle things in your brownstone."

"He never spent a night on the futon." Of course this is not to say I've done more than allow him his side of the bed. "He claims he'll maneuver a deal that keeps the Wellesley house off the table."

Sasha nods. "For your sake and your mother's I hope so. By the way, did the symphony front office ever mention your, um . . ."

"Unfortunate brush with the law, temporary incarceration?" In reply, Sasha splays her hands into the open air. "No. Lucky for me, it seems they missed it."

"Good. That's one less thing to worry about." I make a face at her. "Like or not, Liv, playing the violin earns you a nice salary, as opposed to, say . . . dog walking." She pauses. "Not that there's anything wrong with dog walking. It's a perfectly respectable job."

"If you can't play the violin," I counter.

"I only meant most people would see your job as enviable. As for Rob, aside from this recent misstep . . ."

"And the last one."

"And the last one," she admits. "He's . . . Just don't be so quick to dismiss either thing."

"Uh-huh. As in, my options are limited."

"I didn't say that." It's a staring standoff. "Okay, do you really want to argue your flexibility quotient?"

"Not so much." I sip my coffee. "So, tell me, how is our moody resident writer, Jeremy?" I smile widely, cuing a sharp turn in topic.

"Working hard at his . . . *craft*."

Craft is new to Sasha's vernacular. It's a word she picked up on about a year ago. That's when Jeremy, a writer who wears pajama pants to Whole Foods where he regularly runs up Sasha's credit card, moved in with her. It's also my observation, and Rob's, that since then, Jeremy has no need for *employed* in his vernacular. "And what kind of progress is the burgeoning author making these days?"

Sasha clears her throat and shuffles in her seat. "Let's see. There were the magazine pieces he sold earlier this year." I nod at old news.

"*Writer Unleashed* even asked for a second. Did I mention that?" I stare harder as Sasha alludes to his fifteen-cents-a-word income. "Writing is a full-time job," she insists. "And while you don't appreciate it, Jeremy did win the highly respected Pushcart Prize."

I lower the cup, which was halfway to my mouth. "Two years ago!"

She bristles, her ongoing reasons for supporting Jeremy sounding more like excuses. "Good writing takes time, Liv. And success isn't necessarily about monetary reward." I hear more a parroting of Jeremy's words. "You of all people," she says, "should appreciate how tough it is to make a living with anything in the arts."

"You're right." And she is. Even so, my compassion for a thirty-eight-year-old man, who moved from his second failed marriage into Sasha's bedroom, is small. "But it's not like he hasn't taken a good long whack at it," I suggest. "That and maybe I have my six-figure symphony salary confused with a charitable stipend."

She sighs at a rare Sasha miss—or just the slanted judgment Jeremy fosters. "Okay, fine." She tilts her chin upward. "I didn't want to say anything prematurely, but it just so happens, Jeremy's latest manuscript is in the hands of a big-time publishing house. He's confident it will result in a huge deal, maybe even six figures—like yours."

"For your sake, I hope so. But even Rob agrees that Jer—"

She holds up a hand, unwilling to be tag-teamed by me and an absent Rob. "We all have our flaws, Liv. Guess my big one is wildly evident."

"What's that?" I ask, standing down, sipping coffee.

"An inexplicable need to have moody artist types in my life—whether it's struggling writers or fitful musicians." She eases back into her chair and focuses again on passersby.

"Point taken, counselor." I am reminded that Jeremy's artsy moody behavior has not resulted in owed community service hours. I adjust my sunglasses, maybe hide behind them.

We are silent. Sasha picks up a discarded copy of the *Boston Ledger*. She holds it up as if shutting me out. I narrow my eyes, getting a glimpse of the back page. It's a headline about Boston's endowment-funded orchestra. They've won their district competition and are on to a regional final. An unlikely flutter of self-worth pumps through me before Sasha snaps the newspaper away from her face.

"What are you smiling about?"

"Nothing. The weather." She drops the paper and returns to her latte. I breathe in early-fall air and take in an azure sky. But it's an eerie moment that creeps in—a different September day and the boy fatefully connected to it. My mind wanders from the orchestra headline to Shep Stewart's stories, his 9-11 children. I've never dreamed of dropping in on one—Theo McAdams in particular. Doubt invades. I finish my coffee and focus on impending reality. The bottom line here is that in two hours I will owe ninety-eight community service hours. In two hours my life will only be slightly different—different in a way that no one but me will ever see. But even that small thought draws a cowardly breath. "I don't suppose . . ."

"No," Sasha says, glaring in my direction. "I cannot, nor will I, go back to the judge and attempt to alter your community service agreement. Besides, I've been thinking about it. Your idea to help mentor these kids . . . I think it's a good call, Liv."

"Do you?"

"Yes. Jeremy agrees." She smiles at the opportunity to include his opinion. "Jeremy says you may learn about real human emotion—possibly exhibit some." We trade insulted stares—hers for my less-than-positive remarks about her boyfriend, and mine for now having to endure Jeremy's take on Olivia Klein *Crime and Punishment*. I'm sure he's foreshadowed many a rancorous fate, the kind Dostoyevsky would relish. "As for our opinion on your choice of just deserts . . ." Sasha squints into the bright morning light. "Hmm, how to phrase this so you'll benefit as opposed to being pissed off."

"Go for it," I say, knowing I've got one coming.

"You know how I take pro bono cases?" I nod. "I mentioned that a few of those have been your soon-to-be students." She points toward Braemore, diagonally across the street.

"Right. You have to. Your firm requires it, something like that."

"Yes. But what you don't know is that I take almost double the number required."

"Why?" I'm unsure where she's going with this. Not while my stomach is doing somersaults and the bowl of Special K I had before leaving the house feels like it's on a return trip. "What's in it for you besides extra work?"

"Nothing monetarily—and that's my point. I do it because there's satisfaction in helping someone who, otherwise, wouldn't get a fair deal. And just so you know," she says, sipping her coffee, "I work those cases with Nick Zowzer."

"Seriously? You and Zowz—together, for no money?" I've stumbled on benevolence that exceeds even the Sasha I know. "You loathe working paying cases with him. Why the comradery over pro bono?

"Out of all the things Zowz and I don't have in common . . ." She takes a lingering sip of her latte. "Working those cases appears to be a patch of common ground. We, um . . . we make a good pro bono team." I wriggle my nose at the concept—not the pro bono work, the voluntarily spending time with Nick Zowzer. "It's why we have a justice system, Liv. People have a right to counsel no matter their socioeconomic status." She continues the lesson. "I'm just saying, doing our part . . . It feels good."

I raise the cup to my mouth but then lower it. "I'll let you and Jeremy know how the whole *giving back* scenario works out for me." Choosing not to share my orchestra-funding project with Sasha was a conscious decision. I couldn't imagine her reaction, other than disbelief. I don't want to hear it, how *unlike me* the charitable effort is. Besides, isn't secrecy the definition of anonymity? Admittedly, a small part of me has zero desire to be judged by the Jeremys of the world. Sasha demonstrates this by continuing to educate me.

"All I'm saying is that you might find a benefit in sharing your gift."

My mouth opens. I begin a reply. But the thought and my gaping mouth freeze, enough to capture a passing fly. Everything stops as a man takes a seat at the table across from ours. I sit up taller. Black-and-white photos turn vivid. Theo McAdams drops a canvas satchel onto the chair opposite him and puts down a cup from which a teabag dangles. I study him, my hand moving in an upward V around my throat. My fingers meet with a pulse that requires a Xanax—possibly two. A tall black man encroaches on my view, approaching. A ball cap sits sideways over dreadlocks, and his pants are slouched midway around his ass. I know the black man's features, his face. He was pictured with the city-wide orchestra photo; I've seen him play with the endowment ensemble. He slaps Theo on the shoulder.

"Mr. M—how you doin' this morning?"

"Octavious . . . what's happening, man?" They punch fists in some modern, hip way that I've seen on TV.

"I was just on my way to class when I saw you sittin' here. I, uh . . . I did what you said. I recorded that rhythm I was tellin' you about, the one that keeps showing up at night—like when I'm dreamin'."

"Good, man. Let's hear it," Theo says.

He takes the seat next to Theo and pulls out a cell phone. Sasha starts to say something; I hold up my hand. From the device, sounds emanate. The music I'm most familiar with is, by and large, classical—I've learned it the way a physician absorbs open heart surgery—a delicate procedure with no margin for error. Even I admit it's beautiful when it comes together. But I'm not immune to what I might refer to as *street music*. The air around the Starbucks tables fills with beatbox melody. Theo's fingers tap in succinct rhythm. Octavious is bopping in his seat; his timing is exquisite. Anyone would swear a half-dozen studio musicians are creating the rapid, complex cadence. Nearby coffee drinkers are drawn to the sound. Some appear annoyed, but most look on curiously impressed.

"What'chu think?" he asks as the beats peter out.

"Hey," Sasha says, twisting, and then turning back toward me. "Isn't the white guy your 9-11 kid?" I shush her and shrink back in my seat. But Theo and his student are too engrossed to notice either of us.

"I think that is a seriously good sound," Theo says. "How about we play it for the class? We can head on over right about now." Theo glances at a watch. Octavious laughs. "What?"

"Man, only white dudes from the suburbs would wear something so lame. You need to get yourself a Rolex—somethin' that makes a statement!"

"Not in my budget." Theo gathers his papers; I see the watch. Octavious is right. It looks like an old watch, nothing special. "Besides, it belonged to my father before he died," he says, setting Octavious and me straight. "The fanciest watch in the world couldn't replace it."

As they walk toward Braemore, Octavious says, "Shit, another thing that makes white dudes from suburbia stick out."

"What's that?" Theo says.

"You knew your old man."

Theo laughs.

I watch as they cross the street, pondering this perspective.

CHAPTER NINE

Olivia

A police officer accompanies me to Principal Giroux's office. I am introduced to an African American man who would make a drill sergeant appear passive. His presence is all consuming and, I assume, a necessity. Even so, he could pass for Harry Puckett's brother—tall, a wiry-framed man with cheeks that run wider than the rest of him. Harry is a symphony saxophone player from the French Quarter. I like Harry—we share a swig from the flask he carries before every curtain. We also came by our jobs in the same manner—a proclivity for music, not so much for anything else. But unlike Harry, I sense that Quentin Giroux is deliberate in his chosen position, dedicated to a purpose. His gaze glides over my Michael Kors dress.

"Ms. Klein, welcome to Braemore. I see you've followed basic instructions." I offer him a confused look. "No jewelry," he says. "Although your dress is a little more Beacon Hill than Braemore." I brush my hand over the silky sleeve. I haven't endured a wardrobe critique since moving out of the Wellesley house.

"Yes. I thoroughly read the packet of materials Braemore sent over, cover to cover." This is a slight exaggeration, *skimmed* being more accurate. But it's not as if I'll be in charge of anything, and I assume my presence is cursory. How much could I need to know? Principal Giroux continues to stare.

"I've been curious to meet you."

"Have you?" I smile, deciding it's Principal Giroux's job to be intimidating, and that my dress and preparation is fine. "I hope I can be of some value. I, um . . . I suspect there might be untapped musical talent here at Braemore. I'm no teacher, but I have a usable skill and—"

"Fascinating. Absolutely fascinating." His head tips, like he anticipated a different remark. "For the life of me, I cannot figure you out."

"Pardon?"

"Assessing people between my doorway and this desk . . ." He motions to the entrance, ten feet away. "That's my skill. It's what I do. Nobody surprises me. Granted, I always have a solid head start . . ." He plucks up official-looking papers, with my name in bold print, and drops them back onto his desk. "I assumed whatever I was missing with you would be evident upon arrival. You are a collision of adjectives—capricious, accomplished, ill-tempered . . . eleemosynary." He narrows his eyes at me. "I repeat; you make no sense."

"Seems to be a common conclusion." It also seems to be a safe reply as I'm unsure what *eleemosynary* means. He waits. "I, um . . . I can understand the question. I guess it isn't every day a symphony violinist turns up at Braemore as *part of the system*."

He leans casually onto the desk, though there is nothing casual about him. "Mmm, that's only a small piece of what I'm referring to, Ms. Klein. When I got the call from the DA's office, your name rang a bell."

I roll my eyes, waiting for Principal Giroux to tell me, like Judge Nicholson, he too subscribes to *Musical Notes*. "Fan of the symphony?"

"Never been."

I furrow my brow.

"It took numerous phone calls and days to solve the mystery—where I'd heard your name and why." He pauses, a hum ringing from his throat as he shakes his head. "I had more claims of denial than the regulars from Braemore detention. Trust me. That's saying something. But I'm not easily deterred. I dug; then I tunneled. I know who you are. I know what you do."

"Right. I'm a violinist with the New England Symphony."

"A woman who—when not being arrested for crimes that would earn serious street credit here—also provides funds for music education. A singular program used to serve the needs of students who, otherwise, wouldn't get high-end arts opportunities. The kind kids from well-to-do families are handed. All of it under the stipulation of complete, almost iron-wall, anonymity."

"You must have me confused."

"Ms. Klein, do not call on hubris here. Don't come into my school and think you can bullshit me." He smiles at my slacked jaw. "Don't add to your list of *mystifying* adjectives. If you want to remain anonymous in your benevolence, that's your business. But understand mine. My job, the safety of my students, requires I appreciate the particulars of every person who comes through Braemore's doors. To this point," he says, "you make no sense."

I guess, on this score, the jig is up. "Who told you about . . ."

"The endowment?" I offer a small nod. "You just did." He smiles widely. "I've been doing this a while. I'd overheard your name once—an off-site conference where liquor flowed and mouths moved. I could not, however, get confirmation. Whoever pulls your strings does so with the utmost finesse." I smother a smile. Kudos to Rob's rather brilliant sleight of hand. The source for the endowment is buried so deep, Sherlock Holmes would be hard-pressed to figure it out. "Don't feel bad. Getting confessions out of people who visit my office . . . That's probably like you playing Brahms's lullaby." He looks me up and down. "Now that the field's leveled some, can we stop wasting my time and cut to the chase?"

"Like you said, it's my private business. I'm here to serve out my community service hours. Beyond that—"

"Beyond that I need to understand why you came so unhinged you turned your husband's luxury vehicle into something that couldn't be sold for parts on Craigslist."

"You're exaggerating."

"From the report I read, not that much. Are you mentally ill?"

"Am I . . . ?"

"Do you feel you suffer from mental illness? It's a serious question—a problem highly ignored in this country, but not at Braemore, not if I can help it."

"I'm not—" I lower my voice. "I don't believe I'm any more impaired than the next high-strung musician," I say, smoothing my dress. "Although, I will say not many share my personal history in breeding or background. As for what landed me here, I was drunk . . . It was stupid. Not bragging points, but it does factor into my actions."

"Uh-huh," he says, arms folded. "Ms. Klein, be aware. I can terminate your community service hours more easily than I agreed to them. Enough risk runs through these halls. I don't have time for supposed adults and public tantrums. So unless you'd like Officer Mortman to return you curbside, where you can fulfill your hours elsewhere—"

"I can't undo what happened," I say quickly. "But I take responsibility for it. I'm sure you've read the transcript, the catalyst for the, um . . . unfortunate incident."

"Something about going postal because your husband lost your mother's house in a bad business deal."

"Yes. That's what I told the judge and my attorney—neither of whom is aware of my *connection* to the endowment. Something I wasn't inclined to share in open court. It was my hope that, eventually, my family home—a valuable asset—would provide more permanent orchestra funding. Currently, means are limited and so is space in the program."

"I'm aware. We have a few students who showed an interest. But only one's been granted admission. Octavious Pendleton."

I do not acknowledge the boy I recognized outside Starbucks or from performances where I sat anonymously in the back row. "So, yes—I lost it that night. I blew a gasket on Newbury Street, but not for the reasons everyone assumes."

"I want to ask why you feel it necessary to remain so secretive in your efforts."

"But that would mean going back on your word, that remaining anonymous is my prerogative, my business."

His lungs fill with an assessing breath. "Indeed it would." He waits. As always, judgment looms. "Follow me. But a word of caution," he says, turning back. "If Mr. McAdams gets the faintest whiff of anything more than a compliant professional violinist, serving community service hours, your time here will cease abruptly. You get me?"

He leads me out of his office. It sounds like a phrase often used on the newbies he marches down the halls at Braemore. Fortunately, it is the one thing I can guarantee him. "No worries. Mr. McAdams won't encounter anything more than what's on paper—a professional violinist who owes a hundred-hour debt to society."

"Despite your complexities . . ." He glances at me. "I'm going to accept your word on that."

In my head I hear Sihvola's *Ruins*—one of the most ominous pieces of music ever written. It's a menacing cadence, the kind that makes your belly ache, teeth clench. It continues to play as Principal Giroux and I walk together down Braemore's halls and toward the future.

We arrive at the classroom, which is empty aside from Theo. He sits on the far side of the room, bent over a viola. "Mr. McAdams," Principal

Giroux says with authority, though he lightly taps the door as we enter. "I bring you an adult hoodlum."

It's not the introduction I would have chosen. Clearly, Principal Giroux has zero tolerance for bullshit or formalities. On the other hand, my elevator pitch bio is not his fault.

It doesn't matter. Theo barely hears; he is seriously engaged with the instrument's missing strings. "This is Ms. Klein. I believe you spoke with her . . . *counsel.*" I am grateful for the soft landing; surely Principal Giroux is in possession of legal vernacular to match every introduction at Braemore. "She's your temporary, professional assistance—about a hundred hours' worth."

Theo looks up and looks back at what he's doing. He looks annoyed that he has to let go of the broken instrument. But he hustles across the room, burying any attitude. He smiles and extends a hand. Standing before me is the man Claire McAdams has described to Shep Stewart for fifteen years.

"Hi. Theo McAdams."

"Olivia," I say, taking an up-close inventory. "Sorry—you were busy restringing the viola."

He gestures toward it. "No problem. I'll fix it later. Or maybe you want to . . ." He smiles wider. "I guess New England Symphony violinists have somebody for that." I smile in return, my lungs filling. He knows who I am. "I'm a dabbler by comparison," Theo notes.

"Don't say that. I know you chose music over sports in college. That's a bold choice." His eyes, which are whiskey-colored, look curiously into mine.

"Right . . . Anyway," he says. "I won't lie . . ."

I bet he never does.

"I didn't know who you were until I Googled you."

My heart returns to sinus rhythm, maybe a beat slower. A bell rings and the principal excuses himself. Students wander into the classroom. There is bumping and brushing against my shoulder. "Uh, you might want to . . ." Theo grabs my arm and guides me toward him, out of the flow of traffic. My feet move. My gaze doesn't. His grin drifts away from friendly into *"What kind of dysfunctional flake did they saddle me with?"* We're swallowed by noise, a sewer's worth of expletives, and the beatbox sounds I heard earlier. "If you want, you can take a seat over there." Theo points to a benign corner of the room. "After class we can talk about what it is you want to accomplish while you're here."

"Accomplish?" I ask.

"Yeah. I'm curious. What is it you want out of the experience?"

What a great question . . . But in pure Olivia Klein fashion, I haven't given it any thought beyond this moment.

During class, I feel more like the audience in a theater than a violin virtuoso. Theo makes a quick introduction, and curious stares come my way. "Miss Klein will be sitting in with us . . . *for a while*," he states diplomatically. "She plays with the New England Symphony—she's a professional violinist." They are unimpressed. Theo tightens his brow. "It's about the same odds as playing guard for the Celtics." Amazingly, there are faint sounds that express fascination.

As class moves along, Theo seems to forget I'm here and so do his students. While they are a curious lot, and I am interested in their musical potential, I am ridiculously blindsided by their teacher. Theo and his students compete for my attention, my gaze volleying back and forth. But eventually Principal Giroux's forewarning takes precedence, maybe Sasha's ruminations. How will I benefit society from being here? I will my attention onto the group.

The room is an even divide. About half the class is marginally involved in what's going on, half are passing time. One gets up and abruptly exits. As the boy leaves, Theo says, "Keep going, Ryan, and that will be a yellow card to the office." I assume there is a color-coded system for rule breaking. I wonder if I should have been given one upon arrival. As Principal Giroux noted, defiling a Porsche and mouthing off to a judge is probably worth street credit. Ryan salutes with a middle finger as he exits. Theo doesn't attempt to further engage him. I think this is a wise choice.

For those who show an interest in music, Theo has a deft rapport. He is patient, clearly a natural teacher. When it comes to music, that's saying something, so very few of us are. Octavious has turned up with this group. He appears to be a ring leader. Because he likes Theo, this works to his advantage. Conversation drifts to Octavious's composition.

"Don't matter, man. Ain't nobody gonna hear nothing but a kid from the streets with a foul mouth and some rhythm." This bit of wisdom is imparted by a boy called Jesus who doesn't seem to care much for music class, or Octavious. "Shit that ain't gonna get him anywhere."

"Not true," insists Theo.

"Bullshit." He thrusts a finger in Octavious's direction. "You think what he puts out will ever get respected? Get him paid? People see what they want." He motions at Octavious. I see his point. The sad fact is many symphony patrons would cross the street if they saw him coming. Attitudes like that, like my parents'—it's a big part of what prompted my music endowment.

Theo refuses to give up. "I can't promise that respect will come tomorrow or even before you and Octavious graduate from Braemore. But it will come." Both Octavious and Jesus appear unconvinced.

Theo moves toward a section of wall covered in a myriad of classical masters. "Mozart," he says, his finger thudding against his picture. "Known first for his foul mouth and an obsession with bodily functions. Scriabin . . ." He points to another. "A believer in mysticism and magic—in a time when such outspoken ideas could have easily gotten you institutionalized. Charles Ives," Theo says, moving into the twentieth century. "Nothing short of genius and a Yale graduate. Yet he was best known for bucking the musical system while forging new and never-before-heard music. None of their paths were easy. But they didn't let that stop them from pursing their passions."

Silence settles over the room. Theo's students absorb his point. He might not have changed minds, but he's introduced the idea. And he's right. Like any art form—singing, dance, writing—respect is a hard-fought battle. If you come from this environment, surely it's twice as hard. For a moment, I indulge in the small contribution I have made to this end.

Theo's notes about classical musicians are the highlight as the next forty-five minutes tick off and finally a bell rings again. I field more strange looks as the students exit. But since I've contributed nothing that they know of, they go without a word. It seems evident that Theo has forgotten me. He begins to erase the white board from when the class—which was mostly conversational—took a brief educational turn. Theo drew out a treble clef in attempt to explain a simple three-quarter rhythm. I clear my throat.

He turns. "Oh, geez. I'm sorry." He seems like a curious combination of confidence and absentmindedness—the very definition of a talented artist. He abandons the eraser and makes a beeline for my corner of the room. I'm about to stand when he whips a student desk around and sits opposite me. I widen my eyes at the near nose-to-nose point of view. "So that was a class at Braemore. Better or worse than you imagined?"

I push my back into the chair. "You're good with them. But I see the challenge. There's some talent. The one boy. Oct . . ."

"Octavious. He was a find. I got lucky. Not only is he musically inclined, he's a natural leader. Had he turned on me in the beginning, that controlled chaos," Theo says, thumbing at the empty room over his shoulder. "It would be more like my fourth-period class."

"So this was a good example of music time at Braemore."

"You bet. Stick around. My next class has more the atmosphere you're anticipating—verge of anarchy."

"And you like that atmosphere?"

"I wish I could tell you that was my sole purpose in taking this job, but that'd be a lie."

"So why did you do it?" On the desk, under my hand, is a music theory book. Rhythmically, repetitively, I flip the soft-bound pages with my fingertips. It looks like nervousness. It's not. My hands are almost always in constant motion, and this is a comfort zone. "Why did you take this job?"

He leans back in his chair. I believe Theo felt the next question should have been his: *"So what is it you're doing time for, Miss Klein?"*

"I needed to refocus—find a different starting point." Theo watches anxious energy filter through my fingertips.

"Habit," I say as the book's pages whoosh by. "No instrument, but my fingers don't seem to know that."

"Funny," Theo says. "I do the same thing . . . for the same reason." My fingers halt, clutching the book. Theo reverts to my previous question about why he's taken the Braemore job. "My fiancée and I broke up last spring." He says this as if trying the words out on a stranger.

"I'm sorry. I, um . . . I didn't mean to pry."

"You didn't. I offered." He pauses. "It's not that you asked, just that it happened. India . . . that's her name."

"Pretty name," I say, leaning forward, resting my chin on my fist.

"I always thought so. Anyway, she went back to Long Island where she's from. She works for her parents' catering company. I took the job here."

I wait for more, but there is nothing. There shouldn't be. They are the tidbits you'd share with an outsider. But I hear the sour note in Theo's short explanation. This was not what he wanted. It's a narrow opening to a more personal conversation. I grab it like a kid stealing candy. "I know a little more about you than your teaching status."

"Oh?" he says.

"I've followed the Shep Stewart articles in the *Ledger* over the years."

"Oh," Theo says again. His expression changes, shifting from the fiancée who left him to the father he lost. The pain is completely different, equally intense.

"I'm sorry," I say, sitting up straight. "I didn't mean to—"

He holds up a hand. "You just caught me off guard. The column is my mother's doing. I don't even look at it—or I haven't since I was about thirteen."

"But if you don't want to be part of it . . ."

"I made my peace with Shep's living diary a long time ago. It works for my mother . . . it doesn't for me. We have an agreement. She continues to provide Shep Stewart with basic information, and I politely ignore it." He smiles at me. "Interesting, you're the first person to 'recognize' me from the stories."

"Am I?" I don't know if that makes me sound like a stalker or just ridiculously callous. "But if you don't want to be part of the stories . . . Joaquin Perez, he opted out last year. He moved to Canada."

"Did he?" Theo says. "Wow—you must have us memorized."

Stalker it is.

"I'm sorry. It's such a painful inauspicious date—for an entire country," I say, trying to blend with the masses. "I mean, Shep, he continues with the column because it resonates with readers, right?"

"I suppose," Theo says. "Guess my perspective is more up close." Our stares turn awkward. From Theo's point of view, it appears I've sought him out to gawk at his all-too-personal tragedy.

I stand. "I apologize. This was a horrible idea. I'm very sorry for your loss." *A father . . . Theo has lost his father . . .* It's never sunk in quite this way. My face rarely burns with embarrassment. Currently, it's on fire. "I, um . . . I didn't mean to be disrespectful, following Shep's stories, bringing that up. I just . . . Musically," I say, stumbling like a drunk, "I felt a connection. That's all."

"Listen, it's okay, how you found me . . . or why it is you know me." Theo stands too. "Really." He presses his hands to the air. "I just don't feel any connection to Shep's stories because . . . Well, because I lived it." His hands are still in an apologetic pose, insisting I sink back into the seat. He sits too.

"Sorry," I say again. This may be more apologies than I've cumulatively offered in the past decade. "I didn't think this through from your point of view."

"Doesn't change what is." Magnanimously, Theo eases my guilt.

"Still . . . I got unduly caught up in the stories."

"I've read Shep's other stuff. He's good at spinning drama. What is it now—fifteen, sixteen stories? I can see how a person could get caught up in them."

"But if you don't want to be part of the story, why not take a pass like Joaquin? Why let her . . . your mother keep participating on your behalf?"

"She's my mother. I'd do anything for her." Theo shrugs. "The updates don't alter the facts. They don't help me. Shep's stories keep the memory of my dad alive for her—and I'd guess they sell a lot of newspapers for him. I prefer to remember my dad every day but that day."

"I see. What a thoughtful perspective." *Rational . . . mature . . . enlightened . . . Recognize any of those qualities, Liv? Not so much, huh?* "Well," I say, glancing at the upside-down view of Theo's watch. "I guess I can check some time off my hours owed—although I was about as useful as this music theory book." I've reverted to strumming pages.

"No worries. I assumed this would be an 'observation day.'" Theo's fingers quote the air. "But I thought we could discuss how you might offer some real classroom inspiration."

"Inspiration?"

"Yes. I mean, you'll be participating with students in some way, right?"

"Participate . . . Uh, of course." I'm stunningly reminded of my on-paper purpose for being here. I owe society and Theo. Instead of his watch, I look to the wall clock. "Could we possibly do it next time?

I have rehearsal at eleven." I stand, brushing my hand over my dress. This will be the first time I have ever *not* worn yoga pants to a rehearsal.

"Sure. But wait," Theo says. "Don't I get at least a ten-second Q and A in return?" The brushing stops; I freeze. "I'm not asking your personal business," Theo quickly adds. "But Principal Giroux did share that your community service hours stemmed from a domestic incident."

"That's right."

He misreads my discomfort. "Is it, uh . . . I mean, you're all right at home and everything? I'm not prying. I just feel like I should have some sense of where you're coming from . . . if it's a violent situation."

For a moment I have no idea what he's driving at. Then I connect the word *domestic* to *violence*. How obtuse—on my part. "No . . . no . . . nothing like that. Rob, my husband, he's . . . He'd never . . ." Theo's tender-hearted assumption causes me to flummox so hard I can't form a proper reply. "My husband . . . our marriage, it's hit a rough patch lately. But the community service hours—that was all me. The result of a poor decision. My skill as a violinist is only a close second to making bad choices." I dart past Theo but find myself twisting back around. "It was kind of you to ask, to be concerned."

He watches my awkward, backward exit. I stare, taking in the indefinable mix of genetics. Some children are like that, nothing you can put your finger on. Regardless, whoever Theo is, it's the result of good parenting, nothing more. I turn and exit into the hall, wiping a ridiculous tear from my eye. Nurture has thwarted nature. I've wondered for so long. I have not lied to Theo. Erratic choices have always been my nemesis. Unbeknownst to Theo, he is the exception: giving away the baby who became music teacher Theo McAdams stands as my singular, finest decision.

CHAPTER TEN

Newport Beach, California

Sam

Sam has spent months reacquiring life skills—or adjusting to the fact that he will need some. To a point, Charlene's words have resonated. Sam is determined to prove her wrong, even if he never speaks to her again. He starts by making phone calls. Sure, he's been out of touch, but that is to be expected. He goes as far back as seems necessary to the cause. That means old teammates, good friends. Friends he did not want to burden when he was ill. Sam talks to Andy Palmer and Eduardo Muniez. Athletes have bonds, pitchers even stronger ones. Both are happy to hear from Sam, shocked to learn of his illness. The men are elated when Sam shares his good news. He may live long enough to pitch in a Fourth of July old-timers' game and attend his Baseball Hall of Fame induction, assuming he gets in. He smiles at what is really a foregone conclusion.

The conversations move past history, and the men talk about their present-day lives. Andy, who spent as much time cheating on his wife as he did being married to her, has worked out this particular aspect of his life. A lot of ballplayers are like that—it takes time to transition from the rigors of a pro-athlete existence into an ordinary one. They're really great human beings. A half hour later Andy is still talking, but Sam's ability to relate has slipped. He cannot quite grasp Andy's happy ending, which involves Jesus and something called *Marriage Boot Camp*. He wonders if Andy was bound and duct taped, whisked away into the night, intervention style. When Andy segues into enthusiastic chatter about how coaching Little League for Jesus is his present-day passion, Sam feels as connected to Andy as he did the hot dog vendors in the Big A Stadium. When Andy wants to pray over the phone, Sam agrees if only to end the call.

Somehow, catching up with his old teammate Eduardo proves to be even less relatable. He tells Sam that he is divorced from wife number three, a woman Eduardo describes by way of a litany of unflattering terms that Sam would not use on a prostitute. The former center fielder goes on, spending much of the conversation complaining how the bulk of his earnings go to child support and divorce settlements. He tells Sam he is smart for never having married or had children. When another call beeps in, Eduardo says he has to go, and Sam is glad for the reprieve. Eduardo, he decides, is more bitter than Charlene.

But this conversation ushers in a speck of introspection. With his hand still on the phone, Sam thinks about not having had children. He admits it's not Charlene who is connected to this thought. He did not want a child with Charlene—if this makes him a bad person, Sam cannot help that. Breath trembles out of him, the way it did after receiving various test results from Bogey. During the past year, there were instances where Sam considered changing his phone number, as if this would somehow change his fate. But being as his fate has changed, Sam's brain now floods with ancient imagery. The only child he might have wanted belonged to him and Livy. But, of course, none of that was meant to be.

Sam thinks back to longer nights during his illness. He spent more than a few wondering how life turned out for Olivia. She'd been so devastated when they parted ways. He shakes off dusty guilt. While the end of Livy's pregnancy was his fault, not having children was for the best. Sam would have been no better a father than his own. Hudson Nash was a man who kept two belts—one on him and one in his hand. This thought is enough to quiet Sam's residual regret.

He moves on in the way that's most comfortable, by not looking over his shoulder. Sam continues to make phone calls. He does not feel vindicated; he has not proven Charlene wrong about wasting his life. There's more legacy to life than having reproduced. Sam leaves a few more messages, but his phone doesn't ring. Another week passes before Chaz Thurman returns his call.

Back in the day, Chaz was one a hell of a pitching buddy, and maybe the one person who could party harder than Sam. They lost touch after Chaz was traded to Toronto toward the end of their careers. The start of the conversation proves they still have a lot in common. Chaz never married either, still enjoying the good life and a good party. Sam even learns that Chaz battled testicular cancer a few years ago. With this news, Sam feels the bond between him and Chaz strengthen and Charlene's argument weaken. Sam is surprised to learn that Chaz is now residing in the Dominican Republic. His old buddy says he's found paradise. Sam thinks this may be the ticket for him. After his bout with cancer, Chaz relocated to a luxury oceanfront community. He insists that Sam should visit right away. Sam is tempted, but something about Chaz's nervous energy does not ring true. Still, talk of their past is vivid enough to fuel a conversation.

Chaz understands how living a major league life is different than a regular one. Why a person simply can't walk away and resume a pedestrian existence. It's impossible, he insists, and Sam nods in strong agreement. While Andy and Eduardo's stories are at extreme odds,

Sam offers up their post-ball-playing days as supporting evidence. The two speak again that Friday; Chaz has called Sam. He is wildly insistent that Sam visit him in the Dominican Republic—right away. Sam considers it. No one but Chaz has called. If it weren't for him, Charlene might be right. But enthusiasm wanes, and an inner alarm goes off when Chaz asks Sam if he would do him a solid before coming. On his way out of California, could he stop in Las Vegas and visit a deposit box he keeps at one of the larger casinos? He will FedEx Sam the key. Chaz has been unable to return stateside to collect what's inside. He describes the box's contents as *stuff*. Sam may be cavalier, but he's not stupid. He presses Chaz for more information. After words that Sam hears as double talk, Chaz admits to unsavory gambling debts—including ones on baseball, a line that Sam would never cross. Chaz laughs at this and says, "For real, man?" He sobers, telling Sam that between gambling debts and ex-girlfriends, his life may not be worth much stateside.

"And would I be putting my life at risk if I were caught on camera visiting your hotel deposit box?" Sam asks. Being as he just got his life back, Sam finds he has a renewed desire to protect it. When Chaz tries to laugh it off, Sam says he won't do it unless his old buddy comes clean with the box's contents. Chaz finally alludes to the drugs and illegal winnings Sam will find inside. A few moments later Sam ends the call, deciding he's spent enough time tracking down old baseball friends.

Sam stops by the cancer treatment center a few times. At first the staff is thrilled to see him, ecstatic over his news. Charm, even in the face of death, was easy enough for Sam. But by the third visit, Sam notices that the nurses are not as forthcoming. They are busy with sick people while Sam quietly observes from a corner, hat in hand and hair on his head. Their warm, caring demeanors are now being lavished on the patients in his old chair. But Sam does not perceive them as unfriendly or rude. In fact, he is struck by their seriously compassionate behaviors. He couldn't see it before, as it's decidedly different from this angle. Sam draws an unlikely conclusion: The medical personnel engage in dangerously intimate relationships—the kind he could never acknowledge, no less commit to. The nurses not only care for sick people, but they care greatly about people who may not be here tomorrow. It's an incredible risk. Sam leaves with Charlene's words ringing in his head and a glaring display of human emotion in front of him. He will go home to his sparkling-clean condo and oodles of memorabilia to sit alone until the sun sets. The phone will not ring. No one will come to the door. Unless Sam Nash changes something, his second chance at life will be worth no more than his first.

CHAPTER ELEVEN

Boston, Massachusetts

Olivia

While Holst's *The Planets* is on this season's schedule, I wish I were in another universe. I escape my morning with Theo by diving into a lengthy symphony rehearsal. I don't stumble but stagger through the first and second movements. An hour in and we take a short break—union rules. Concertmaster Rolph Buhr shoots a nasty look over his shoulder to assistant concertmaster Renee Fisk. Conductor Manuel Gutierrez loudly blames Rolph for the egregious musical faux pas. In turn, Rolph blames Renee and she blames me. That's how it works—Rolph is the concertmaster and responsible for all violins, as well as all instruments. Renee does the talking for the violin section. Naturally, I blame the stand behind me.

When we continue, I bow the wrong way twice, irritating my stand partner, Mary Alice Porter. I am the outside chair, she is the inside. Bowing the wrong way, especially in more fervent sections, can result in an eyeless stand partner. But Mary Alice and I have a longtime partnership—she envies my musical talent, and I quietly note when she is half a beat behind. As the bow lunges toward her, she only ducks and furrows her mousy brow.

I sit up straighter and navigate through "Mercury"—aptly defined as the "the Winged Messenger." Its volatility suits my mood. But as we continue on our planetary tour, flowing into "Saturn," the fifth movement, the music's dark edges are foreshadowing. There is a cliché about music speaking to you. Right now it is screaming at me: *"What have you done, Liv? What have you put in motion? All this time . . . all these years . . . It's your worst decision yet, dropping in, in disguise, on Theo's life . . . What the hell are you thinking?"*

The movement of "Saturn" enhances intense emotion, maybe the panic attack I am fending off. I bear down on my bow and the notes, the layers of foreign feelings. There is no rest; I keep going. What I'm feeling, it's not the emotion that drives my relationship with Rob or my close comradery with Sasha. It's not the cloak of inadequacy that my mother swings over me—or my father's dead yet perennial disappointment. It's not even the ancient devastation of Sam Nash after looking into his son's eyes. It's more about having opened Pandora's box.

I deserve shame; the ridiculous stinging aftereffect of knowing that Theo McAdams was not overcome by an intrinsic connection, whether it be blood or music. We did not spot each other on a mother-child level.

The orchestra eases into "Neptune," the culmination of *The Planets.* Mary Alice flips to the next page. It's an easier section, which only allows my mind to wander. Like a clashing of symbols, anxiety hits on the beat—for being dishonest with Theo, for not thinking through the mother of all impulsive decisions, a willy-nilly choice that never should have been the fix for my court-ordered punishment.

The music underscores the circumstance—a lonely conclusion of connected notes that drift, almost unnoticed, into the vacuum of space.

It ends. I rest my violin in my lap. Rolph turns to Renee. Renee turns to tear into me for my continued sloppy performance. The sight of a damp-eyed Olivia Klein is enough to keep them both at bay. I hear generic excuses being passed forward, conveyed to Manuel. Mary Alice asks if I'm all right. I don't answer. I stare at the last pages of Holst's masterpiece. Really, he should have written something with more of a finite ending. Instead, all he has done is lead us into the abyss of the unknown.

I don't spend the walk home thinking about how I will deal with the sudden existence of Theo, but rather how I'll avoid the tentacles of emotions our meeting has unfurled. With a lifetime of practice, I am crafty enough to do this. Eventually I will cut it off—one extra twist of the tourniquet. Navigating a purposefully orderly late afternoon helps. I buy fall flowers and the new wineglasses Crate & Barrel has on display and keep moving toward home. I slip into my evening feeling calmer in the safety of the brownstone. It's not as if Theo will show up at my door.

The ruse becomes more intricate during dinner, though if I were cleverer the meal might be a distraction. Among Rob's less dangerous talents, he can cook and has made lamb chops. It's a favorite that I've barely touched. He reads my silence as ongoing punishment. Enough silverware clinks to be mistaken for Morse code, and Rob's knife makes piercing contact with his plate.

"Liv, could you just spell it out? Is this how it's going to be until the Wellesley house situation is resolved, the rest of our lives . . . or what?"

My usual comeback stalls. The one good perk in the day, I'd nearly forgotten about the house. But I can't tell him what's at the crux of my silence. Like everyone else, Rob knows I was briefly married to the man who eventually became baseball icon Sam Nash. He even knows there was a pregnancy. But like all the significant others in my life, with the exception of Phillip, Rob believes the pregnancy ended in a miscarriage. Years have gone on and the story hasn't changed, only the number of people to which I've told it.

Until today, their misinformation felt like the truth—at the very least something I simply chose not to share. That's allowed. I consider it now, but see no benefit in coming clean. It would be like explaining the Earth's climate to someone born and bred on one of Holst's planets—maybe Mars. Unless you experienced it personally, you couldn't possibly grasp the atmospheric conditions I faced all those years ago—Sam and my parents.

"Liv?" he says as my silence lingers.

"I wasn't thinking about the house," I say. "It was just an odd day." I take another stab at the lamb chops. "These are delicious."

"How was your first day at Braemore? You haven't said a word about it."

"It's an interesting place." I gulp a mouthful of red wine. "A lot of what you'd expect and a little of what you might not."

"How so?"

"There's some talent in the room, which was gratifying to see. And the instructor . . ." I can't help myself. Theo has consumed my frontal lobe. "This Theo McAdams, he does a good job given the environment."

"Right. The 9-11 kid. What's he like?"

A forkful of lamb chop freezes in midair. "Why would you ask?"

"I don't know . . . making conversation."

"Bright. Thoughtful." I take another drink of wine. "He wanted to know if I was living in a situation of domestic abuse."

Rob's glass is midway to his mouth. He places it back on the table and pinot noir sloshes over the edge. "Why the hell would he ask—"

"He jumped to a conclusion. I think maybe he thought I'd been railroaded by the judge or the system. Apparently, he knew my community service hours were connected to a *domestic incident*. But he didn't have the details, so he assumed . . ."

"Jesus, Liv, I hope you set him straight."

"No worries. I told him my husband, while a wild card with assets, bore me no serious threat—other than monetary." Rob makes a face.

"I didn't even hint at that. You're safe." Rob appears relieved that I have not painted him in that unsavory light and returns to his meal.

My husband is a master of introvert and extrovert, a trait I still find fascinating. He's an expert at extremes. Rob can be aloof, often deeply lost in his own thoughts. Yet take him to a dinner party, and you'd swear he's running for mayor. He grew up in a house that came with expectations, but nothing as resolute as the ones I faced. Because of this, he liked his lone-wolf lifestyle and claims he never came close to marrying until Sasha's matchmaking effort. Beyond his personality tics, Rob is an animal lover and would like to have a dog—an on-again, off-again, lesser point of contention. Long hours go by in the house with no one at home. It'd be unfair to an animal. Often, it's unfair to us. Above all, Rob is a pull-the-trigger kind of guy. His aim—like the Wellesley house proves—can be off. But anyone who knows him will insist he's a man of action, a decision maker, who does not waver no matter the crisis or circumstance.

Silence settles in again. I force my mouth to move, although it's thoughts about Theo that dominate. "He was exactly what his parents . . . his mother raised him to be." Rob looks at me as if he's already forgotten the topic. "Theo McAdams, the 9-11 boy." The light in Rob's eyes comes back on. "It was only a couple of hours and a short conversation, but I can see he's a wonderful young man, perfectly lovely."

Rob motions his glass toward me. "Here's to recognizing that when it comes to parenting, leaving it alone was the way to go—our childless choice."

And for whatever his misses, Rob's pinpoint accuracy plunges right into my skin. Early on in our relationship, both of us noted that neither of us wanted children. It was a bonus tidbit—most men do want to reproduce. Unbeknownst to Rob, our reasons for remaining childless have nothing in common. His is about an inability to see himself in that role. Mine have something to do with punishment—I surrendered my right to maternal instinct when I gave away Theo. I had no business asking for another chance.

Conversation picks up and we talk about Sasha. I share her latest hope for Jeremy—that he may actually sell a novel. As I reminded Sasha, Rob feels that Jeremy is taking advantage of her generous nature. If not for a nudge or two from me under a table, he would have expressed his feelings, emphatically, ages ago.

"If he doesn't sell the book, Jeremy '*the thinker*'" he says mockingly, "won't suffer, not with Sasha's money covering incidentals, like food and rent."

I poke at my baby red potatoes. "I raised the point with her."

"But what can you do?" I look up. Rob is focused on me. "Sasha is hopelessly drawn to artsy romantics—be it musicians by default or novelists by claim."

Our smiles connect. "Funny. She said the same thing too."

Rob is also a wildly smooth talker. It's as natural as it is genuine—something that also takes time to figure out. It's different from the pseudo mayoral race he runs on occasion, more intimate. Pockets of Rob can make you feel like the only other human being on the planet—well, on his planet. A long-ago taste of that was like heroin to me; it has made Rob tempting and dangerous. From our start, his positive opinion of Olivia Klein was a high I craved, even if I could never make the feeling last.

After dinner, we go into the living room. The blinds are drawn and the light is low. A bottle of wine has been split between us. It's enough to make us comfortable, soothe our prickly week. Things start out as quiet sex on the sofa. I've never used sex as any sort of punishment with Rob. In fact, over the years, the best sex has often been the heated kind, where raw emotion spills over and into our bed. But that doesn't happen here. I'm not angry with Rob—I'm too appalled by my own actions. I breathe hard at the reality of what I've done. I find myself clinging to Rob. In the whole of my life, he's been the constant.

It's comforting and real. He feels it too—kissing me again, and again. He says my name in some airy way that's been missing for a while now. Grasping for a physical fix, I dig my fingers into the muscles of Rob's back and run them through his dark hair. The scene inches toward an intense climax for both of us—one where I almost blurt out who I am, what I've done, the imperfections Rob has not yet seen. But then it ends, abruptly. Sex and emotion go out of sync as Rob shudders into a release that has likely been building since I deconstructed his Porsche with a baseball bat. Breathlessly he asks, "So we'll survive this?" I want more from his words. *"I love you, Liv . . . You can tell me whatever's on your mind . . . I'll understand . . ."* He doesn't say it. It isn't there because aloof Rob has invaded.

"Don't we always?" My arms, which were around his neck, push against his shoulders. I catch the defensive gesture and curl my hands into soft fists. "It's a house . . . a car . . . stuff . . . In the end, they're not the things that really matter, right?" He furrows his brow. I sound like a Hallmark card. My gaze rests on his perfected BMI chest. My eyes inch upward into cool blue irises. I'm distracted by genetics—any child of ours would have been fair eyed. Chunks of fallen sky and smoky green irises run in our families, every person I can think of. The color, the shape of Theo's brown eyes came as a startling surprise. I haven't seen them in years. I dislodge thoughts that don't belong between Rob and me, never mind in my head.

He stands, butt naked, in the brownstone living room. His physique has only improved since we met—sinewy, his fair complexion almost snow white in contrast to his dark hair. Wisps of gray mingle with the smattering of black hair on his chest. Rob is five years younger than me, though grays intruded at his temple years ago. Then the hint of middle age vanished. At the time, I didn't think much about it. A few months later, I found a box of hair color for men in a bathroom drawer I don't use. Of course, this is nothing compared to the eyebrow waxing and alpha beta facial peels he schedules religiously. I ignore Rob's vanity the way he disregards my dislike for small talk with strangers, often people we know. He pulls on his silky boxers, and I casually drag the cashmere throw across my bare midriff.

My figure hasn't changed much either, though it's never been as toned as his—or Sasha's. I do sometimes think if I were to get fat, Rob might use it as grounds for divorce. I am being facetious, and he's not that shallow. But he might buy me a trip to a fat farm, disguised as a Christmas gift. Attention to physical fitness is another benefit of not having had children—well, not in this century. We have time to devote to heightened personal interests. Exercise routines are maintained, and diets have never been invaded by the temptation of junk food. Aside from my mother, the only things that come into this house are the ones we willingly invite.

"You know," Rob says, drawing my attention. "I feel like I could still burn some energy." He picks up his clothes and exits toward the lower level where a treadmill, rowing machine, and his world, removed from ours, is located. Lying naked on the sofa, I stare at the fire. I remain there, covered in the throw, longing for the place that was once a fascinating hollow of belonging, where the nerve and desire to confide in Rob proved to be my saving grace.

CHAPTER TWELVE

Boston, Massachusetts

Seven Years Earlier

Olivia

"So call him," Sasha says. She sits curled on my apartment sofa, sipping spiked hot chocolate. In the past hour the conversation has segued. We've moved from my latest dog-walking gig to her new job with a prestigious law firm, and now onto the reasons why I'm avoiding one Rob Van Doren.

Rob Van Doren—he even sounds like somebody I'd date.

"I can't call him," I insist.

"Why not?"

"Because I ignored his last two calls. How would that look?"

Her expression goes goofy. "Uh, like maybe you're interested, as opposed to your usual 'Thanks for applying, Mr. Van Doren, but my hard-to-hold interest has expired.'" Sasha checks her watch. "Though the timing is about right."

"Meaning what?" Taking my hot chocolate with me, I pass by an over-stuffed chair where Dumpling, a King Charles spaniel, is perched. He lifts his head and bares his teeth, growling. "Oh, shut up. I could have left you to do your business all over Mama Lowenstein's Kenmore Square condo." I take in my Bay Village apartment view, a Boston winter wonderland.

"You know exactly what it means." I turn back to Sasha. On the coffee table is a mixture of vodka and Baileys; she pours another shot into her steaming cup. We're really not the straight-hot-chocolate types. "Although props to Rob for outlasting prior suitors by two dates."

"Three," I say absently, observing a blanket of fresh snow.

Sasha mumbles a faint, "I stand corrected . . . Not to mention further impressed," and crosses to Dumpling. He does not bare his teeth, but rises and turns, knotting himself in a ball to face the wall. "How long is Mrs. Lowenstein away?"

"Until next Thursday. I figured bringing him . . . *Dumpling*," I say, rolling my eyes at a name I have a hard time saying, let alone attributing to the persnickety beast. "It's better than trudging over to her place, considering the winter we're having. That only leaves me with the Greens' cat downstairs, and the boxer in the building next door. It won't be so bad." Sasha hums and raises a brow. "Okay, Sash, add that to your complaint about the recently dismissed Rob Van Doren. Is there something you want to say?"

She frowns. "I know better than to press. If you're happy walking dogs, scooping litter boxes . . . happy here alone . . . I respect that."

I narrow my gaze. "Bullshit."

"Okay, maybe it's more like I've exhausted all intelligent avenues on the subject of you and men, especially given the abrupt dismissal of Rob." She glances toward the music stand and a violin parked in a remote corner of the living room. "Did you play today?" I half nod and shrug. I refuse to admit an interest in music, even to Sasha. "And yesterday?" she presses.

"Pet sitting doesn't exactly fill my day." Sasha stares. "Playing gives me something to do with my hands, okay? I'm used to it." My voice tenses and she backs down.

"How's your father doing?"

My gaze shifts from the violin and returns to the window view. "It's inoperable."

"Liv, I've been here for an hour! Why didn't you say anything? I'm so sorry."

I fold my arms against the cold that penetrates from a wintery window.

"Because it was one sentence of diagnosis followed by an entire fresh angle of browbeating. Only my father could find the 'Eureka!' in dying. While my parents refer to it as a 'disturbing diagnosis,' they feel it's a sign."

"A sign of what—other than the obvious?"

"Something like, 'It's fate, Olivia. Can't you see it?'" I say in a well-worn Asa Klein tone. "My lifelong desire for you to play for the symphony, to be a part of something worthy of *our* gift . . . It's now or never." I stop, staring at Sasha. "Apparently he thinks turning his forever demand into a last wish will sway me."

"Sounds more like blackmail by death."

"Thanks for saying as much. I'm so fucked up on the subject, I was afraid it was just me." I stride toward Dumpling and attempt to pet him. He snaps at me. "You nippy little bastard," I hiss and challenge him by leaning in. "You're lucky I don't drop you into a three-foot snowbank." Instead, I toss a fuzzy throw over his ill-tempered ass and turn back to Sasha. "Anyway . . . you can understand why seeing Rob again just isn't possible."

Despite the grim news and deplorable manners of my canine guest, Sasha laughs. "Actually, Liv, based on what I've observed, I would have thought Rob Van Doren is exactly what you need."

The table is beautifully set. It's one of a few positives instilled in me by my mother's Southern sensibilities: an antique damask linen complements the dishes I bought in Europe last summer. Today, I've unpacked the china for the first time. A spray of white winter roses sits center on the table, candles glistening—tiny tempting glimmers of light. Silverware that belonged to my grandparents and never-used crystal glasses make for a glossy magazine-ready spread. I glance at Dumpling. "What do you think? Too much?" He lifts his head and offers a whine of discontent. It's nothing new; the only time the dog is marginally amenable is when his leash comes out. However, in this instance, I agree. "You're right. The flowers are overkill." I transfer the arrangement to a side table, blowing out two other candles and turning on a lamp. It's a dinner invitation, not a seduction scene.

I called Rob the other night, not at Sasha's prodding but despite it. Generally, when given a direction, I will go the opposite way—habit. My call went to voice mail. The truth is I missed Rob's first call earlier in the week because I was out walking the Gallaghers' schnauzer. On his second call, an hour later, I got it in my head that perhaps, he too, was feeling the same thing as me—a desire to be in the same room. When I realized I'd memorized his phone number, it spooked me enough to keep me from calling him back.

We had conquered what should have been an awkward first date. Rob and I met up in the North End for coffee, which turned into dinner, then drinks, finally ending when someone started vacuuming the carpet around us. On subsequent dates, Rob didn't suggest a Boston sporting event—nothing short of miraculous if you live in this city. Instead, we did things like take in a new Monet exhibit at the Museum of Fine Arts. Although, on our next outing, Rob demonstrated his range—or insisted that I show some—by booking us two blank canvases at Paint Nite, hosted by a trendy Boston bar. I admit; it was something different, as is he.

Rob doesn't know a damn thing about music, yet he smoothly navigated his way through conversation after running into Leland Solder. Leland is a charming, dedicated cellist I've played with on occasion—an ensemble group hired for various catered events. It's a counterweight to pet sitting, and facilitates a use of my gift that my parents find equal to playing in a bordello. Leland insisted on buying us a drink. Rob said, "Sounds great," smiling and hanging in deftly as Leland dominated the conversation with talk of mutual musician acquaintances and ending with, "Liv, when will you ever do the obvious and audition for a symphony chair?"

When it became apparent that Rob was not going to grab a cab and flee, Leland left. Rob wanted to know for how long he'd had *a thing* for me. I was surprised. "How did you know . . . ?"

"I have eyes, Liv. And you seemed to like him enough." Rob then leaned into the table and said, "So if you don't mind me asking, is it an *in the past* thing, or a *something I should be aware of* thing?"

"More like never a thing at all—not that he hasn't tried. I don't date musicians. They're temperamental and require copious amounts of attention."

"You don't say," Rob grinned and downed the last of his drink—some high-end Scotch delivered over a mammoth ice cube. "Too bad old Leland couldn't figure out the obvious way around that."

"How so?"

"If it was me, I'd just quit playing the fucking cello."

And my surprise turned to flattery.

That was our last date. Instinct said to cut it off at the pass—nothing good could come of it. Really, I was doing Rob a favor. Yet I have not been able to dismiss Rob's easy confidence, a presence that feels absent since ignoring his calls. After my unreturned call, I texted him. He didn't reply to that either, and I figured we were two for two. Then it pissed me off. I wasn't going to be ignored, or at the very least Rob wasn't going to get the last word by way of a non-reply. I texted him once more, inviting Rob to dinner at my apartment. He only texted back to ask if he should bring white or red. Then the real problem dawned on me—I'd have to cook.

"All right," I say to Dumpling. "Assuming he's impressed by a stunningly set table, we may be fine." My gaze moves to the tiny galley kitchen, which is a disturbing contrast to the organized table. I didn't realize the state of turmoil I'd left it in, abandoning my "make ahead" beef Wellington to take a shower. Under a flour-sprinkled iPad is a recipe with 635 positive reviews and what are promised foolproof directions. I decided pre-make ahead might work even better and turned up the oven before heading to the shower. Sniffing the air, which smells beefy enough, I also suck in a breath of confidence. I can cook a meal if I choose to and have dismissed the fact that I've done little in this kitchen other than pour wine. I waver slightly, eyeing a deep drawer that contains thirty-three takeout menus, all with delivery service.

Flour has also found its way onto the small silver chafing dish I plan on using to serve. I dust it away, catching a glance of my polished reflection. *Not too bad . . .* I was surprised to learn that Rob is five years younger than me—not that it matters. But I do gaze into my silvery image, wondering if I look more like ten years older. I huff at absurd silliness. I look perfectly fine, though there it is again—something Rob has, by his mere existence, brought to my attention.

I don't have another moment to ponder this or add another layer of foundation as the intercom sounds. Rob has never been further than the steps of my apartment building. The urge to invite him up last time was palpable but overruled by the thought of what he might find given a closer look. I take a turn around the small but smartly decorated space and glance in a wall mirror before granting him entrance. As I open the door, it occurs to me that my true concern was never about age or décor.

"Hi."

"Hi." He flashes a brilliant smile, a trait that has left me curious. Does Rob rely solely on over-the-counter whitening strips, or is the snow-white enamel professionally maintained? Either way, it's dazzling, causing a fluttery feeling. I stop smiling, aware that the flutter has little to do with his smile. I am nervous, which I hate. I particularly hate being nervous in my own home. "Okay if I come in?" he asks as I linger in the doorway.

I brush my fingers to my forehead. "Yes . . . of course." I step back and he moves forward into the living room. "Sorry." He hands me a bottle of white wine as my pitchy laughter betrays any confidence.

"You okay, Liv?"

"Yes. Perfectly fine. Sorry—I don't throw many dinner parties for two."

"Three," he says, pointing. "I didn't know you'd have another guest."

"Oh, him. I, um . . . One of my clients." Aside from our brush with Leland, I've mentioned my skill set and part-time violin gigs, though Rob also didn't flinch when I stated *pet sitter* as my day job. "With the weather, I thought it'd be easier to bring him here. He's kind of old, grumpy . . . *Dumpling*, his name is Dumpling, if you can believe that. I mean, what are you supposed to do, call him Dump for short? You might not want to get too close, he's a bit testy, especially with people he doesn't . . ."

But Rob's already crossed to the chair that Dumpling has claimed. He slowly holds out the back of his hand, which the dog sniffs. My eyes draw wide as the dog proceeds to lick Rob's hand. I want to ask if he used liver-scented hand soap before arriving, but from the masculine whiff of cologne that just passed by me, I'm fairly clear as to which one of us Rob has dressed for this evening.

He scratches the dog behind the ear. "Hey, buddy," he says. "What were you saying about him?"

"Uh, nothing. I guess it just takes the right person." He leaves the dog and takes a turn around the apartment. "Nice place, Liv. Have you lived here long?" Rob removes his overcoat and scarf, which I take from him.

"Almost two years. I kind of bummed around, bounced around before that—parents' guest house, a couple of different roommates, didn't really work out."

"Not the roommate type?"

"Not so much."

He nods. "Me neither. I bought a co-op near Fenway a couple of years ago—first thing on my to-do list post law school."

"Your finance business must be doing well. Though it does seem odd that you put all that work in and you don't want to be an actual lawyer."

He uses the smile. "Didn't you say something about studying the violin for years? Yet . . . ?" He points to Dumpling.

"Point taken, *counselor.* Anyway, I just thought putting your law degree to work in a traditional way would have made your Boston co-op goal easier."

"Maybe." He shoves his hands in his trouser pockets. "But what's expected has never interested me, and I've never cared much for things I didn't have to work for."

"Well," I say, swallowing. "You may be in the right place." I head for the bar top that separates the living space from the kitchen. "I'll open this."

"Oh, I thought we could have it with dinner, but that's fine." He meets me at the bar and peers into the dim kitchen, which now occurs to me could be captioned: "Post Normandy Invasion." He clears his throat and recovers. "Sorry, you said to bring white."

"I did."

"Kind of smells like beef." We are facing each other, and I think I'm thinking about kissing him. He's an excellent kisser, and I have wondered, in a three a.m. sort of way, if it's a skill that extends to more intimate actions. But instead of leaning in, he says, "Burning beef."

"What?"

Just as he points, the smoke alarm blares and all hell breaks loose: Dumpling begins to howl like the Baskervilles are calling, and Mrs. Rosemount, who lives above me, starts banging her cane into the floor—a standard signal that me playing the violin at one o'clock in the morning is pushing it. But it's invading smoke that takes precedence, and I rush to the stove, hitting buttons. "Shit! I read the directions first!"

"For what you're cooking?" Rob asks, appearing beside me.

"No. For how to work the stove." We trade a glance that assures him I'm not joking.

"Uh, pot holders?" He opens the oven door to a thicker rush of smoke. I shake my head no; he reaches past and grabs a flour-covered dish towel. I have no idea where the grease-splattered, charred mess in front of us came from, but this is not the promising meal I put into the oven an hour or so ago. Rob exits the kitchen, leaving me with the pastry-crusted meat, which looks more like it's been wrapped in the tires of an eighteen-wheeler. A burst of coldness seizes my attention, and I turn to the welcome air of an open window. As quickly as that's occurred, Rob has climbed onto a dining table chair where he disconnects the battery from the smoke alarm. He hops off and puts back the chair. In the abrupt quiet, he scoops up a whimpering Dumpling like a baby and says, "It's okay, pup, just a drill." Cradling the dog, amid my disaster, Rob appears calm and at ease. "Liv . . ." he says in the most serene, gentle voice.

"What?"

"Just toss some flour on the grease fire behind you."

A half hour later, aside from the slight lingering odor of burnt beef Wellington, things settle down, or feel more like they've hit a groove. We closed the window and Rob opened more wine. "Is it okay with you if I make us something?"

"Sure. If you want." From there he heads into my kitchen, where he forages for spare edible items. When I offer to assist, Rob holds up a hand.

"It's a small kitchen. I've got this."

"What will I do, besides drink?" Looking at the kitchen mess, I'd say getting drunk in a corner sounds about right.

Rob points to my violin. "I wouldn't mind hearing you play." My gaze holds onto his. "I mean, you've mentioned it—I heard old Leland talk. Either you're that good, or he lays it on pretty thick." He shrugs. "But only if you want to."

Never once, not since my grandfather passed—or after the chain was attached and the grind began—have I wanted to play to please somebody. I can't even imagine what that would feel like. Rob doesn't say anything else but retreats to his impromptu meal prep. I sip the wine and eye the Amati. It's an inanimate object capable of evoking volatile emotion, mostly from me. Perhaps it is the combination of challenge and request, or oddly enough the man it came from. I put down the wine, pick up the violin, and hesitate. Rob cheers a wineglass in my direction, then helps himself to all my kitchen drawers—remarking on what is apparently a disgraceful selection of knives. I begin to play—*The Lark Ascending*, a piece sometimes defined as *pastoral romance*. Between Dumpling's fascination with our visitor, and mine, it seems fitting.

I watch as Rob continues to go about the business of feeding me. The music isn't the thing that has my attention; I play this piece from memory, the way most people recite the alphabet. It's my comfort level, which I fumble with at first, wanting to be annoyed or bored by the request to perform. I am not. Instead, I find myself sinking into an enticing pocket of warmth. I can tell Rob is listening, his dark brows rising as he cracks eggs—hearing measures of music that would cause even a pedestrian ear to take note. That or it's a musician thing; you just know when someone is moved by music. Normally, I could not care less how my playing moves anyone. Eventually, I glance toward Dumpling. He lowers his head and closes his eyes, seemingly at peace.

A short time later, Rob and I have finished the bottle of white wine and scrumptious French toast—who would ever think to pair two such contrasting elements and end up with a winning combination. "By the way," he says, downing a last sip of wine, "the table setting is beautiful."

"Thanks. Of course, I did choose it with a bread-based dish in mind." I smile, the two of us having segued smoothly from burnt beef Wellington to stale bread that Rob repurposed on a miracle level not far from fishes and loaves. "The French toast was outstanding. Is breakfast your forte?"

"Maybe. If we make it to tomorrow morning and eggs Benedict, you can let me know." I don't smile but breathe deep.

I retreat from the table to the window. A light snowfall is in the process of turning into something less than charming, a blustery storm that, by morning, will disrupt usual patterns and require heavy machinery to correct. The whole thing will be not only costly but forgotten by June. It's beautiful but pointless.

"Sorry," Rob says, following. "That was presumptuous. I can, um . . . Maybe I should get going." A moment later, he's gathered his coat and said good-bye to the dog. He offers a parting remark. "For what it's worth, Liv, thanks for the attempt."

"The attempt?" I turn, ready to inform him that the playing he heard was nothing short of virtuoso quality.

"Yes. The beef Wellington. I appreciate the trouble you went to, even if it didn't work out."

"Oh. I didn't think you meant . . ." Since the smell of burnt pastry has faded, I'd nearly forgotten my initial attempt to impress Rob.

"Right. Thank you—for coming . . . For cooking. Not too many people . . . men make it as far as my kitchen."

"Doesn't look like you do either. But that's okay; nothing pisses me off more than a person who excels at everything. I mean, we all have certain gifts, right?"

"I suppose. I'm guessing yours isn't necessarily cooking." He continues to scratch Dumpling's head, closer to the exit than me. "Despite your knack for crotchety canines, I assume it's not that either."

"You're the dog whisperer, not me." He flashes a quick smile. "If I said I'm still trying to figure it out, would that sound lame, especially to someone whose talent is so obvious?"

"Ah, now you're talking about the violin." I raise a brow at him. "No. I'd say it sounds disturbingly honest."

"For the most part . . ." He hesitates for a moment. "With the exception of one recent incident, you can put a check mark in my honesty box."

"I wasn't keeping score."

"Liv, why don't you want . . . ?" He appears to rework his thought. "I was going to ask why you don't want this to go any further, but I'll keep it simple: Why don't you want to date me?"

"I never said . . ." He is prepared to leave, and I have, once again, hit my Rob wall. "Honest, right?" I say hurriedly.

"Probably might be best, given the moment." I look curiously at him. Rob cocks his chin toward the bedroom. "I don't need to spend the night, nothing like that. But if we leave it like this, I'm not going to call again. I don't do vicious circles."

I stride away from the icy window and toward him. "What happened earlier, with the dinner I was going to make—it was just kind of comical, right? Not really a big deal. I can't cook."

"I hate to break it to you, but there are other ways to a man's heart than through his stomach."

I ignore his attempt at mid-century humor. "If we went on more . . . *dates*"—I focus on his hand, which continues to stroke a softly snoring Dumpling—"it wouldn't take many to find out I'm not exactly, or even close to . . . *perfect*."

"Wow. You're kidding?" He frowns, nodding deeply. "Spoiler alert, Liv . . . I was already kind of betting on less than perfect. And the imperfect part—just so you know—that's the part I've been wanting . . . waiting to get to." My gaze jerks to his. "After a third date and a fourth . . . It's really all I've been thinking about. Who is the woman beneath the one that is so carefully—and not with great success—watching her every move? The glimmers of you, in case no one has ever said, are spellbinding."

"Thank you . . . or not." I half laugh. "But seriously, Rob, be aware, I'm more trouble than—"

He leans past the dog and kisses me. For a moment I indulge in the exquisite feel of Rob's mouth, the smell of him, which is precisely the scent you'd want to find on your sheets, and the feel—the words *hot* and *steady* come to mind.

"Here's an idea. Why don't you let me decide about imperfections for myself?"

"Really, you don't understand—"

"Liv, listen to me, we're all imperfect." His head tips back and forth. "Granted, varying degrees of imperfect . . . So let's get a few basics out of the way. Have you committed a felony?" I shake my head. "Are you wanted for murder, grand theft auto, or forgery in this hemisphere? Have you committed treason? Do you have a drug habit I should know about or walk thoughtlessly past homeless people muttering, 'Let them eat cake'?"

"No, not recently . . ."

"The drug habit or homeless people?"

"I've smoked my share of pot; I always give to the homeless."

"Okay then. Like I said, we all have flaws—I might even have a few of my own. I think it's more about deciding who you want to be imperfect with."

"You make it sound so easy."

"Only if you want it to be."

I glance back at the snowy view. "One thing I have to insist on."

"What's that?"

"No eggs Benedict. If we're going to move on from *dating*, I'd like to start off right, do my share in this relationship. Out of thirty-three takeout menus, six deliver breakfast. After this storm, one might be open tomorrow morning."

Rob glances between me and a dimly lit bedroom where the door is slightly ajar. "You can totally be the judge here—but so you know, I don't really consider French toast a high-ranking item on my list of usable gifts."

CHAPTER THIRTEEN

Boston, Massachusetts

Present Day

Theo

Theo and his mother are finishing a pleasant downtown lunch on Newbury Street. It's a Saturday, and Theo has promised for two straight weeks that he would make time for this. Post India, he's gained a better understanding of his mother's love and loss. After his father died and life was nothing but the two of them and devastation, Theo was uplifted by his mother's devotion. It appears she's trying to do the same thing again, fix the gaping hole India's left. When he was ten, her dedication made a tremendous difference. At twenty-six, Theo isn't sure Claire's effort will have the same result.

"How's the new book you're editing? A romance, right?" Theo asks, downing a mouthful of the brownie sundae his mother insisted they split. She has taken two minuscule bites, nudging the plate closer to Theo with each one.

"Upmarket literary fiction," Claire corrects as her phone rings. "Debut novel. Ah, there's my young *author* now." Reluctantly, she surrenders to the call. Theo knows Claire does not like the interruption, but she's committed to everything she takes on—work, charitable causes, her son.

He wants to look at his own phone, but he'd only be looking for a missed call from India. Theo is growing tired of self-inflicted disappointment, so instead he half listens to his mother's conversation. The young novelist is fresh out of Sarah Lawrence and younger than Theo. After his mother's lunch meeting with the girl at Booktini—a Manhattan bistro she frequents when in New York—Claire was quick to voice her displeasure. The new author arrived late, ordered a drink out of the gate, and used words like *awesome* and *stressed.* Yet his mother did accept the freelance assignment of editing her book. Claire is only being Claire. "One must choose their battles, Theo. Carefully assess, then choose," is a common Claire idiom.

She holds her hand over the phone and mouths "One minute," to Theo, though the pitch of her voice tightens as she continues the call. Their back-and-forth exchange exceeds a minute and Theo's interest.

As his mother prattles on, Theo thinks back to his freshman year at Cornell. It's when he learned that, after his father died, his mother turned down offers to return to her former life with New York publishers. She refused to uproot Theo. Perhaps she had no desire to be so close to ground zero, or move him on top of it. When Theo went off to college, he thought it might be a signal to Claire that she had done a good job. Her life could be about more than overseeing his. But after college, when Theo returned to Boston, Claire was firm in her choice to remain there as well. His attention reverts to his mother as she ends the call.

"I'm too old and out of touch for this," she says. "Most authors are less than half my age. So are in-house editors. Neither has a clue." She stabs at the brownie sundae, taking a more believable bite.

"Maybe the key is to get more involved with your publishing house." Theo does not want to be the reason, twice, that his mother puts her life on hold. "Years ago, after Dad . . ." A lump lodges in Theo's throat. "You could have gone back to your career. It bothers me—you didn't get your chance because you chose me over your work."

"Theo! I can't believe you'd even think such a thing." She smiles. This is a gesture Theo associates with warmth and protection. "You know how difficult you were to come by in the first place."

Theo has heard the story many times. After a decade of failed traditional methods and advanced science, Theo's parents decided to adopt. Claire often tells Theo she is sure he's the reason all other avenues were unsuccessful—it was simply meant to be. Theo pushes the plate away. He is full to the brim and cannot eat another bite. Lunch is to include shopping, at the very least a stroll down Newbury Street. Theo isn't much for shopping, but his mother likes to peruse store windows, always insisting on purchasing him some article of clothing.

They exit the restaurant and walk all of twelve feet before Theo realizes the shopping pattern is in motion. She points to a sleek leather jacket in an upscale men's clothing store. The jacket probably costs more than Theo's entire paycheck. Claire makes good money with her editorial work, but it was David McAdams's advance planning that made sure his family was provided for.

"Do you like it?" she asks. "It looks like it belongs on the cover of *GQ*—maybe with you in it." While it's a typical Claire compliment, she will not force the issue. If Theo is opposed to her garment of choice, they will continue to shop until they find something he does like.

Theo puffs out his cheeks and blows air, staring at the jacket. He does not agree with his mother's *GQ* take. When it comes to her son, Claire sees an inspired oil painting. Theo sees more of an evolving sketch—a musician, who, if not for his mother's steadfast guidance, then India's input, would likely vanish into his music.

His gaze drifts from the jacket, catching his reflection in the storefront glass. Claire is five-nine, so Theo's five-eleven stature never looks particularly tall next to hers. There is enough of a plausible resemblance that no one has ever said, "How is *she* your mother?" Although she does have blue eyes and so did his father—a piece of biology that he recalls startling him in the eighth grade. *Two blue-eyed parents cannot produce a brown-eyed child* . . . In the classroom, for a moment, Theo wrestled with the sensation of falling—suddenly not so secure in the place he belonged. The feeling passed back then. It passes now as he refocuses on the jacket.

But a moment later he blinks into his reflection and Claire's, her blond bob bobbing. Surely his mother's hair color says nothing about genes. Only her hairdresser would know that information. Their features are comparable—oval faces and Reese Witherspoon chins. His hair is a river of messy waves, the color of past-prime fall leaves. David McAdams had brown hair too. Theo wonders if he would be less secure had he been a redhead, like India, or a different ethnicity. What if his parents had adopted a baby from China or Mexico? Would that boy have stuck out on the McAdamses' family Christmas card? Of course, if his parents had done that, a whole other person would be Theo McAdams. This bit of happenstance makes Theo's head swim. They are the thoughts only adopted children will think.

His mother interrupts Theo's questions with one of her own. "Shall we go in and try it on?"

Theo has forgotten the jacket. "You know, Mom, it might not be the best thing to wear to a place like Braemore."

"So wear it somewhere else, out with your friends or . . ." She doesn't finish the sentence that should end with India's name. Theo moves on to the next shop. They are mutually lost in a bookstore for a time, separated by genre—he scans the latest thriller titles while Claire plucks women's fiction novels from an end cap. Theo does not know if she wants to size up the competition or simply enjoy a book.

In some instances, Claire's motivation can be hard to read, like the time she arranged a dinner with Sophia Beauregard and her mother, Pamela. Sophia is a ballerina, and the Beauregards are family acquaintances. Theo thought it odd, his mother's sudden interest in the ballet and the need to have dinner with people he barely knew. But he didn't think more than that. The matchmaker scheme only dawned on Theo *afterward* when his mother bluntly asked, "So what did you think, son? Sophia comes from such a fine family. Can't you picture her on your arm, so smart and delicately boned?" Theo gave her a look and said, "Yeah, and we'd be on our way to a deli so I could buy her a sandwich, where we would continue to find nothing in common. What is *Downtown Abbey* anyway?"

Standing in the bookstore, Theo snickers at the memory, which his mother was quick to correct: "It's *Downton Abbey*, Theo." Maybe encouraging his mother to take on more New York work wouldn't be an awful idea.

After making their purchases they continue down Newbury Street. It's the height of Saturday shopping in early October. People are shoulder to shoulder on a historic street meant for a much sparser population. So it's amazing when, through the thick of crowds, Theo spies red hair from half a block away. Of course, Theo would likely spot her from the moon. His stride lengthens to close the gap. Moments later, his and India's noses nearly mash in an almost head-on collision. Claire drops her package; books spill everywhere. He thinks Claire has said an unlikely expletive, but he's not sure. It's India's voice that rings in his ears.

"Theo," she says, breathlessly, as if spying a Newbury Street ghost.

"What . . . why are you here?" And for one glorious second, Theo entertains a lifetime's worth of fantasy. India has come back to him. She's driven like a madwoman from Long Island to Boston, and is just making a quick stop in Victoria's Secret before surprising him at their apartment. They won't emerge from the bedroom for days. Before and after they make love, she will tell him what a terrible mistake she's made—that she's realized her abrupt breakup was an overreaction to kissing an old boyfriend. She's even feeding into his fantasy by saying the word *wedding*.

"You remember . . . it's tomorrow. Colleen and Jeff's wedding."

Theo slams so hard into reality he's too blindsided to speak. Claire steps in on his behalf.

"That's right. Your cousin's wedding—you're a bridesmaid." India is clutching a garment bag. "Of course you'd need to be here for that, your parents are even doing the catering, right?"

Theo hasn't forgotten the wedding, only the date. Of course, looking at India, standing on the same slice of Newbury Street, Theo is lucky if he can recall his address. She is quite possibly more beautiful than he remembers.

"Yes. And at a healthy discount," India says, though she's looking at Theo.

He looks back, fighting an urge to step up and kiss her. Theo remembers everything about kissing India and the way her body fit perfectly between the bedsheets and him. He wants to believe she's thinking the same thing. Her wavy red head swings toward Claire, and India takes a step back. It douses any ideas about sheets and day-dreamy kissing.

"I'm sorry. I never imagined I'd run into . . . Boston's a big city, and Theo doesn't like to shop."

"Just the extension of a mother-son luncheon," Claire tells her. "How's your move back home, India? Things working out?"

Theo hears protective instinct.

"Fine. Busy. The Boston leg of the business is doing good. Well, it is thanks to you." There is uncomfortable silence. Not long before India and Theo broke up, Claire hired Take Me to Church Catering to host her upcoming fall fundraiser. It isn't her personal fundraiser, but she is the committee chairperson. The event, for Boston Public Schools, was a boon for the small business, and it was magnanimous of his mother not to switch caterers after India broke her son's heart.

"Yes, well, I've been in touch with the woman they've hired to replace you. I'm sure the event will be fine. And your sister?" she says, changing subjects. "How is Helen doing?" It's charitable small talk, at which his mother excels. She knows India and her parents dedicate themselves as much to Helen as Claire does to Theo. "I hope your parents continue to cope. I've thought about giving your mother a call . . ." Her words trail off.

"Helen's doing better—it's difficult. It will be a lifelong struggle."

"Yes, it will," Theo says, though he is hardly talking about India's sister and her heroin addiction. Helen's drug problems were the one thing that stuck out in his and India's, otherwise, storybook relationship—three a.m. trips to the emergency room and panicked calls from Helen, who was always one good hit away from total self-destruction. But even with this, Theo viewed Helen as a strength. Not a strain on their relationship. He and India did life better as a twosome. Helen was proof that, together, he and India could navigate obstacles. It's part of the reason Theo's so stunned that one misplaced kiss was their final undoing. Theo cannot help himself, asking, "Will you be in town long—maybe we could get a cup of coffee or something?"

He recognizes her reaction. India is a careful thinker—she weighs pros and cons. She will even make lists on a white board. Right now she is thinking how to say no without further crushing him. Theo swears her hazel gaze is watery, but it is likely the fall breeze in her face. "I don't think it would be a good idea, Theo." She has found the gentlest way to drive another nail through him.

Even so, Theo wants to reach for India and an ending like one of the many romantic comedies she insisted they watch together. While Theo objected, he enjoyed the date-night movies a great deal. Maybe he should have told India he loved them. Standing on the sidewalk, Theo still imagines they're living in one. India's mouth is slightly agape, like she's so very close to saying something perfect and personal. Theo is getting even more personal, as the mere presence of India is causing an unexpected physical reaction. But instead of reaching for India, Theo shoves his hand in his coat pockets. He's no longer reeling from the pain of losing India. He has grown accustomed to that—a wound that won't heal. This feels more like contempt for her vague glassy gaze. He is pissed off at a hard-on that will be resolved by way of a cold shower or some pathetic fantasy. Theo knots his hands. He's angry and yet he wants to throw his arms around her.

India crushes the garment bag tight to her. "I'd better get going. The dress will be a wrinkled mess."

"What color is it?" Claire asks.

And now Theo is angry at his mother for perpetuating small talk. India's gaze travels from Theo to Claire, looking as if she has asked her to solve a polynomial equation. A swallow rolls through India's silken throat, porcelain skin that Theo can still smell and taste and feel. He focuses on her hands. It doesn't help. Her small fingers are crunched around the bag, and Theo can only think of the diamond she wore, tucked in the cedar box on his dresser. On India's finger now is an amethyst ring he doesn't recognize. Theo wonders where it came from—if perhaps India has a new boyfriend to go with her new life.

"Lavender." India looks past Theo and his mother. He knows he sees tears. "I have to get going. I flew up to Boston. My flight was late, and I'm the last one to pick up my dress. The rehearsal dinner is in an hour."

"Enjoy the wedding," Claire says. India doesn't reply, but pushes past them. Theo twists around to watch as she vanishes into the crowd of shoppers and sightseers. Theo jams his fists harder into his pockets. Claire loops her arm through his. "You know, I think we've done enough shopping for one day." Theo turns back, allowing himself to be guided down Newbury Street.

CHAPTER FOURTEEN

Olivia

I return to Theo's classroom with increasing guilt. It's one thing to be curious about a twenty-six-year-old question, to wonder about the human being you gave away. It's quite another to perpetuate a relationship based on facts about which only one of you is aware.

A reputable attorney handled the adoption, providing dossiers on a dozen potential parents—I only had to make the final selection. How wrong could I go? Someone else narrowed the choices. According to the attorney, every couple was wholly deserving of a child. But when I saw the McAdamses' suburban Boston address, I found reasons to eliminate all other candidates. Before 9-11 and Shep Stewart, I had the consolation of knowing the baby I gave away lived within a twenty-mile radius. And, I admit, this fact sometimes led to fantasies about bumping into Theo in a restaurant or a shopping mall.

Once, however, in a movie theater line with Sasha, a rowdy group of teenagers drew my attention. One boy was the perfect mix of Sam and me; he strongly resembled the grainy Theo photos in Shep's stories.

He was popular. Throngs of kids flocked to him like they did Sam. I didn't eavesdrop; their boisterous chatter was impossible not to hear. I tuned in tighter as the *Theo* boy talked about baseball. He was a pitcher, just like Sam. Another boy taunted him about continuing with band, a not-so-cool activity. The Theo boy defended his love of both things. My heart swelled. Then it deflated like a Macy's Day Parade balloon, smacked into a live wire. The same teenager called the boy "Dan." *Theo.* By then, thanks to Shep, I knew my son's name was Theo.

Sasha and I proceeded into the theatre. I was relieved to sit in the dark with an excuse not to speak with her for the next two hours. Otherwise, who knows what I might have confided. Back then, it was all so clear. But now—is Theo still part of my past I've chosen to keep private? Or has he become a certifiable secret, or worse, a lie? By not telling Sasha or Rob about Theo, I avoided answering for choices I made at twenty-one.

Going forward now, I resolve to make sounder decisions. As the weeks move forward, I continue to play my part at Braemore: a classical violinist, here to bring a dose of court-ordered culture to the students. They're the focus, not Theo. For a short time, it works. Organized chaos and varying degrees of outbursts is a staple among these at-risk kids, enough so that one is kept busy from the beginning to the end of each class.

I work three days a week in Theo's classroom, for a total of eight hours a week, meaning I should complete my community service by the time Braemore breaks for the December holiday. I both dread and look forward to the date. Once it sinks in that observing Theo's class will not count as participation, I attempt to dive in. While I'm wholly dedicated to supporting school music programs, there's a reason I'm not a hands-on participant. My effort goes about as well as a thirty-foot leap into three feet of water, concrete bottom. We start with small teacher tasks, me overseeing students who showed an interest in string instruments. To be honest, my proclivity for music allowed me to dart past a yawning learning curve a lifetime ago. Conversely, it doesn't take long for all of us to discover my low tolerance for students with a desire to learn but little aptitude. I struggle for patience while truly trying to teach a girl named Eden a one-octave, C major scale. Later in the week, I work with Tyler, a boy with slightly more promise. But as I remark, "Why can't you follow what I'm saying? The sound needs to emanate organically, as opposed to what you're doing, which is just so . . ." I suck in a huge breath, blurting out the word *mechanical.* It takes a moment to realize Theo's grimace is directed at me, not his student.

Nearly a month into my educational efforts, Theo suggests I stick to demonstrating various musical techniques, like rhythm, pitch matching, and vibrato. There isn't much margin for error or interaction. It keeps me at a distance and us in a group setting where Theo remains the teacher in charge. Not only have I come to respect Theo's gift for music education, I feel thoroughly guilty about the many teachers whose patience and dedication I've trampled.

In addition to menial tasks, Theo gently steers me to a back corner of the room, putting me in charge of string maintenance. Mercifully, he says he'll tend to the woodwind and brass instruments, which includes things like water keys. My in-depth inventory of the string instruments leaves me appalled—warped violins and violas, brightly colored ones no less—a horrible fate for any string instrument. The cellos, of which there are two, look like perhaps they survived the *Titanic.* Bows are in no better shape, black and tattered beyond belief. I determine that the most beneficial solution for all the string instruments would be a bonfire.

Despite the defective instruments and unpredictability of the room, Theo continues to navigate with a steady hand. One particularly raucous afternoon, he employs the finesse of a UN diplomat. He introduces his music appreciation class to the Jazz Age, and I am mesmerized as he makes the cultural and social struggles of the time relevant to this room's populace. When he tells the students about Earl Hines and

Dizzy Gillespie, he captures them. For once, the music is the only sound in the room. They are involved and intrigued, swayed, if only temporarily, from their everyday fates. But as the class absorbs the period's music, it's Theo's soft remark that seizes my attention: "I must have inherited the art of persuasion from my dad." He whispers this to me, observing the rapt faces of his students. "If there's one thing I know about my father, David McAdams could get anybody to listen."

After class, Theo goes on to stack chairs; I stand, stunned. In the Jazz Age, a person could live their whole life and not know they were adopted. Like other societal prejudices, adoption came with a stigma. But surely not now, not today. Is it possible? Could Theo be unaware Claire and David McAdams are *not* his biological parents? My face flushes and my pulse hammers—covetous and confused. I want to ask him while fighting an urge to say: *"Your ability to captivate a crowd is inherent, Theo—just not from the man you're thinking of . . ."*

The unlikely moment dips deep into Sam Nash history. Something I deftly avoid, memories of those distant days in North Carolina. But hearing Theo's misguided thought, his voice so like Sam's, it unearths the past. Theo is the result of everything I felt for the man from Tennessee. My tender, disfigured memories should come by way of yellowed love letters or a crushed corsage, not a living, breathing person. And yet, there he stands.

My next visit to Braemore is out of order, more so than usual. Theo has asked me to come by and observe Antonio Graham's private music lesson on an October Friday. Among Braemore's music students, he is the standout—a gift far beyond Octavious's ear for rhythm. He's never applied to the city-wide orchestra, but I understand why. A recent arrest record is an automatic disqualification. Unfortunately, Antonio fits this profile. Standing in the music room doorway, I raise a brow, guessing the same could be said for me. Perhaps we should look at that rule on a student-by-student basis. I'm a few minutes late. Antonio is playing

Bach's "Gavotte en Rondeau" in E major. Even with a dime store instrument, the music filters out with amazing promise.

Antonio is lost in the music as Theo spies me. He cocks his head, a silent invitation to come inside. My stare lingers on Theo's profile. His arms are folded and his frame is lean and defined. I feel like I'm looking at old photos. Yesteryear rushes me, clobbering me, intense and disturbingly unexpected. A flutter of emotion invades, but I force my focus on Antonio.

An unusually peaceful expression fills the boy's face. I have never seen Antonio's features display anything but discontent. He still doesn't look like a violinist, but I have learned not to judge these kids based on appearance. Truthfully, at best, most will end up with mediocre lives; some will end up in jail. But there are glimmers of hope, and Antonio is the brightest. You could tour every high school in the state and not come across a gift like his.

Antonio continues with Bach's "Gavotte"—the first masterful piece most violin students learn. Before he gets to it, I anticipate the snag. Theo and I trade a glance. He knows the same thing as two measures of double stops approach. They are sticky widgets of music that take time and practice. The blunder is to be expected. I accomplished the piece at ten, but I faltered just as Antonio has. He hears it too. He stops playing. Peacefulness drains.

I know a little about Antonio—he stole his mother's car and went joyriding without a driver's license. More troubling, he's been caught with meth and prescription drugs, trying to sell them to an undercover cop. In between, Antonio has paid some attention to his talent—enough to read fairly complex music, which only emphasizes the depth of his ability. I don't get the drugs part, but I understand how Antonio feels about playing the violin. We see it the same way, even though we've never had a conversation about it. Antonio is like me; music is an undeniable piece of his brain. Although he's not sure, given a choice, he'd want it that way.

"Antonio," I say. "You are doing beautifully. Mastering those measures is the kind of challenge that will only make you better. Trust me." I remember this line of encouragement (which I labeled bullshit at the time) from many an instructor. I glance at Theo, who appears surprised by my benevolent reaction. Twice Theo has asked me to play for them, music beyond basic technique and theory. *Polite* is an abstract concept at Braemore, so I knew they were honestly impressed when I played. But I am too old and too removed from their world to be more than a three-minute fascination with a fiddle.

Antonio's expression turns more fretful—frustrated. For as much as playing can be a gift, it can also make you want to tear out your hair. Repetitive errors like this can be a cliff-diving scenario for someone like Antonio. If exasperated enough, he may leave here and rob a liquor store or ingest enough drugs to land him in the morgue. Theo will take it personally. It's his encouragement that got Antonio this far. I won't allow it. I move closer to the teacher and his student. Theo attempts to verbally convey the difficulty of measures 72 and 73 in Bach's piece. The violin is not like a piano where mistakes can be hidden by a clever hand.

Antonio shakes his head. "This is a fucking waste of time. Even if I get it, what's the point? Why should I even bother to try?"

His attitude is one of the more exasperating obstacles at Braemore: the loud impatience of these kids' lives. They flail about, grabbing at things which they think they are owed, unable to grasp what it is they've earned—which in most cases is nothing. On the other hand, if a kid like Antonio could focus, stick with it, he might achieve something to which he is entitled—a life far away from this one.

Theo looks at me. "Hang on, Antonio. Why don't we let Miss Klein take a run at it? I know the measures seem impossible. But I just want you to listen—*listen* to how the piece should sound. You're so good at interpreting music. It's how it *will* sound if you give it time."

Antonio and I pass a look between each other—it's the solidarity of understanding my lack of influence. Theo takes the violin from

Antonio and holds it out to me. I shake my head and push it back toward him. "I think it would be better if you showed him." Theo gives me a queer look. He is a high school music teacher. I am a violinist with the renowned New England Symphony. Only in this room are our credentials irrelevant. Stressing my point, I back up and sit in one of the student seats. Antonio is quiet, as if waiting to see if Mr. McAdams will rise to the challenge. Theo is smart enough to get my point—even an average interpretation of Bach's "Gavotte" from him is more likely to resonate than any notes I might offer.

Theo begins to play. Antonio listens. For a moment, I do the same. It occurs to me that I have heard Theo talk about playing the violin, but in my time at Braemore I have not experienced it. I don't know what I'm expecting, but a few measures in and I hear so much more than music. Everything in the room fades to a backdrop. I become the backdrop. My presence as a wayward violinist, committed to community service hours breaks down. The intricate melody plays on, serving as a lovely underscore to the banned emotion inside me. The splendor of Bach's "Gavotte" winds through. It's like the tail of a kite string I've been chasing my entire life. One measure after another, Theo's ability comes clear, matching the music—or more precisely, the musician. At first he focuses on sheet music. Then Theo closes his eyes, sinking into the grandeur of the composition. There's an inherent unmistakable gait to what he's doing, an authenticity that is utterly organic. I press my fingers to my mouth like a prayer. I've seen my father do it in old home movies, ones he could never bear to watch. I experienced it with my grandfather before he passed away. On Sunday afternoons we would play together—call and response. He would play a musical phrase, I would mimic it, and for finite bits of time, music was good. The four of us—me, my grandfather, his son, and now his great grandson—we hear and translate and play with exactly the same gift.

Antonio and I trade an awestruck glance as I attempt to make my eyelashes soak up tears. The music weaves on, perfectly executed peaks and valleys of connected notes that make the most beautiful sound. Theo masterfully handles the troubling double stops as if they are grace notes. My God, he's better than me, and I realize why: Theo possesses all the passion I lack. For the first time in my life, I see why my gift with hands and instrument, ear and melody exists. It exists so it can belong to Theo McAdams.

The "Gavotte" comes to its understated melodic close, a relief from all the angst its interior measures deliver. The sudden silence is piercing. Antonio and I stare. Theo shrugs at the music stand. "Maybe not too bad for an amateur."

I am practiced enough to keep my reaction composed. Not a mother who has just heard her son execute a stunning rendition of a complex piece of music, something he has achieved, not because of Claire's good mothering or his adopted father's admirable talents, but by way of a gift he has inherited from me—only me. But I know my place. I won't lose sight of it. After Antonio packs up, leaving with renewed hope and the promise of practicing this weekend, Theo asks if I want to grab a cup of coffee. I succumb to the impulses that have driven so much of my life. I say yes.

CHAPTER FIFTEEN

Olivia

The café down the street from Braemore is cozier than Starbucks, and I fear more intimate. We order coffee. Theo was oddly quiet on the walk over; a nervous vibe wafts off him. It fills me with paranoia. Maybe he's figured it out. But then I remember I'm not sure if Theo knows he's adopted. He smiles at me, and I smile back. Damn, if it's not the same smile. Could Theo have figured it out from that—a mirroring smile? I run the rationale through the spin cycle that is my brain. Would you approach someone who is no more than a friendly acquaintance and say, "Gosh, I've noticed we favor a bit—could you possibly be the mother who gave me away twenty-six years ago?" I look out the window into a snarl of traffic. It doesn't begin to reflect this mess.

"Olivia? Are you all right?"

My gaze flicks to his. "Perfectly fine. Why?"

"You look startled, which is kind of funny, because I'm the one who has the nervous question to ask."

"Oh?" For once a waitress has impeccable timing. She delivers coffee. I busy myself with artificial sweetener and a spoon. I don't look at Theo; it doesn't matter. He reaches across, and in a surprising gesture clasps my shaking hand.

"My gosh. Tell me what's wrong? You seemed fine until I played Bach's 'Gavotte.' Was it that awful?" He grins as if it's a proper joke.

"Yes. I mean, no. Theo, you know damn well it was nothing short of magnificent."

He lets go of my hand; his expression shifts to slight embarrassment. "Magnificent . . . More like mysterious, at least the origin."

If I was the fainting type, now would be a good moment.

Look at him, Liv . . . You did this . . . You screwed up again . . . Now face it . . . "What do you want to know?" He'll ask. I'll answer. We'll part ways—just like we did twenty-six years ago. I'll go to jail for not fulfilling my community service or decent-human-being requirements. "Well?"

He's taken aback by my tone. It's the one Sasha points out on occasion, the one that frightens store clerks and is not suitable for small children.

"I, uh . . . I was wondering if you think the symphony might offer a summer internship to a kid like Antonio." He stirs black coffee.

"What?" I lean in, squinting at his request.

"I understand. It's probably totally out of the realm of possibility. It'd be a hard thing to finagle for a talented kid from Brookline. I can see where a student from Braemore would be a long shot."

"A summer internship." I lift my cup, and coffee sloshes over the edge. Fortunately it's tepid. The cup makes a shaky landing back onto the saucer. "I, uh . . ." I smile our smile. "I didn't think that's what you were going to ask."

"What did you think I was going to ask?"

"Nothing that matters." I stiffly shift my shoulders. "An internship. I'll talk to Manuel Gutierrez, our conductor. See if he'll speak to the front office."

"Great," Theo says, breathing deep. "If it works out, your *assignment* at Braemore will have delivered more than I could have imagined."

"And what did you imagine? A snooty symphony violinist, banished to a timeout for bad public behavior."

He frowns. "Not really. I don't make judgements based on occupation. As for the timeout . . . Well, after getting to you know a little, I can't see that either."

I have been careful about the Olivia Theo knows, crafting the woman I would like him to see. While she is clearly not a teacher, she tries. She is reserved. She does not act out or take baseball bats to luxury vehicles. Theo still doesn't know the transgression that landed me in his classroom. Of course, that's nothing compared to the other things Theo doesn't know. I flounder between small talk and a ridiculous well of emotion. "You know, Theo, you're extremely talented."

"So I've been told."

"You're being modest."

The diffident tip of his head turns into a nod. "It took a while to realize it . . . grasp it."

"You thought your life should be dedicated to athleticism."

"How do you know . . ." He knots his brow; then it relaxes. "Oh, that's right. You've followed the Theo McAdams chronicles, the Shep Stewart stories."

"Yes, the stories." Thank God for the stories. More than once they have explained my innate knowledge of Theo. "You, um . . ." I feign a struggle to recall facts. "Didn't you win a scholarship or something based on athletics?"

"To Cornell. A full ride for lacrosse."

"Cornell. You must have had the grades to back that up."

"My parents—my mother," he says, alluding to David McAdams's limited time with him. "Schoolwork always came first, whether it was music or sports."

"Tell me, were you class president too?"

"Vice president," he admits.

I am blindsided by the miraculous correction that can be made to DNA. "She . . . they," I say, giving an absent David McAdams credit. "Your parents raised an incredible human being—so gifted yet so selfless and smart about your talents."

"When it comes to sports, music . . . education, they instilled good values. But the gifts themselves . . ." Theo's gaze moves around the café, taking in the strangers that surround him. His eyes settle back on me.

"What?"

"I'm adopted."

I bite down on the inside of my cheek and concentrate on forming normal steady breaths. We're doing okay for just having stepped off a cliff. Right. I've stepped off, but I am holding his hand. "So you always knew that you were adopted?"

"Mmm," he murmurs. "The same way you know your birthday. It wasn't a big deal."

"Even when it falls on New Year's Eve?"

Theo thuds against the booth and his jaw slacks. "How do you know . . ."

My fingers flit nervously through a layer of bangs. "Subconscious recall. Claire must have mentioned it in one of her many updates." His surprised expression doesn't change, but he can't argue. Theo hasn't looked at the stories in years. "Or maybe you brought it up in passing."

"I don't think I've ever mentioned—"

"So you were saying, you've always known about your adoption."

"Uh, yeah." His face relaxes. "I remember my mother rocking me when I was about four or so. She'd say 'You're my sweetheart, you're my lamb . . . you're my adopted . . .'"

Brava, Claire . . . how brilliant.

"Just another word for love," I say softly. But a wedge grows so large in my throat it feels as if I've swallowed a sea of jealousy.

"So, actually," Theo continues, "I don't know where any of my abilities come from. I don't know how it is I stepped onto a soccer field at five and, hands down, was better than every kid out there. Of course, at that age, when your dad was a college All-American, you just figure it somehow comes from him."

"I can see where a boy could draw that conclusion." Aside from the McAdamses' zip code, David McAdams's athleticism was a boon. The savvy athlete turned business executive and accomplished woman with a publishing background. Intelligent (which is different than smart), unselfish, focused, and success stamped on their DNA. Those are the things I wanted for a child who might have all the inherent gifts in the world and be sorely lacking an ability to navigate them.

"I liked believing athletic talent came from my dad. It kept him that much closer. But it all blends. I love to read, and I know that comes from my mother—despite biology. She has a background in publishing. It all fit naturally, less the music."

"Couldn't attribute that to either of your parents."

"My mother is tone deaf, and, well, my dad was so good at sports . . . How many talents can one person have?"

I lean in and my gaze turns questioning.

"Right." He laughs again. "I do wonder more about the music, where it comes from. Don't get me wrong, there can be beauty on a field, in that sort of accomplishment. But it isn't anything like music. Not for me."

I'm sitting on my hands to keep still, silently willing him on. He is saying all the things about music that I've been told but never truly experienced.

"At first music was like sports. It was something that came naturally; it just existed. Then, after my father died—the way he died—that changed. The meaning of music changed."

"It's music. How does it relate to what happened to your father?"

"Chaos," he says. "That time in my life was chaos. The world was chaos. Afterward, no matter my mother's influence, my life could have become chaos. Music kept that from happening. All the questions, all the anger. Music is the one thing where every note is where it's supposed to be."

I lean back into the booth. It's such a profound thought. Theo is so fortunate to have the capacity to think it. Yet the other end of that equation sinks in. "But if you hadn't been adopted, nothing on 9-11 would have been so personal—a father and the tragic way he died. You wouldn't have had to go through that."

Theo shakes his head. "The tragedy would have been not knowing him at all." I am too awed to reply. Theo continues on. "David McAdams was an exceptional father. After 9-11 . . . My mother certainly gets all the credit. I couldn't have asked for a better one there either."

Touché, Liv. You had that coming . . .

"But she couldn't give me everything. Wherever my musical wiring comes from, that was my saving grace."

"How incredible," I murmur. "It's been nothing but a burden for me."

"How so?"

"That's a long story." I glance at my cup. "They probably don't have enough coffee on hand to get through my formative years."

"I'd love to hear it. It'd be fascinating to know how you interpret your musical gift. It's not a conversation I can have with a lot of people."

"I suppose it isn't." I take a deep breath and we order more coffee. "It's a twofold story. My gift was *my* father's. His life was all about music. All he wanted . . . all he could see was a career as a symphony violinist. While on his way to achieving his dream, he got into a car accident." I breathe deep and so does Theo, who sinks further into his grandfather's story. "A stupid, reckless accident. He was out joyriding with some friends from Indiana University."

Theo nods. "One of the best music programs in the country."

"The very best in the early 1960s. He lost his left index finger in the accident," I say, bending mine at him. "He suffered severe nerve damage in his hand. Suffice it to say a finger wasn't all he lost that day. In so many ways, he never recovered. It affected the rest of his life—and mine."

"But he could have done other things, maybe taught music?"

Theo's naïveté is sweet, the ease with which he pinpoints a simple solution. "You, Theo, are a born teacher. For my father, music and the violin became nothing but instruments of torture. Playing . . . performing, it was the only aspect he deemed worthwhile."

"And he ended up putting all those unlived, lost aspirations onto you."

I widen my eyes at the café window, the steadier flow of traffic. "Is it that obvious?"

"After listening to you play . . . I see the talent—clearly. But I also sense the lack of passion." Theo shakes his head. "Maybe it's only something one musician can see in another."

"Like a slight note of imperfection that only a well-honed ear can pick up on." I pause; he waits for more. "Without sounding too '*poor me*,' I was bound to Asa Klein's crushed dreams from the age of five, when I made the god-awful mistake of playing Carl Bohm's *Moto Perpetuo* flawlessly."

"Interesting. I suppose my parents only saw my talent as a pleasant surprise." Theo pauses for a moment. "I guess you never know what you're going to get with grab-bag DNA. Still, they never pushed me musically."

"No disrespect. But they probably didn't appreciate the depth of our gifts." This comes out wistful, my gaze reverting to the window. Then it darts back to Theo. "Speaking in general, of course, about musical talent. The only good memories I have about music belong to my grandfather, which is ironic."

"Because?"

"Because, compared to me or my father, his connection to music is the true tragic story." The intent look on Theo's face deepens. "My grandfather was a Holocaust survivor. His ability to play saved his life. He was in Dachau," I say, informing Theo of family history he has no idea exists. "They kept him alive and barely fed to play at the commandant's house parties and for the guards on duty. Jacob Klein's experience left him with a hard-earned appreciation for life and for music. Being with him . . ." I breathe deep at what I view as a sacred memory. "We used to play together on Sunday afternoons—memorable rounds of call and response. Those are the fond thoughts I associate with the violin." I stare at the coffee cup. "My grandfather died when I was eight." I look at Theo. "There, um . . . there just weren't enough Sundays."

Sharing this story is not something ordinarily I do. Although we surpassed extraordinary the moment I intruded on Theo's life. "I have my grandfather's violin. My father would never allow me to play it. I'm not sure if he considered it substandard or too much of a treasure. It was impossible to tell how he felt about things like that."

"And because of his behavior, for you, music became nothing but a job."

"More like a requirement. The organ grinder's monkey. Over the years, only the organ grinder's face has changed: my father . . . even my mother, time served at various musical institutions, and the symphony." I pause and smile at Theo. "You're not going to say it, are you?"

"What?"

"That if playing music makes me unhappy, why don't I walk away? Open a flower shop, travel the world, pursue something I do love."

"Because you can't. I know what it is to have that gift, Olivia. I'm sorry you're so torn by it, your experiences so negative. But I also know you can't deny it. Maybe that's the bottom line of what troubles you."

I tilt my head at Theo. "Have you ever considered psychoanalysis as a career path?"

"It wouldn't work for me the same way a flower shop wouldn't work for you." He smiles wider. "No matter what, music dominates."

"You're so talented," I say, steering away from emotion. "And yet you've never considered playing professionally?"

"My fiancée—my ex-fiancée used to ask the same thing. Who knows . . . Maybe I was still trying to figure it out when India walked into my life. It didn't matter so much after she walked out."

"The effect one person can have, it's so curious . . ." I think of Rob and Sam, the profound ways both men changed my life. "I definitely know what you mean."

"Do you?" Theo asks.

"What, um . . . What happened between the two of you?" If I keep the conversation slightly off balance, I may make it through this. "If you don't mind obvious prying."

"No, I should talk about it, or at least be able to by now." But Theo's drifting gaze falls to his hands, which are clamped around a cold coffee cup. "India works for her parents' catering company," he says. "She was setting up a cappuccino machine at a Cornell alumni event in Boston. I'd just graduated and was trying to make connections. I didn't get a job—but I got a hell of a lot more, or at least I thought so."

The loss on his face is awesome. I dive toward inconsequential information. "Did you help her with the cappuccino machine?"

"No. The way I told her to put it together was completely ass backward. India put her hands on her hips, insisted I was an idiot, and fixed it herself." He drifts into a deeper memory "She was total fire and passion—between her personality and that flaming red hair . . . I would have done anything to prolong a conversation."

I nod at Theo's deliberate path to a first impression. I suspect he's more than capable of assembling a cappuccino machine. "But things didn't work out?"

He takes a regretful breath and a big gulp of coffee. "Last spring India attended a catering convention in New York. She ran into an old boyfriend. I suppose he was more than that. They'd nearly gotten engaged. Anyway, that afternoon . . . *Tom* invited her for coffee—some swanky Midtown martini bar."

"And it turned into something else?"

"A few martinis." Theo's jaw goes rigid. "Then a kiss. She called me that same night, confessed everything. It was hard to hear . . ." He breathes deep. "But I trusted India. I trusted what we had."

"But that wasn't the end of it?"

"It was as far as the old boyfriend is concerned. As far as I know. I thought India rushed back to Boston to try and smooth things over. She came back to end our engagement."

Theo's words are heavy. Anyone can see he is still madly in love with the redheaded India. His brooding mood is so dense it clouds the café air. "Maybe you'll work it out," I offer.

Theo shakes his head. "Not long before we broke up, India's sister, Helen, hit a rough patch. I saw it myself when she and India came to collect her things. Helen looked . . . *bad*."

"Is she ill?"

"Not exactly . . . Not in a way that makes you completely sympathetic," he says. "Helen is a heroin addict." My eyes widen at this tidbit. "She's overdosed a couple of times. Dealing with Helen can be like being trapped on a roller coaster."

"But a ride that India is willing to take."

"India is fiercely loyal to Helen." He is quiet for a moment. "Actually, India is like that with anyone she loves. But I imagine the timing of moving back home was a relief to all the Churches. Once India made her choice . . ." Theo flashes a smile. "Did I mention that India is stubborn? I heard through mutual friends that they got Helen into a private treatment program this time. It was good news. India's parents were never able to afford more than the ninety-day variety offered through the local hospital. Her mother and father, they've got their own issues, aside from Helen's. My guess is once Helen completed the program, having India at home . . . Well, my loss probably turned into their saving grace."

I let the clanking of dishes and noise of café patrons dominate. "I . . . I'm sorry that happened to you—all of it." A bizarre compulsion to physically reach out to Theo invades.

"I guess it's rawer than I want to admit. But being angry at India isn't going to solve anything. I hope it all works out for her—I really do."

It may. I'm far more concerned about how life works out for Theo. I know how long bitterness can last. I'm surprised how badly I don't want this for him. I take a breath, start talking, and stop. Then I dive headlong into our past. "When I was at UNC," I say firmly, "my last college stop, I fell madly in love."

Theo's glance shoots to mine. "But not with your husband?"

"No. Not with Rob. This boy . . . *man*, he was a baseball player." Boldly, I fill in a few more details. "His name was Sam." It's so simple and generic, downright Dr. Seuss. Surely Theo is only hearing a narration of topsy-turvy verses. "Sam was carefree and wicked . . . Or maybe just wickedly handsome." I look in Theo's eyes. *Sam's eyes . . .* "We were so different. I came from old Massachusetts money. Sam came from the middle-of-nowhere Tennessee—dirt poor, a childhood more caustic than mine. I was the number one fan of the man from Tennessee." I reflect on an old joke about an even older song that Theo will not get.

"But Sam was also honest. And I don't mean that in a selfless way. He just made no apologies for who he was. And that seemed like the thing sorely lacking from my life."

"But you didn't end up together."

"No. We didn't. Shortly before our climactic *end*, Sam was recruited by a major league team on the West Coast. I'd already been dismissed from the Boston Conservatory . . . and MSM. UNC for the Arts was my last stop. In my parents' minds, it was their last hope for success."

"So no pressure," Theo says.

I laugh. "Let's not forget why it is I'm in your classroom in the first place. Failing at what should be an obvious expectation is my real talent."

"I take it your dismissal from all those schools had nothing to do with your ability as a musician."

I squint toward the ceiling, thinking about what light I'd like to paint myself in. Michelangelo would be perplexed. I go with the truth. "After my grandfather died, acting up, acting out, became my focus. Pressure from my parents increased and bad behaviors ranged." Theo awaits examples. "Surely my teenage years make the highlight reel—showing up to practice wasted was a favorite. Running away from home was also a go-to resource." Theo's face sobers. "I'm lucky I didn't end up like India's sister. But in my case, Sam turned into my addiction."

"And your parents disapproved."

"He baffled them. They despised him for a variety of reasons."

"Like what?"

I weigh my reply. "Sam wasn't a bottle of booze that could be dumped or the shock of my smart mouth. He even exceeded the terrors of having a runaway daughter. Disturbing as these things were, my parents saw them as . . . controllable, to a point. Sam, on the other hand, was a strong-willed human being they suddenly had to deal with."

"And someone who had more influence."

"Exactly. Trying to take Sam away would have been like taking air out of my lungs."

"Were they right about him? Was he a bad person?"

"No . . . Nothing so black and white. In lots of ways, Sam was as mixed up as me—all the talent in the world and a horrendous starting point. We, um . . ." I stop and regroup. The point is Theo's loss. "You couldn't pin Sam down—even when it came to me. 'Hey, Livy'"—I say, employing the twang seared to my brain—"'let's take a road trip to Memphis, and bring your fiddle.' What for, I'd ask? 'Because we're going to Graceland. I think Elvis would love to hear you play.' At that point, the way Sam loved me, it was the exact opposite of anything I knew."

"So why didn't it work out?"

"Sam came from nothing. Because of that, he had a stronger sense of need. When he was offered the baseball contract, he knew this was his chance at a different life. At first, he was all for me coming with him. Of course, Sam knew my parents would strongly object. But he also knew they'd have less of an argument if we were already married. Naturally, I said yes, and on a windy May day we drove to Maryland and did just that."

Theo laughs at this bit of history. "You are a live wire, Liv. I kind of admire your impulsiveness. But I'm guessing your parents didn't take the news any better after the fact."

"You're kidding, right?"

"But California has plenty of great choices for music education. Surely one would have accepted you." Theo offers this with the steadiness of a guidance counselor.

"Maybe." As the positives of the story come to a close, I lean back in the seat. "Sam was signed by a California team, but reassigned to their farm system in Cedar Rapids, Iowa—not exactly fertile virtuoso feeding ground." Theo's expression says he's trying to put the puzzle pieces together. He doesn't have enough information. "My parents reacted worse to the location than they did the *married* part. To make sure I didn't miss their objection, Mr. and Mrs. Klein cut me off without a dime. Eventually," I say, skipping the middle of the movie, "Sam and I parted ways—"

"Because you didn't like the location? Because your parents wouldn't give you money?"

Well, that's not very becoming . . .

"No. That's not . . ." Theo's lack of facts is mudding the point. "Location, my parents' financial support . . . our breakup had nothing to do with that."

"But you just said . . ." Theo pauses. "Then you must not have really loved each other very much."

I consider stopping there. It would be complementary reasoning for India and Theo's breakup. My continued impulsiveness foils the greater good. "You have no idea how much I loved Sam."

"I'm not following. If that's true, and you say he didn't leave you . . . It sounds to me like you passed on happiness because it affected your credit limit and zip code."

Anger flushes through; facts never meant for Theo's ears spew out. "I got pregnant."

Theo is startled. Of course he has no idea how startled he should be. "Oh. I didn't . . . Sorry." He mentally scrambles to shove pieces in a puzzle. "And that didn't work with Sam's future plans."

"To say the least. By the time I found out, Sam had already left for Iowa. He wasn't ready for a child, and it, um . . ." I examine the tabletop, a scattering of sugar crystals and truth. "I don't want to give Sam a pass, but is it fair to cast blame on someone for being who they are?"

"Sam had a responsibility," Theo insists. "He was already married to you. If he loved you, he should have done the right thing. Hell, he should have done the right thing if he didn't."

Oh my, he has been wholly trained in accountability. I would have been lucky to teach him not to steal candy from the 7-Eleven. "He tried, Theo. In his own way, Sam tried. After some tearful phone conversations, he came back to North Carolina. It wasn't as if he abandoned me. But the marriage was so impetuous; I was still living in a dorm. We drove to a little place on the outskirts of Winston-Salem, a honky-tonk we frequented, the Pour House. I thought he'd come to say 'It'll work out, Livy. Iowa's not so bad—we'll make a life.'" I smile at Theo. "To my disappointment, it wasn't his first suggestion."

Theo expression goes flat. "He wanted you to get an abortion."

"He put it on the table. He wanted me to consider it."

"That's horrible."

"Theo, I wasn't even twenty-one. We'd been married barely a month. There was no plan . . . no money. There were a ton of obstacles—not the least of which was my parents. Sam lived in an apartment with four other guys. We were still figuring out life between the two of us, never mind throwing a baby into the mix." I swallow down the rest of the confession, but it bobs right back to the surface. "I had enough trouble taking care of me. At that age . . . even now . . ." I take a deep breath. "Theo, I'm not mommy wired."

He is speechless. In Theo's mind parenthood is illustrated by people who are willing to go around the world to get you.

"Oh, so you didn't . . ." Theo says. "You don't have children, do you?" My mouth gapes. "Sorry. I assumed, at some point, you would have wanted . . ."

"A part of me did want that fantasy, for Sam to react like he was supposed to . . . in a book, in the movie. In reality, Sam's coldhearted suggestion only made me lash out." My fingers make a prayerful knot, a physical diagram of the web I'm weaving. "He, um . . . Sitting in the Pour House, he didn't exactly come around."

"So what did the two of you decide?"

I'm stymied. My mind can't close the gap between the grown man across from me and a bundle of black-and-gold blanket, made from a sweatshirt. A sweet smell forever embedded in my brain, tiny fingers curled around mine for a few hours. I never said good-bye. I just said, "See you, baby boy . . ." I breathe deep at him and a fortuitous choice of words.

"Liv?" Theo prods.

"Sam and I concluded nothing about—" The word *you* almost tumbles out. "His hesitation was evident. So was his fear. Sam had a rough life, and he was halfway to a golden-ticket future. Instead of being the person he wanted to share it with, I was suddenly the person stopping him."

I sink back into the booth. "On the way back to campus our discussion turned into an ugly argument. I pushed Sam. I wanted him to say he loved me more than the shiny future in front of him. I demanded to know what he wanted more, a career in the big leagues or us."

"I guess he was leaning toward the big leagues."

"He was leaning toward the wrong side of the road. It happened so fast, a car was coming straight at us. Sam swerved. We hit a ditch. The next thing I knew we were hanging upside down from our seatbelts. Really, we were lucky."

"Jesus . . . That's incredible . . . *and lucky*."

He has no idea how much.

Theo's eyes fill with compassion and question. I don't let him ask the one on his mind. I let him assume the accident ended in a resolution—a miscarriage. According to the doctor who treated me, it should have. Apparently, Theo's will to thrive was always deeply seated. For as many times as I've told this part of the story—to Sam, to my parents, to Sasha, and even Rob years later, I've never imagined conveying it to the subject.

But what does it matter? In little more than two months, Theo and I will part ways again. He'll go on with his life and meet someone better than India. It's why I began this story. "It worked out for the best. Sam went on with his big league life, which told me something about our chances. That kind of all-consuming love, Theo, it's not the best recipe for a happy life." Theo is quiet, perhaps applying the lesson to himself and India.

"Afterward . . . I stayed with my brother for quite a while. I'd lost Sam. I couldn't stand the idea of living with my parents. But eventually I came back to Boston."

I ignore more intimate details, the handwritten footnotes that belong in Theo's baby book: *I wonder if you mind competing with a holiday on your birthday? Sorry about that. Twenty hours of hard labor . . . The seasons in New Zealand, they're opposite ours; it was ninety degrees the day you were born. I always think of you as a summer baby . . .*

I rehash other truths: After the accident, at the hospital, Sam came to my room—he'd been discharged. It would be the last time we'd see each other. I told him there was no longer any baby to be concerned with—that if he was looking for a fateful solution, he'd found one. Sam sat on the side of my bed, looking chagrined. It wasn't as if he could sit there and tell me how sorry he was. He tried to take my hand, and I told him to leave—to go back to Iowa. I told him it was over. How could it be anything else? Hours later, I told my parents the same thing.

"And the happy ending?"

Theo startles me out of my mental rewind. My gaze meets his. More than two decades have passed since I made that choice for everyone. I don't get Theo's question. He repeats it.

"And your point, Liv? The reason you told me your story . . . you ended up with someone you loved more than Sam?"

"Rob?" I blink furiously. "Yes. Of course, I married Rob because I loved him."

"More than Sam?" Theo presses, looking for his happy ending.

I look toward the now shadowy street. "Differently," I say, acknowledging that it is. "When you fall in love in your thirties, it's bound to be different than what you feel at nineteen or twenty. Brain chemistry, maturity, desires, it all factors in—you're just not the same person. You need different things. Does that make sense?" I ask, looking oddly at Theo and waiting for an answer.

CHAPTER SIXTEEN

Olivia

After parting ways with Theo, I walk—Boston is well suited for that. While I would not have predicted ending up in Theo's classroom, I am less surprised at the depth of information I shared. It's the sort of error—self-inflicted or stumbled upon—that defines me. So I walk, because I need to stop and think. Mostly, I think of Theo. How this misguided, but not malicious, idea has spiraled.

Between David McAdams and Theo's fiancée, I don't want to be the third thing Theo has to overcome before he's thirty. Worse, what if he can't? So far, Theo has rebounded from difficulties that would test anyone. What if I'm the person who breaks him? I play it out—picturing Theo's shock, labeling me the mother of all mistakes. Theo would hate me; a person he seems to like. I trudge slowly down Boylston Street, searching for different avenues of resolution.

I could pick a nasty fight with Theo or show up to class as myself. He wouldn't be interested in having coffee or a conversation after that. But I'm too taken by even a simple friendship to jeopardize it. The more

I get to know Theo, the more I want to see how his life will turn out. For so long Shep Stewart provided that window. Going forward, I'll want all of Theo's year—not two paragraphs, courtesy of his mother. I snicker at the sidewalk. Maybe that's the rub. Envy is nice payback—an *up close but don't touch* look at the relationship Theo shares with Claire. Ambling onto Gloucester Street, I settle on a rational strategy. I'll quit while I'm ahead—or at least before I have been slapped with a restraining order.

Not that I'd ever let it go that far. Nothing could make me confess the things Theo doesn't know. I keep walking. I am on track to complete my community service hours before the holiday break. With that in mind, I vow there will be no further friendly bonding, certainly no shared coffee and heartfelt stories. I stride forward with fresh affirmation. For the second time in Theo's life I am determined to do the right thing.

My phone chimes Brandenburg's Concerto no. 2. I retrieve it from my purse. Damn. *It's Theo*. I stop moving. A cooler more distant Olivia answers the call. Theo apologies for bothering me after taking up so much of my afternoon. His manners are impeccable. Fresh determination melts like April snow. Listening, I lower myself onto a bench. He's likely forgotten to tell me about a Braemore schedule change, or it's an afterthought about Antonio. Just as I'm poised to tell Theo we'll have to talk about his students during my official classroom hours, he derails my new attitude.

"My mother," Theo says. I squirm a little. "She's on a committee that raises funds for the arts in Boston Public Schools. Braemore is part of that. She's hosting a black-tie gala at the Boston Public Library. Would you come, Olivia? She'd get a kick out of it if I brought a real live symphony violinist. You'd lend some clout to the event."

It's unexpected, the invitation and the lure. I stall, asking Theo the date. *We can't . . . Rob has Bruins tickets that night* (I've never set foot in the frozen rink) . . . *It's my mother's birthday* . . . Her birthday is in May. *The symphony has an engagement that evening* . . . An actual possibility . . . A million easy lies are on the tip of my tongue. I choose to perpetuate the one I'm living. "Uh, sure, Theo. I think I can make it."

"Bring your husband." He laughs. "I wouldn't want my mother to get the wrong idea about me inviting you."

The call ends. I roll my eyes at Theo's stab at humor. Claire might prefer an older love interest to the truth. Of course, unless I'm wearing a sash that says *Theo's Birth Mother*, Claire won't know me. We've never met. She's never seen a photo. The baby handed to her could have belonged to anyone. Her facts are purposely limited. When people are desperate to adopt a child they'll agree to anything, even borderline anonymity.

As far as the McAdamses knew, the woman who gave up Theo lived in New Zealand. Surely, Claire and David McAdams saw this as a bonus perk—no one from Down Under would turn up on their doorstep. The distance screamed *"Take him away . . . take him far away . . ."* During the adoption process, the McAdamses were given a few morsels—Claire knows music and athletics were part of his birth parents' backgrounds, along with Caucasian, and no known diseases. She also knows both parents were under twenty-five and over eighteen. Since this accounts for millions of people, she won't think twice about me. Theo is such a blend of genetics, I have trouble seeing where I end and Sam begins. I sigh at my phone and the ten seconds it's taken to break my new vow. I hurry away from the bench and the deeper hole I've dug for myself.

I walk until the shoes I'm wearing blister my feet. Finally, I grab a cab but ask to be dropped a few blocks from the brownstone. Enduring some level of physical pain seems appropriate.

Gingerly, I cross the street, heading toward Commonwealth. I pull my cell from my pocket and hover over Sasha's name—she's first on my favorites. There's a trendy corner bar nearby. I need a drink. But if I have a drink with Sasha, the odds of this entire story spilling out are too great. I can imagine her appalled reaction—to the fact that I have a grown son, to the fuse I've lit by dropping in on his life. *"Liv, what were you thinking? Knowingly asking to serve your community service hours with the son you gave away. Furthering things by agreeing to a social event . . . That's disgraceful—even for you . . ."* I withdraw my thumb. I wonder if I've committed a crime beyond ethical; I wonder if Sasha can get in trouble for this. Best not to invite yet another opportunity for open sharing today.

I let recent history dominate. Instead, I call Rob.

He meets me at the bar, taking my invitation as an olive branch. On the surface, things at home have settled into the pattern of this past year—two people who cohabitate and share complementary shortcomings. After a drink and some benign conversation, I ask Rob if he's made progress on the Wellesley house. I've avoided two calls from my mother today. Rob says he spoke with her. I cheer my glass toward him. "The specifics are still in motion, which is what I told her. But no, I don't have it nailed down yet. The house is still in jeopardy. It was, um . . . a strange conversation."

"Why?" I pick a peanut from the bowl in front of me. "She wasn't happy to hear from you?" Usually a conversation with Rob under any circumstance makes her happy.

"Not so much that, but while we were talking she came across her watch, which apparently had been missing."

"So . . ."

"She said it was in a coat pocket."

"That is a little peculiar; she's never without it. I wondered if she took it off during her last manicure. But I am glad she found it." He tips his drink, staring at the Macallan in his glass. "Rob?"

"She said she found it in the pocket of your father's brown mackinaw."

I inch back on the barstool. That is odd, especially since I helped her pack up the bulk of his belongings ages ago. Among his clothing was the sheep-lined, belted coat he favored. The one he wore every winter day to his job as an economics professor at Tufts. "Maybe you misunderstood."

"Yeah. Could be." He sips his drink. "Sometimes, when your father's name comes up, I wonder if he's come to haunt me—gaslight me at the very least."

"Well," I say, returning the gesture with an even larger sip, "I wouldn't necessarily count it out." The mention of my father, or more to the point, Rob and my father, softens my mood. "It was good of you to call her, keep her up to date, even if the house issue isn't resolved yet."

"I am sorry, Liv."

His remorse is palpable. I don't doubt Rob's sincerity. I suppose I should be grateful that he came clean with the facts long before the only answer was to auction off a violin. But I'm also aware that Rob is a risk-taker. I don't get involved in the particulars of his day-to-day business ventures. But now I'm wondering if he's dangled close to financial ruin before? Maybe I've only been clued into the big wins. It could be that he's kept losses to himself. I can see it—aloof Rob controlling the flow of information. I sip my wine, thinking it's a good thing casino gambling has never interested my husband. It might have left us stripped bare years ago.

Exhaustion and distraction keep me from currently pursuing a financial Q and A. "Just . . . maybe next time you could make a point of *not* including the roof over my mother's head—or an asset we were counting on—in your business deals."

"If it comes down to it, if we do lose the house, I'll find a way to make it up to you." He raises his glass to his mouth and lowers it. "Of course, I'm not exactly sure what we'll do with your mother."

"Maybe that will work out too. Maybe she'll find a seniors' cruise line with an ongoing bridge tournament." He laughs at what has always been our grandest plus, a similar sense of humor. "But whether it's tomorrow or years from now, you're the one who planned out how we'd go about funding the city-wide orchestra, Rob. The money I inherited from my grandfather—those investments." This is a question I have to ask. "Tell me they're not at risk too."

"They're completely protected. You know that—earning steadily in low-risk investments."

"Good. That's good to hear." For a moment, the bar noise dominates. "So, I have a different question about that, my inheritance. Can the money we're using for the endowment be filtered elsewhere?"

"Elsewhere how? Like a trip to Aruba or something within the music program itself?"

I smirk at his remark. "I know the point was to make the endowment airtight—no room for misguided funds; it was one of your big concerns, right?"

"More or less," he says. "If you wanted to remain anonymous in your efforts, I thought it prudent to strictly limit the use of the funds."

"Is there enough wiggle room to buy classroom instruments for one school in particular?" He looks harder at me. "I understand that overall public school instruments are going to be mediocre. But I've noticed that certain schools, maybe due to reputation, are supplied with instruments that don't even qualify as inferior."

Rob narrows his gaze and takes out his cell, poking at the notepad. "What's the street address for Braemore? I'm sure between your money and my scheming, something can be arranged." I smile as he makes the note; at the same time, his cell rings. "Duly noted on the instruments. Just let me just grab this quick." He ducks outside, away from the crowded bar.

Drinking my wine, I reflect in the bar mirror. The Wellesley house was the future cornerstone of Rob's endowment plan, actually one of his most brilliant moments as a financier. Honestly? It was kind of sexy. When we were dating, after things turned serious, I told Rob about the money I inherited from my grandfather—money that wasn't mine until my thirtieth birthday. I saw the point of an age stipulation: giving the money to me before then would have been like storing water in a sieve. Once the inheritance was mine, I did consider shiny objects, trips abroad, and a fancy car. I did a few of those things. But none of it wooed me. The cash altered my net worth, not my self-worth; it only padded the room a bit, rented me a cute village apartment. For the most part, the money sat until Rob turned me onto the idea of funding a city-wide music program.

We concocted the plan in his bed, on a Friday, during a thunderstorm while eating Chinese food. By then I'd auditioned for and won a symphony chair. A week's worth of draining rehearsals sparked the impromptu conversation. A handful of private school kids had been invited to perform with us. I'd listened to them play all week. I wasn't impressed. Picking at Rob's crispy duck, I said, "Why do people assume money implies talent? I bet there are dozens of kids out there with twice the aptitude—probably real passion—and simply no chance."

He plucked a wonton out of my container. "So why don't you give them one?"

I put the Chinese food on the nightstand and rolled on top of Rob, thunder and rain making for a sultry setting. "Right. Because that's such a natural fit." I kissed him, Rob's hands traveling in a way that still lights a fiery memory. "Hey, maybe I can give lessons too."

"Well, no. Not that." He kissed me back, dominating me and the mood. "Be realistic. But you do have other options." Through candlelight and the glow of a muted TV, sex and talk of unrelated ideas continued. "If it bothers you, fix it. God knows a little purpose wouldn't kill you." For a second, the idea teetered. It could have easily succumbed to the moment. Rob was poised just below my navel when he glanced up. "Lots of people talk, Liv. Very few have the means. Fewer still will put their money where their mouth is."

With Rob's mouth on the verge of making me forget any talk about music and opportunity, I hauled myself upward, my knee accidentally colliding with his chin.

"Son of a bitch," he said, grabbing his jaw.

I apologized as Rob rubbed his chin. "I have no idea how to go about something like that." I looked hard into his candlelit eyes. "But you would."

From there Rob became the wizard behind the curtain, making connections and filtering orchestra funding anonymously. I was impressed by the intricate plan he devised, and proof that a man so interested in money wasn't silently coveting mine.

As for me, I liked—and still do—my back-row view. More than anything, I love what my grandfather would think about the use of his hard-earned money. If wisely handled, Rob said the inheritance would last about fifteen years. He encouraged me to seek out other benefactors, future funding solutions. I encouraged him to think harder. While Claire McAdams's social standing will pack a Bates Hall fundraiser, mine wouldn't fill a Porta-Potty. It's why the Wellesley house became key years before. Eventually—assuming my mother doesn't have the power of eternal life—the property will be ours. While technically Rob has equal ownership of the house, he said to do whatever I liked with it. The plan was nothing short of genius—until the genius gambled it away.

In the bar's mirrored reflection, I see Rob come back inside. I spin around on the barstool. "Before your call, you were saying . . ." He furrows his brow. I sigh. "You indicated a plan B if we do lose the Wellesley house. It's a lot of money, Rob. I know you can make money. But the Wellesley house is worth what? Over a million dollars?"

He signals the bartender for another Macallan. "North of two."

"North of two," I repeat. His future financial plan for the orchestra funding is based on at least two million dollars. That's a lot to make up for. Investment wise, I suppose it's the kind money Rob shuffles around on a spreadsheet. We trade a glance as his drink is delivered. "Producing that much cash . . . Can you really do it?"

"We've been at this a while now, Liv. I've been known to do all right by you."

He's insulted. He possibly should be. Despite our current circumstance, Rob has brought an abundance of positives to my life and closure in a most precarious moment. "So," I say, looking for better footing, "did you go to your office today?"

"No, I stayed home. I knew you'd be gone all day, and I thought I could concentrate better. The brownstone is great for pacing while I talk."

I can see it. Rob's office is boxy. He probably broke his Fitbit record walking miles through the narrow but deep brownstone. "Did you stop to eat lunch?"

He grins, less irritated. "Worried about whether or not I ate? How sweet, Liv."

I stare at my wine. "Just anticipating the cranky mood and headache you'll have in the morning."

"Makes more sense," he says, taking a solid mouthful. "And yes. I did eat lunch, compliments of Sasha."

"Sasha?"

"Yeah. She brought lunch by for the two of you, but she didn't know you were going to do your community service hours today."

That's true. I don't usually go to Braemore on Fridays. But before I decided on nomadic wandering, I did tell him about some errands, a stop by Symphony Hall. "So you and Sasha, what? Had an impromptu picnic on the living room floor?"

"No. We used your music room. The sun floods in there beautifully that time of day." Typical Rob sarcasm hits my ears as he looks coolly past my head. "We had deli sandwiches in the kitchen. Talked for a while."

"About what?"

"Why?"

"Because I just find the image of you and Sasha and lunch a curious talking point."

The glass, halfway to his lips, halts. "You wouldn't find it stranger if she showed up with food, realized you weren't there, and said, 'I guess I'll take my lunch for two back to the office.'"

"Either way, that was generous of Sasha," I say. "She's like that, an always susceptible soft spot." I am thinking of Jeremy and the number of pro bono hours she admitted to working. But perhaps Sasha was thinking of Rob, the hard time I've given him in recent weeks.

"Sasha's good people." Rob finishes his drink with one massive gulp. "She had some things on her mind. I was grateful for a change of subject. She talked; I listened. That's all." I nod at his explanation and we are quiet. Then he looks at me. Really looks at me, like he hasn't in a long time—long before I beat the shit out of his Porsche with a baseball bat. "Liv . . ." The sound of my name seems to carry more weight than the rest of the slightly crooked conversation. "Sasha, we, uh . . . We talked about . . ." My body tightens, almost braces. "Are we going to make it, Liv?" he asks. "Is the Wellesley house going to push us over the edge? I know it's been a rough year. But is this . . . Can we fix it?"

My gaze drops to our shoes. Mine are hiding blistered feet, whereas his are covered by fine Italian leather loafers. Hard to see past. A quiver comes with my inhale. Lately, we don't discuss our marriage in fine detail or even full sentences. No one says, *"Honey, let's talk."* Of course, this is not to say that Rob and I haven't individually considered the shakiness of our union—clearly, it's a concern we've both now shared with Sasha.

In my mind's eye, there isn't a conversation about the marriage having deteriorated beyond repair. I just come home one day and find Rob, his rowing machine, and smartass remarks gone. There'd be a forwarding address and brief exchange about putting the cable bill in my name. Eventually, Rob would go on, find someone more appreciative of his tolerant nature or in less need of it. She's not perfect either—maybe she doesn't quite get his sarcasm and will merely smile and say dopily, *"We'll live on love,"* should he lose everything. She can be described by a useless word like *nice*, and is competitive with Rob in the kitchen. She looks good in turtlenecks, which she wears well into May. Rob's second wife is thinner, more toned, but also a slightly less attractive version of me.

"Liv?" he says again. I look up from our shoes to his face.

"In the most critical moments you sure are a brave bastard."

"I thought maybe one of us should say it out loud."

I trace the rim of my wineglass with my index finger. The slim band of diamonds on my left hand sparkles. I see that it's sparkling more than usual as I stare at it through a prism of tears. I blink them back and face him. In a brief knot of honesty I reply, "I don't know anymore, Rob. I don't know."

CHAPTER SEVENTEEN

Olivia

Rob and I walk silently, side by side, toward the brownstone. A half a block away my tentative shuffle turns into a full-on limp. Rob touches my arm, stopping us. "Did you trip or something, turn your ankle?"

"Nothing quite so timely and romantic. New shoes. Nasty blister." In the chilly air, on the middle of the sidewalk, I discard one shoe. It's an incredible relief, and I hang on to Rob's arm while bending my leg upward to reveal a raw spot on my heel about the size of a quarter.

"Ouch! Why didn't you say something?"

"What were you going to do? Lend me your shoes?"

"We could have called a cab."

"To go two blocks?" I slip off the other shoe, which hasn't produced quite the same wound, prepared to take my chances with dirt and jagged sidewalk debris. "I'll survive."

"Yeah. I know. No matter what."

Having walked a few steps ahead, I turn. "What does that mean?"

"Nothing. Just that you are a survivor, Liv. Things haven't always been so easy for you."

"Where did that come from?"

"Just some thinking I've been doing. I understand that your parents are responsible for a lot of who you are. I have an amicable relationship with your mother, but some of the reason for that isn't lost on me." I shake my head vaguely. "Her love for me is a dig at you. I get it."

"You shouldn't take it personally—I don't. She can't help it. Instead of the Mayflower, I've often thought her descendants were more closely tied to arachnids or certain amphibians."

"Because?"

I glance around the empty, lamp-lit street. "Because some species actually eat their young."

It's typical humor between us, but Rob doesn't laugh. "I never knew your father well, but I got a good taste of him in his closing moments. I can see where a lifetime of being a Klein would make you say something like that."

Tell me something I don't know. While Rob and my mother get along famously, my father was ill when we started dating. It kept them at a distance. It was just as well. The chair of Tufts Behavioral Economics department would have likely made a lab rat out of him. *"Fascinating specimen, Olivia . . . Intelligent, yet possesses risk factors more common to the corner bookie."* From there my father might have poured himself a drink and demanded Rob detail his family history: social, monetary, breeding. It would have wrapped up with a comment directed at me: *"I suppose he's more suitable than your first husband. But if you can keep it to two . . ."*

I sigh and tune back into Rob, who continues lamenting my mother. "It's all part of Genie's motivation, the reason her son-in-law gets such a high approval rating, even after he jeopardizes the roof over her head. Kleins are calculating, your father certainly was, right up until the end—such as it was."

"Yes . . . well, when it comes to calculating, I suppose I do my fair share to keep up tradition." I start walking again.

"I didn't mean it like that."

I did.

Rob latches on to my arm and I stop, facing him. "I get that growing up in that house was toxic, Liv. Hell, your brother had to put an entire hemisphere between him and them. Not only did you stay, but you survived it."

"Rob, where in the world is this coming from? Have you been cramming back issues of *Psychology Today* online?"

"Lunch," he says. "Today, at lunch, it's one of the things Sasha and I talked about." The blip of information grabs my attention. "Sometimes I don't give it enough consideration, how your parents affected you. And . . ."

"And what? You and Sasha determined the mental divide between personal responsibility and what can be directly blamed on Asa and Eugenia Klein? Is there a psychiatric intervention in my future, maybe some shock therapy?"

"Hardly. No one's that brazen—or nuts. But we did have a serious discussion. The kind you and I don't seem to have anymore."

"Well, bully for you and Sasha." My face grows warm. That I was the subject sandwiched between the mustard and ham on rye. That such a deep exchange took place about me, between my husband and best friend.

Rob tucks his hands in his pockets, tipping back on the heels of the Italian loafers. He sees my discomfort. He reverts to banter more suited to us. "No worries, Liv. Although, if you'd benefited from some therapy years ago my Porsche might still be in one piece." The look on his face, I haven't seen it in some time. It has something to do with concern. "I just . . . Sasha reminded me that there are a lot of complexities that resulted in Olivia Klein. Sometimes I forget to factor that in."

"Thanks," I say, nodding. "I appreciate the introspection. But do me a favor."

"What's that?"

"Don't discuss my complexities with Sasha." I glance down the street. "Together you'll likely conclude that the damage is beyond repair—certainly not worth her effort." I take a deep breath and give Rob the respect he's earned in this moment, the effort he is making. "Or yours." He grins and closes the scant physical distance between us. His arms fold around me. On the sidewalk comes a kiss that belongs to people who describe their relationship as bliss. I kiss him back. "Aside from that . . ." A fall breeze couldn't squeeze between us. "Can you imagine the price tag for therapy? You'd need two Wellesley houses to pay for it." We both laugh.

Then Rob does something wildly spontaneous. He picks me up, like we're starring in some cheesy date night movie. "What are you doing?"

"Liv, I'm a few questionable things, but I'm not completely unchivalrous. I can carry you a block."

"And after that?" I ask as we move along, arms wrapped around his neck like this is status quo for us.

"After that . . . Maybe I'll head to the basement, skip the rowing machine, and polish my armor. Or maybe I'll get lucky."

"You might," I say, kicking my bare feet through the breeze.

Rob looks where he's going. I am afforded the benefit of admiring him. I see past coifed hair and skin that's benefited from alpha beta peels, beyond his surface. I see what matters—Rob, focused on us, thoughtful, and, yes, even chivalrous. It's not something you'd find on his résumé, but they're some of the more complex parts of Rob I fell in love with. I'd nearly forgotten how appealing those traits could be.

He enhances the softer mood with just the right note of humor. "But if you think I'm carrying you up the brownstone steps, you're crazy." Then he pauses. "Although if you want me to carry you to the bedroom . . ."

I turn my head toward the brownstone, just to see how far off we are. The streetlamp right outside is like a spotlight. Romance pauses. Sitting on the steps is a man. The homeless rarely venture to this part of town. His knees are bent and his head is cast downward. In his frozen pose, there's something familiar. We slow to a stop. The man looks up. Rob's heroic gesture was a smooth swoop and scoop. But this is more of an electric cattle prod moment as I lurch from his cradling hold. The man glances between Rob and me. He stands. Despite a beard and twenty-six years, he's exactly as I remember him.

"Livy."

My bare feet shuffle backward and onto Rob's shoes.

"Sam?" I cup a hand to my mouth. He comes down the steps, meeting us on the sidewalk. In the back of my mind, I've always known he and Rob are precisely the same height—wildly different men. "Oh my God. How . . . What are you doing here?"

He takes a deep breath, and the brown of Theo's eyes meets mine. "I came to apologize."

CHAPTER EIGHTEEN

Theo

Theo doesn't drink. Not like this. But that is what he's been doing since stopping at the liquor store and arriving home from coffee with Olivia Klein. On the table in front of him is a flask-size bottle of Jack Daniel's. The tea-colored liquid vanishes with each sip, revealing more and more of the unsettled thoughts in Theo's head. He hasn't spoken aloud about India in forever—a subject that, on its own, can get him drunk. Adding to his mood was Olivia's story about her brush with an unwanted child. It gnaws at him still.

He leans harder into the sofa, where he's confronted by talk from a long-ago family get-together—his Uncle Kevin, cousins, other relatives sitting around a dining room table. It was the two-year anniversary of his father's death—or the anniversary of his birthday. However they needed to look at it. His father's favorite, a slice of plain cheesecake, sat in front of Theo, the other pieces slathered in gooey strawberry sauce. Everyone knew strawberries gave Theo a horrible rash. His younger cousin, Kyle, was perched in Uncle Kevin's lap, mashing the red goop into the cheesecake with a spoon.

Their grandmother leaned in, first trying to get Kyle to take a bite. He refused the way four-year-olds do. "So amazing," she said, looking wistfully at Kyle. "He barely resembles you."

"Or me," said Aunt Celia, Kyle's mother, who looks every bit her Italian heritage.

"I think it's the nose." This observation came from Aunt Julie, his father's sister.

"Yes. Definitely the nose," Theo's grandmother agreed. She cupped Kyle's chin. "And the eyes. Those are David's blue eyes." His grandmother's teary gaze stared into Uncle Kevin's—whose eyes were decidedly not blue.

"It's a gift, Mom—Kyle's the spitting image of David." Uncle Kevin kissed the head of his squirming son.

Theo recalls an awkward silence and Claire glaring across the table like radioactive beams might shoot from her eyes. Even so, if it weren't for Claire's prolonged reaction, Theo might have easily overlooked the exchange. But the entire way home she vehemently reminded and reassured Theo that *he* was David McAdams's son; that no look-alike cousin could come close.

It was an isolated incident. Honestly, Theo has never felt anything but wanted. It's only on days like that, and this one now, that he ponders things like whose nose he has. Theo knows very little about his background, aside from his New Year's Eve birthday and that he was born in New Zealand. He's read about New Zealand. It's a highly mixed populace, meaning his ancestors could be Dutch or cannibals. Theo quit Googling New Zealand years ago.

On occasion, he's wanted to know more, curious if his biological parents were good people or had prison records. Did he come from low-life trash or accomplished, well-educated types? He has gently asked his mother, who cited a deplorable lack of information. The only memento

Theo has is a tiny black-and-gold blanket. It looks homemade, a shield-like emblem on one side. Claire doesn't even know the first names of his birth parents. That was part of the private adoption agreement. The arrangement worked for his parents, who desperately wanted a child. It worked for whoever gave him away. But Theo's not sure anyone thought how it might work for him years later.

Still, the memory has only surfaced because of Olivia's story, her first husband and the child he would have aborted. Theo is hyper-focusing because alcohol accesses parts of his brain that, otherwise, do not get out of control. When he and India were together, he was particularly disinterested in his past. It didn't matter. Everything was in front of him. But after sharing his sad tale about India, Theo's not sure Olivia's story had the intended effect. She was not terribly convincing in her message—that after tragedy a greater love is sure to come along. He thinks Olivia Klein is not a happy person, perhaps mixed up in her own past, though he suspects she was only trying to help.

Theo sighs and swallows down the kind of gulp that goes with unhappiness. He wonders if Olivia Klein drinks. Theo shakes off the thought and digs his cell phone out of his pocket. He glances at text messages between himself and Zach Lawlor. Zach was going to be Theo's best man; they have been friends since high school. But Theo has passed on Zach's current invite to court-side seats at the Celtics game. It's a sporting event that used to pique Theo's interest and provide the "wicked good time" Zach's message suggests. But his decision to decline isn't about tonight's game. It's about the games he passed on last season. In those instances, Theo preferred to be with India.

On a Friday night they might have gone to a small downtown pub and split a pizza, walked hand in hand back to the apartment, and made love until the exhaustion of the week and sex wore them out. At some point, Theo would have mentioned the spare Celtics ticket and Zach's invitation. India would have chided him for spending the evening with her instead of going out with his friends. Then she would have laughed, kissing Theo, and telling him how much she loved him for choosing her instead.

With a shaky hand, Theo reaches for the bottle. He still cannot grasp how quickly things changed between himself and India. Until his conversation with Olivia, Theo thought he was making progress with his life. In fact, before stopping at the liquor store, he called Olivia and invited her to his mother's charity event. Inviting her was impulsive, but expanding his circle of friends and encouraging forward motion, it's the goal nowadays. When Olivia sounded so befuddled, it occurred to Theo that he's trying too hard, hurling himself in too many directions.

Feeling awkward about his invitation and even more displaced, Theo continued to walk the streets of Boston, which he sometimes does when in deep thought. Eventually, his sober mood delivered him to Pop & Cork Liquors. But after walking a few blocks with the small bottle, it was Theo's mother that caused him to hurry home. He was taught better than that, wandering aimlessly, his booze and sullen thoughts hidden by a brown paper bag.

Staring at his phone, Theo considers calling his mother. She would insist he come home for the night, to the suburban Boston house he grew up in. Once there, his mother would listen thoughtfully, curled up on the sofa as he rehashed India's unceremonious dumping of their future. She would be sympathetic. Claire would make hot chocolate and suggest several good books that Theo hasn't read. They might look at family photos and indulge in memories of David McAdams, reminisce about the hopes he had for his son. Hopes Theo has lived up to, aside from this drunken stupor. If he sought out his mother tonight, Theo would end up sleeping in his boyhood bed and waking up to the delicious smells of pumpkin pancakes with powdered sugar and a side of made-from-scratch apple compote. His mother is an excellent cook. But because Theo also likes to think of himself as a grown man, he does not call Claire.

He rests his neck into the curve of the sofa cushion and closes his eyes. Being a man means self-assurance. Despite the bump of a flask of Jack Daniel's, he's doing fine—without his father, without India. Theo sighs hard. The declaration is total bullshit. He's not doing fine at all. Theo jerks forward on the sofa, eyes wide open. Since India left, Theo has been doing anything to keep himself from thinking about her. Braemore is helpful, but hearing Olivia's disturbing story of lost love and seeing a text message about having a "wicked good time"—an ability Theo does not currently possess—has ripped open a tender wound.

He stares at the bottle. Theo knows his limit with liquor. And while puking all night would give him something to do, the overall idea is unappealing. He picks up his cell. He only means to scroll through some pictures. They are photos his mother suggested he delete, or at least move to a file on his computer. She's probably right. His mother is right about most things. Almost all the photos include India, her fiery hair and smiling eyes. When India smiles her whole mood is evident. Not that India is flawless. She has irritating habits, like leaving old razors in the shower and ATM receipts all over her car. She's a vegetarian, and Theo loves a good steak. He sips the liquor again. Most stunning, India can read him like no other human being, though Theo knows this is not a flaw but the thing he misses most. Together, Theo could drown in his music while India steered and supplied the outside air to their life. But perhaps this is part of why India left. In retrospect, it's wildly selfish behavior.

The photos on his phone flick by like scattered pieces of Theo's heart. There are hundreds of pictures of India: at parties and other people's weddings, Red Sox games and big holidays. There is a favorite photo of a lazy Saturday morning, the memorable shot doused in pancake batter. India did not wish to have her photo taken quite so early, and the image was captured through batter flicked in Theo's direction. Finally, he gets to the photo of the day they got engaged. He has to scroll back quite a ways.

Under the pretense of leaf watching, Theo and India went to a rustic Maine inn. Theo didn't give a damn about turning leaves and pumpkins, but he did make some accidental romantic remark about how India's red hair fit so beautifully into the fireball of a waning fall sun. She smiled wider than usual. India said that in elementary school she was often teased about her red hair. Theo felt a pulse of rage, wanting to seek out every kid who was mean to her and pummel them, or at least tell them off. But Theo's outrageous thoughts subsided as India told him that she often wished for blond or brown hair—something ordinary. And Theo knew there wouldn't be a more perfect moment. "You can't help it, India. Everything about you is extraordinary. Take me on—spend the rest of your life showing a simple music teacher how you do that."

Theo had carried the ring around in his pocket all weekend, terrified he might lose it. Normally, India would keep track of things like this. He thought a romantic dinner that evening might be the right spot. But standing in a sun-streaked field of orange and red and amazement, Theo knew this was the place.

On the screen of his phone, Theo runs his finger over India's face. Her name is tagged, which reroutes Theo to his contacts. And not just contacts but FaceTime. It connects. Theo holds his breath. He would hold on to his heart, but it's in too many pieces. And just like that, they are staring at one another.

"Theo . . ."

He says her name, but it is followed by silence because drunken fate has placed this call.

"Are you all right?" she asks. "You . . . you, um, don't look so good."

Theo attempts to sober his expression, at least close his slacking jaw. He doesn't recognize India's location, though it's a restaurant—tables behind her, a hum of patron noise. Perhaps she's working an event for Take Me to Church Catering. But maybe she's on a date. Humiliation bears down on Theo, imagining a strange man seated across from her. He'll wait, patient and curious as India stumbles through a conversation with her intoxicated ex-fiancé. After this poor showing, the man will think his odds of taking India home and to bed have improved significantly. Theo reverts to ideas about puking all night.

"Theo?" she says, her head tipping at his. If India is with someone she does not say so.

"I, uh . . ." Theo is a terrible liar. He doesn't even try. "It was an accident. I didn't mean to call. I was looking at my phone . . . well, pictures of you . . . *of us*, on my phone. You know how stuff like that is, so sensitive. I touched your face, and the next thing I knew . . ."

"It's okay," India says. "I can see how that could happen."

Her tone is forgiving. Bits of Theo's broken heart scramble toward one another. "Sorry. Like I said . . ." Theo stands, abruptly grasping at dialogue. "How was the wedding?"

"The wedding?"

"Your cousin's wedding."

It has been more nearly a month since the wedding, since Theo ran into India on Newbury Street. Even longer since she kissed an old boyfriend and returned to her life on Long Island.

"Oh. Right. It was nice. My Uncle Roger got drunker than usual." Theo wonders if the bride's father was as drunk as he is right now. His head is spinning and he presses fingers to his temple in a vain attempt to stop it. "He fell into a fountain at the reception," she offers. "It wouldn't have been such a big deal, but he was dancing with the bride at the time. A total catastrophe if she'd fallen in with him."

"But I bet you all laughed."

"We did." Despite Helen's issues, India and her family have a good sense of humor. He admired this about them. When Theo's father was alive, the McAdamses laughed like that. It was never the same after he died. His mother's humor is more refined, less belly laugh.

"How . . . how are you?" Theo is now pacing the small apartment. There's silence on the other end of the line.

"I'm good," she finally says. "Theo—" He waits. He hears a glimmer of hope in her voice. He believes he can see it in her face. "I, um . . . I heard about your new job. Ashley and Mike mentioned it," she says, referencing mutual friends. "How's it going? Do you like it?"

It's not the emotion-filled statement Theo wants, but at least she hasn't disconnected the call. If India is with someone else, she is being incredibly rude, which is completely unlike her. Theo decides she's alone.

"It's good . . . interesting. The students are interesting," he says, separating drunken babble from rational conversation. He can do this. Years ago, he came in from his senior prom drunk as a sailor on leave and carried on a ten-minute conversation with his mother. She never suspected.

"I'm sure it's different from Weston schools."

"Just a little—though rich kids can be trouble too. You remember. The money and endless understanding. Sometimes it makes things worse." Theo thinks of the parade of public and private psychologists accessible to Weston students, the way he complained to India about the pitfalls of entitlement. Maybe he complained too much. Theo sticks to Braemore. "Kids at Braemore, some have worse issues than others, but none are trouble free." Theo holds the phone away, providing India with a view of an area rug that needs vacuuming. He digs his fingers into his skull. *Duh . . . why else would they be at Braemore . . . ?* India is saying his name. He looks into the phone again, into India's eyes. They are so beautiful. *Get a grip, you idiot . . .*

"It's complicated," Theo says. But his remark is met with silence because *it's complicated* sounds more like their Facebook status, if they were still Facebook friends. Braemore and its populace are too big of a topic for this delicate discussion. Theo scrambles for something smaller but relevant. "I have some help in the classroom—Olivia Klein. She's a violinist with the New England Symphony."

"Oh?" India says. There is an uptick to her tone. "A violinist? The two of you must have a lot in common."

Theo nearly panics. "No—well, yes. Musically. Nothing else. She's married . . . older. We're friendly. She's quirky interesting. She ended up in my classroom because she's doing community service hours."

"Really? What did she do, steal a Stradivarius?" India laughs.

He hasn't heard India laugh in ages, and at the moment, Theo is so very grateful for the simple existence of quirky Olivia Klein. "You know, I'm not sure. Maybe I'll ask her and her husband when I see them at—" Theo thinks and breathes for a second. "I invited them to my mother's charity event . . . It's soon."

"Yes. It is," she says, and the gears of small talk slow. "You're not worried about the fundraiser, are you, Theo? Believe me, your mother would never settle for anything less than perfect."

He hears tension in India's tone. "I'm sure it'll be fine. She mentioned the woman they hired to replace—" Theo does not finish the thought. It will only lead to the reasons India no longer lives in Boston. He tries a different approach. "They've kept the theme you came up with—the Edwardian era."

India smiles again, but it looks forced. She glances around the restaurant. "Good to know."

Theo paces backward. He scrambles for more soothing conversation. The back of his legs hit the leather sofa, a piece of furniture where he and India had sex more times than he can count. His sluggish thoughts and memories of the sofa make it increasingly difficult to think about catering. "Anyway . . . at the fundraiser, I'll ask Olivia what she did to end up in such a spot."

India is wearing a silky dark-blue blouse. Theo watches her delicate chest rise and fall with a sigh. "Sounds like you're moving on . . . New job, new friends . . ."

"India." Theo suddenly feels sober. If he just says the right thing, right now, India will see the mistake was not kissing an old boyfriend. Though, yes, that sucked. The mistake was letting the incident end them. He hears vacillation. India misses him. She misses them. But India looks away from Theo's limited view. She puts the phone down.

"India, how nice to finally meet you." Theo hears a man's voice. "I'm so sorry I'm late." The phone is facing the ceiling. The strange man leans over the table and shakes India's hand. The man finds India attractive. Theo can tell by the way he cups his other hand over hers, an otherwise unnecessary gesture. The man is slightly older—polished, dressed in a suit. It's at least a full five seconds until he releases India's hand. Jack Daniel's rushes up Theo's throat. He very simply wants to kill him.

In a reciprocal greeting, India says the name "Claude." She glances nervously downward, into the phone.

Claude? Theo immediately decides Claude is a snooty, tight-assed dick-wad who led hazing rituals in college. A man who would cross the street to avoid homeless people and is cruel enough to leave a dog locked in a hot car. He should not be within a mile of India.

"Would you excuse me for one minute?" India says, picking up her phone. "I just need to finish a call."

In his snooty voice Claude tells her "By all means . . ." and apologizes again for being late.

Clearly, Claude is a complete ass with no manners whatsoever.

It's Theo's turn to view industrial-grade carpet as India leaves the table. Then she looks into the phone. "Theo—" Her harsh tone halts his fluttering heart. Her parting words to Claude ring in his ears—"Excuse me for one minute . . . I just need to finish a call . . ."

"India, wait!"

She is standing by a rack of coats, shrouded by a gray overcoat and bright floral print. "Theo, I have to go." Her voice is low, like she doesn't want Claude to hear her conversation. The light is much dimmer, but Theo swears he sees tears.

"Who . . . who is he, India?"

"Who?"

"The guy. *Claude*."

"Nobody . . . Just a man who owns a couple of boutique hotels. They're thinking about hiring an outside caterer."

"I thought your father usually handled those kinds of meetings."

"Theo." Their gazes tangle. "This, um . . . this, calling me, wasn't a good idea—even accidentally. It might be easier . . . better if you deleted me from your contacts."

Theo's ass hits the sofa like someone has slammed his stomach with a baseball bat. "Delete . . ."

"I, um . . . I'm not saying it to be mean. But it's not like we can be friends . . ." Her voice is tight, the way it was the day she got into a fender bender on Athens Street. India was shaken, because it happened, because it was her fault. She was driving and talking to Helen, who was doing what she does best, disrupting India's focus.

India is right. They can't be friends because they should be married. Theo drags a hand through his hair. His eyes are wet and his throat closes. It feels like everything around him is closing. "No . . . of course not. We can't be friends." Theo says this because he does not want to look like a complete loser, because he has a modicum of pride left. "Like I said, I dialed you by accident."

"I know. It's okay," she says again. Theo swears she is choking out the words. He does not want her pity. "I'm just thinking it might be easier for us to move on . . . if you can't call me accidentally. I, uh . . . I'll do the same."

"Right. Makes sense." Theo forces a tremendous lump through his throat. "Well, good-bye then, India." He disconnects the call before she can have the last word. Through blurry eyes, Theo stares at his phone.

He will move the pictures to his computer first thing tomorrow, but he will not delete her number. He's not ready for that. If India is so determined to forget him, let her get a new number.

Then India's last thoughts echo through his head: "I'm just thinking how it might be easier for *us* to move on . . . I'll do the same." Maybe he is only hearing what he wants to hear. Maybe there is too much Jack Daniel's in him to have heard right at all. But India left him. She could have deleted him from her phone months ago. Better still, if this is what India wanted, what is there for *her* to move on from?

CHAPTER NINETEEN

Olivia

On the sidewalk outside our brownstone, Rob's chivalrous behavior continues. I am too stunned by the sudden appearance of a ghost to move. He invites Sam Nash inside, perhaps because I don't, and guides me by the arm. We all move cagily into the living room. Rob is aware of our known history. He's cognizant of the fact that Sam was once the love of my life. It could be that Rob believes he is not. Compared to the dizzying whirl of events, furniture seems wildly heavy and anchored. A glance passes between Rob and me. He's as curious as I am. I sit on the sofa and Sam sits in the adjacent chair. On any other Friday night, this moment would register as a shock. But because I had coffee and bonding conversation with Sam's son, his unlikely presence carries the foreboding of a head-on collision.

Rob offers Sam a drink. I remain uncharacteristically mute. Sam thanks him and says a glass of water would be fine. For a second, I think he is an imposter and this is a Halloween prank, courtesy of Rob's twisted humor. Sam asking for water is a dead giveaway. Water with three fingers of bourbon—maybe. As Rob exits I say, "I'll have a drink too." My gaze bounces between the two men. "Anything with alcohol in it." Sam grins and my brain confirms his identity. Not even Hollywood could so perfectly recast his smile. My gut clenches as my mind fills with haunted memories and cherished ones.

"How . . . how have you been, Liv?"

"Do you mean in the past five minutes or twenty-six years?" He snickers at well-timed sarcasm. "Good—until now." I'm immediately annoyed I have allowed even cursory insight to my emotions. Last time Sam asked how I was, it was in a hospital room. The one where I told him that there was no baby to be concerned with and he should go live his life. That's what he was supposed to do—*forever*. I curl my blistered feet beneath me and sit up taller. "What are you doing here?"

"Like I said, I came to apologize."

"For what?"

"For the past."

"Our past?"

"Yes."

"Why?" I narrow my eyes and he looks oddly dumbfounded.

"Uh, maybe I'd best back this up a little."

Rob returns with two drinks. A medium-size glass of water, no ice—the kind you'd offer a repairman. The one who's asked to use your bathroom and you just want to leave. In the shorter, fatter glass is a double Macallan on the rocks. I suspect the odd beverage choice, Rob's usual, is meant as a marital show of solidarity. I wonder if we're supposed to share it.

Sam thanks him for the water. His gaze stays with Rob as he delivers the Macallan. Sam is absorbing the man I've married. I don't know the meter for how straight men assess one another, but I'm suddenly grateful my middle-age husband is a fitness freak, self-absorbed enough to get facial peels and use hair dye.

"Thanks," I say. I almost tack *honey* onto that, but why startle Rob with more surprise than what has descended upon our living room. My husband stakes a claim in the middle of the Oriental rug—it's a round robin of glances: Sam looking at me, my darting gaze moving between him and Rob, Rob most decidedly focused on Sam. It's Rob's call. He looks between the sofa, where there is plenty of room, and the chair next to Sam. He defaults to trust; my chin tips upward, poised not to fail him.

"I'll, um . . ." Rob glances at his watch. "I have a couple of overseas calls to return. Guess I'll go do that." Sam stands. "It was, uh . . . *interesting* to meet you."

"Same here." They do not shake hands. "I . . . I've always wondered about the man Livy might have married."

Rob nods. "Oh. I just meant it's interesting to meet a baseball icon." He exits, though his remark zips through like a dart. I hear him head down the basement steps where his home office and man cave are located.

Sam sits again and sips the water, putting the glass on the coffee table. He rubs his hands over denim-covered thighs. "Funny," I say, reaching for the upper hand. "I don't remember a nervous bone in your body."

"Yeah. Well. Me and my body have been through quite a bit." Sam clears his throat. "Regret and humility are still new to me." My ears tune to the unlikely admission. Sam Nash, in addition to being free-spirited and fun-loving was also a cocky son of a bitch. Most everything about him camouflaged that last fact, though it is clear in my memory. "I've been sick this past year. Very sick."

As only Sam Nash can do, cockiness fades, melting under the warmth of my sudden concern. "Sick. I'm sorry." But a flush of adrenaline rushes me. If my life-altering past has showed up to tell me he's going to die, I'll kill him. "Sick how?"

"Leukemia." Sam removes his ball cap—which to me is still an extension of his body—revealing a head full of hair. It's wavy and thick, the brown salt and peppered. That would be the surprising part, except for the fact that it's the hair on Theo's head, less the gray. I squeeze my eyes shut. Then my gaze turns questioning. Sam doesn't look sick. "I almost didn't make it," he says. "Can you imagine that—Sam Nash succumbing to a disease?"

"That wasn't alcohol related?"

"Agreed. I mean, seriously, Livy. You didn't think I'd end up parting this world by cliff diving or . . . I don't know, maybe by wrapping a four-by-four around a tree?"

"You did that." And the empathy in the room defaults to me.

He rests his elbows on his knees and focuses on my empty fireplace. "Right. Sorry. I'm still working on thoughtless remarks."

"You have a ways to go."

"Exactly my point."

"Have you come here hoping to recall the more vague, less sober parts of your past? Maybe you're writing a memoir." I take a gulp of the Macallan and silence a gag. *How does Rob drink this shit?* "Could be that you're fuzzy on the extreme highs and lows of your life. Maybe you were right to come. I'm a great choice for a refresher."

"Yeah. It, um . . . That very thing made you first on my list. When my trip to Boston came up, it seemed like fate was tapping me hard on the shoulder. You weren't hard to locate."

"So I'm not even the point of your visit. How very flattering."

"You don't—" His lips purse. "It took a lot to come here, Liv. I didn't know what I'd find or if you'd just slam the door in my face. I have meetings at Brandeis, a coaching position. When that happened . . . I knew I had to take the chance. Sorry if that's not white knight enough, but we're really not living in that moment anymore, are we?"

"Yes, and you fell off the horse the first time around." I deviate from our past, which I'm still trying to fit into the present. "Didn't you win a World Series or something? As my husband alluded, he was fascinated when it came up."

"He, uh . . . he seems like a nice person . . . your husband." The expression on Sam's face flattens. "What does he do?"

"Rob's a lawyer on paper, but he doesn't practice. He's in finance . . . investments. Real estate, small companies, other . . . *ventures*. He, um . . . he buys things, sells off some. Makes money . . . or not. Starts over." My explanation is vague. The Wellesley house is the most in-depth conversation we've had in recent memory. The mental footnote makes me think of my mother. I clamp down on a smile, envisioning her shock if she knew Sam Nash was sitting in my living room. He reads my mind.

"Your parents. How are they?"

"My father's dead," I say matter-of-factly. "Cancer." Sam's eyes widen. "Sorry . . . I mean, you just said you were sick and . . ."

"No. It's not that, I just thought you were going to say he had a heart attack."

"Why? So you could say *'I didn't know he had a heart?'*" He doesn't reply, but we both laugh. Sam focuses on his water glass. "My mother," I offer more soberly, "she still lives in the Wellesley house."

"Sorry about your dad." Sam clears his throat and sips the water. "Did, um . . . Did the two of you ever . . ."

"Make peace? Find common ground in the gift we share?" I shake my head. "Though I did play for him while he was dying. It probably sounded like submission."

"They knew how to enforce control, make an impression . . . Or they liked to think they did. And that house, I'd never seen anything like it . . . or maybe it was your parents, people so determined to . . ."

"Turn me into precisely what they wanted?" He nods. Sympathy and history nudge me. I recall how acutely Sam did not fit into their plans. Honestly? I had no idea my mother could be so cunning, insulting without ever saying anything directly. "You know, I'm from the South too, Sam . . . It's amazing, the obvious distinction between social class. Even nowadays—old money versus trailer trash . . . College athletics, you say? So fascinating; the opportunity to attend school predicated on the ability to toss a ball about . . ."

The discomfort of that long-ago Christmas is vivid. Sam had never been on an airplane or north of the Mason-Dixon Line. I didn't imagine my smooth-talking boyfriend could be so out of his element. My father was first to make an impression. Ten minutes into the car ride from the airport to our house, I thought it might be kinder to drop Sam in a crime-ridden Roxbury neighborhood. He could have held his own there. Between my parents' icy reception and a lifestyle he'd only seen on TV, he was like a trapped animal, woefully out of his natural habitat. Eventually, Sam escaped through a bathroom window. I found him hours later, miles away, in the closest corner bar. Sam sits up straighter. I imagine we are reliving the same memory. He switches subjects.

"Been married long?" His gaze moves around the room. He is looking for family photos, perhaps ones that include children. I swallow down the irony and more Macallan. He spots the lone wedding photo behind my head; it sits on a marble-topped table.

"Six years." I tuck a thatch of hair behind my ear. "Rob and I married a little later. I was busy with other things." Then I eyeball Sam. "My first marriage left a bad taste in my mouth." I clear my throat. "Your glory days . . . a World Series win, right? Didn't you do something in spectacular Sam Nash fashion?"

"Uh, yeah. Ninth inning." His tone reverts to the younger Sam I recall—the one who fed off glory moments. "Giants last at bat. Pitcher before me loaded the bases, no outs. A hit and the Giants would have won." I nod, frowning, waiting for the Sam Nash heroics that never touched my life. "I struck out the side."

I force the frown the other way. "So wouldn't that be the focal point, the thing of interest? The thing that matters most if you're recalling biographical memories?"

"I'm not writing a memoir. While a World Series win is a nice highlight, it's the only one."

"Sam, you're going to have to be more specific. Surprise again. You've caught me off guard. Is your visit in reference to our overall past? Or just the extreme memories of—*us*?"

"When I was sick, my prognosis wasn't good. In fact, it was pretty grim. My brother . . . You remember Tate?"

"The only person more unpredictable than you? Hard to forget." Tate once blew into Winston-Salem like a vortex of debris-filled air. He said he needed a place to crash. He consumed every bit of food in Sam's apartment, ran up his phone bill, and ordered cable porn. He left, stealing what little money Sam had in his wallet. "In comparison, he did make you look sedate."

"He hasn't changed much. Doc Bogart . . . *Bogey*, he's a leukemia specialist. According to him, Tate was my best shot—siblings are by far the most realistic possibility for a bone marrow match. Tate and I lost track about eight years ago. I hired a PI to find him. He traced Tate all the way to Washington State before the trail went cold. Anyway . . . lucky for me, I didn't need him. Long story short, the chemo treatments got me into remission. That was six . . . almost seven months ago. It's taken time to restart my life . . . Understand that I might actually have one."

"So you're cured." It's my turn to sit up taller. Whatever my mixed feelings about Sam, I do not want this to be his fate.

"Bogey says *cured* is a relative term with leukemia. But my remission is holding, and my most recent test results are better than expected."

"I see."

"I realize it's a lot to take in, Liv. But this fresh at bat, it got me thinking what I might fix. What I might do better."

With the Macallan in hand, I point an index finger at Sam. "And so what, after I grant you absolution, you'll move onto Africa, spend your good health and second chance feeding starving children, maybe hammering nails for Habitat for Humanity."

"Wow."

"What?"

The grin emerges. "I'd forgotten the hell-on-wheels attitude of Olivia Klein. Don't fuck with her. You were the only person . . . *woman*, who ever saw right through Sam Nash bullshit." I simper at the remark and information Sam has unwittingly offered. No one has taken my place—not in that sense.

"Look, it's been a long time. But you know me well enough to get that I'm a good-intention sort of guy. Altruism, on the other hand, is not a good fit. I had a near-death experience. I didn't have a personality transplant."

I raise my glass to this snippet of honesty. "Hear, hear." Sam would donate a million dollars to a good cause. He'd likely show up and sign baseballs at whatever charity event. But rolling up his sleeves and pitching in on some elbow-grease level. *That* I wouldn't believe for a second.

"But this isn't bullshit either, Liv. It's a lot of cliché—I get it. A fresh start and all that. But I'm here because I need to do more with my second chance than take it out drinking and dancing." He sips his water and avoids my stare. "It was, uh . . . It was sharply pointed out that before I got sick, I might have taken life for granted."

"Really? And what is the name of this wise woman?" A tiny piece of me doesn't want to know. While Sam never cheated on me—not to my knowledge—I'm positive he had ample opportunity. It crossed my mind, or more like grated on it, particularly as I reached whale-size, pregnant with his child. Perhaps he married one of the long-legged groupies who liked to stalk athletic types with big-money potential. Maybe she was wise and beautiful. I down another swallow of Macallan. On second thought, the swift onset of numbness might be worth the taste. I take in his lanky, now healthy frame, folded in my living room chair. I consider the way his clothes fit his body. The body beneath them. It's my turn to look away.

"Charlene," he says. The name of the woman who so intimately understood Sam draws my gaze to his. "She's a good person. She put up with a lot of shit—as much as you."

"I sincerely doubt that."

"You're probably right." He takes one more sip of water and stands. "I'm sorry about the way I behaved all those years ago, Liv. The way I walked away, left you in a bad moment."

"Bad moment?" I huff as angry beads of sweat prickle out of me.

"It, um . . . it was beyond selfish, how I behaved, especially after you lost the baby. I'm sure it was tough."

"You've no idea." Chagrined is a strange look for Sam, but that's what I see.

"After we left the Pour House, the argument . . . Upset as we both were, God knows I never should have gotten behind the wheel of a car. Then later, at the hospital . . ."

I stand too. "I get it, Sam." My voice rises to a tone that I wonder if Rob can hear. If he does, it doesn't bring him pounding up the basement stairs. "You regret being a complete jerk and for proving my parents right." I shrug. "Really, the *I told you so* kept them busy for years. And since you've come all the way to my living room to admit your folly, let me tell you how I see it: Bottom line, the only thing you don't regret is how the problem resolved itself. I'm sure it was a tough balance—your dollop of guilt versus the relief of not having to deal with an unwanted pregnancy, or a—" I clamp my mouth shut, stifling the word *son*.

He is silent. The look on Sam's face does not match any that I recall. "Yes," he says. "I am sorry for the way a twenty-one-year-old kid handled things."

I fold my arms and stare. Age is emphasized by the lines on Sam's face. Damn the clarity that comes with it. Back in North Carolina, I saw my young lover as a grown man. I expected him to do what Theo said earlier, to act like one. At the time, Sam was five years younger than

Theo is now. Still, I have little sympathy. He got to react like a kid. I had to be the grown-up.

"In the moment," Sam says, "I ran from that hospital. You're right." I roll my eyes, slightly appalled he's come so far to confirm what I've known for decades. "But after that . . . After the lightning-fast annulment your parents arranged, I'm sure you think I went right on, partying away my life. You wouldn't be completely wrong." My arms clench so tight I'm cutting off circulation. "But I never forgot what happened that night, Livy. I thought of it more than you'd ever believe." He clutches the ball cap and shifts his focus to a spot on the Oriental rug. "But I was too ashamed. Back then, I was too charmed by my own life to do anything about ours." His gaze travels from the carpet to me. "Part of my second chance is making peace with that. I regret—"

"Fine." My chin cocks toward the foyer, a *get the hell out* gesture. "You regret leaving the way you did, ending things on such a sorry sour note. You're forgiven."

"That's not what I regret. Not if I'm being honest." He moves closer to the door. My face burns and so does the past, which is flaming up in front of me. "My regret isn't about bad choices I made out of immaturity. Hell. You can think whatever you want to about that." Sam looks over his shoulder, toward the basement door where Rob exited. "My regret is what we missed out on."

"What does that mean?" Something at my core says I shouldn't request a clarification. Something says *"Just let him go, Liv . . . You don't want to know . . ."*

"What if you hadn't lost that baby—or we had another eventually? What if after I got back to Iowa, I'd picked up the damn phone, like my gut said to?" A remorseful breath seeps out of him. "Once the baby was gone . . . It made my sorry-ass excuses easier. It allowed me to accept the end . . . *of us*. Anyway . . . either way, a whole different life could have been lived. It might have been as nice as this one." He gestures at tangible esthetics. Sam is too far from me, too close to the door. He can't hear the gasp drawing between slightly parted lips. He glances, again, in the direction Rob has gone. "Looks like your life has worked out. And maybe showing up like this . . . Could be all I did was disrupt your Friday night. But back then, I wish I'd made a different choice."

"Different . . ."

"I don't know how long it took you to get over us, or if maybe you checked out of that hospital, picked up, and moved on. It was believable. It was the thing I loved most about you—resiliency. For whatever it's worth, what I regret is giving up on us." Sam reads my frozen pose as a reply—anger, maybe indifference. "I regret losing what we might have had."

He leaves. The brownstone door clicks shut behind him.

I don't move, mentally floundering for my footing. I'm surrounded by familiarity—the slight rush of fall air as it darts in the door. The mantel clock ticks. There are nights I come down here at three a.m. and sit, desperate for the music and mania to stop. A new reality unfurls in front of me: In Sam's great need to apologize for the life we missed out on, he's revealed a chasm I did not know existed. He's admitted to wanting everything I gave away—our life, our son. "You bastard. Tell me I didn't just hear that?" And as only Sam Nash is capable, he's shoved me, body and mind flailing, headlong into a past that might have been.

CHAPTER TWENTY

Olivia

I'm in my nightgown, standing in dreamy moonlight that streams through the brownstone's bedroom window. In any other life, in any other bedroom, this might serve as a stunningly romantic vignette. On my way upstairs, I glanced toward the basement light. I heard the rhythmic strokes of the rowing machine. Bypassing Rob was the only thing I could think to do. He doesn't fit into any of the thoughts in my head. Sometime later, when I hear heavy breathing at the bedroom door, I know he's rowed five or six miles away. Yet, here he stands.

"So . . . do you plan on telling me what that was about?"

It's such a muddled, mind-fucking mess. I go with what explains my frazzled state, something I won't be able to hide from Rob. "He was sick." I tip my head toward the moon.

"Sick like what? Needs a kidney, or . . ."

I turn. Rob is dripping in sweat, his chest heaving, and his expression unsure. "Like dying sick . . . at one point," I clarify. "He came to apologize for past mistakes. You know—the whole long-before-you-existed North Carolina debacle."

I squirm inside and out. Awkwardness is a natural reaction, having been pregnant with one man's child. Then openly choosing to remain childless with the one to whom you are married. Rob doesn't squirm; he's too practiced for anything so common. But I know it's what he's thinking. As to what he's feeling . . . Lately, that's a million-dollar Rob question. "Anyway . . . Sam is hell-bent on a second-shot-at-life mission. Making apologetic speeches was on his to-do list."

"So is he going to live?"

I almost laugh. It's such an honest Rob remark. The question is not out of concern for Sam, only an inquiry as to whether or not this subject will further affect Rob.

"Apparently he is."

"And that was it?"

Hardly. But I've reached the precipice of what I'm willing to share with my husband about Sam Nash. It might blow a gaping hole in what is already a fissured marriage. "For anything that matters . . . Yes."

Rob crosses the bedroom, discarding his sweat-soaked T-shirt as he goes. He pauses at his dresser and removes his wedding ring, placing it in the drawer—a habit. He can't sleep with anything touching his body. He peers into the dim reflection of the mirror. "So that was the famous Sam Nash?"

As predicted, Rob forays into cursory conversation. "Famous how?" I ask.

He frowns, shaking his head. "Miracle ace reliever of the 2002 World Series? Or maybe the in-flesh phenomenon that affected Olivia Klein in ways no other human ever has."

I widen my eyes at the less likely remark. Over time, I have confided some of the painful parts of my relationship with Sam to Rob. When I don't respond, he does.

"Interesting, whether we're talking about you or his World Series win, either accomplishment could make a headline." Rob sheds his sweatpants and underwear, moving naked toward the bathroom.

I turn back to the window, imagining how exposed I would feel if Rob knew everything. Tonight, Sam and Theo and myself—we'll sleep within a few miles of each other. The last time we slept in the same place it was a cramped dorm room on a college campus. It's a curious reunion to say the least.

I glance in the direction Rob has gone. This is reality and I am being absurdly sentimental. The sudden, outrageous facts Sam Nash delivered are bittersweet, but they don't matter. I scrub my hands over my face, brushing away the layers of revelations. *Disrupt my Friday night?* It draws a snicker.

Of course, there is a natural resolution here and I cling to it. If everything remains *as is*—and I see no reason why it shouldn't—tonight and Sam and Theo will all eventually go away. With the moon bearing witness, I decide this is no more than karma biting me in the ass. I've had it coming since I shoved a newspaper under Sasha's nose and uttered words about a better idea than green space beautification. I walk into the bathroom. My intention is to brush my teeth and tend to my blistered foot. It's the one raw spot I have a decent hope of healing.

The shower water runs hot, and steam has settled over the vintage bath. It's been restored to modern perfection—a splurge after one of my husband's better investment deals. A soapy Rob stands with his back to me. It's a deep shower, custom tiled, with a partial glass wall. I recall where our night was headed before we arrived home to find my past sitting on our doorstep. I consider what I alluded to as Rob valiantly carried me down the sidewalk. I ignore regrets and think of spelled-out promises, the kind said in front of a judge six years ago. Promises I meant. Instead of reaching for healing ointment, I go for a flash fix. I tug the nightgown over my head and skim off my underwear. I step into the shower.

At first it's just the water beating around me; then it's the feel of Rob's hands as they make firm but intimate contact. His mouth is a little open, like he's thinking about saying something, but can't decide what. Just like with Sam, I have to stand on tiptoe to kiss Rob when barefooted. His mouth has something to do, and he runs with it. It's a rain shower of emotion in an ongoing drought—soaking kisses, anxious greedy touch. Our fingers lock and I know my grip is as firm as any man's, years of practiced movement with a bow and strings. I squeeze Rob's hand and he squeezes back. But he lets go as his hand crooks behind my neck, kissing me harder in some claim-staking gesture. A few moments later I'm between him and a limestone wall. Both are ridiculously hard, one is more porous. If not properly maintained, limestone can rot right out from under you.

For a brief second, almost suspended animation, the kissing stops. Water beats on him, Rob shielding me. His mouth is pursed to a firm line, his gaze taking a possessive inventory. Impulsively, my hands thrust around either side of his face and I stretch to kiss him heatedly. Then I am weightless as Rob hoists my body upward, between him and the wall. My legs wrap around him. He thrusts inside of me with the well-played accuracy of a *Cosmo* article on hot, aggressive sex. Panting sexual noises aren't commonplace in here, not lately. Now they override the pounding of dual rainforest showerheads.

The sex doesn't last long, but long enough to put a dominant satisfactory look on Rob's face. The limestone scratches against my back as I slide down, my feet meeting the river-rock shower floor. But I don't let go of Rob, feeling both our hearts pound. His mouth opens again. "What?" I ask. Rob doesn't respond. "He doesn't mean anything. It's old—maybe just an old sting." Water and emotion continue to pour down around us. I take a chance. "Did I look at him like he meant anything more to me than an unlikely surprise?"

Rob shakes his head ever so slightly. "It wasn't how you looked at him. It was the way he looked at you."

CHAPTER TWENTY-ONE

Olivia

Ass-biting karma. I stick with it as an apt explanation for yesterday. It's cosmic payback, perhaps a reminder that I am not immune to having to answer for my actions, even if Jack Nicholson is not presiding. Rob and I spend Saturday enforcing normal. He devotes his to a companion headset, pacing the brownstone while doing business. Outwardly, I spend mine practicing. Quietly, more covertly, I absorb Sam's rise from the dead and the almost unbelievable presence of our son in my life. When my mother calls, I take it as confirmation that the universe is not yet done with comeuppance.

I keep the conversation short, though I do tell her about Claire McAdams's charity event. It's a Eugenia hallmark social gathering—a black-tie soirée, mingling deep pockets of pretty people. She coos at the notion of me joining her ranks. But while speaking, my subconscious dishes up large servings of wiseass narration: *"Yes, a lovely charity event, Mom . . . I was invited by your grandson . . . You remember him . . . After I told you he no longer existed, you patted my arm and said 'See that,*

Olivia. Sam proved us right, and mercifully everything's worked out as it should . . .'" Regardless, today's call ends benignly. My mother is going to look into Claire's event, see if any of her friends are on the guest list.

On Sunday I refocus on practicing "Jupiter" and "Saturn," movements four and five in Holst's *Planets*. The symphony schedule picks up next week, and I've been distracted. If one violin is off, the rest of the violins will suffer. Since violins are the heartbeat of any orchestra, other instruments will follow. The entire performance will be lacking, and it will be my fault. My work ethic is enough for this to matter. I take "Jupiter" and "Saturn" by storm. An hour later, when the house phone rings, it breaks my concentration. But Rob picks up after two echoing shrills, and I begin again. Ten minutes later, the phone rings a second time. Rob answers, but it's too late; I'm out of the practice zone. My mind drifts, imagining how Theo would approach the challenging measures of music. I would love to hear the passion with which he'd play it, passion that I masterfully fake.

I sink further into the Theo thought, blindsided by a fantasy. My daydream is facilitated by the new information Theo's father provided—maybe a life where his biological parents worked it out, awed and able to foster their son's gifts. When it comes to Sam's talents and mine, the only common denominator is their existence. But it might have been enough. We wouldn't have handled Theo's gifts perfectly, but we would have grasped them. That's something. Well, something less the obvious tug-of-war. I half smile. Damned if I wouldn't have encouraged Theo's musical instincts. What I wouldn't have done was made it Theo's only option—surely Sam would have doubled down on that.

I finger the complex pages of sheet music, lost in family dynamics: mothers and daughters, mothers and sons. The son's uncle crosses my mind. The only souls who know about Theo are my brother, Phillip; his husband; and the moon. It's strange for such a long-ago, cloistered secret to breathe new life. Phillip and Scott visit every other year from New Zealand. While the visits are pleasant, my brother has rarely spoken of the son I gave birth to on the other side of the world, which is the way I wanted it. I believe his silence is compensatory. I'm the sibling who remained stateside—the adult child who sat beside Asa Klein as he lingered in this life, playing on demand while Phillip waited on the other side of the world. Then it was Rob, not Phillip, who came to my aid, taking the cool necessary action needed to end my pain and my father's.

I raise my bow. It drops dejectedly. I am stuck on all sorts of notes from the past. Sheet music turns misty. Theo so eloquently described music as the order in his life. The thing that made sense when the world turned to bedlam. I imagine it's something similar to what my grandfather might have experienced by way of music. I don't know how they did it, and I strongly beg to differ. No piece of music will quiet the fact that Theo's father stood in my living room last night, altering what I thought was truth: if Sam had picked up a phone—or I hadn't lied—our lives would have turned out so very different. Different good or different worse? That I do not know.

I breathe deep and assure myself everything has worked out as it should. I begin to play again, but find I'm too distracted, too stuck on Sam's unexpected confession. The light on the music room phone is still lit. I give up on practicing and head to the kitchen, guessing my mother now has Rob's ear. She's the only person who can keep him talking this long. But as I pass through the narrow dining room, soft peals of laughter waft toward me. It's not the way Rob jokes with my mother, which is more of an ingratiating laugh. I hit the swinging door hard, and Rob looks startled. The laughter ceases, and he tells the caller to "hang on a sec" before holding out the phone. "It's Sasha—something about having lunch."

"With you?"

He looks perplexed. "No. With you." But before handing over the phone, he presses it to his ear. "See you, Sash." He turns it over to me. I listen to Sasha but watch as Rob picks up his cell, texting someone. Earlier, he mentioned watching football at a sports bar with friends. Sasha and I are supposed to have lunch today. To my disappointment, she says she has to cancel and proceeds to apologize. "I'm sorry I've been so out of touch lately," she says. "It's just things . . . odd things have come up."

Her words about *odd things* sound like they should have come from my mouth. Sasha goes on to explain that Jeremy insists she go with him to some musty bookstore reading; she feels obligated. I roll my eyes at the imagery, an outing where Sasha will pretend to be enamored by literary prose, spoken by some reclusive author she's never heard of and can't think of now. I know Sasha's reading tastes. Like a drug dealer with a stash, she once hid a plastic-bag-bound copy of *Fifty Shades of Grey* in her toilet tank. She spent so much time in the bathroom Jeremy thought she should see a gastrologist. She actually made an appointment, telling me it was easier than confessing her bathroom book habit to Jeremy. "He'd be mortified . . ." But I say nothing about Jeremy, including their lack of common interests. Instead we confirm a Tuesday lunch date.

Sunday night, Rob announces that he's taking an impromptu business trip to New York. He's coordinated a few meetings with past investors, hoping to bring them onboard with his golf course project, which would ultimately take the Wellesley house off the table as collateral. On Monday morning, when he slips from the bed at five a.m., it's raining. He's booked on a crack-of-dawn flight. I roll to his side of the bed, which has turned cold, and think of David McAdams, who also visited New York on a beautiful September morning. In a half-awake state, I shuffle my body across wrinkled sheets. There's a lesson and a sudden urge to talk to Rob. My call goes to voice mail; he's probably already boarded. I don't leave a message, but I do relax once the sun has pushed through gloomy Boston skies and planes have landed safely in New York.

A short time later, Sasha sends me a text. Her busy calendar has changed again. She can't make lunch on Tuesday—an emergency deposition. It happens with regularity. Jeremy tends to get annoyed by abrupt changes like this, so I make a point of being purposefully understanding. It's my hope that eventually Jeremy's demanding behavior will dawn on Sasha—or maybe mine will just look good. I text back and suggest dinner on Wednesday. And hour passes before Sasha replies, saying our dinner date will be fine.

When I arrive at Braemore, I learn that Theo's called out for the day. I don't wonder but fixate on his absence. My reaction is out of whack. Someone fulfilling community service hours should only be concerned if the hours will still count. I walk aimlessly for hours after class wondering if Theo is sick or heartsick, and it occurs to me that this is something only his mother would do. When a police car passes by for the third time, the officer asks if I'm lost, can he point me in a direction? Well, yes. But hardly the kind involving a compass.

Finally I make my way into the Boston Public Garden and sit discreetly on a bench. My phone turns up in my hand, and the urge to call Theo is a gnawing itch. I resist the impulse that is both foolish and dangerous. I also eliminate calls to Sasha and Rob. My husband is, no doubt, in the midst of his New York business, and Sasha is just plain busy with her life.

Instead, I succumb to a different temptation. I call not one but three hotels that are nearest to Brandeis University. On the third try, I find Sam Nash registered at an Embassy Suites. I ask to be connected to his room. There is no answer. I recall Sam saying something about a coaching position. The excuse for his jarring visit and subsequent confession. Sitting on the bench, an anger that reaches all the way back to New Zealand consumes me. How dare he? How colossal is Sam's nerve and his ego, after all these years, to sanctimoniously drop in on my life and apologize for mistakes that forever changed it. I don't care if he was dying—he isn't anymore. I head straight for our parking garage. Fury gets into the car with me, and I blindly follow the GPS to the Embassy Suites. "Your reward for not dying, Sam Nash, isn't absolution. That's for damn sure."

Once I find my way to the lobby of the Embassy Suites, it occurs to me this is not a well-thought-out fit of rage. They never are. What are the odds of Sam traveling with a baseball bat *and* owning a Porsche? I bite down on a thumbnail. Not likely—he was a pitcher; he flew into Boston. Plopping onto a stain-resistant sofa, I people watch for a while. It could be that Sam won't come back here until evening, if at all. I don't have his phone number. I have no idea where he lives, if he returned to Bulls Gap, Tennessee, or remained on the West Coast after his baseball playing days—I was too flummoxed to ask. Strangers come and go. After all this time, I wonder if Sam is anything more than that. I do the thing that I've resisted since the invention of the internet—I Google him.

For the next half hour, I take a Cooperstown-like tour, skimming baseball history and noting stats. I have no idea if the stats are good or bad. Good, I suppose. There's a lot of fuss about his pitching prowess. The sums of money that he was paid make my eyes bug. Attempting to attach this kind of money to Sam is like picturing him as the wallflower at a party. Impossible. When we were together, he never took me home to Tennessee. I know it was because he was too ashamed of where he came from—especially after his chilly trip north to the Wellesley house. But his reasons for keeping me away went deeper, centering on a childhood that made mine appear pedestrian.

Sam grew up without a mother, but he didn't know if she was dead or had abandoned them. According to Sam, his father spun various tales depending on his state of sobriety. Sitting in the hotel lobby, I recall one in particular: "Sometimes my old man tried to scare us, saying there was a body buried out back. Saying it was our mother—sadistic son of a bitch that he was. It kept Tate and me away from the shed, the piece of yard behind it. When I was thirteen or so I got up the nerve and went out to see for myself." At first I thought Sam was telling a humorous story, one that had a punch-line ending. It did. It just came by way of his father's fists. Hudson Nash caught Sam where he wasn't supposed to be, staring into a finely farmed patch of marijuana.

Every so often, mostly when Sam was drunk, his guard would slip and he'd share more of his tumultuous past—growing up in a trailer not fit for raccoons and a father wholly unfit for parenthood. I vividly recall Tate, the older brother who dropped in on Sam's life in Winston-Salem. I remember remarking to Sam about his brother not being housebroken. "Aw, Tate's nothin', Livy . . . If you think he's rough around the edges, you should meet my old man . . ."

I didn't need to lay eyes on Hudson Nash to see his effect. The first time Sam took his shirt off, sexual tension turned to shock. My aroused gaze traveled his muscular frame and a half dozen circular scars—the size of a dime. He froze. "What happens if you don't get the beer to the TV fast enough when the Vols play." In comparison, my scars were wholly internal. Thinking they couldn't be real, I touched them. Sam grabbed my fingers. "Don't." He squeezed until I retracted my hand and my eyes met his. Then he smiled. "When I started winning baseball games, Hudson backed off. When they offered me a full ride to Wake Forest, he actually said I might amount to something. He came to a game once. Afterward, he told Coach how proud he was—like it was somethin' he said every Sunday after church. That's the only part I think about, okay?"

Our brewing sexual encounter escalated into something deeper, a connection we lived on for a year and a half. As unlikely as it was, we understood where the other came from—mine the demanding beleaguered childhood, Sam's something that should have been reported. But we both survived, and it made for a solid bond. Outwardly, friends saw us as the party couple, loud and raucous. No one ever got a glimpse of the tender moments that fed us—I know that Theo was born out of one in particular.

Sam had gone home; his father was in the hospital. One of many attempts to dry him out. He called me at school, asking me to meet him at a cabin west of Winston-Salem. The cabin belonged to a teammate of Sam's. It was a great place to party—no authority figures within miles. But that night it was just the two of us, a fire, and Sam wearing the kind of emotion that he would never display in public, barely in private. In hindsight, I know it's the reason he chose the secluded cabin. It wasn't as romantic as it was a respite. Sam had a fresh bruise on his face. I assumed it was his father; he alluded to a drunken brother. "Doesn't matter," he said. "They swing the same." Apparently, a call from a major league scout set the whole thing off. Sam said it didn't matter. He was never going back. Thanks to the scouting call, he wouldn't have to. Then he asked me to marry him. Together we would have a fun, fabulous life, our pasts erased. It sounded like nirvana. Looking into a blazing fire that night, I remember wishing I'd brought the Amati. I would have happily tossed it in.

The rural cabin sat on the outskirts of the future, where caution was easily dismissed. Like all seductive settings, we lived only in that moment. Sam was in pain and I was the fix. I loved being that person—I'd only known what it was like to be someone's goal and subsequent disappointment. That night made me believe Theo was meant to be, even as I boarded a plane alone, three short months later, to New Zealand.

Sitting in the Embassy Suites, staring at an online photo of a younger Sam, the varying disappointments filter out. I recall the subtler motivation for my choices. Forcing parenthood in Sam's path would have stopped his future from happening. The one he needed so desperately. At least this was my interpretation until Sam showed up and altered those facts. Facts I believed to be the truth since before Theo was born. "Jesus, Sam," I murmur, touching the screen on my phone. "Why couldn't you have just stayed away?"

CHAPTER TWENTY-TWO

Olivia

A distant Southern drawl startles me. At first it's a memory. Then it's there. I inch my gaze upward, past jean-clad legs, a plaid shirt, and onto Sam's bearded face. I blink into the hotel's bright lobby light as the past turns into the present.

"Liv. What are you doing here?"

My rage has petered out, replaced by more poignant feelings courtesy of the internet and memories. "I, um . . . I don't . . ." I fight a wave of nostalgia, faltering.

In turn, he does not. "Can I buy you a drink?" Sam holds out his hand. I take it and follow. On the way to the bar, we're stopped twice—long-time fans that recognize a baseball icon. They want to regale his career and World Series win. I suppose Sam has secured his place in sports history. The second man shakes Sam's hand like he's pumping a well, and finally we break free. He tries, again, to finish his thought. "Sorry," he says as we settle in at the bar. "That happens sometimes. And

I'm sorry about blindsiding you the other night. I should have called, maybe friended you on Facebook first."

"Do you have a Facebook page?" I ask.

He shakes his head. "You?" I offer the same response. "Party's in the room, right? Never could get my head around cyber socializing."

Loud distractions, it's how we both lived life when there was a party. Sam starts talking as if not a day has passed. Perhaps his brownstone appearance was the icebreaker, because this feels disturbingly comfortable. He hits the highlights of his glory days. It's an easy starting point, and then he drifts to more personal stories that match the fun-loving man I knew.

Years removed, I now know that Sam's "fun-loving" nature was a façade, self-preservation. I was an enabler of wild behavior, as ill-equipped as Sam to deal with his father and the abusive childhood he lived. An hour later, Sam is drinking his third bourbon blend and I'm nursing a second. Maybe I'm still an enabler. The drinks are concoctions Sam supervised after making fast friends with the bartender. He too recognized Sam and was openly giddy at the idea of the celebrated athlete sitting at his bar. The drinks taste like the South—all burning warmth and quixotic lure. It's just after lunchtime, and the bar is in a lull, hours before patrons invade looking to escape life. It takes Sam a while to ask about mine.

I talk about the symphony and having made reasonable peace with my violin. I don't go anywhere near community service hours or how a music teacher at an alternative high school, who was a star athlete in college, makes this a deceptive conversation and beyond surreal. Yet I keep going, mentally retreating to a place where Theo doesn't exist. Why not? It worked for me until Shep Stewart showed up with annual updates.

There's a flutter of pride when Sam says he's pleased I ended up pursuing music. I don't move as he brushes back a strand of hair, remarking, "You're so talented, Liv. No matter your parents' influence, anything else would have been a shame. *I* would have been a shame." He turns toward the liquor-backed bar and sips his drink. "It would have been my fault, making you sit in East Bumble-Fuck, Iowa." He turns toward me and grins. It's as familiar as the bourbon and even more intoxicating. "So, can I ask, what did you do after . . . *us*? I've always wondered."

Adrenaline surges—a jarring stab of reality. I thought I'd packed Theo away, at least for the afternoon. The sensation drills on. Wait. It's my phone, though my heart pounds furiously as I answer. It's Rob. How timely. He's checking in. It feels like a jerky conversation, but I suspect this is paranoia. I am sitting at bar in the middle of the day with an ex-lover. The father of my son. Rob says his first meeting was canceled and that he's unsure if he likes staying at a boutique hotel, something new for him. While he describes his surroundings—an ultra-tiny room and non-Rob baroque décor—I don't mention mine. He winds down, defaulting to mundane talk about me picking up his dry cleaning and asking if the insurance company has called. When I don't reply, he says my name. "Uh-huh, right. I heard you." Truthfully, I am half listening, maybe a quarter, focused on Sam's profile as he chats with the bartender and pretends not to overhear my conversation.

The moment I hang up, Sam swivels his neck in my direction. "How's that going, Liv . . . marriage?"

And for all the lies I've told, the truth slips out like a silk knot. "Not so great."

Sam narrows his eyes and sips his drink. "When I was on my way out . . . sick, I thought about us."

"Isn't that what dying people do, count their regrets? Maybe dwell on them."

"You may be right. But not in my case. Dwelling on us came after I got the good news." I don't say anything, running my index finger around the rim of my glass. "Not great as in you're doing your best to work it out?" Sam asks. "Or not great, it's just a matter of pulling the trigger, ending it."

I dodge minefields of complications. "You never married . . . never found—"

"Anyone like you? No."

"But you said there was a woman, you lived with her. There had to be others."

"None whose name I recall, except Charlene." Sam pokes at the ice in his drink with a swizzle stick. "She got the short end of that deal, for sure. Last time I saw her, Charlene had no qualms letting me know I was more trouble than I was worth. I couldn't argue the point."

"You overcame a lot, Sam. You had a great career. That's obvious from a short walk through this hotel. You must have terrific memories."

"And a clean condo filled with memorabilia, an upgraded view of the ninth hole." He lifts his eyes from his drink. "You were smart to walk away after the accident, especially after there was no reason to stay." A swig of bourbon sits in my mouth; I can't swallow. "As it is, I probably got more than I deserve. I'm alive." He doesn't speak directly to me, but stares into the bar's mirrored backdrop. "If Charlene was right about karma, dying on my living room sofa wasn't the worst thing I had coming my way."

I'm dazed by Sam's melancholy conclusions, fearful of what's heading in my direction someday. Nervously, I click on my phone. The time lights up; still midafternoon. Yet I use an evening rehearsal as an excuse. "I have to go. Symphony practice."

He nods. "Probably best. You in the parking garage?" I nod back. "I'll walk you to your car." He winks. "Big cities."

While I'm certain the security in the Embassy Suites outside Brandeis is perfectly safe, I allow Sam to accompany me. The gait is familiar, the rhythm returning. He strides like an athlete, slowing down to match my pace. Halfway through the dim garage, his hand wraps around mine. It should strike me as inappropriate. Instead I squeeze back. The physical contact feels like a silent note of reverence. "There,"

I say, pointing to the Audi sedan. At the car door, I let go of Sam's hand, fishing for keys. I pop the lock, standing with my back to him.

"Livy . . ." I turn. Old energy connects to the sound of my name, the way he says it. It explodes into a ferocious kiss. It goes on longer than a kiss should, long enough for Sam to say breathlessly, "Don't go. Come up to my room."

Touching him turns time back. But the feel of him is nothing compared to the smell—Sam skin laced with bourbon and possibility. When Sam left for good, he left behind a Wake Forest University sweatshirt—black and gold colors, the shield-like emblem on the front. When I left for New Zealand, I took the sweatshirt with me. The scent enveloped every memory—good and bad. Right before Theo was born, I cut the sweatshirt up, and with a little help from Phillip's neighbor, who was a whiz with a sewing machine, we fashioned it into a tiny Wake Forest blanket. I assume the nurse who cared for Theo on his journey home discarded it along the way. It was easy to imagine; the McAdamses' new baby would not arrive with second-hand labeling.

Instead of backing off, I burrow closer to Sam. He's still a drug. He still erases the life I don't want to deal with. Sam kisses me again, and a hum of confusion pulses from my throat. I push away from the kiss but hang on to the man. *Confusion?* I should be unconscious from the potential fallout, not the least of which is the husband I currently have. "I can't do that, Sam. Go up to your room." But it comes out weak, barely an objection. I glance toward the underground entrance. "Let me guess. Top floor, penthouse suite?"

He shakes his head. "Sixth floor, room 644 . . . Old ballplayer superstition—forty-four was my number."

"And the six?"

His mouth gapes before he answers. "June sixth."

It's my birth month and day.

Of course, it's also D day. Foreshadowing, I think.

Holding on, Sam does the sensible thing and takes half a step back. "I'm sorry, Liv. I shouldn't have suggested it."

"Because you realize it's a residual reaction to *not dying* . . . Because a couple of drinks made us both nostalgic for the parts of us that were good?"

He shakes his head. "Because I don't want to cause bigger problems than I did all those years ago."

His son would be proud of his father's improved high moral ground. "It might not take much to do that." Hastily, I reach forward, hugging him and holding on. His grip is equally tight. In his ear I ask, "How long will you be in town?"

"A while . . . At my meeting today I agreed to a tryout coaching position. See if the team's a good fit, vice versa. Not sure how I'll do with regular life. I never was much good at it."

And from the man himself, I am reminded of the reasons that I made the choices I did years ago. Choices that were starting to take on the feel of regret. "Well," I say, opening the car door, "isn't it incredible that you have a second chance to figure it all out?"

I decide I'm not going to rehearsal this evening. I go home to the brownstone and draw all the shades, sitting in the living room until it's dark. When my stomach grumbles, I think of food but only light a candle and check the time. It's not nearly as late as I thought, just a lack of lunch and a fast-setting fall sun. I can't get out of this day fast enough. I go to the wet bar where there are equal supplies of Macallan and Crown Royal. I wipe the back of my hand across my mouth, which still smells of Sam, and reach for a neutral, already open bottle of merlot. I fill a stemless wineglass with zero deference to what society deems an appropriate amount. After emptying half the glass, good sense relaxes. I pick up my phone and dial. In an effort to avoid one problem, I grasp at its blood-related mate. Theo answers.

"Liv . . . hey," he says.

He sounds sleepy. "I was just wondering if maybe we're suffering from the same thing. You weren't at school today, and I ended up staying home from rehearsal." Compared to everything else, it's the tiniest of white lies.

A rumble of Theo laughter cuts into the line. Less the Southern drawl, the mirroring depth of his and Sam's voice is uncanny. "Not unless you were suffering the aftermath of a binge weekend, thanks to a busted heart." I am quiet and he is embarrassed. "Sorry. I didn't mean to be so . . . *dramatic*. Really. I'm fine. Braemore kids take a lot of attention and energy. I didn't have it today—that's all."

I should tell Theo how we functioned without him. Until Principal Giroux came in, acting as security guard, the room was chaos, even with a substitute music teacher. It's the appropriate subject matter between friendly classroom acquaintances. "I'm sorry you're having such a rough time, Theo."

"I called her."

"India?"

"Yes."

"And?"

"It was an accident, the call. Long story. Anyway . . . we talked for a few minutes. It was weird and comfortable all at once."

I swirl the wine and say absently, "I know what you mean."

"How so?"

The swirling stops. "Uh, recently—someone from my past turned up. We had that sort of weird-comfortable conversation."

He laughs. "Not the guy you were madly in love with in college?"

I nearly fall off the sofa, and the wineglass does hit the coffee table with a sloshing thud. "Your call with India. Tell me about it," I say, deflecting facts.

"Like I said, odd and comfortable. I don't think she'd been sitting by the phone waiting for my call." He is quiet for a moment. I let him think. "But she did . . . Hell, it was probably my imagination."

"What was your imagination, Theo?"

"It was so tiny, but it was there. I'm sure of it. India made a comment about her needing space to get over us. Does that make sense, Liv? She broke up with me. What is there for her to get over?"

Misinterpretation or a valid observation, I have no idea. But I find myself desperate to fan Theo's spark of hope. "It does make sense. Maybe . . . maybe don't give up completely on the two of you. Not yet."

"Why do you say it like that, like you're rooting for us?"

I take a deep breath and draw on what might be motherly wisdom. "If you give up too soon, you might miss the chance of a lifetime. If you're too stubborn or rash, Theo, you could miss everything you were supposed to have."

CHAPTER TWENTY-THREE

Olivia

On Wednesday, Braemore is closed, an educational day for teachers. This is good; it will put distance between Theo and me. I shouldn't have called him. Nothing positive can come from furthering a relationship. But between the quiet of the brownstone and looming catastrophe, I've thought of nothing but Theo and Sam. It's crazy. A couple of months ago, one was a tender memory I visited on a day of New Year's Eve mourning—it seemed appropriate, allowable. The other was like a distant shadow—Sam, hovering in the yesteryear of my life.

I called his hotel twice on Tuesday, but hung up both times. Afterward, I did the right thing and minded my business, even heading to symphony rehearsal early. As I took my place next to Mary Alice, who is perpetually early, she asked if I was feeling okay. I muttered, "Fine. I just, um . . . I had nowhere else to be." Normally, my ass hits the chair with two minutes to tune.

When Sasha calls and tries to back out of dinner, citing an overload of work, I don't relent. I need to change the subjects in my head.

I convince her to meet me at Neptune Oyster in the North End. After arriving, we find so much food and flavor that distraction seems possible. But after the oysters, which are succulent, breezy conversation stagnates. Avoiding what's foremost on my mind leaves few talking points. I don't mention Sam, his close call with death, or his more startling appearance in Boston. I don't because Sasha and I are too close—one dubious confession will lead to another. I also don't want to test the odds. Would Sasha believe my questionable behavior stopped with a heated parking garage kiss? I smile, unable to decide where she'd come down on that point, and order another martini.

Sasha isn't much help with alternative topics. She's distracted and not her usual, on-point self. It's a state of mind I use to regulate my own, and something I need desperately this evening. But since her late entrance, I sense that I'm the one holding it together. Sure-footed Sasha literally tripped as she approached the table and glanced sheepishly around the restaurant before sliding into the booth.

With nowhere else to go, I bring up Theo. I keep it benign as in "the music teacher at the alternative high school." Sasha fidgets and I push the topic, like a child trying to get her attention. How far can I go? She's not listening, and I succumb to a pinch of Jeremy's demanding behavior. She shows cursory interest in my add-on thoughts about Octavious and Antonio, the idea about asking Manuel if the symphony would provide a summer internship. Her haziness drifts to obtuse when I say, "Both students, they have so much promise . . . I wouldn't mind teaching them myself." It's perfect fodder for a Sasha comeback.

Her lackluster gaze bumps over mine. "What a great idea."

"In what universe?"

She smiles vaguely. "Didn't you say something about planets being part of the symphony's upcoming pieces? Maybe that will work out."

For a winter-ash brunette, it's the blondest moment I've ever heard from Sasha. Her tiny frame pops taller, and she keeps her hand tight to her side. I'm sure it's gripped around her phone. "Trial starts tomorrow," she says. "Huge case. Zowz and I are handling it."

"Oh, you and Zowz beyond your pro bono hours. How cozy."

"What's that supposed to mean?"

"Nothing . . ." As the waitress delivers dinner, I glance around the otherwise sedate setting.

"Opening statements," she says, examining her meal. "It's always comes down to the wire which one of us will do that. I, uh . . . I'm also hoping Zowz will track down some last-minute evidence. The whole thing, it's got me on edge."

I can't recall a time when the law or Nick Zowzer put Sasha on edge.

She cuts into her steak. It's what Sasha would order in a seafood restaurant and so rare it should have arrived on a leash. She's also a food sniffer. At least her dining habits don't appear ruffled, performing this ritual before tasting a fancy potato dish laden with a thousand-calorie-per-teaspoon sauce. Sasha has the metabolism of a gazelle. The lobster and sea greens salad is placed in front of me. She slices into her bleeding meat and says, "So what about this Theo? He broke up with his fiancée or something?"

"Right . . . his fiancée." I pick up my fork, amazed she's retained this much. Since Sasha's asked a direct question, I convey what I know about Theo's love life. Her interest perks up a notch. As I talk, the soft crease in her brow deepens to a groove. Sasha's stare drills into me as I wind down with Theo's recent call to India. She's abandoned her filet. I read Sasha's body language like a mood ring. I've said too much. "Soo . . ." I go on in a drawn-out breath. "What's new with Jeremy?"

Sasha doesn't reply, studying my poker face. I imagine it's the look she gives when deciding if the witness is lying. She stands down and picks up her steak knife. "Not much . . . or I'm not sure. Jeremy's been . . . distracted lately."

"And why is that?" I dab at my mouth with a napkin and down another Liv-like gulp of martini. "Writer's block?"

"Since you ask, more like relationship block."

I'm in luck. The conversation's leapt from me to her. "Oh, sorry. I guess we haven't talked in a while." This is unlike us, for me not to be up to speed on Sasha's love life. Sometimes I'm sure I know too much, like the fact that Jeremy enjoys kinky lingerie and that last Christmas Eve they had sex in my powder room. I clear my throat and the holiday memory. It's not so much the sex, but sex with Sasha's moody live-in boyfriend. Sex is something Sasha puts a lot of thought into. She once pulled me into Victoria's Secret dressing room, anxious for an opinion about the lacy scabs of fabric covering her body. All I could think was, *Seriously, this is the performance you put on in addition to room and board? Jesus, I'd never leave either . . .* That and she must keep the woman who does her waxing on a retainer. I erase the visual and pay attention. "What's going on with you and Jeremy?"

Her slim shoulders shift, and her silky gray blouse opens wider in the front. Among her many talents, Sasha has the impeccable gift of fashion. It only heightens her bizarre willingness to dress like a hooker in the bedroom. It also makes me think of Jeremy's staple wardrobe—threadbare Red Sox pajama pants and a rotation of eighties rock-band T-shirts. I rephrase my Jeremy question, attempting to give him the benefit of the doubt. "Didn't you say a big publishing house was considering his new novel?"

"They were. They did." My head cocks and her penciled eyebrows arch. "They passed."

"Oh, that's too bad."

"But this time it's not just the rejection—it's the aftermath." Her silverware clinks against the plate. "And it's not getting any better."

"Has he stopped writing?"

"He's stopped bathing."

"You're kidding?"

"Not so much."

Unfortunately, this is almost too easy to envision.

"We had an agreement. It wouldn't have worked for everybody, but it worked for us. I was the breadwinner while Jeremy had all day to write. In turn, he did the domestic detail. I hate to sound like some 1950s, Ward Cleaver character, but I liked someone doing all that—cooking and cleaning, running errands. But it was more. I liked that Jeremy's head is so filled with imagination while mine spills over with reality. And now . . ."

"Now what?"

She sighs. "With Jeremy's latest setback, things have changed. I find myself avoiding him. I don't feel the sympathy I should. I . . ." She looks harder at me. "To be honest, when I talk to him, I'm starting to sound like you and Rob."

"Ouch!" I say, scrambling for something positive to note about Jeremy Detweiler. Before I can, Sasha continues to spill.

"It just hasn't been good for a while now. Not good at all, you know what I mean?"

I'm not sure if this is rhetorical, or if Sasha is looking for my take on rocky relationships. She clarifies by turning her troubles into a direct cross-examination. "I've just never been here before, Liv. Not like this." She focuses harder on me. "I suspect it gets obvious when two people just aren't suited for one another anymore, right? But it's probably an over-time realization. It's not one fight. Nothing makeup sex will fix."

Shower sex with Rob jumps to mind. While effective in the moment, sex will not cure what ails us. Of course, the sudden resurrection of Sam Nash won't either. My attention shuffles back to Sasha, who seems to be looking directly into my head.

"Is this how it goes when a relationship stops thriving and starts feeling like it's dying on the vine?"

"Are you asking me specifically?" I narrow my eyes.

She forces a smile. "Sorry. I, um . . . No. I meant generally speaking. It wasn't a dig at you and Rob. I wouldn't do that . . . You know that, right?"

I sigh and poke at my salad. Sarcasm is a welcome part of our friendship; direct stabs at open sores are not. That said, Sasha is struggling and I should be a better friend. I open my mouth in an effort to lend support. Then it clamps shut. I don't know that encouraging her is the right thing. Perhaps her relationship with Jeremy has run its course. As much as I don't like to see Sasha hurting, this may be something she'll have to get through. Like I told Theo, her breakup may lead to someone better. I take the middle of the road. "You're smarter than me at relationships, Sash. I'm sure you'll work it out, make the right choice."

She draws her phone to table level and glances at it. "Don't be so sure. I'm not beyond reproach. I'm as likely as the next person to make impulsive decisions when it comes to men." I offer a weak smile and imagine how much better I could make Sasha feel by admitting to a cheap make-out session in a parking garage.

I deviate. "So Theo, his mother is hosting a charity event on Friday at the Boston Public Library. I told you about it. I even managed to finagle a chamber ensemble to play pro bono for a couple of hours."

"Ah, see that. Your newfound benevolence is already expanding."

I make a face, but at least the remark is more on point. "The symphony only has a Saturday-night gig. I thought Rob and I would go. I'm curious to meet her . . . Claire. That's Theo's mother."

"Why?"

"Why what?" My sea greens–crammed fork is midway to my mouth. I shove it in and chew.

Bad decision. Allowing Sasha time to work the angles is never a good idea. It's why no one will play board games with her.

"What is it with this kid, Liv?" She's annoyed—that I have not fought the Jeremy cause on her behalf; that I've taken my Theo talk one sentence too far. "I don't get it."

I chew until my molars are chomping on nothing. "Get what?"

"Since you started at Braemore, every time we've talked, Theo McAdams has been your sole focus. First it's his classroom, his students . . . Then it's his incredible musical talent, your almost hand-wringing question if he's wasting his time as a music teacher when he should be pursuing a career more like yours. I swear when you said that you sounded like your father."

I dart back, dodging the comparison. "I did not either."

"The hell you didn't. It was like Asa Klein incarnate. And now you know the intimate details of what sounds like a rough breakup between Theo and this India."

"India, huh . . ." I bite down on my lip.

"India Church, whose parents own Take Me to Church Catering." Sasha has that *gotcha* tone, the witness she just tripped up on the stand. "Now you're anxious to meet his mother. You're way too interested, Liv. Fess up. What's going on?"

"Nothing," I insist. "I find Theo interesting—we've gotten friendly. Is that so difficult to understand?"

"For you?" Sasha cheers her wineglass toward me. "Quite frankly, yes."

"I don't think so. Musically, we have a lot in common—I can appreciate his talent. I'm sympathetic to Theo's past, the way his father died. In the present, we hit it off. We get along."

Instead of her cabernet, Sasha takes a drink of water. It strikes me as a head-clearing action. Her gaze pans the white tablecloth and crumbs, a drop of red wine stain. Then she looks directly at me and hauls in a breath that consumes her tiny frame. "Tell me the truth, Liv. Is there something more going on between you and Theo?"

"Something like what?"

She rolls her eyes. "I don't want to make accusations—but I know you. I also know . . . Without it sounding like a dig, I know things between you and Rob have been shaky since you came back from Italy last year."

"Not Italy, Sash. Just his first financial catastrophe—the one he didn't feel the need to mention until it was almost too late."

She nods in a consolatory gesture. "And certainly things haven't improved with this second monetary misstep."

"Not so much," I say, feeling a sudden loss of appetite.

"So I can see it. I can see how an attractive, vulnerable younger man, one who you clearly like—"

I widen my eyes at her twisted inference. "Whoa . . . Wait. Sasha, listen to me . . . It's not—" But I stop, bewildered as to how I will neatly fill in that blank. "There's nothing going on between Theo McAdams and me. I admit, I like him. Maybe more than most people. But I swear to you, there's nothing *romantic*."

"An affair can be a lot of things aside from romantic, Liv. It can be comfort, escape . . . even accidental in the right circumstance."

"Okay, but—"

"I know it sounds irrational, but sometimes affairs aren't even about sex. Or it doesn't start out that way. Sex is just where need ends up. One minute it's what seems like a straightforward relationship," she says, her hand darting at me. "And the next . . ."

Before I can respond, her phone rings.

"I have to take this . . . Hi." She tucks a piece of hair behind her ear and her gaze drops to her lap. "You're back." Noise rises around us, enough that she presses a finger to her ear. "Good. No, I ended up at dinner after all." Her tone sounds like confirmation that I have dragged Sasha to Neptune Oyster. "Could we talk about this later, after I get home?" Her glance drifts back to mine. I feel as if I am eavesdropping, and I busy myself with the sea greens and lobster. She ends the call abruptly and announces, "I have to go—tomorrow's case. But, Liv, about Theo . . ."

"I swear, Sash. You couldn't be more off the mark." *Theo's father, on the other hand* . . . I clear my throat and point to her phone. "The call. Did your last-minute evidence turn up?"

"Something like that." Sasha reaches for her purse, which is newer. This fall's Kate Spade line—a deep hobo bag that I warned her would be a bottomless pit when trying to retrieve her wallet or whatever.

I say not to worry about the bill. But in true Sasha form she's diligently conscientious. She digs for her wallet, discarding random bits of her life on the table: three lipsticks (I own one), hairbrush, checkbook, dry cleaning receipt—I didn't know we used the same dry cleaner. While I wait for the kite string and skate key, she plops a boarding pass, rubber-banded notebook, and a claim check stamped in a gold fleur-de-lis pattern, and a bag of peanuts. Finally she comes up with her wallet. She looks at the mess on the table and hurriedly scrapes it all back in before paying her share of the bill.

"Don't say I didn't warn you, Sash." Rising from the table, she looks startled. "The purse." I point. "When you insisted on it, I said important things would plunge right to the bottom, you'd lose them forever."

She grips onto the edge of the booth and offers a shaky smile. "I think you were probably right about that, Liv."

CHAPTER TWENTY-FOUR

Olivia

The brownstone is dimly lit. But I hear Rob's voice and I follow it, turning on lights as I go. A trail of talk and the smell of food leads to the kitchen. Upon seeing me, he quickly ends a call. "How was your trip?" A tofu hot dog is on the downdraft grill. I should have packed up the remains of Sasha's filet; he would have gratefully gobbled it down. He doesn't reply. "Rob?"

"Uh, not exactly what I was expecting in some ways . . . No great surprise in others."

"Could you be more cryptic? A little more information, if you don't mind." Rob concentrates on the grill. I wonder how long he can remain in iron-chef mode while roasting bean curd.

"I don't have a lot of positives to share, okay?" He continues to focus on fake tubular meat, applying grill marks meant to make it look appetizing. "What'd you do while I was gone?"

Turning away, I drop my purse onto the counter and flip through the mail. "Nothing much." I tap envelopes on the quartz edge. For a brief moment I consider telling Rob about my visit to Sam—less the kiss. I glance over my shoulder. I don't. It would only add tension, not alleviate it. I put the mail down. Damn, maybe I'm more concerned there wouldn't be any tension. *"Hell, Liv, you should have gone for it . . ."* I stay in the neutral zone. "Mostly rehearsal. Braemore was closed today. Don't forget we have that charity thing on Friday." He nods, retrieving a plate from the cabinet. "So are you going to tell me what did happen while you were in New York?"

"You mean about the house?"

I move my hands in a vague gesture. "Unless something of greater interest transpired?"

Abruptly he abandons his hot dog and decides to take out the garbage. I wait as he knots one Hefty bag and replaces it with another. Rob stalls until he is forced to return to the grill. "I haven't gotten the house issue resolved yet. I sought out some new investors. It didn't work out. It's late. Can we leave it at that?"

"No, Rob. We can't. I'd like to know if my future funding is really gone. If I'll need to go to this charity event prepared to do my own schmoozing. Maybe Claire McAdams has a tip sheet."

"I think you'd need more of a crash course."

"Precisely. The beauty of a no-brainer asset."

"Liv, I don't need another reminder." Irritation colors his voice. "Deals like this take time to finesse. You can't bully your way into getting people to loan you that kind of money."

I've steered clear of particulars long enough. "Exactly what kind of money are we talking about—the whole golf course deal. Bottom line?"

He shuts off the cooktop and transfers the hot dog onto a plate. Rob doesn't take his eyes off it, his hands planted firm on his waist. He glances in my direction and runs a hand through his dark hair. "Almost three million."

"Dollars?" I'm suddenly more sure why Rob is standing in the kitchen, cooking a tofu hot dog that is likely past its sell by date. No

wonder the Wellesley house is a load-bearing wall in his collateral package. "So it's the house . . . and more? That's what you need to raise?"

Rob does the brave thing and makes firm eye contact. "Yes. I'll have to liquidate some additional assets."

He's referring to smaller holdings, at least compared to the Wellesley house. Things he's rebuilt since his last financial debacle, stocks, maybe our retirement savings, which the Amati auction had previously spared. But the house, particularly ones like this, people stalk them, waiting for vintage Wellesley properties to come on the market. His creditors would snap it up and sell it in a heartbeat. I take a turn around the kitchen.

"I never thought it'd go this far, Liv. I've tried pooling other resources. It's just a lot of bad timing, cash that is tied up in investments I can't touch right now. My usual go-to sources . . . Well, they're—"

"Let me guess, not overly anxious to buy into whatever you're selling."

"Not fair, Liv. I've made far more money than I've lost. Solid returns for my clients—and for us." He splays his hands in front of him, noting the brownstone.

I shake my head. "Then could it be that this time, *after last time*, you're looking a little too high stakes? Maybe sounding a wee bit desperate?" He doesn't answer, abandoning his healthy meal for the drink on the counter. "What? No quick-witted comeback?" The crystal winces in his grip. He is quiet, staring at his Macallan, which he does not drink. But who knows how many he had before I showed up.

"While I was in New York, I went to see my father about the money."

Oh. Quite a few drinks, I imagine. The statement crystalizes the desperation meter. While Rob might discuss the New York Knicks, Grand Prix racing, and foreign markets with Robert Van Doren Senior, they do not talk about Rob's business ventures. He's unaware of his son's previous financial skid. His father never got over the insult of Rob's refusal to join his successful accounting firm. Honestly? I could see Rob's point. He would have languished in the minutia of book-balancing other people's trite money. He needs to be where the action is. The rift between father and son has been a sore spot since I've known them. From the time Rob decided to go into business for himself, his father has been waiting for an *I told you so* moment. I suspect he found one. "Your father. Sorry if that doesn't ease my mind."

"Thanks for the vote of confidence."

"Just imagining his reaction."

"Yeah. Not too difficult. Interesting. On my way home, I could only think of one thing that might have been more humiliating."

Neither of us needs to say it, though I do. "Confessing it to my father."

He snickers. "I'm sure the chair of the Tufts econ department would have had a field day with this." Rob's frustration hits tilt as he shoves the tofu hot dog and plate across the counter, where it careens into the backsplash. Italian pottery breaks into pieces; a wall tile cracks. "Hell, Asa Klein would be so appalled he'd probably insist you should have stuck with your first husband."

"Sadly," I say, knowing my father, "I can't disagree." I stare at the broken things on the counter. Rob's gaze cuts to mine. "I didn't mean it like that." I take a step toward him. "I wasn't talking about Sam, only that my father would be livid about the house."

"Either way, it's astonishingly convenient, isn't it? The prized athlete, good ole boy—loaded, no doubt—recently surfaces, and with a clean bill of health. What the fuck more could you ask for?"

Ashamed by the accuracy of Rob's angry ideas and a heated parking garage kiss, I look away. "I only meant the house," I repeat softly.

Rob reaches for his drink and downs a vile swig. He puts down the glass and focuses on melting ice, maybe our melting marriage. "Right. Anyway, be aware, Liv. I don't know if I can fix this. I honest to God don't know what else to do."

"How much time until . . ."

"Until the house is lost for good?" I nod. "About sixty days." He takes another sip of his drink. "Part of my New York trip was to negotiate an extension." He smiles a cunning Rob Van Doren smile, a weighty asset that was once the smallest part of what had awed me. Now it just looks . . . fraught. "I didn't secure that either. So short of a monetary miracle . . ."

I glance around the stylish brownstone. "Great. At least I know what to get my mother for Christmas."

"And that would be?"

"A key to our house." The moment I say it, I realize how badly the sarcasm misses.

"Touché, Liv." Rob cheers his glass toward me and brushes past, disappearing into the basement.

Seconds later I startle at the sound of glass shattering. There's an exposed brick wall at the bottom of the stairs; I suspect the last of the Waterford just met with it. I am rushed by a wave of sympathy. Last time Rob fucked up, it didn't come with such an explosive level of guilt.

Years ago, when I added his name to the Wellesley deed, it was so much more than what I said to Sasha—a reciprocal gesture for buying his bride a brownstone. I was making a statement: the benevolent venture of funding the orchestra belonged as much to me as it did to Rob. I know he felt equal satisfaction; we'd done something good. Something noble—particularly noble for two people who wouldn't ordinarily be defined this way. *"Do you know the Van Dorens?" "Why yes, lovely couple, so generous and charitable . . ."* It's not what people say about us. For me, it wasn't necessary that they did. It still isn't, but that's not to say it didn't feel good. *Noble.* It's a word more suited for someone like Claire McAdams.

Poised at the top of the basement stairs, I almost go down and assure Rob the house issue will resolve itself. What is it people say when faced by irksome tragedy? *"It's only a car . . . a house . . . it's just money . . . meaningless stuff."* My mother has assets and options. In reality, she probably wants to live in my spare bedroom as much as I want her there. It's the orchestra funding that's widening this smear of bad blood between Rob and me. We both feel it, an already shaky marriage strained to its breaking point. Overwhelmed by all of it, too burdened by the past and future, I give up on the present and head to the bedroom.

Routine is comforting; I take to my nighttime ritual like a bow to strings—favorite nightgown, the umpteenth book I've started at my bedside, face cream that costs $90 an ounce. It promises to revitalize a youthful glow. It's fitting; the falsehoods in my life continue. Seated at the vanity, I stare into my eyes, paler blue than Rob's. Once my best feature, they are now sinking into the sockets, outlined by years of cynical squinting. I rub equally pricey cream into my hands, which present no better picture. Fingertips that are permanently ribbed, and I see another age spot to be counted. It peeks up from between my thumb and index finger. While playing, I'm provided with a permanent, up-close view.

On the bathroom counter is Rob's travel bag. I know what's inside: shaving gear, man moisturizer the aesthetician who does his facial peels talks him into, his toothbrush. I abandon my routine and decide to put his personal items away. Rob will notice when he comes upstairs, a subtle peace offering for what happened downstairs. Unzipping the leather case, I withdraw the expected belongings, picking out a travel-size bottle of cologne. I gave it to him for Christmas—a suggestive manly sexy scent that Rob wears particularly well.

A sniff takes me back more than a year. It was a time exceedingly less complicated than this one, or so I thought. I was on a week-long symphony break and Rob insisted on a spur-of-the-moment trip to Italy. Who does that? I thought we did and the two of us went, forgetting the rest of the world. While abroad we had the most exquisite time. Even now, the cologne seems like a sign, a happier, more believable us. Two days after we returned, instead of a gondola in Venice, I found myself aboard Rob's quickly sinking financial barge. I don't subscribe to whimsy, like finding lucky pennies or the meaning of butterflies. But I allow for a touch of that now, breathing in the positives the cologne still elicits. For a good long while, Rob and I, we got this right.

I stay on task, standing over the travel case and digging for his toothbrush, groping at spare change he tends to toss in. I come up with a cotton shoe shine cloth. It is marked *The Bed, Manhattan's Most Exquisite Small Luxury.* I'm about to toss it into the trash, but instead lay it out flat on the marble counter. The sexy tagline is complemented by a gold fleur-de-lis. I stare at it, feeling a wallop of déjà vu. I can't place it. Then I do—the claim check from Sasha's hobo bag. My butt hits the vanity chair with a heart-rattling thump.

The past few hours, maybe days, rush like an express train through my head—Sasha's vague demeanor, and the phone she kept tucked beside her, out of sight. Her odd behavior during dinner and her quick exit before it was even over. I blink into the mirror. A queasy feeling that I haven't experienced since my first hint of Theo weaves through my stomach.

It's ridiculous.

I look away from the mirror. Then I look back. *Is it?*

Recent memories propagate—Rob and Sasha's impromptu lunch. *But it was hardly their plan. They didn't know I wouldn't be home . . . It wasn't their lie being perpetuated while I was out bonding with Theo . . .* I pay no heed to wild imagination. I put back the shoe shine cloth and scrape the spare change back into the bag. But the action jars another fact that spilled from the hobo bag. Among Sasha's lipsticks and personal items was a boarding pass. I didn't see the date or destination. But I can't recall a recent trip she's made, one where a boarding pass would end up in a purse she's owned for little more than a month. An innocent call from last Sunday rolls through my head, so does tonight's. Both times Rob was talking on the house phone, definitely with Sasha the first time. A call to the house phone wouldn't look out of place, not like a call to his cell phone. Come to think of it, other than last Sunday, I can't remember the last time Sasha called on the house phone.

I hear Rob come into the bedroom and quickly shove the rest of his belongings back into the case. As he comes into the bathroom, I dart from the vanity bench. He puts his arm across the door, blocking my way. "No matter what happens with the house, Liv, I think we need to talk about some things."

I don't look at him; the accusation would slip too easily from my mouth. I can't believe it's true. I don't want to know. Like a game of limbo, I duck under Rob's arm. He doesn't turn but enters the bathroom and slams the door. I shuffle across the bedroom floor. *Houses.* The brownstone and the Wellesley properties are in both our names. It would be a cleaner, more amicable split if Rob were to simply remove himself from the Wellesley deed, giving me sole ownership. It would also give me somewhere to live—*immediately.* It would be an even divide of assets. In a jumbled haze, I plunge my arms into a heavy robe. It does nothing to warm the chilly air surrounding me. What if Rob's sudden remorse is really a mad dash to the exit? It matches his style, maybe more so than anonymous charitable endeavors.

At the window, I take a few deep breaths. The glass fogs and clears. I need to do the same thing with my mind. This is absurd. I watch a man walk by with his dog; another man jogs past wearing reflective clothing. I wonder what they will go home to—warm beds and trusted lovers? I glance over my shoulder. The shower is running. My head tips against the cool glass as the most telling memory surfaces. It's not about a brownstone or a mini estate tucked into a prestigious Wellesley neighborhood. It's not from last week or even the past few hours. It's a conversation with Sasha from seven years ago.

"Liv, just meet Rob for coffee."

"Why? He's your castoff date. What do I want with him?"

"I don't know, maybe nothing . . . To me, he just had a strong Liv vibe—quick witted, good looking, Teflon coated."

"Thanks so much."

"You know what I mean. He seems sort of indestructible, like a Rock 'Em, Sock 'Em Robot, but way sexier."

"So why aren't you interested?"

"Because when I kissed him he didn't turn into my prince."

"Great. Make that your used *castoff date."*

"Oh, come on, Liv. It was a kiss. Nothing more, I swear . . . I did consider it; then I thought of the greater good that could be served if I passed. What do you say?"

"I say if you're this high on him, maybe you should think about it a little more."

Maybe Sasha should have.

Maybe she did.

I cover my mouth with my hand. Maybe I've busted my Rock 'Em, Sock 'Em Robot and I am the center ring cliché: a wife whose husband is cheating with her best friend. I hear the bathroom door open; Rob flips off his bedside lamp. I listen as he punches the pillow. His body falls so hard into the mattress I feel the vibration ten feet away. I turn and look at him in the moonlight. What I see is Sasha's flawless sexy frame—the one that seems ageless—lying beside him. She is wearing a puddle of silky nightgown. Rob would like that so much more than tarty, lacy scabs of red lace. So would Sasha. I'm absolutely sure of it.

CHAPTER TWENTY-FIVE

Theo

Theo has spent time thinking about how he will get through his mother's Boston Public Library gala. Perhaps he will find a remote corner and get lost in a book. It seems like the safest alternative. When India first left him, his mother was all for canceling her contract with Take Me to Church Catering. "Theo, forget the cost . . . I'll find another caterer. I was merely doing India a favor by hiring her parents' company. If it saves you any pain, I'll gladly do it." She meant it. His mother would fire Take Me to Church Catering and move her fundraiser to Toledo if it benefited Theo. He appreciated the thought. He would never do it. Besides, the Church's contract is not with Claire, but the charitable board on which she sits. It would be beyond embarrassing to have his mother intervene on behalf of her son's broken heart. Theo insisted she let it go. He also doesn't want to be the thing that comes between Brown Bag Dollars, his mother's slogan name for the event, and success.

He prepares for the evening at his boyhood home in Newton, aware that he may have to face Daisy and Charlie Church, India's parents. He may even encounter Helen, who they employ in a less visible capacity. But it's unlikely India will be present. While she may have dumped Theo, she is not cruel. Unless India proves to be someone he didn't know at all, Theo is certain she will not be there. At least this is what he hopes.

Standing in front of his father's dresser mirror, Theo rips at a crooked bowtie. He does not hope this at all. In fact, he's spent all week wagering that if his mother's expectations are on par, the event may demand India's presence. Before they broke up, the theme and dining portion of Brown Bag Dollars was in India's hands. The committee has dedicated the bulk of its annual fundraising budget for this one of a kind night. It's imperative that it be a success. Theo wonders if this can be accomplished without India.

His mother has hired a limo for the evening, and Theo's agreed to ride with her. After she's helped him with the tie, Claire asks once more if he would prefer to stay home. She's more than capable of making his excuses. Theo considers it. He declines for three reasons: His father did not raise him to hide from uncomfortable circumstance. Secondly, he's not five; Theo is man enough to face unpleasantness. Lastly, a small part of his brain will not let go of hope. What if he did hear regret in his phone call with India? Maybe tonight is the chance for a different outcome. As they get into the limo, Theo recalls the last time he and his mother did this. He wonders if she is thinking the same. They rode in a limo to a packed memorial service for his father, where there was nothing to bury. Theo climbs into the limo wondering if any passenger gets into such a vehicle destined for normalcy.

Halfway through the ride Claire breaks the silence. "Theo, you can always leave. You know that, right?"

While his mother hasn't spoken India's name all week, they both know to what she is referring. "I'll be fine, Mom." He smiles in her direction. She cannot help herself, raising pink painted fingernails and brushing them through his wavy brown hair. While it's not really possible, Theo is certain that Claire sees his father when this gesture occurs. She confirms as much. "He'd be so very proud of you."

"He wouldn't have lost the girl in the first place."

"Ah, so she's still on your mind." Claire smiles sympathetically. "Theo, what makes you think I was your father's one and only dream girl? Perhaps there was someone before me. Someone he was madly in love with."

"I was only ten, but I remember. The way he looked at you."

"Maybe you don't remember everything."

Theo is unsure if his mother has just admitted to being the second love of David McAdams's life—something that has never crossed his mind—or if she's trying to make a point. Maybe, prior to his mother, there was a girl David McAdams loved. Theo cannot fathom it. But if so, her innuendo should give him a different perspective. It appears to be the exact point Olivia tried to make when she went on about an ex-husband. Of course, his mother has done a better job, especially since she turned out to be the love of his father's life.

A short time later, Theo looks toward the approaching lights of the Boston Public Library. The stately Copley Square site has been transformed. It looks, indeed, as if his mother has outdone herself. A Hollywood red carpet event has dropped into the middle of Boston. Some people will view tonight as the upper crust deigning to do their part for the masses. But Theo knows they will also come with fat checkbooks and worthwhile connections. Boston Public Schools will benefit greatly. Claire knows what she is doing. His mother always has a plan. As Theo escorts her inside, he is proud to have his mother on his arm. Local press and TV news crews are on hand. In the giant marble entry, a reporter shouts Claire's name. She turns and smiles. "Shep—how good of you to come!"

Theo stops dead. He has never spoken to Shep Stewart. He doesn't want to start tonight. Animosity bubbles. Theo keeps forward motion moving, heading toward the grand staircase. But since his mother's arm is looped through his, he has little choice but to follow when she glides in Shep Stewart's direction.

"So this is the famous Theo," Shep says. Theo is certain that "famous" achieved by way of his dead father is the last thing he wants to be. Shep extends a hand. "Great to finally meet the flesh-and-blood man. Kind of feels like I've been writing about a ghost for the past fifteen years, you know?"

Theo doesn't shake Shep's hand. "To do that, you'd have to interview my father. Try that one. Excuse me." He unloops his arm from his mother's and heads toward the staircase.

She is not far behind. "Theo!" He turns. "That was incredibly rude. The man was just anxious to finally meet you. There was no reason to be so sharp with him. He's just doing his job."

"And the only reason he has his bottom-feeding job is because you continue to supply him with annual updates. Not my choice, remember?" Claire rises to the next step up so she is looking down at Theo. She glances past his head. She seems suddenly, acutely, aware of the throngs of event-goers flooding in.

She smiles at him and moves to the base of the steps, where they are not on display. Theo is obliged to follow. His mother looks very regal in her blond updo and navy gown, though her nostrils are flaring. She speaks in a softer but no less irritated tone. "If this is any indication of how you plan on behaving, perhaps it would be best if you left now. I have a lot riding on this event."

Theo feels like he's twelve and thinks if Brown Bag Dollars were taking place in his mother's living room, he'd be sent to bed before the main course is served. Before he can recover, a voice interrupts. It sounds leery, as if it has been listening.

"Theo, this must be your mother." A hand extends, reaching toward her. "I'm Olivia Klein. Maybe Theo's mentioned me?" This is the most forward behavior he's ever seen from Olivia. Her nervous smile and abrupt entrance is fidgety, quirkier than usual.

Like blades over ice, his mother's expression skates deftly toward amicable. She smiles widely. "Of course, you're with the New England Symphony. You're assisting Theo in his classroom."

Theo hasn't mentioned that Olivia has landed in his classroom because of her community service hours. It isn't Claire's business. He's aware, however, that Olivia's made a much better pre–first impression by appearing philanthropic, like his mother. Olivia further impressed his mother after offering, via Theo, to secure a chamber orchestra to play for the first hour. As Claire's hand meets Olivia's grip, Theo is struck by the contrast—his mother's hand is delicate and refined, meant for turning book pages and touching his hair to brush back pain. Olivia's grip, he knows, is firm, her fingers rough and permanently ridged. All of her is talented in a way that feels sublimely natural to him, something to which he connects. It occurs to Theo that together, each woman's strengths—while vastly different—complement the other.

A man clears his throat. Only after Olivia looks over her shoulder does she release his mother's hand and gaze. "I'm Rob. Liv's husband," the man says. The introduction seems to ground Olivia, who repeats what he has just offered. He looks much like what Theo expected, a good fit for Olivia. He stands just to her side, partially behind her, as if she is on display and he is there to make certain all goes well. Theo can tell that his mother finds him attractive. Her head tips to the left and her conversation continues beyond cursory introductions, though it's mostly directed at Olivia's husband. She points toward the staircase, inviting them up to Bates Hall. She takes Rob by the arm.

Theo offers his to Olivia and says, "Thank you for coming."

"I wouldn't have dreamed of missing it." Her eyes are on the back of Claire's head, though a sideways glance cuts to Theo. Her expression is mischievous. Then it fades. "Although, for a second, I thought I might have to come alone."

"Why's that?" They make the wide turn on the marble staircase and head toward the grand room India secured. Olivia breathes deep and glances at him, taking in his tuxedo-covered appearance. "Rough week at home. Nothing you need to worry about."

"Sorry to hear that." Theo is disappointed at the blip of information. He's stuck on his first impression, and he wants it to be true. Rob is the love of Olivia's life, the one she never would have met if she'd stayed with her first husband—some baseball player with the scruples of an alley cat. He sighs, aware that he's only relating Olivia's personal history to his own. Otherwise, Theo wouldn't think twice about Olivia's personal life, this husband, or her last.

At the entrance to Bates Hall, Theo's gaze travels the vast room. Early last spring he accompanied India to the Boston Public Library, where she insisted on its grand room. India was inspired as they walked through the hall with its majestic barrel ceiling and arched grilled windows. "Vintage—we'll do an Edwardian-era gala and curate period books, original manuscripts for display! The library is the perfect setting. Oh, Theo, your mother will be so pleased!"

She was. Claire was over the moon about India's idea. She thought it was brilliant. The grand historic framework is the perfect canvas, just as India had envisioned. A waiter, wearing early-twentieth-century manor house garb bows gracefully, offering flutes of champagne. Theo hands one to Olivia and takes one for himself.

It appears Take Me to Church Catering has outdone itself with period décor supplied by a theater company. The event's theme is highlighted by the glass-encased original works of Dickens, Lewis Carroll, the Brownings—Elizabeth and Robert—in addition to Mark Twain and Thoreau. India was in the midst of curating the on-loan literary treasures when she left Theo.

The air fills with the smell of hors d'oeuvres. India had partially planned the menu, choices that mirrored Edwardian delicacies. Although she did tell Theo that for the sake of authenticity, and in deference to the have-nots the event is meant to benefit, boiled potatoes and stale bread should also be served. India shared this in private after Claire insisted that gamier fare like rabbit and trout be avoided—"Seriously, Theo, the idea is to entice people into writing five- and six-digit checks, after paying $500 for a ticket. You cannot feed them gruel." He supposes his mother had a point, and Theo sees that India has obeyed. Trays of mini tarts, lollypop lamb chops, and oysters on the half shell are being circulated.

"Theo, is, um . . . is she here?"

By asking the question, Olivia has read his mind. But the room is packed and it is impossible to tell at glance. If India is here, chances are she's wherever the food staging area is located. He does, however, spot Helen, who is talking to a waiter. Theo points with his still-full champagne glass. If there is any chance of seeing India, the last thing he wants to be is drunk. "That's India sister."

"The one with the drug problem?"

Theo does not like to define Helen by her addiction, but it's true enough. Besides, if there is one thing he's learned about Olivia, she does not sugar coat. "Yes. Helen. She looks good." Theo squints. "Very good, in fact." Theo and Olivia look in Helen's direction just as she looks back. Awkwardness washes through like spilled Edwardian-era punch. India's sister quickly turns away and disappears into the crowd. "They don't favor each other much."

"The way they look?" Olivia asks.

Theo remembers telling her about India's red hair. Helen's is a dull shade of brown, her years of drug use making her frame, which is inches taller than India's, look like a wilted flower, the bloom hanging on for dear life.

"Everything about them, really."

Olivia nods. "Your mother seems . . . lovely."

The sight of Helen has pummeled Theo's ability to navigate pleasantries. He imagines what running into India will do. He would excuse himself if he were talking to anyone other than Olivia. But she has an uncanny ability to dial into Theo, to know if she should say something or just shut up. "My mother's in her element. It'll be brilliantly successful. Something her social circle will gush on about for the next year. It's all that matters." Theo changes his mind about this one glass of champagne and guzzles it. When he looks back, Olivia's blue eyes are staring wide into his. "Sorry. My mother is doing a very good thing here tonight. I didn't mean to sound so cynical."

"It's not that." She's still staring. It's almost trancelike. Olivia shakes her head and closes her eyes for a moment. "You could have been describing my mother. That and you sounded so . . . *like me.*" She looks away and downs her champagne faster than Theo did his.

CHAPTER TWENTY-SIX

Olivia

It's difficult not to be further impressed by Claire McAdams. Between her son and her event, I wonder how flawless one woman can be. I observe Claire from a distance. She exudes all the confidence I lack. She glides from guest to guest, appearing to have something meaningful to say to each one. It's an annual battle with Rob to avoid a holiday party of twenty at the brownstone. My aptitude for party planning and small talk would max out in an elevator.

Rob and I manage to avoid each other much of the evening, which mirrors the past few days. He took a business trip to Denver and was gone overnight. I thought it within reason to see if Sasha was traveling too. A call to her office and a quick chat with Carly, the receptionist, confirmed Sasha's busy court calendar. Carly asked if I wanted to leave a message, but I said "Don't bother" and ended the call abruptly.

Since then, I have ignored the two messages from Sasha. Neither call was made to the house phone. I don't know what I might say to her, or if I should say anything at all. I did spend a solid chunk of time talking myself down. If Rob were going to cheat, he'd at least have the courtesy to do it with a stranger.

Yet, the inexplicable gnaws at me. Rob plainly stated, before leaving for New York, that this was his first stay at a boutique hotel—so the shoe shine cloth couldn't be from a previous trip. In an effort to explain evidence that Sasha might label circumstantial, I went as far as to concoct a theory by which another woman previously purchased the hobo bag. Then she returned it after one use and one visit to New York where she stayed at The Bed. It's only coincidence that Sasha then bought the returned purse.

I keep turning it over in my mind, the reasons our marriage has deteriorated. There are Rob's money misadventures. There are my imperfections—idiosyncrasies and issues more deeply seated. Any of them would fit fine on an analyst's couch, not so much in a marriage. But then another point occurred to me, new logic why lifestyles, vacations, and common goals like music endowments aren't enough to sustain a marriage. Late one night, I Googled statistics on childless couples, curious if the percentage of failed marriages is higher. It's not something I thought about before walking into Theo's life.

Sadly, the facts were not in our favor. Apparently the absence of children can lead to a disconnect, making it markedly easier to walk away. I took our marriage woes one step further: Is it unbelievable that Rob would have an affair? A year ago—yes. But now? Not entirely. It could be that a lack of children was only one less roadblock to an affair.

It's Sasha's motive that's less explainable, and the safer hope to which I have clung. Sasha's been my champion in life and in court. She practically threw Rob at my feet. My happiness has always made her happy. But it's not Sasha's behavior that I ultimately question. It's mine. In our relationship, have I been too much of a taker? Perhaps Sasha concluded that she and Rob have suffered enough.

With an unsure breath, I take another flute of passing champagne. I face the crowd. Rob works the room. He knows a number of people in attendance. If he makes the right connection and ends up saving the Wellesley house, Claire's event may benefit Boston Public Schools in ways she'll never know. The clock is ticking. Barring a miracle, the house will be lost, my future music program funding gone. Assuming she does not want take an extended holiday in New Zealand, my mother will be mine. Sipping champagne, I turn back to Rob. He is talking to a state senator—varying degrees of handshaking and backslapping are traded. But Rob stops his conversation abruptly to look at his phone, which must be ringing. I assume it's an important call because he whirls away from the senator to answer. In the swarm of noise, he plugs one ear with his finger. He keeps moving, heading toward the marble-clad hallway and exit.

I turn the other way, but Theo's disappeared too. The chamber orchestra members, the only other people I know, are busy playing. I glance in their direction, slightly surprised they accommodated my request. I don't do favors like this, so I don't ask for them. But Mary Alice Porter is popular with fellow orchestra mates, and I suppose being a good stand partner has earned some benefits. In the name of charity, she commandeered her friends to play.

India's sister, Helen, catches my eye. She's alone in a corner, observing the festivities. Her antsy demeanor is evident—a leftover from her drug-addicted days, or maybe she's currently high. Out of curiosity, I make my way over. "Take Me to Church Catering has put together a lovely event."

"You think?" She looks permanently tired, like something more taxing than this evening has taken a toll. Sunken eye sockets rimmed in too much black eyeliner or dark circles—could be one is meant to blend with the other in a punk rocker way. Helen's tall frame is missing about ten pounds, making her cheekbones jut out; it's more of an ill appearance than super model. If Theo thinks she looks good now, I wonder how bad she looked before. She's wearing a simple black dress, one that someone probably insisted on, the kind that makes you blend.

"Mrs. McAdams was determined to get everything she wanted tonight. She won—*everything*." Her gaze flicks around the room like there's a bee buzzing through. It stops on Theo.

"The Churches, you're their daughter, right?"

In Helen's peripheral glance there is a distinct attitude of *"Why the fuck should I talk to you?"*

I can respect that; it's even relatable. I've often used it on music teachers and my mother. "I'm not the daughter people usually think of, but yeah."

"So India's your sister."

Her expression reflects the idiotic remark. "Why? Do you know India?"

"No. But I know her ex-fiancé, Theo McAdams."

Helen's sideways gaze turns steadily onto me. I have said something very wrong. "Don't tell me you're fucking Theo?" She takes an appalled step back. I do the same. But she comes right back at me, devouring personal space. "Am I supposed to send that message back to India? Their breakup isn't enough?" She snorts indignantly. "Don't count on it."

A loyal drug addict. How fascinating. Helen makes my usual candor feel like a feather duster. "Uh, hardly," I say, clearing my throat. "We're just friends. I'm doing required community service hours at Braemore, in his classroom."

Helen appears intrigued. "You've been arrested?"

"Yes. Even did a little time. The community service hours are how Theo and I met." Helen looks me over, my gray beaded gown not fitting with the confession. Yet my admitted break from society evokes solidarity. "Theo's confided to me about him and India . . . their breakup. I feel very bad for him . . . *them*. I was wondering if she's here tonight."

"Here?" Helen's deep-socketed eyes spring wide. "Uh, no. Look, my sister is tough and giving and she'd do anything for me. But she's no masochist."

"And why would being here make India a masochist? The way I understand it, she broke up with Theo. I get it if she felt her presence here would cause Theo more upset, but . . ."

Helen reaches into her pocket and pulls out a pack of cigarettes. "Look, I need a smoke. Can't do that in here. I don't know what your interest is in Theo and India, but filling in your blanks isn't my problem—or your business."

She starts to walk away. I go for it. "One more question—a really giant one that isn't my business either. But I only want to help." Helen turns back; she's annoyed but listening. "Is it true? Did India leave Theo because she ran into an old boyfriend, because she kissed him and became wildly unsure about marrying Theo?"

"India did run into Tom. She kissed him; it's true. Surprised me. I'm the one who's supposed to fuck up in this family." Helen's gaze pans the pristine event. "But mistakes aren't allowed when it comes to Theo—even by someone as good as India."

Helen and her cryptic reply vanish through a door. As she does, a man cozies up to the tiered tray of pastries displayed beside us. "That girl is a piece of work," he says.

"You know Helen Church?"

"I know *of* her. Didn't catch your conversation, but I caught her attitude." His gaze travels my formfitting gown. In turn, he is one of a handful of men in the room not wearing a tuxedo. He extends a hand. "Shep Stewart."

Jackpot . . .

"Olivia . . . Van Doren." My grip and gaze hang on to his. "Did you say Shep Stewart, as in the *Boston Ledger* reporter?"

His roundish face lights like a bulb. "Do you know me?"

"I know your work. Who doesn't?" I edge closer. Helen's instinct was to tell me to fuck off. Shep may be more forthcoming. I clung to his articles out of an aching curiosity. The fascination they arouse in most readers is herd mentality. Shep is the leader of the herd. Surely he'd enjoy expounding to one of his followers. "I'm a fan," I say, smiling flirtatiously, in a way I haven't since high school. "I'm also a violinist with the New England Symphony." He nods at the instant integrity *symphony violinist* elicits. It will get you a dinner reservation at Mistral and give you street credit with people like reporters. "Actually, it's your 9-11 stories I recall most vividly. They're riveting." He beams; I've plucked the right string. "I, um . . . I *volunteer* at Braemore. I didn't realize Theo was one of them . . . your 9-11 kids, until I ended up in his classroom." This fib will put me in Claire's league, one of the many do-gooders in Bates Hall. "In addition to playing, I've always wanted to teach."

"Commendable, wanting to mentor young minds." Shep shifts the topic back to himself. "Yeah. Those stories have been my bread and butter, assured me a place at the table. *Ledger* sales jump forty percent every year on 9-11." He grabs a mini meringue tart off the display. "Uh, of course the tragedy itself . . . Well, awful, goes without saying." He shoves a tart in his mouth, dabbing a napkin at a bit of runaway cream left at the corner.

"Yes. Absolutely . . . of course." If smarmy has a carbon footprint, I believe Shep's covers a chunk of Earth, at the very least New England. "What a complex and interesting experience, your stories. You must have developed an intimate rapport with the children . . . their parents over . . . How many years is it?"

"Next year would be seventeen. And definitely." He points to Claire. "None better than her. When the kids became adults they took over the annual interview. Kind of made young Theo different, kept him at a distance."

"That's right. He may have said something about his mother being his go-between."

"Mmm . . . more than that. I'd go as far to say that I've become Claire's confidant, maybe her annual source for venting." He pauses and looks me over. "And you? Do you know the McAdamses well?"

I play this tightly. He is not asking out of polite interest. "I only met Mrs. McAdams this evening. I don't know her at all."

"Yet you know Helen Church."

"No, not her either. Just Theo." Shep is intrigued because, really, he doesn't know Theo at all. I enhance my innocent bystander role by grabbing a salmon puff from a passing tray, showing more interest in it than the conversation. "Just some friendly facts I learned from Theo—gossip at his school. You know. Bad habit of mine." I chew. He assesses.

"So is it the sensationalism of my chronicle that you find *riveting*?" He snatches up a berry-covered mini tart and waves his arm at the crowd. A berry or two tumbles off.

"Oh, not at all. Not on the whole. I mean, who wouldn't be drawn in to the tragedy and triumph of your stories. But it's the content that's so compelling. You're a magnificent writer." Actually, Shep's writing strikes me as hackneyed: repetitive introductory clauses, an overuse of superlatives, trite *see ya next year* conclusions. "After meeting Theo, eventually he mentioned his broken engagement. We've gotten chummy. Naturally, I was even more moved. It was such a shame to hear. Theo's an outstanding young man." I press my hand to my heart. "His mother must be so proud. Did you say you're friendly with her?"

"Definitely on a first-name basis with Mrs. McAdams," he says, noting that I am not. I smile warmly and wait. "You didn't read about the broken engagement because Mom makes certain readers only get the upbeat, positive points of Theo's year."

"Oh yes, understandable. But it must require such wisdom on your part—knowing what to print, what to keep private."

"Part of being an ace reporter is rapport." He wallows in his prowess. "I'd say there isn't anything in Claire's life, or the kid's"—he points to Theo—"that I don't know . . . On, *or off*, the record."

"I see . . . Like maybe the nitty-gritty details of her son's breakup."

"Maybe," he says.

"I'm impressed." I back off the topic but ease so close to Shep I'm sure he can smell my perfume. He's one of a handful of media people permitted access tonight. Claire has great trust in him, the kind one-sided listening and years of preening will earn—it's like having a lady's maid. "So there's more to the story about Theo's breakup? Come on, Shep, entertain me! This event," I say, nudging a shoulder at the crowd, "while incredibly elegant, is kind of . . ." I wriggle my nose at him. "Boring. Wouldn't you say?"

He doesn't disagree. "The engagement fiasco is all water under the bridge, so . . ." He looks toward Claire, who is out of earshot. "During our interview two years ago, Claire—off the record—shared that she'd learned the particulars of the hooked-on-drugs sister, Helen. It wasn't sitting too good with Theo's mom."

"In what way? As far as I know, India and Helen weren't sharing needles." I listen harder, wondering if I've misjudged Theo's fairy-tale version of his beloved India. Maybe it's Claire who's seen the harsh truths. "I thought the ex-fiancée's life was the opposite of her sister's?"

"Sure. For now." Shep licks sticky spots of meringue from his thick fingers. My grossed-out stare is averted by his next fact. "But then India went and kissed the old boyfriend." He makes a sucking sound as his mouth disconnects with his thumb. "Claire caught her red-handed."

"Excuse me?"

"Yeah. Apparently it happened at some swanky book-slash-martini bar Claire frequents when she's in New York, meeting with her 'literary types.'" He throws finger quotes in the air, his animosity for other "writer types" evident.

"How devastating . . ."

"For Claire or for India?"

I stay right on point. "Claire, of course."

"It was the meringue on Claire's cake," Shep says, scooping up yet another mini pastry. "Based on India's family history, she was already leery of the girl."

"I'm not sure I follow. Why does India's family history matter?"

And since telling stories is what Shep does, he settles into this one. "It might be a stretch for some, but . . ." Shep looks toward Claire's captivating frame; she is the centerpiece in a room filled with priceless objects. "Between India's bad move with the old boyfriend, Helen's drug use, and the rest of the family skeletons . . . I'm pretty sure Claire decided Theo could do better."

"What family skeletons?"

"Nothing horrific . . . Not unless you view the world through Claire McAdams's eyes. From the start, she was concerned about the Church family. Did you know Daisy Church is a recovering alcoholic?" I shake my head no. "Yeah. The daughters were younger, so it's not something the Churches dwell on. But Claire found out about it, along with a history of depression. Somewhere between Helen and India, Daisy tried to kill herself."

"My heavens. That is quite a story."

"And one Claire would never confide to her fellow committee members or these people." He cocks his chins at a room where no one knows another person's private business, particularly suicidal tendencies.

"But what you said about India's mother. It's old news."

"Ancient history, until you get to Helen."

"I get it. Addiction on the whole can be intrinsic."

"Righto." Shep tips his head back and forth. "Between that and India's indiscretion, it was enough to justify Mrs. McAdams's caution when it comes to her son—at least in her own mind."

"Theo seems capable of smart choices. You have to give him credit for that."

"Maybe. Or it could be that she takes the credit, and sees it as necessary to oversee the balance of his life." Shep leans close, as if we're exchanging dark alley information. "Did you know Theo was adopted?"

"Is he?" Shep and I are so close now that if Rob glances over he may think we're having an affair. "Goodness. But, um . . . didn't the stigma of adoption go out ages ago, like forcing lefties to be righties because it's a sign of the devil?"

"Claire's never dissed adoption directly, but I also happen to know it was David McAdams who pushed for that. When Theo's father passed, her concerns became more acute. When the kid was ten and fifteen, I got her caution. Boys do stupid stuff. Ones without fathers can do even dumber things. Those that come with unknown DNA require a scrupulous eye—at least that was Claire's take. In those formative years, she felt the pressure of raising a kid herself."

"Seems like she did a good job. So what is she still guarding against?"

"Theo being adopted was off the table in terms of my stories. I knew better than to test that boundary. But Claire's always been concerned about his *biological origins*. She knows very little about Theo's background."

I nod deeply. "What, exactly, has her so concerned?

"Anything beyond her control," he says matter-of-factly. "For example, is Theo the product of two scientific geniuses who weren't interested in being parents, or is his biological father a rapist?"

I do an excellent job of suppressing the urge to slap Shep Stewart. "That's a wide-ranging scale. Maybe Theo's biological parents were just two college-age kids, too young to raise a child."

"Maybe. But there are endless combinations in between. Claire's always been concerned about wild-card influences, things she can't control."

"So in her mind, it's always been about nature versus nurture. She is determined to be the stronger force."

"Yeah. But don't get me wrong. Claire feels like she hit the jackpot when it comes to the kid. She adores him." He gestures in Theo's direction. "He's proven that wherever he comes from, the gene pool was pretty potent—Cornell, lacrosse champ, musical prodigy."

"Proclivity," I correct.

"Excuse me?"

"Theo's musical talent, it's a proclivity. *Prodigy* is a pedestrian interpretation of aptitude and hard work. His musicality is a proclivity."

"Sure," Shep says as if he's learned a new word. "Whatever. Anyway, Theo's roots were always a concern for Claire, less so once Theo proved himself. But then he hooks up with somebody whose gene pool has an obvious shallow end."

"I see. The genes and demons that run through Helen, and Helen and India's mother—India might succumb herself, or worse, she could be a carrier."

"Now you're catching on."

"My, that is a lot for Claire to try and . . . *oversee*."

He smiles. "You mean control."

"Either way, brava to Claire for doing her part, making sure Theo and his future offspring dodged a bullet, staved off a possible lifetime of hardships, risky behaviors."

Shep thinks I am referring to the Church family genes. Hardly. I look toward Theo, who is by his mother's side. How lucky for Theo that he did not inherit Sam's never-ending thirst for Jack Daniel's and a good time, or our mutual proclivity for making bad decisions. Even more unnerving, what if Theo had inherited my specific list of questionable qualities? Imagine if Claire's son had my picked-last-in-gym-class coordination or terminally smart mouth. How incredibly fortunate for Theo that he chose wisely from the grab bag of genes. How would his adopted mother feel about a son who was less than a standout athlete, sweet soul, and a gifted musician? My envy and admiration for Claire swan dives off a cliff. "So Theo's mother, she wasn't terribly sorry when India left him."

"If that's what Miss Church did." Shep helps himself to more champagne. "Anyway, getting back to the 9-11 stories; don't get too attached."

"Oh? Why is that?"

"Readership has fallen off. That forty-percent spike was down to seventeen this year. But the better news is I'm left with a thumb drive of less feel-good moments."

"Ah, the less flattering, off-the-record parts. I guess Claire isn't the only one who confided those." I down the remainder of my champagne. "How is that 'better news'?"

Shep hesitates, then doesn't. "A tell-all book about the less pleasant outcomes of 9-11 kids might make my retirement more comfortable." He too finishes his champagne, depositing the empty glass and used napkin beside the exquisite tier of tarts. "Enjoy your evening."

"Enjoy my . . . Wait. What unpleasant outcomes?" I ask, following.

Shep glances around the room, assuring that Claire is still a good distance away. "Joaquin Perez, he opted out last year, moved to Canada. A few weeks ago he died from a drug overdose. He was never able to make peace with his father's death; it haunted him. But that was only the latest in years of domino tragedies. Andrea Wakefield, her mom remarried—they live a happy life in New Hampshire, right? I also happen to know DCF has investigated a few times. She's hinted that the new stepfather has acted not quite so 'fatherly' toward the girl. Stacy Roche was just a toddler when her father died on 9-11. It might have worked out if her mother didn't gamble away the life insurance money earmarked for her education. She was recently indicted for fraud. Just a few ways 9-11 went on to make victims out of its victims."

"And you'd put that in a book? Why?"

"Because I know what sells—particularly when it comes to American tragedy."

"That's your incentive?"

Shep narrows his eyes at me but continues. "Survival is my incentive. Mrs . . ."

"Van Doren," I say, glad I did not share *Klein* with him.

"Any idea what a newspaper salary pays compared to the earnings of a bestselling author?" My gaping mouth furthers Shep's defense. "You can't hold me responsible for the public's desire to watch a train wreck. Don't blame the messenger."

"But you're fine with the public plunking down fifteen bucks to read it."

"More like $24.95. My agent's sure it'll be hardcover, maybe a bidding war." He gives me a long once-over. "Hey, don't worry about your buddy's heartbreak. If Theo had married the Church girl it might have made for a juicy mention. As it is, who cares? Of course, being as I know the adoption detail . . ." I widen my eyes. "I might be more curious than Claire about Theo's pre-adoption past. Is there anything there that makes his story worth telling?" Shep winks at me. "It'll take some digging, something I excel at. But don't sweat it. What are the odds the kid's biological roots will make my book any more of a page-turner?"

CHAPTER TWENTY-SEVEN

Olivia

My heart pounds the way it did the day I gave Theo away. It won't be tragedy, but it will be tabloid fodder if Shep Stewart learns the facts about Theo's adoption. I made it private. I didn't seal it in a tomb. With Shep's admitted dogged determination, he'll figure it out. When it turns out Theo's biological father is a household name, famous athlete, it will be Shep's book hook. Theo didn't want to be part of Shep's human interest pieces in a Boston newspaper. Imagine how much he'd hate being part of a twisted best seller. I glance into Bates Hall and at the corner behind me, the one into which I've painted myself. What the hell am *I* going to do about it?

I could confide Shep's end game to Claire. But what are the odds she'll believe me? And if she does, she'll want to know why I'm so interested in protecting her son's private life. Worse, I do not like what I've just learned about Theo's mother. It sounds like something my own mother would have orchestrated: "Olivia, your friends are a reflection of you . . . and us. Sarah Schaffer's parents are divorced; her mother had an affair. It's all over town." Then years later, with Sam: "Olivia, what is he exactly? The icing on your defiance cake? Did you go to UNC looking for the boy with the most unsavory background? What did we do to deserve this?"

It could be that Claire McAdams is a stealth-like version of my mother. Through the crowded room, Claire soaks up the many accolades being cast upon her. She is popular and well received. Her personal tragedy gives her status that will never be questioned. Everyone wants to be her friend; everyone wants to help make her life easier. But my chat with Shep brings a different lens. It appears much of Claire's unconditional love for Theo is tied to his inbred perks—something for which she can thank his biological parents.

Shep's other bombshell slides back to center: Theo and India. According to Theo, Claire was devastated when his fiancée left him. Maybe it was just a good disguise for relief. The urge to do something with Shep Stewart's information is palpable—Claire's controlling nature and the potential fallout of Shep's tell-all book. Yet I'm wary. This is the place where I generally make a colossal mistake. I can't afford one. Talking it through would be wise. Of course, at the moment, my list of viable confidants is shorter than Claire's. I can't tell the whole story to Rob, though he seems like my best bet. Rob's entire wheelhouse centers on being smart with slippery information. The exit into the library hall, it's the direction Rob went. A few twists and turns through the crowd and hall and I spy him on an exterior balcony. He's still on his phone. I keep moving, formulating an abbreviated version of the facts as I go.

Two separate French doors frame the balcony. The one to the right is partially open. I slip through without touching it. Rob is alone, facing the library courtyard. Behind me is the garbled noise of partygoers. His words carry crisply on November air. "Sash, it has to be done. We agree on that much. All I'm saying is it'll be better coming from you. The way things have been between Liv and me lately . . . It'd just be one more blow up I don't need—" I freeze and listen. His voice sounds soft, tender. "Yeah, well, I don't know that saying it was *accidental* is going to carry much weight in terms of an excuse . . ." If biting down on a gasp is possible, that's what I'm doing. "Hey, you know Liv. She'll be pissed. But she's fairly indestructible." He looks at his phone. "Listen, I've got another call. It's important. Can we talk about this later?"

Fascinating, a call more important than the one easing his mistress's guilt? But Rob doesn't take it, ending the call with Sasha and tucking his phone in his jacket pocket. It could be that my husband has too much of a hard-on to do business. Rob turns away from me, heading for the other French door, and disappears inside. He never sees me as I step farther outside.

Scenes from a heated affair and covert rendezvous plummet into my gut. Champagne and a salmon puff rise back up. Pinning myself to the balcony's concrete rail, I note that I am two stories high. The fall will not kill me. However, it may maim me to the point of permanent injury, surely a lengthy hospital stay. I am rushed by images of my husband and best friend keeping vigil at my bedside. Each holds a hand as their gazes tangle over me, one part remorse, two parts unbridled passion. Clearly, it's not the way they're used to spending time together near a bed. Sasha and Rob would be forced to wallow in their guilt while tending to my every need. God knows I have no child to step in and assist me.

I pull in a stabbing breath of icy air. It's cold and it hurts. I grip concrete that's as dense as my body feels. A different vision slips into focus. Rob and Sasha's bedside manner only lasts for so long. Rob is too bottom line and Sasha is too busy. Soon it's a convenient fact that I'm a broken body in a vegetative state. It leaves plenty of room and excuses in my brownstone bed. Before long Sasha's moved her straightening iron and drawers of cosmetics into my bathroom. I wonder if Rob has seen her without makeup—still attractive, but it does cause a double take the first time. Regardless, my clothes are relocated to the guest room.

Even a size-four wardrobe needs closet space. On the empty balcony, a sound emanates from my throat, something like a slowly dying animal.

The holidays. It would have to be close to the fucking holidays. I will spend them alone—with my mother, packing up the Wellesley house if Rob can't do me the exit courtesy of saving it. Eugenia and I will move in together, to a walkup rental on the outskirts of the city. Someplace with a zip code that she won't want to share with her friends; she'll keep a Boston post office box. Once we're settled, my mother will spend the rest of her life telling me how I went wrong with mine. Wait. That doesn't seem quite right. She likes Rob better. There's a good chance she'll choose him. I am divided on the outcome of this particular scenario.

"Liv?" I hear my name, but my feet don't move and my body won't turn. "Liv, the folks from the chamber orchestra are done. It thought maybe you'd want to say thank you . . . or good-bye . . . Liv?" I force myself about, swiping at streaks of mascara. The light out here isn't good, but it's bright enough. "Liv, what's wrong?" Theo has never looked or sounded so much like his father.

"Nothing." Tears and visibly shaking hands call me a liar. Theo rushes toward me, and I sidestep him with the utmost caution. An outpouring of sympathy, exacerbated by Theo's own broken heart, is hideously disturbing. *Again . . . thank yourself, Liv . . .* "Rob," I start rambling, folding my arms in *keep your distance* body language. "I just overheard . . . Remember I said it'd been a rough week between us." He nods. "I have confirmation it's about to get rougher. Rob . . ." I slap my arm the direction my husband has gone. "He's having an affair. I overheard a conversation . . ." I force out the rest. "I think he's in love with my best friend."

"With your . . ."

Theo cannot fathom anything so sordid. I recall his strong reaction to Sam's response to him. Things like loyalty, obligation, and doing the right thing; these are the qualities that define Theo McAdams. No wonder India was so devastated by her own act of weakness. Theo is hard to live up to. I whip toward the courtyard view and blink furiously. *My God, imagine from how many angles I'd be a disappointment . . .*

"Jesus, I'm sorry, Liv. Are you sure?"

"About as sure as I can be, short of the two of them sending me Snapchats from a motel room." Through a dripping of tears, I smile. "Seriously, it's not totally unexpected. It was probably always a matter of time."

When I married Rob, I lived in the moment. I was thirty-nine. Our union wasn't focused on dreamy *rest of your life* visions that come with marriage in your twenties. I'd done that. It imploded. Rob isn't driven by romantic ideals—or at least he wasn't. It was part of what worked. I didn't require rose petals; he didn't have the first clue what to do with them. Seems he's figured it out. We squeezed our wedding date into a judge's tight schedule, the symphony's fall dates, and Rob's intense negotiations with a Japanese-based business venture. It was fine. Come to think of it, the judge declared us married without ever mentioning forever.

"My friend. Sasha." I swallow and grip my stomach. "I never thought she'd . . ." My teary gaze connects to Theo's drier one. "Though maybe I should have . . . Did I tell you that's how Rob and I met?" Theo shakes his head, understanding that he shouldn't speak right now. "Sasha, she went on a date with him first. She kissed him. She even told me he was a good kisser—can you believe that?" I graze fingertips over my lips. "But because Sasha is always looking out for my happiness, she passed him off to her best friend. The one who's a whirlwind of unstable energy."

"Liv, you might be impulsive and say what's on your mind, but I don't think—"

"Theo." He shuts up. "Do you have any idea what I did to earn one hundred community service hours?" He doesn't reply. "I was upset over a bad business deal. Instead of talking to my husband about it, I beat the shit out of his Porsche with a baseball bat. Then I mouthed off to a judge, telling the man to go fuck himself."

He manages to keep shock in check. "Okay, so everybody does stupid things, Liv. Everybody makes mistakes."

"Not at my level. For me it's an art form. I may be even slightly better at it than I am at playing the violin."

"I don't believe that. And whatever you've done, it doesn't justify what your husband and friend did—or are doing."

I draw in more cold air, maybe enough to freeze dismal pain. "You're very sweet, Theo. You're also naïve. I've been building toward this particular disaster for some time."

"You talk like you deserve this."

"Trust me. I'm not the person you think I am."

"I'm not a bad judge of character, Liv. You don't give yourself enough credit. You're a good person. I watch you with those kids at Braemore. You've tried." My expression turns doubtful. "Okay, so teaching is not your thing." He looks to the courtyard view and back. "Look, I didn't say anything because . . . Well, you didn't. But last week . . . You're responsible for the brand-new instruments that turned up in my classroom, aren't you?

I pull in a shaky breath. "That's a bold assumption given the circumstance."

"Only proves how sure I am about you. Hands-on mentoring isn't the only meter for being a good person." His gaze jerks toward the crowded library. "Neither is executing a soirée that, while beneficial, will also make all the society pages. In fact, it could be argued that anonymous efforts are the most selfless."

"Don't do that, Theo. Don't take one episode of unselfish behavior and slap my image on it. It's distorted and it's not true."

"Listen, my mother is so absorbed she won't notice if I'm gone. Why don't we get out of here, take a walk." He waits anxiously for a reply. "I do that," he adds, "when I need to think. I take long walks."

The mirroring habit startles me. But because I have so thoroughly deceived Theo, my only option is an acquaintance-like observation. "When India told you what happened with her old boyfriend, is that what you did—walk?"

His expression sobers, but he's not about to deny a near-hysterical woman some truth. "No. That part I dealt with because I wanted to convince us both we could fix it. That it was jitters, a few drinks—maybe some risky memories. I did the walking when India told me it was over, when she left me. I save walking for really shitty moments."

"How many of those could you have possibly had?" I squeeze my eyes shut at the obtuse remark.

"On top of everything else, on 9-11, the Boston Police Department had to go searching for a ten-year-old boy. I'd managed to make my way from our house to Fenway. My dad and I had gone to so many games . . ." Theo's shifts his shoulders. "I thought for sure I'd find him there." He crunches his forehead—another recognizable mannerism. "At the time, and to a ten-year-old, it seemed more rational than what did happen to him."

"I'm sorry. My question was incredibly thoughtless."

"Thoughtlessness is understandable given the circumstance."

A fresh stream of tears comes. They aren't all connected to Rob and Sasha. While it was not a future I could have predicted, I am culpable for Theo's fate and the fate of my marriage. This may be the largest cumulative Liv mess ever. I'm struck by how far and how long it would take to walk to the Santa Monica Pier. Rob alone, Sasha alone, I don't know that they could drive me to that. But together, with Theo's lifelong loss tossed in . . . I should start heading west right now. I can't; I'm wearing completely the wrong shoes. But with Theo waiting, I am forced to make a believable recovery. "I get the walking part, Theo. More than you know. But walking, right now, together, it's not a good idea."

"Okay, so we'll go somewhere. Talk. I'll buy you a cup of coffee . . . or maybe a drink."

Great, even worse . . .

"Please, Liv . . . Let me help."

"Why?"

He pauses. His mouth, so like mine, gapes a bit. It forms the same O of vagueness when we are at a loss for words. "I can't explain it. Not in sentences," he says. "But since you've come into my classroom . . . maybe my life." He shoves his hands into his pockets. "I don't know . . . you just make sense to me."

I move my hand through sprayed hair. He's picked a wonderful moment to acknowledge blood kinship. Our eyes meet. The compassion in his is something I need more than my next breath. But I haven't completely lost touch with reality. I tell him no thank you—I have an old friend in town. I don't want to burden Theo with my problems. I head for the set of French doors that Rob used to exit. I turn back. Theo so wants to help. If he knew the truth, he'd likely toss me over the balcony rail. "Can you do one thing for me?"

"Sure. Name it."

"Would you tell Rob I wasn't feeling well and that I left?"

"Would you mind if I punched him in the face first?"

It's the grandest show of support I've ever felt. My heart swells. Then it deflates because it makes reality hurt all the more. Theo is a wonderful caring human being. It's no thanks to Claire—so I've decided—or me or Sam or even a dead David McAdams. Theo is proof that not everything is a result of nature or nurture. There are anomalies. I glance back at the drop overlooking the courtyard cement. I'm sorry we're not on the roof. My husband, in all likelihood, is in love with my best friend (I'd hate to think it's just about sex). The child and relationship I forfeited twenty-six years ago stands five feet away. Yet for all the good it will do me, I might as well have left him in New Zealand.

Infants and small children weren't my strong suit at twenty-one. That fear lent rationale to giving up Theo. But a relationship with an adult child—I might have been better at that. I sigh into night air. None of it matters. None of it will ever happen.

Worse than this, Theo's heartfelt offer of friendship and empathy isn't what I crave—not in the part of me that acknowledges him as my son. And right now, it's unconditional love that stings the most. It's the love of a husband that now belongs to my best friend. It is the love of a son that doesn't belong to me but to Claire McAdams. It seems I have lost everything, even the things I never really had.

CHAPTER TWENTY-EIGHT

Olivia

It's close to midnight when my cab pulls up to the Embassy Suites. This location was not my first intention, nor my first stop. In the past two hours I have learned there are four friendly bars between the Boston Public Library and here. All of them served Macallan on the rocks. Icy rain hits the cab window as the driver asks if he has the right hotel. "Right hotel. Different life," I slur. But there's no one left to confide in, only the long-lost comfort zone that is Sam Nash. For a moment, I debate going home. I shove two twenties at the driver, signaling my choice.

Like I told the last barkeep, turning back time is the only way to avoid what's in front of me. Sid, a chatty Brit who poured large portions, agreed. "Love . . ." He said in the way Brits do. "If you can turn time back, I say run off and bottle the stuff." He thumbed over his shoulder, rows of liquid forgetfulness lined up behind him. "I'd never peddle another drop of that, but I'd sell second chances by the bloody pint."

A half hour ago, it sounded like a suggestion. I left Sid and his eighty-proof potions, grasping at alternative ideas about turning back time.

Getting out of the cab, I trip on the curb. The thickly accented driver rushes around to my prone position. Even this drunk I'm embarrassed. Whether it's Farsi or Turkish, I hear phrases of acute concern. It heightens my urge to escape the public eye. He helps me to my feet. Having face-planted into concrete, I am impressed by alcohol's ability to do its job. The sting is dulled. Seconds later, someone from the hotel is there, bracing a bloody elbow, asking if I'm all right. Dabbing at my cheek, my fingertips come away bloody. Regardless, I swear I'm fine and push past the cab driver and hotel employee, mumbling that I won't sue if they just let me get to my room.

Memorizing musical notes is what I do; I have the same ability when it comes to numbers. The sixth floor and room 644 are stuck to my brain like a G clef on a stave. I don't think; I don't waver as the elevator floors click by. Then I don't even knock. I pound. On the second round of fist beating, a woman at the end of the hall pops her head out. I had no idea women still actually wore curlers to bed. There's a full-on flash of memory of my mother in curlers. "Olivia," she said from the edge of my bedroom, her hair in torturous rubber knots. "Time must move faster in your room. That's hardly two hours of practice . . ."

I blink at the woman staring me down now; surely she has stumbled upon a nasty husband-and-wife rift. She has, just not the correct husband and wife. I narrow my eyes. She retreats, though I suspect she will call the front desk if the disruption continues. The police may arrive. I could be arrested—again. Fuck. In addition to everything else, I suppose I've lost my legal counsel.

Sam opens the door. I'm safe.

His sleepy face jolts to wide awake. "Liv . . ." The door opens wider and I spill inside, my heels snagging on the carpet, my dress whooshing past him. "I'm guessing Cinderella had a shitty time at the ball."

Anger bubbles. I consider taking off one shoe—decidedly not glass—and beating the shit out of him with it. If assigning blame to the taut threads of this moment, a number of strands can be traced back to Sam Nash. I glance from a mirror to him. On the other hand, while Sam is accountable, he's not the one hanging onto one hell of a secret. I banish all thoughts of Theo. In doing so, I lower the mental shoe. In the meantime, Sam grabs at a bleeding arm. "What the hell happened to you?"

I bend my arm to look at a nasty scrape. My eyes meet his, and Sam's fingers come forward. "I tripped coming into the hotel."

"You're sure?" he asks. I nod, assuming the liquor on my breath helps confirm this. He hustles into the bathroom and returns with a hand towel, shoveling in ice cubes from a bucket. I jerk away at first, but my cheek is throbbing. Ice is more rational than any other idea I dove into during in the past two hours. "How drunk are you?"

"Not enough to forget the past few hours." I stare. Sam stares back. Unsteady emotion pumps through me. When Sam manned up to old regrets, he brought new *what ifs* into my already fragile marriage. I stand down. While Sam has fueled the Cinderella bitch moment, he did not cause it.

"Liv, are you going to tell me why you've been drinking like it's a Friday night at the Pour House? What the hell is going on?"

"I, um . . ." I look right at him and hiccup. "Can I . . . Could I spend the night here?"

The smell of coffee wafts into my dry nose. It triggers other signs of life—some more pounding than others. I open an eye, which proves to be a feat. Individual false lashes are tangled with real ones, crusty tears making for a better bond than the glue applied last night.

Fuck.

Last night.

If it weren't for a steamroller effect, I'd spring up in bed. It's the appropriate response to my current circumstance. I don't do it. I need more specific information. Like maybe what, besides sleep, happened here. A cotton T-shirt rubs between me and the hotel sheets. I'm not sure if I'm wearing underwear. A crease of light blinds my periscope view. Cutting through the blackout curtains, Sam's silhouette glows in a sliver of brightness. He peers into intense sunlight. In his hand is a coffee cup. He's dressed—jeans and an undershirt. Had I woken to a naked Sam looming over me, I'd have a clearer picture of last night. I roll into the pillow and imagine how I will feel upon confirmation—the cheated on or the cheated with? It could go either way. I remember a thunderous release of words about Rob, then falling into Sam's waiting arms. Less romantic, I used the bathroom—but whether it was to pee, vomit, or tend to bloody scrapes, who knows? I was always a lousy drunk.

One thing I do know, I said nothing about Theo. Neither vulnerability nor booze could pry that from my daft mind. Theo is a secret I will take to my grave. It's the only constant, given the unraveling of recent hours. Sam's relaxed stature affirms this. Even the world's most casual man would register flustered if he suddenly learned he had a son. I clear my throat. I don't possess enough saliva to get my tongue off the roof of my mouth. Sam turns from the window.

"I was trying to remember how long I used to let you sleep it off." Sam is the proverbial early riser. It's as if energy has accumulated in his body overnight and he needs to expend it, starting at the crack of dawn. He used to expend a lot of it on me. Grumbling noises of agreement make their way out—I haven't been this hung over since New Year's 2015. I woke up with no memory of that evening either, but I do recall the morning visual: Sasha and Rob in the kitchen, chatting over coffee.

"Wait," he says. My cloudy mind drifts to Sam, who's said something about coffee. "I do remember what comes before talking or coffee." I sit up and confirm that I am wearing his T-shirt and my underwear. "Or anything else for that matter," he adds.

He smiles a Sam smile. Then he disappears into the bathroom. We both know what "anything else" refers to. As spontaneous as sex was . . . *is* . . . ? My stomach rolls. Either way, I am a stickler for brushing my teeth first. Years ago, it caused more than one playful argument, which always ended with unbelievable, fresh-breath sex. On occasion Sam would compromise. He would follow me into the bathroom, and since I was already bent over the sink, he took full advantage of my position. I'd spit toothpaste, and he . . . Well, the steamy memory seems hotter than the visual at a banged-up forty-six.

In an adjacent mirror, I get a glimpse of my cheek and lightly float my fingertips over a tender spot. Sam returns holding out a complimentary hotel toothbrush. I throw back the covers. Sam hands off the toothbrush as I pass by. He does not follow.

Inside the bathroom, I peer into the mirror. A definite bruise and slight black eye, my forearm looks worse. I pee, brush my teeth, and think. On the sink is a bottle of pain reliever. I take three—then a fourth. I consider rummaging through Sam's medicine bag for something stronger. I recall what I found last time I combed through a man's travel bag. I stay in the bathroom and seated on the closed toilet lid. I review last night's balcony confirmation and stumbling into Sam's room. And after that? What was my response to Rob and Sasha's affair?

With my palms planted firmly on my thighs, I let reality sink in. Did I take refuge in my all-too-convenient past and retaliate by having sex with Sam? It seems like a *count on it* Liv move. Perhaps Rob and Sasha are having coffee right now, debating the odds or just what hotel Sam and I woke up in. I wonder if in a knee-jerk reaction I took pictures last night. Hell, I took a baseball bat to a Porsche. I look up, staring at the bathroom ceiling. It could be that I went as far as to text photos to Rob. Caption: *Suggest a collage holiday card* . . . Panic erupts. My gaze darts to the mirror. It's not inconceivable. I can't remember if I had sex. I could have easily forgotten selfies.

I fling open the bathroom door and start scouring the room. "My purse . . . My phone. Where are they?" Sam's returned to the window; light streams in like a beam looking to skewer me. He points to a chair, where the dress lies in a heap. The purse is underneath. I fumble for the phone. Sam watches. My heart slows a bit. Multiple texts and calls from Rob, a few from Sasha, scroll past my line of vision. There are no replies from me.

"You didn't make any calls. You didn't even take your phone out." I calm and shove the phone back into the purse, retrieving a hair elastic—like maybe this was the purpose of my purse siege. Sam mumbles under his breath. "Not that he doesn't deserve a few choice words . . ." I grapple for organization, gathering my bedhead into a ponytail. "Liv, I just need to ask you again . . ." He points his coffee cup in my direction. "Swear to me the bruises are the result of you, booze, and clumsiness."

I close my eyes. This is the third time Rob has been accused of the one behavior I could never imagine. He is so many things, but never, not in a million years, that. "No . . . It's exactly what I said. Ungraceful and humiliating as it is, I tripped getting out of the cab."

He gives me a long once over. "Not bad. But not near as humiliating as waking up in a brothel in New Orleans, stripped of everything but Mardi Gras beads."

I arch my eyebrows. "Oh. That would be . . . *rough*."

"*My date* ran up five grand on my credit card before I managed to put a stop on it. So if you need to feel better . . ." I nod. "Do you want to talk about last night?"

"Which part?"

"You told me a pretty grim tale. Your husband . . . Somebody named Sasha. That's when you started crying. She's your friend. You said . . ."

"That they're having an affair." The jackhammer at my temple adds a nice note of assurance—this is all for real. "My very best friend." My bottom hits the mattress and a rumple of sheets. I try to sort out how what I've done compares. "Sam . . ."

He sits next to me and curls his arm around my shoulder. It's reminiscent of yesteryear and last night. My gaze catches on a bruise on Sam's left arm—likely from his workout at Brandeis. Closing my eyes, the tears seep through. Sam's presses his mouth into my pounding head. I consider asking him to close the room-darkening curtains and climbing back into bed. Sam has always equaled escape—pressure, my parents. He possesses the ability to spirit me away from everything that's wrong in my life. Now seems like a good time for that superpower to reemerge.

"What do you want to do, Livy?" I am at a loss for a clear thought. I offer a massive shrug. "How about if I made a crazy, perfectly timed, Sam suggestion?"

"Like what?"

"Like one that made us . . . *us*." My head dips onto his shoulder, luring comfort closer. "Pack up your things and come back to California with me. I don't need to take any coaching job here. You'd like Newport Beach. It's sunny . . . warm. They might even have an orchestra somewhere."

I laugh. "A little group. California Symphony Orchestra—world class."

"So do that. Grab your fiddle and the parts of your life you want to keep. Do what we should have done all those years ago."

I pull away and blink at him. There's a world of difference between what Sam believes he walked away from and reality. I can't forget that. Yet I also can't help toying with the notion. "You make it sound so simple. Pick up where we left off?"

"I'm not that naïve. All I'm saying is let's see where it takes us."

The thrill of distraction and escape. No promises. No real plan. How very Sam. But his words are tempting, as is the sound of his voice. His superpower lives on. My expression is blank. My mind isn't. "What? Find out if I'm still the number-one fan of the man from Tennessee?"

He laughs. "If you don't like California, we could always try Denver."

They are old song lyrics. It's an even older life. Maybe it was just the *please come to Boston* part that never stood a chance. "We were always good at running, weren't we?"

"We were," he says.

I keep playing along. "And by sheer luck, in California or Denver, there'll be an open symphony chair?"

"Why not? I'm supposed to be dead, remember? Crazier things have happened." He looks me over, looking so very much like the past. And then he kisses me. It's so present and sweet. I meld into it, my fingers gathering knots of soft cotton T-shirt. Sam is on a faster track, his hand slipping beneath the T-shirt I am wearing, his fingers sliding from my breasts to my back, hooking around the edge of my underwear. Does it get any easier than this? Hell, we're in a hotel room, sitting on a bed. There is no first-time sexual hesitation. It's more like old-home week. The difference between now and last night is that this time I will remember having sex with Sam. It's enough to stop me. I push the hand that is between me and my underwear away. Yet I don't let go. In fact, I hold on tight.

He whispers in my ear. "Okay, I get it. Sober retaliation is a deep line in the sand. But, Jesus, Liv . . . don't tell me you don't want to do it."

I ease back from a moment I want badly—the comfort, the idea of nothing mattering but Sam and me. To my surprise, I can't do it. I stare at a carpet stain. It looks terribly permanent. A lot of things are permanent. Sam has no idea how big those things are. "Want has nothing to do with it. I can't. Not for a million reasons."

"Didn't sound that way to me last night. It sounded like your husband's a serious shit and your best friend isn't much better. Maybe worse. Isn't there some sort of girl code that says 'do not touch,' even if she did date him first?"

"Was I that specific? And it was one date," I qualify. "Hardly a blip on the radar."

"I suppose. But you did hit more recent Rob highlights." The way Sam says Rob's name, it's as if he's the intruder in my life. "What's he into the Wellesley house for?"

"I told you about the Wellesley house?"

He sighs. "Damn, you always were a scary, aftermath drunk. Yes. You said he used it as collateral in a business deal. You thought the reason he's so desperate to save it was because it would make for the easiest settlement."

"Oh." I flutter eyelids at my candidness and detail. "Weren't you incredibly sober last night, not to mention a good notetaker?"

"I told you, I've tried to put bad habits behind me. Going to bed sober *is* an improvement. No notes necessary. I always listened to you, Liv."

"You did," I admit. "But why do you want to know the specifics about Rob using the Wellesley house as collateral?"

"Because you told me what the money is for. While it wouldn't hurt my feelings to see your mother's address downgraded, I thought the part . . . What you've done for those kids is pretty amazing. It shouldn't be jeopardized by your husband's bad business move."

I am caught off guard. Aside from the forced acknowledgment to Principal Giroux, I've never told anyone—except Rob, of course—about the orchestra funding. "I guess it's hard to get your mind around. Seriously out of sync with who I am."

"I don't think so." I paste a squirrelly-eyed glance on him. "You never could see it. You could never look at yourself in any other way than what your parents saw. Do you really think that's the girl I fell in love with?" I inch back. He tucks a runaway piece of ponytail behind my ear. "The woman who would give away her family home for a greater good. That's the girl I fell for."

"Sam," I say softly, capturing his hand in mine. "Even so, it's just as much Rob's endow—"

"It's your house, Liv. Your money." Our hands part and he rubs his over denim covered thighs. My eye catches on the bruise again, or is it a different one? Before I can ask about it, he presses the subject. "So tell me, what's old Rob into the house for?

I laugh. "All of it. He owes close to three million. He can probably scrape the balance together, but the house is major collateral. It's worth . . . I don't know, about two and a quarter million."

A frown overtakes Sam's bearded face. I still can't get used to it. I'm not sure I recall kissing it last night. Kissing him in the parking garage is far more vivid. "Okay," he says, nodding. "So we'll fix that part first." He gets up from the bed and reaches into what looks like a gym bag, producing a checkbook.

"What are you doing?"

"Cleaning up after your husband—saving your house. I'll just make the check out to you, and you can give it to him. In return, his name comes off the Wellesley house deed." He glances at me. "Get someone other than the lawyer girlfriend to handle the legalities."

"Wait. What?" I stand and shuffle toward Sam. I see that he has written out a check to Olivia Klein for 2.5 million dollars. "Sam, you can't do that."

"Why not?"

Old sarcasm slips out. "Even if I was the world's best hooker, that's a ridiculous price tag."

"Don't say things like that, Liv. That's not why I wrote it."

"Then why?"

His face is awash with serenity, born out of age, maybe a life-threatening experience. It wasn't there twenty-six years ago. "Because it feels like the right thing to do."

"Sam. You can't." I glance at a check that looks a lot like a pot of gold. "You can't write a check for over two million dollars like it's a fifty-dollar donation."

"Trust me. Without being what your mother might call *vulgar*, I can afford it."

"Yes, but you can't go around handing out that kind of money to old girlfriends . . . ex-wives," I correct. In truth, ex-girlfriend is my memory. The marriage shattered so easily. Being Rob's ex-wife will surely be a more vibrant image.

"You forget. I excel at doing whatever the hell I want. Take it." He holds out the check. Our eyes meet in some way that both negates and embraces nostalgia. Here is where I should offer something tremendous in exchange: *"In gratitude for your generosity, Sam, I have something stunning to share . . ."* But telling him about Theo this way seems stilted, badly timed at best. "Sam." He holds the check steady. "I can't take your money. I can't go to California with you."

"Why not?" And for all his personal growth, innocence invades. We lived fine on *Why not?* . . . until we didn't.

"Because my life doesn't fit in a backpack anymore. I can't up and run away from this—not like I did from my parents."

He narrows his eyes. "You ran from your parents because you didn't want to be with them or near them. I know a shitty family life when I see one, Liv. It doesn't matter if the scars aren't physically visible or what the address implies."

"Yes, but—"

"And what about your husband? Are the two of you just shitty family history repeating under a different roof?" I'd forgotten Sam's abruptness. Despite the remark, laughter ignites a zing of pain through my cheek. "I'm afraid that's going to hurt worse before it feels any better."

"Are you talking about my face or my husband?"

"Like I said, is history repeating?"

"I'm not sure what you mean. Rob's not my parents."

Sam places the check on the dresser. "I don't know enough about your life or your marriage to get how you feel about it . . . *him*. But you are standing here. You told me a hell of a story last night. You did . . ." He stops. "From what I see, you still don't have a lot of love for the girl who looks back in the mirror." I glance away from him and all nearby mirrors. "There's a big part of you that likes people to see nothing but the trouble part. I get it. It's self-preservation, kind of like readying the beers before ole Hudson burns you with a cigarette. I understand how far a person would go to avoid that kind of pain." My gaze cuts sharply to his. "But you're a good person, Liv, and you should know that." I attempt to speak; he cuts me off. "And another thing I've learned in the past year or so, life's not that long, sweetheart. Whether it's a house or a husband, know what to save. Know what to walk away from. Don't waste time."

Instead of looking at Sam, I glance at the rumpled sheets. Hotel room beds are amazingly telltale compared to everyday ones. "Last night must be is a good indication of how I feel about my marriage . . ." Something sinks hard into my gut—sleeping with Sam, it's one giant counter argument to everything he's saying about me. Good people don't make these kinds of mistakes. "And last night, no matter your opinion of me . . . It's right on par for the girl in the mirror. I'm not wrong about myself, Sam."

He takes a deep breath. "Yeah. I can see why you might think that given the circumstance." Sam's line of vision travels the same route as mine, landing back on me. "If it weren't for one thing."

"What's that?"

He points to the culprit bedding. "Nothing happened, Liv. Nothing that should make you dislike the girl in the mirror even more. You cried . . . you bitched. You bled. Once that all calmed, it did get hot and heavy. Then, um . . . then you stopped." I narrow my eyes at Sam's recollection. I honestly have no idea what happened last night. "The same way you did a minute ago."

A weight I might not have imagined lifts from my entire being. "Nothing . . ."

He comes closer. "Don't give yourself all the credit." He hesitates and grins. "But you know me—that was never my style, doing other guy's girlfriends . . . wives."

"But the other day, in the parking garage. You all but . . ."

"Hell. Clearly, I'm tempted. But I was a few drinks in the other day." He frowns. "Weaker moment. But it didn't happen then . . . Or last night. Got it?" He studies my bruised face. "You don't remember any of it?"

"No. I don't." Sam pulls me close, and I hang on for dear life. "Back in the day," I say, "it's one reason you always stuck so close. One of us could handle our liquor . . ."

"The other was there to make sure nothing bad ever happened."

"Right." I feel tears soak into the undershirt that Sam is wearing, the one matching mine.

"Last night, you needed a body in the bed. That was all."

"It's still hard to believe nothing . . ."

He holds on tighter. "Don't push it, Liv. I'm reasonable. I'm far from perfect, and I just did ask you to run away with me."

"But you weren't serious."

"I wasn't not serious."

"Thank you for saying that." I feel his mouth on the top of my head. "Thank you for wanting me . . . for not making a bad situation worse. No matter what Rob's done, I don't know how I could face him if we'd . . ."

My words trail off as his lungs fill with air. And in this moment, I'm so very grateful Sam Nash is alive.

CHAPTER TWENTY-NINE

Olivia

Street parking is full, the sidewalk thick with joggers and people enjoying a late-fall day—shopping, coffee at a café, sightseeing if they are in town for the weekend. As I hurry up the brownstone steps, the glances of strangers brush over my bruised and gowned appearance. My thoughts layer like falling leaves, piles of them. Maybe Rob isn't home. Of course, the alternative to that is more disturbing. With my hand on the knob, I stop. I imagine the three of us in a showdown. One where Sasha has rolled out of my bed, her pixie frame and silky toffee-colored skin wrapped in Rob's wrinkled white dress shirt.

Conversely, my appearance will come with its own shocking statement—the combo of streaky mascara, a burgeoning black eye, and unknown whereabouts lending curious talking points. My hand brushes over the beaded gown—surely a frock worn so early in the a.m. equals an admission of guilt. I step inside the brownstone and hear a low rumble of voices, including Rob's, along with a strange man, and . . . *my mother*?

I inch around the corner. A policeman is in my living room. There is a pang of déjà vu; it's about thirty years old. "Jesus, Liv!" Rob puts down his coffee cup and darts across the hardwoods. "Are you all right? Where the hell have you been?" He grabs my shoulders and gives me a shake that's hard to label. *"You bitch; you kept me up all night"*? Or *"Darling, whatever became of you? I've been worried sick . . ."*

"I take it this is Mrs. Van Doren?"

"For the moment," I murmur. Rob offers a confounded look before replying.

"It is." He turns back. "For God's sake, Liv, what happened to you?"

"I fell." Although I suspect it's not what he's asking.

My mother, who has the advantage of previous vanishing acts, is more direct. "Too much to drink, Olivia? And is it still considered running away from home when you're forty-six? I'm curious." I purse my lips and my gaze turns evasive. She jerks upright from the sofa—age not slowing her accusations. "I told you," she says, speaking to Rob and the policeman. "Whatever *stumbles* my daughter made last night, she'd ultimately be fine." Her glare drops from my bruised face to my hands. "Fingers in one piece?" I flex them and nod obediently. "I guess that's something." The police officer and Rob's mouths are agape. "This is precisely what I said, Olivia reverting to old behaviors, bad habits—two authority-related episodes inside ninety days. It's classic. Her father will be disgusted but hardly shocked." Her misspeak draws my glance, but I don't say anything. She turns to me. "Of course, now that I know the catalyst—Sam Nash having pulled a bad penny trick—it all makes sad sense."

"Eugenia, please. You're not helping," Rob says. But clearly he's brought my mother up to speed on the many things that are not her business. "Where have you been, Liv? We checked the local hospitals."

"Did you check the local bars, hotels?" she asks.

"Eugenia." This time Rob's teeth are gritted. He reverts to me. "What do you mean *you fell*?"

"Tripped," I offer. "Getting out of a cab last night."

"Did the cab get lost?" he asks. "Or should I assume your destination wasn't home?"

The questions are a blend of accusation and concern, as if Rob is unsure what side he should come down on. Although the cop in the room indicates he was leaning toward concern. On the other hand, it could be that Sasha has advised this scenario. Having his state of mind on the record is surely in Rob's best interest. Can't say I'm surprised not to find Sasha here. It reads like a bonus confirmation of their . . . *relationship*.

"Mrs. Van Doren," the cop says again. "I'm Officer Wheeler. Your husband contacted us early this morning, like three a.m. early. He says last night, without any warning, you left an affair."

"Or she went to one . . ." my mother chimes from under her breath.

The officer, who is a sizable African American man, absorbs much of the energy. He ignores my mother and presses the question. "Mrs. Van Doren, did you leave the event of your own volition? Are you all right?"

"In what sense?" My tone mimics the one I used with Judge Nicholson—unresolved authority issues. "I'm fine . . . Well, except for the obvious," I say, holding up my scraped forearm. "I'm sorry for the trouble. The bruises are my fault. I'm not in need of police assistance."

"End scene!" My mother claps her hands like she's at the opera. She sits again, looking blankly at the officer and Rob. "What? I've attended this performance before. Though I will say her creativity has dampened—perhaps her stamina. Home in less than twenty-four hours? Vanishing to New York for five days when you were sixteen, then another four six months later—now there's a showstopper meant to get your attention."

The policeman flips closed his notepad. "So solely a domestic issue then? One that doesn't reflect on your injuries?"

"That'd be one way of describing it." He continues to stare at my rumpled appearance. "I fell. I swear; Rob wasn't anywhere near my collision with concrete."

"Still, Mrs. Van Doren, if you're feeling at all unsafe . . ."

My mother interjects. "Honestly, officer, if you knew my daughter . . . Tell me, Olivia. Do you ever think? It could have been broken fingers instead of scraped-up arm, bruised face. How would that look—"

I hold up a hand, speaking louder than my mother. "I don't feel unsafe." I assume this is proper code for *abused spouse*. "I'm perfectly fine in my own home. Again, I'm sorry for the confusion."

The officer taps his pen against the leather-covered notepad. His gaze moves around the inviting interior of the brownstone. I believe we all feel his point. Socioeconomic status is not an indicator of domestic harmony, or lack thereof. He starts for the door, but passing by Rob, he stops. "This is my regular beat," he says to us both. "One way or another, work it out. Let's keep this to a one-time visit if we can." He exits, the door shutting hard enough to rattle bric-a-brac.

Rob comes back into the living room; his eyes don't move from my disheveled appearance. But it's my mother who attacks first. "What do you have to say for yourself, Olivia?"

"As you can see, Mother, except for some slight wear and tear, I'm fine. The rest really isn't your business."

"The hell it isn't." Her coffee cup hits the coffee table with a startling thud.

I move as far as the matching club chairs, and my fingertips dig into the plush back. "No, it isn't. When I was fourteen . . . and sixteen . . . and even twenty, you got to do this. But the window has long passed. I appreciate you rushing over here because . . ." I narrow my eyes. "Exactly why are you here—just for the floor show?"

She stands. "Because your husband called at three a.m., wanting to know if my daughter had shown up. I found the question disconcerting since you haven't spent a night in the Wellesley house in more than twenty years."

"And if only I could have avoided the twenty plus years before that!"

"Typical ingratitude. See it however you like, Olivia. But—"

"Enough—both of you!"

Rob is standing near the bar, hands clenched in tidy fists of anger. "Your mother came out of concern, Liv—no matter how you translate it." My mother only has time to smile before Rob finishes his thought. "Other than that, Eugenia, Olivia is right. This is between my wife and me. I appreciate you coming over, but as you can see, she is . . . basically in one piece, so . . ." His hand waves toward the brownstone door.

Her head tilts compliantly at Rob. If he looked good before, I'd imagine his stock has risen in multiples since three a.m. She makes a slow gliding exit, as if mentally forming each word on her approach. She leans in. "You're right, Olivia. This isn't about us, something far beyond repair. But remember the things I warned you about." A whoosh of fall air rushes past as she exits.

Silence fills the space the police officer and my mother invaded. Rob is at the bar, his arms leaning into it. I have no urge to speak first. Sasha and Rob—by not making an audible accusation about the two of them, it won't be true. Or maybe I just want them to confess it.

Rob does no such thing.

"Are you all right?" A sideways glare cuts to me. "Physically?"

"I'm fine. Nothing a little hydrogen peroxide and pair of sunglasses won't fix."

"Good." He stands erect. "Then do you want to tell me where you were all night? Or better still, why?" He is in negotiator Rob mode—demanding yet coaxing.

He can be cunning to a fault, and I do not wish to be on the receiving end—at least not until I've had a shower, used the hydrogen peroxide. "Not really." I turn and start to head up the stairs.

His bare feet thunder across the hardwoods. At the stairs, he pounces and grabs my unscathed arm. I lose my balance. Rob closes in, pinning me between him and the wall. A safe recovery or cornering his prey? "I don't think so, Liv. You can beat the shit out of my car with a bat, but you don't get to do this. You show up looking like you've spent the night in an alley—which might be easier to hear. Wherever you've been, on top of that, I'm notified of your abrupt departure via a cryptic message from the other spare man in your life."

"Cryptic message . . . Spare man?"

"Yes. Theo McAdams. The other thing—since your ex showing up—that's turned you into someone I don't know. From the moment you met him, something's been more off than usual. So start there. Why does some kid you barely know approach me like he's going to take my head off, and then inform me you've 'left the fundraiser'?"

"Did he?" I feel a tickle of motherly pride. "Theo and I are friends. Don't let him bother you."

"He does. But forget the kid, Liv. Get to the point. Where have you been and why?" His hand is gripped like a rope around my wrist. It's unlike Rob. Keeping cool is his MO. But is he rattled because of what he's done, or because I've gone off script? He breathes out anger and I suck it in. Then he draws his own conclusion. "You're fucking kidding me? Tell me Eugenia Klein did not hit the nail on the head about your ex . . . whatever he is," Rob says, his free arm thrusting upward.

I don't shrink from the innuendo, my back scraping against the wall as I rise up one step. We're eye to eye. "Wow. I can't decide who has more nerve, you or my mother." I come at him with bolder words. "Or maybe it's Sasha." He knots his brow. "You go first. Then I'll be glad to have a discussion about Sam Nash and my night."

He lets go. He looks startled, like negotiation tactics have taken a sudden nosedive. "Are you admitting that's where you were last night—with him?"

Anybody else would find his offense appropriate. But I'm well versed in Rob Van Doren bluffing. "Yes," I say, smiling. "I spent the night in Sam's hotel room."

"Liv . . ." Distress settles over his face and his tone is riddled with disbelief. Nice touch. He swallows hard, like there's no spit in his mouth. Rob backs off the step and retreats into the foyer. "Honest to Christ, you're just going to stand there and tell me you spent the night with your old boyfriend . . . ex-husband, whatever the fuck he is? You're not even going to preface it with 'Honey, we need to talk . . .'" He shakes his head. "Who . . . who the hell are you?"

"I said I spent the night at Sam's hotel. I didn't say I had sex with him," I say, empowered by Sam's disclosure. "Of course, I can see how deflection is a smooth move here, considering."

"Considering what? And why are acting like you're the injured party? Better still, why are you so pissed off at me?"

While I'd like to play Rob's cat and mouse game, I don't have his for taste blood. Emotion wins. "Shut the hell up with the injured-husband routine, Rob! I'm not the one sleeping with somebody's best friend."

He blinks at me, his head almost vibrating back and forth. "What the hell are you talking about?"

"I know about you and Sasha. You can cut the stunned-spouse crap anytime."

He is painfully silent; his mouth hangs open. "Sasha?" My tears from last night begin to well. He runs his hands through his dyed haired. "Liv, hold on a minute. What is it you think . . ."

I come down the three steps. I'm sorry I do. The false height felt like the upper hand. "I don't *think*, Rob. I know," I say sharply. "But I'm not so terribly blind or self-absorbed not to get it. Everything from impromptu lunches to cozy phone calls."

"Cozy phone calls?"

"Yes," I say, teeth slightly gritted. "First it's a chummy call on the house phone—a number Sasha rarely dials. Then it's a more telling conversation, or maybe I should say intimate one on the library balcony."

"Do you know how paranoid that sounds?"

"Do you know how evasive you're being?"

He widens his blue eyes, shaking his head tersely. "If I was talking to Sasha on the house phone, it's because she did the dialing—ask her. As for the library balcony . . ." He stops. "Were you eavesdropping?"

"You bet. And worth the Miss Manners slip considering the earful I got. Something like, 'Sure, Liv will be pissed, but she's tough. She'll get over it.'"

"Sasha was returning my call. I'd asked her, lawyer to lawyer, if she'd review a long shot but potential loophole in the contract involving the Wellesley house."

"And I'd need to get over that because . . . ?"

"I don't even remember saying that to her." His expression is a designer-worthy ensemble, fall's dumbfounded look. "I did rush to end the call because she went off on a tangent about . . ." He takes a deep breath. "Jesus, Liv. This is just absurd."

"Not from my perspective. Particularly after you add it to the lovely tip-off souvenir from The Bed?" His face perplexes. *"The Bed,"* I repeat. "Manhattan's Most Exquisite Small Luxury. You stayed there recently."

"Right," he admits.

"So did Sasha." He continues to look queerly at me, like he can't follow the conversation. "In your travel bag." I fold my arms, the raw scrapes showing. "There was a shoe shine cloth, compliments of the romantic boutique hotel."

"So?"

"The same night you came home, I had dinner with Sasha. She spilled a bunch of junk on the table. There was a claim check from The

Bed—the date stamped on it. Same date you were there. She also had a boarding pass. Care to explain that?"

"No."

"No?"

"No, because I have no idea what the fuck Sasha was doing with a claim check from . . . *that hotel.*" His mouth gapes for a moment before continuing. "Look, Liv, as far as Sasha and I currently . . ." His blue eyes blink into mine and he appears truly at a loss for words. "It's ridiculous."

"Is it? You take an impromptu trip to New York; stay at a boutique hotel that is *so* not your usual choice . . . She's all but unreachable for the same amount of time. You both show up with souvenirs, hers stamped with the date. You stand here, look me in the eye, and tell me you're not sleeping with Sasha. Stand here and tell me you never—not once—have fucked her."

Then it's like a murder confession when a stunning "Yes . . ." seeps from his throat. "Once."

On the confirmation, I take a step back. "Once . . ."

"Jesus, Liv, I had sex with Sasha *once*—seven years ago."

"Seven . . ." I'm suddenly as flustered as he looks.

"Yes. It was the chemical equivalent of trying to light a match under water. It was enough to . . ."

Now it's my head that's vibrating. "You and Sasha . . ."

If Rob didn't look caught before, he does now. "Christ almighty . . . I didn't . . ." His full lips purse and he takes a turn in what suddenly appears to be a tight space. I have a much clearer picture of where those lips have been. Now I'm wondering for how long. "But it's ancient history. You're standing here now, accusing me of . . ."

"Sleeping with the woman who introduced us," I deadpan. "My God, how far back do the lies go? Both of you went a mile out of your way to swear it was never any more than a good-night kiss."

And now he's stuck explaining the past and the present. "Liv. Listen to me." He's back to negotiation mode. "After one . . . *one* date with you, I called Sasha. I said I felt sure there'd be another. She laughed. She said you'd already called her and said the same thing. Is that untrue?"

"No. But apparently I'm the one who was given a different version of *your date*."

"I said you were everything she warned me about—fiery, challenging, irreverent, and dazzling in so many ways that I'd never want anything ordinary again. She was right about all of it. I can't argue Sasha's on-point predictions."

"Damn, Rob, I'm not sure talking her up is a great idea this second."

He holds up a hand. "In that single conversation Sasha and I made a pact—maybe not the most honest one, but we thought it was in all our best interests. We dumbed down a meaningless one-night stand to a one-time-only kiss."

"And you think that's commendable—particularly given the moment?"

"What moment?" he fires back. "I told you, Liv. I'm not sleeping with Sasha." He takes an angry breath. "Ask her yourself. Ask her who she's been . . ." A growl erupts from his throat and his face angers. "I'm not going to defend this. I'm not the one who just rolled in from a night with their ex—whatever."

"No. If I recall, you're the one who didn't even suggest having sex on our first date—unlike Sasha, who nailed you out of the gate." I turn and start up the stairs. "Go ahead and add *that* to the list of things Sasha does better than me."

CHAPTER THIRTY

Olivia

Rob and I spend the rest of the weekend avoiding each other. When we are in the brownstone together he's in the basement. I assume he slept on the futon; he only went up to the bedroom after I vacated it in the mornings. At lunchtime on Sunday, he heads into the kitchen; I retreat toward the music room. On the hall table is his phone. From the kitchen I hear a knife clink in a mayonnaise jar, a plate making contact with the counter. I eye the phone.

Over the years, I've inadvertently heard the large and small jealousies that invade the personal lives of my orchestra mates. I scoffed at their rocky romances, rolled my eyes at the drama—artistic types can be high strung, many thoroughly distrustful. Despite my flaws, I've never viewed myself as prone to these capricious emotions. So when I pick up Rob's phone, I tell myself it's merely my right to know. Interesting. He hasn't changed the pass code. I scroll through his texts. The only one from Sasha is months ago. She asks where he's left the key. I was out of town with the symphony; Rob was away on business. Sasha was going to take in a package I was expecting. It doesn't matter; both are far too clever for such a pedestrian trail. There could be a disposable phone I know nothing about.

However, there are several calls. The first is from Friday night, their balcony chat—perhaps Rob and Sasha decided the need for complete discretion has passed. The next is from much later that night, most likely the two of them discussing my disappearance and what it might mean. I imagine their spy-like chatter:

"Do you think she knows?"

"She might. Listen, Rob, if you want to come away from this with the shirt on your back (which I'll be glad to remove later) call the police, play the concerned husband—for now."

Four more calls followed. It explains why I have not heard from Sasha—not to inquire if I turned up, not to ask what's happened. Clearly, she's been updated. Besides, I've purposely let my cell die. She'd have to call the house phone. How ironic would that be?

I continue on to the music room. Focusing on Holst's *Planets* is my plan. I don't want to wallow in the one I'm stuck on. I practice more than I have in ages, moving from *The Planets* to Brahms's Symphony no. 4—stunningly emotional music from a man best known for a lullaby. Rob won't interrupt the sanctuary of this space, certainly not the fervor of the rehearsal. For a time, music becomes a Band-Aid. Interesting. It's so often been a weapon.

The Amati was precisely that the day I tried out for the symphony, not long after my father died. I did not endure the arduous, sometimes humiliating hurdles and hoops of the audition because it was a lifelong goal, but rose to the occasion motivated by retribution. I remember my surrounding competitors, their nervous chatty whispers and them shuffling shoeless onto the partitioned stage. Several hopefuls threw up before and/or after. I never flinched; I just walked out there, barefooted, and delivered the performance I'd been trained for my entire life. As I recall, mine was the only audition that drew audible murmurs from the judging panel. For any other musician, triumphing would have earned a magnificent burst of pride, the culmination of years of dedication. As it was, I managed a pleasant "Thank you" to the symphony's front office director, who delivered the news of my win. I exited the building and nearly stumbled into traffic, blindsided by my immense lack of satisfaction. Later that evening, it was Rob who turned things around, pointing out an alternative perspective: "Forget your father, Liv. His demand died with him. Take the chair and opportunity and make a fresh start with music." To a limited end, I have tried to follow through.

I segue from one piece to another now, going from the baroque era to more modern compositions, even deviating to classical Indian music. I stop and start, on a search for the comfort Theo and his great-grandfather derived from music. Not a weapon, but a way to uplift myself from swirling turmoil. Another few minutes pass: clearly, I am a more skilled violinist than I am a person. The refuge Theo described and the optimism of music that kept my grandfather, his great-grandfather, alive does not materialize for me.

Eventually I give up on the violin and decide that instead of lunch I want a drink. While standing at the wet bar, Rob comes down the stairs, which I never heard him go up. He's changed—Sunday bar wear. He stops in the foyer and pauses, staring into the empty music room. I keep silent in a darker corner of the living room, which he doesn't turn toward. He puts on his jacket, all the while staying focused on the music room. He punches his fists into the pockets. Heaving a sigh that is hard to read—more thoughts about denial or just the exhaustion of not wanting to go another round—he leaves without a word.

For a moment, I listen to the silent, music-less brownstone. With a wineglass in one hand, I pick up the Sunday *Ledger*. I aim for pedestrian distraction, aided by aged Bordeaux. Shep Stewart has a big piece on big city construction. I rehash my conversation with the reporter, his promise to pen a tabloid-type book about his 9-11 kids. In the midst of my current crisis, I haven't forgotten the book. I just can't concoct a reasonable way to stop it. More to the point, a confession from me wouldn't stop Shep—it'd just be a road map. Any action would seem out of place. I think of Claire. What would she do? I imagine Shep Stewart swinging by his balls.

Of course, that's not to say it would be kudos to Claire for protecting Theo. Between Shep's insights and Claire's harsh judgments about India, appearances may be Claire's strongest motivator. Granted, having caught India red-handed, kissing an old boyfriend, Claire's anger was understandable. India is responsible for that. But tacking India's family history onto her crime, making her accountable for the future, seems wildly unfair. I know Theo well enough to surmise how he'd feel about Claire's conclusions. He'd be angrier with her than he ever was at India. The whole sordid story makes me ponder Theo and India's breakup—a girl he was prepared to forgive. A girl he still loves. With a near-empty glass in hand, I retreat to the computer where I Google Miss Church.

There isn't much—though I did imagine an online snippet, maybe a social media post. I hear Facebook can be as regrettable as it is engaging. Perhaps there's more, like a circulating photo of India kissing her ex-boyfriend. Nothing so damning appears, but what I do find are published engagement announcements. It produces a lump in my throat. India is a sweet-looking girl, freckled, with a brilliant smile. I squint, envisioning hair redder than the black-and-white photo allows.

I run my fingertips over Theo's picture. I am drawn to the intricate combination of Sam and me. Mothers and fathers must marvel over markers like this, one at a time, at appropriate stages. I imagine their exclamations about a similar chin or a mirroring nose, an allergy, or inherent gifts like the ones Theo possesses. My intense fascination is a cumulative response, years of pent-up wondering. I force it quiet and read a little more about India.

She has a degree in humanities from UConn. I half smile. *Humanities* . . . No wonder she ended up working for her parents' catering company. While a humanities degree from UConn is commendable—and more than I accomplished—I don't believe it will feed you. But the short blurb also notes that India will pursue her master's in clinical psychology. I wonder if she's done this. I wonder if Theo was right about his phone call with India. Does she miss him, or has she gone on with her life? What's more obvious are Claire's feelings on the subject. She's satisfied much the same way my mother was when Sam and I ended things. Future calamity averted. I click off the webpage, sipping on mixed memories and wine.

Just as I'm about to leave the computer, Skype buzzes in. It's Phillip. I'd avoided telling him about my dubious choice, to serve community service hours in Theo's classroom. In order to do this, I would have to explain how I got there, really got there. While Phillip knew my best-kept secret, he didn't know about the orchestra funding. It seemed small and sort of "so what" compared to Phillip's life, which is dedicated to service.

About a week ago—before all hell broke loose with Rob and Sasha—I e-mailed my brother and divulged the Theo part of the story—every detail, including the endowment. When I didn't hear back, I concluded that perhaps, he too, finally had enough *Liv* in his life.

Cautiously, I answer the Skype call. "Phillip," I say too cheerily. In only a way Phillip can, he reads my tone, which translates like the pop of a flare gun. Yet I stick to my cordial greeting. "How are you, besides tan?" Phillip has been perpetually tan and happy since relocating to New Zealand. Not even a fuzzy feed affects his rugged good looks, and I am reminded of the throngs of disappointed girls from his high school days.

"I'm good, Liv." He leans closer to the screen. "What the hell happened to your face?"

"I fell." He cocks his head. "I was drunk," I state more plainly.

He only nods in reply. "Sorry it took so long to get back to you. Scott and I were away, barely electricity, definitely no internet."

"Visiting another school?"

"Actually, a refugee camp in Nauru, an island north of the Ditch. A tentative agreement with the Australian and New Zealand governments will allow a limited number of approved applicants asylum—mostly Syrians, as you can imagine. Scott and I volunteered to assist during the process."

"Of course you did," I murmur. I shake my head at my snarky tone.

"I think Granddad would be all for it."

"Yes, he would . . . And that's wonderful, Phillip." It is. Regardless of any orchestra funding, it's also a reminder of how removed Phillip's life is from mine. Scott, a New Zealand native, is a pediatrician. Together, he and Phillip have devoted themselves to causes like this. Phillip is a teacher, though his inability to secure a teaching position stateside helped to facilitate his move abroad decades ago. It was a time when elementary schools found more reasons to deny an openly gay man a job than to give him one. Between this, my parents, and the luck of finding Scott, his ticket to a new life was easily punched. "So along with this latest project, I assume you continue to spend your inheritance on the needs of others?"

"Where it's most beneficial . . . yes," he says. "Not that I don't get some serious surf time in too." Phillip smiles, a feature that does not belong to either of our parents. It's our grandfather's smile—a man who took care to live a meaningful existence after his unjust imprisonment. Once stateside, Jacob Klein made his fortune by writing musical scores for big Hollywood productions—a stupefying twist compared to his past. He also made connections, turning his earnings into even bigger money, ultimately giving a huge portion of it away. Despite Phillip's tin ear, they are alike, in temperament and in purpose. Conversely, I suppose it's obvious who takes after our father. When it comes to Granddad, I also like to believe he would have responded to Phillip's sexual orientation by saying: *"Abi gezunt!"*—"As long as you're healthy." I smile at Phillip, who says, "Sounds like you've been doing some philanthropic spending of your own."

"Nothing compared to yours, but yes. I'm sorry I didn't tell you about the orchestra endowment sooner. I just, um . . ."

"Didn't want to brag?"

I smirk at his teasing reply. "How did you know?"

"Experience. Better still, I know how you don't see yourself." A few seconds of silence passes before he says anything more. "That was a hell of an e-mail you sent. I'd congratulate you on your endowment endeavor, ask the details, but you kind of eclipsed it with your Theo news."

"You know what they say about no good deed going unpunished."

"Interesting choice of words, Liv." Phillip shakes his head. "All these years. Except for what happened to Theo on 9-11, you haven't said a word about him. What were you thinking?"

"I wasn't thinking, hence the current mess."

"And how long have you been 'helping out' in his classroom?" Phillip puts air quotes around the phrase.

"Since mid-September."

"Thanksgiving's next week. Telling him a while back might have been the smart move."

"So did you just Skype in to reiterate what I know—I've exceeded all expectation in terms of fucking up?" I pick up my near-empty wineglass and cheer it toward the screen. "Maybe you do have a little of Mom and Dad in you after all."

He doesn't flinch at the dig, but his face sobers. "I don't think you have to be them to agree this is a bit of a . . . *predicament*."

I make the cheering motion again. "Fair enough."

"Here's a thought. Why don't you try confiding in your husband? He might have a reasonable solution. Granted, it'll all come as a bit of a surprise, but Rob—"

My posture pulls pole straight. "I can't do that. Not now."

"Why not?"

I draw the wineglass to my nose, breathing in alcohol-filled air. "When I sent you that e-mail, things weren't great between Rob and me. Now . . ." I linger for moment. "Let's just say we've gone from bad to worse inside a week." For a brief second, I toy with the idea of spilling everything. I can't. It would cross a new threshold of humiliation. "We're, um . . . Rob and I aren't really speaking at the moment."

His sober look morphs to concern. "Do you want to talk about it?"

"No," I say emphatically, downing the last mouthful of wine and placing the glass on the desk.

"Okay . . ." he says carefully. "But, Liv, when it comes to Rob—"

I slam my hands on the desktop and jerk closer to the screen. It's abrupt enough to startle Phillip, nine thousand miles away. "Oh my God, if one more person points out how Rob is so well suited for me, I swear—"

"Liv," Phillip says in a loud but calm tone. "If you're finding that statement overplayed, it's because it's true, and something you already know."

"What's that supposed to mean?"

He leans back, lacing his fingers behind his head and shifting ridiculously broad shoulders. "Okay, let me take a page from the Liv handbook of blunt: Accepting everything Rob has to offer means accepting yourself, admitting that you've earned that kind of happiness—a man for whatever his flaws, loves you a great deal. For reasons maybe only you and I can understand, I get why acceptance is a monumental task—more so than playing a Bach minuet at the age of five."

"It was Bohm's *Moto Perpetuo*."

"Whatever. The point is, from what I've observed about you and Rob, it's always been two steps forward, three steps back. You're never going to get to happy doing that dance, little sister. You've got to take the chance, when it comes to Rob . . . sounds like, maybe, when it comes to Theo. But only you can do that, Liv. It's not that you don't want it; it's that you don't believe you deserve it. That's a problem."

"That you solved for yourself twenty-five years ago." I suck in a sigh. "You were always the braver one."

"Hey, my transgressions weren't nearly as heinous and devastating as yours. I get that. I only fell in love with a man. You refused to hang on a cross and be Dad's musical savior. Believe me; I'm aware of which flaw came at a greater price. And yet you stayed. I'm not the braver one of us, Liv . . . Not even close."

"Your point of view is slanted."

"My point of view is distant—clearer perspective." I am quiet; Phillip knows we've reached an impasse. He sighs and leans forward into the screen. "So tell me, what's my nephew like?"

Our Skype conversation goes on for the next half hour, until the screen freezes twice and the desk phone rings. The answering machine picks up and we hear Rob's voice, and Phillip says, "Liv, maybe you'd better get that."

"What for?"

"Liv . . ." he says in a warning tone. "Three steps back . . ." Before I can act, Rob hangs up.

Phillip and I end our Skype call and I mumble into the blank screen. "Yeah, but what you don't know is that those last few steps were off a cliff." The phone rings again. It's Rob. This time I answer. "Yes?"

"I called your cell an hour ago."

"It's dead. That's the best way of avoiding people I don't want to talk to. At the moment, that's just about everyone I know." If Phillip lived closer, had a better grasp on the myriad of troubles that plague my marriage, he might have had a different opinion, or a more lasting influence with the one he offered. As it is, I hang up on my husband and head into the kitchen, rummaging through the refrigerator.

Seconds later the phone rings for a third time. Rob's voice echoes. He's angry, but he also sounds off-kilter. I can't make out what he's saying. I peek around the refrigerator's stainless-steel door, hearing words so tense they would snap a Slinky. It ends with "So come here if you want. I'm not sure what else to do for him—or you." He hangs up.

Back at the desk, I fumble for the play button on the answering machine. Rob tells me he's at Mass General—with Sam. As he does, my hand rises to my mouth. He's in the emergency room. I don't call Rob back. I just throw on a coat and grab my purse. It's a jumbled drive between city construction, the muddy hues of a sinking sun, and my life. Right turns and wrong ones, unexpected twists in the road.

When I arrive at Mass General, I'm not entirely sure how I got there. I can't find a spot, so I park in an obvious tow zone—the brilliance versus the inconvenience of Boston hospitals. At the emergency room entrance, the double doors open automatically. Rob is coming down a corridor, hands shoved in his jacket pockets, the front of his Pats jersey smeared in blood—like maybe they put him in the game this afternoon. I stagger to a stop.

Wild scenarios erupt in my mind, ones where Rob confronted Sam at his hotel. A fight ensued. But how or why Rob is blood splattered, yet appears unscathed, makes no sense. While Rob is a fitness freak, Sam is a professional athlete. Better still, avoiding a punch is the thing Sam learned best growing up. "What happened?" My head shakes with questions.

"I went to see your ex."

"What the hell did you do to him?"

"What did I . . . ?" Rob thumbs at his chest. "Yeah. I guess that'd be your next wild claim." For a moment I think he's going to stomp right past me and out the doors.

"Well?" I say, pointing to the blood streaks he just pounded. "What am I supposed to think? You're upright, making phone calls, and Sam's—"

"In with the doctor." I look past Rob and down a busy corridor. "I didn't hit him. Christ, Liv, do you really think I went to see your ex-, pro-athlete husband with the intention of punching him in the face? I like risks; I don't have a death wish." His gaze glosses over me. "And don't flatter yourself. Beating the shit out of him because of you wasn't on my to-do list today."

I think of my accusations about him and Sasha. He's right; a jealous confrontation wouldn't make sense. "Why would you go see him at all?"

"Because I can't figure out what's going on with you—or us." I glance away. "I was desperate. I thought maybe he could enlighten me. It was, um . . . *educational.* He knows you well."

"What did you want to ask him?" I lower my voice. "Maybe see if my claim about *not* having sex with him matched his?"

"Actually, that came up here at the hospital."

"And he told you nothing happened, right?"

For a moment, Rob doesn't respond, though his eyes narrow and his nostrils flare. He stares, pursing his lips before replying. "He said you were drunk. That eventually you passed out." Rob scrubs a hand over his face and pushes past me. "He's in treatment room four. See him or don't." I turn; he continues to walk away.

"I'm sorry." The loud and abrupt apology stops him. "I'm sorry about the other night. No matter what, I shouldn't have gone to Sam's hotel. It was a bad choice. Will . . . will you tell me what happened?"

He turns. "If I had any sense at all, I would do exactly that—word for word." His face is uncharacteristically solemn and he draws a deep breath. "As I said, I thought a conversation with him might give me a clue about what the hell is going on. We didn't get very far. When he opened his hotel room door, his nose was already bleeding. I cracked some joke about the husband of somebody else's wife getting there before me. He only said 'I wish.'" Rob looks down the hallway. His face is a disturbing mix of compassion and anger. "He was white as a sheet, sweating. A minute or so later, he fell forward into me." Rob's hand grazes over his jersey. "I caught him. But he caught me by surprise. I lost my balance. He fell. On the way down, he hit his head on a piece of furniture. Once he was out cold, you kind of became an afterthought. I called 911."

I'm wobbly myself. I reach for Rob's arm. He yanks it back. "Is it, um . . . So you ended up here because . . ."

"I rode in the ambulance with him. It seemed like the decent thing to do. He regained consciousness by the time they got him on board. From what he said to the EMTs, he's clearly concerned that his leukemia has relapsed." Rob shakes his head. "All the shit you've put me through the past few days—to be honest—the past hour, and I end up feeling sorry for the son of a bitch. When we got here, they ushered me into the room with him. But even prone, your ex managed to leap to your defense. While waiting for a doctor, we talked. First, he asked point blank if I was having an affair with Sasha. Dying or alive, the guy's definitely got a set."

"He always did." A tear surprises me, dripping off my chin.

"Guess you two did a lot of personal sharing. He certainly provided me with an earful."

"About what?"

"Your past with him." He looks me up and down. "Your present."

"What present?" I say, incredulous. "Yes. I spent the night in his hotel room—I was angry, upset . . . I admit it was a poor choice. But I told you, nothing happened."

Rob stares, breathing deep again. "He said that's what he told you. Interesting, I told you the same thing about Sasha and me—aside from one night of unremarkable ancient history." His blue eyes meet mine. He speaks more softly. "Tell me something, at this point, if I was having an affair with Sasha, why wouldn't I just admit it? What would I be fighting for, considering where . . . where we are right now?" He whips around, heading toward the doors again.

Rob's interpretation clarifies a stunning point. He's right. If he was having an affair with Sasha, the last place he'd go would be to Sam Nash's hotel room. "Rob, wait." My breath catches, my heart fluttering. "Don't walk away like this." My plea is loud enough to draw the stares of waiting patients and medical personnel.

He stops and turns, though I can tell it's more a gesture of obligation than desire. On his face is a rarely seen look of loss, maybe judgment. I get the distinct impression he's about to say something devastating. Instead, he snickers, his tone defeated. He shakes his head. "I can't do this, Liv. Not now. Maybe today . . . the other night was meant to be. Maybe this is just the push we needed."

I take a step back, Rob's words hitting like a physical response I would never associate with him. "You're pissed off about where I spent the night. I get it. Probably something like learning you and Sasha slept together all those years ago and that you both kept it from me."

"Mmm . . . something like that, though not quite. Not after my talk with Sam."

"But I told you—"

Rob holds up a hand. "I'm up to speed on you, booze, and bad choices."

"Fair enough," I say quietly, knowing he's right, wishing he didn't have quite so many go-to examples. "As for you and Sasha, I can't explain the hotel souvenirs or what it looks like. But, um . . . but given the ledge we're standing on, based on what's happened . . . You and Sasha, it doesn't seem so likely."

"That's great, Liv. Glad to hear it." He nods and his mouth dips to a frown. "Here's the bad news." He looks past my head, down the hallway. "Knowing the ledge we're standing on. Given what's happened, I don't know that I give a shit anymore." He turns and leaves.

CHAPTER THIRTY-ONE

Olivia

"We should have your labs back shortly. We'll go from there." Dr. Travers pats Sam's arm. She's an overtly caring emergency department physician. Or so I have determined in the past hour.

"Dr. Bogart?" Sam asks.

Standing beside him, I just listen and look at the stress-filled clench to Sam's jaw. It's in confirmation of what he already knows, or doesn't want to hear. "We've got a call in to him," she says. "Why don't we just get some solid numbers before drawing conclusions? The fever may be a combination of an infection and a still-weak immune system. As for the nosebleed—it's hardly conclusive. The shift in climate for you and Boston's dry fall air could do that to anybody. We don't know until we know . . . Let's keep a good thought until then." Sam nods; the doctor and her chipper disposition exits.

"Not terribly convincing, was she?" he says.

"She may be right. Like she said, positive thoughts. You don't know."

He leans his head back against the pillow. "Yeah, Liv. I do." I reach over and squeeze his hand. It's hot. In addition to the bloody nose, he has a temperature of 103. IV fluids are being pumped into him for now. Separately, you could make a hopeful argument for his symptoms. Together, I suspect Sam knows better. I squeeze tighter. The bruises on his arm. I'm suddenly aware they're not a result of his workout at Brandeis, or like the fresh bump on his head. A drip of blood puddles at the top of his moustache. I hang on to my poker face and subtly hand him a damp cloth the nurse has left. He takes it and presses it to his nose. We both suck in a sigh. Even while clinging to my hand, he trembles slightly. "It was, um, good of your husband to come here with me. Did he leave?" Sam glances at the clock, disoriented.

"Rob left. He, um . . . he had some business things to see to."

Sam cinches his brow. "You should know, after we got here, I asked Rob if he was shagging your friend." He shakes his head. "At least I think I did. Sorry . . . am I making that up? I, um . . . we talked about a lot of different things." He sinks his head deeper into a pillow.

"No. You're not making it up. Don't worry about Rob and me. What I thought about him and Sasha was, I think, just the last straw." I take an even deeper breath. "Hey, why don't we find something more positive to talk about?"

"Compared to my health, I thought your marriage was a more positive topic."

Levity dominates for a split second. "You don't know," I say more soberly, squeezing his hand harder. "And you got better before. Nothing says you can't do it again. You're a man who beats incredible odds—all kinds."

"I don't think so, Liv. Not this time. When it comes to this disease, I got lucky once." He lets go of my hand, brushing his over the fresh bruises on his arm. "But I ignored these . . . I've been feeling lousy for a while. To be honest, since you've turned back up, it's occurred to me . . ."

“What’s occurred to you?”

“You know I’m not a big believer of fate or even fitting endings, but maybe there’s a reason we didn’t stay together all those years ago.”

“I’m not following.”

“If we had, we’d be old history by now—I mean, considering you . . .” He glances at me. I shrug. “Considering me, what were our odds of keeping it together? Our departure from one another would have been something uglier than an awkward conversation in a hotel room.”

“I still don’t—”

“These past few days, I’ve been thinking about the thing that’s scared me most. It isn’t dying. It was dying alone. You’re here. Maybe fate’s seen to just that much.” He turns his head away and focuses on a blank wall. We are quiet as he composes himself. I assume it’s a distraction when Sam reaches for his cell, tucked beneath the sheet. He clicks on the screen. There are two calls from Brandeis, no others. He glances at me. “Sorry. I didn’t mean to imply that you’re suddenly responsible for me.”

“That’s not how I took it. Can we just not allow fate to have the worst-case scenario? Not yet.”

He clicks on the phone again, one contact in particular. “I’ve kept in touch with Rex Simmons, the PI I hired to find Tate. Even after I got better . . . Well, I thought it wouldn’t be the worst thing to know where your closest kin is.”

“Tate,” I say breathlessly. “A bone marrow transplant. It’s why you went looking for him in the first place.”

“Yeah. A sibling is your best bet. After that, blood relatives become . . . Well, not even a distant second. I have a few cousins. Bogey said it was lottery-ticket odds they’d be a match, but they insisted on getting tested anyway. They weren’t.”

I inch away from Sam, my rough fingertips running over my mouth. “I, um . . . so if a sibling is your best chance, and cousins are at best a lottery-ticket shot . . .”

Naturally, he does not follow my lead. "There's the national marrow donor registry, but so far no match. Of course, back when this all started, Bogey talked about a haplo match."

"Haplo . . . ?"

"Yeah—a *half match.* Longer odds than a sibling, more realistic than a cousin; a newer treatment compared to traditional bone marrow donor matches." He clicks off the phone and looks at me. An effort to smile collapses to a shudder, visible through his bearded chin.

"And what, um . . ." My chin shudders back. "Who qualifies for this half match?"

Sam shakes his head. "Parents . . . a kid. For whatever good that doesn't do me."

My heart pounds furiously. A male nurse with a wheelchair comes through the door. It's best he takes Sam away; otherwise he'd hear my heart thumping.

"Mr. Nash, since you did hit your head, just to be on the safe side, Dr. Travers has ordered a CT."

"Right. Because I'm sure a brain bleed would be a worse way to go."

A few moments later, he's helped Sam into the wheelchair. As he does, the nurse goes on about a historical and dramatic last pitch, a final out—what an extraordinary thing a World Series win, like that, must be. As they back out of the treatment room, Sam's damp eyes blink into mine. He replies with phrases that sound canned, like he's answered this question a million times. I suspect his perspective changed in the past year, maybe to "it's only a game."

The moment Sam is gone I snatch my phone from my purse. I scroll to what may be Sam's last pitch, the one that's in my possession. It's a curve ball, listed under Theo McAdams.

CHAPTER THIRTY-TWO

Olivia

The next few days are a hazy whirl—I've jumped from one shaky life (my own) deep into another. Subsequent tests confirm what Sam suspected. At the hospital, he hit me with a rash of numbers, white counts, and other medical jargon that I couldn't interpret. Regardless, Sam's grim summation said it all: "Hell, if they were baseball stats, I would have never even made the minor leagues." Sam was admitted to the hospital. He's too ill to travel. Like a single snowflake falling, there is one speck of good news—Mass General is the best. They excel in treating his particular type of leukemia. But the snowflake is quickly swallowed by the surrounding storm. Because Sam has relapsed after remission, treatment options change. His best chemo hope is lesser-proven clinical trials. I guess having *the best* is all about perspective.

I take a crash course online and learn pedestrian facts about myeloid leukemia: age has a lot to do with odds in this particular disease—if Sam were younger, his chances would be better. Of course, if he were older, they'd be worse. So he falls to the middle. Yet cure rates are greatly affected by the type of treatment—numbers vary between stem cell transplants and traditional treatment, or even trial chemo therapies. Even though the overall numbers are not wildly encouraging, people have survived; they beat the odds.

I want their names. I go from website to website, searching for more positive outcomes. I find none. Mostly I learn the differences between remission, relapse, and a cure. When I left Sam in his room, I was all about curing him. No wonder he just kept smiling and nodding. Remission is the realistic hope. It's what he achieved back in California. It's what he was hoping would last longer than six or seven months. I continue, absorbing more grim statistics, the latest clinical trials, and quality-of-life studies. As Sam said, his best hope for a bone-marrow donor remains his brother.

Unfortunately, *hope* is not a word I equate with Tate Nash. Sadly, it's far easier to imagine him turning Sam down than agreeing to help. If this is the case, maybe it's best he never turn up. I consider this avenue closed. There is the National Marrow Donor Program, but, so far, no match for Sam. Finally, I find the word Sam mentioned in the emergency room—*haplo*. Or as a Johns Hopkins webpage points out, Haploidentical Transplantation—a treatment by which parents and children—once considered an automatic non-match—can have life-saving potential.

Of course Sam did not see this as an option.

Yet I do not contact Theo immediately. My hesitation isn't about fallout—I am stunningly unconcerned about how this will bode for me. My hesitation is approach. I want to be wiser, steadier about what I do next. Years of rash behavior finally serves as a lesson, but most glaringly these past few months. Impulsive Liv is the last thing anyone needs here. I've no one but myself to blame for the loss of a husband, possibly a best friend. I've not heard a word from Sasha. As it is, Rob left a curt note about being *out of town* for a few days. The way it was written, he could have left it for the cleaning lady. He does not say where he's gone. He doesn't call.

Frankly, at the moment, it's for the best. My crisis mode isn't that high-functioning. I put "wiser" to work. I don't waste time cobbling together a plan whereby I only share the truth about Theo on a need-to-know basis. I get it; the jig is up. Telling Sam will be a shock—ultimately a welcome one. Rob may reply with the same answer he did in the hospital corridor—"I don't know that I give a shit anymore, Liv . . ." As for telling Theo . . . I suspect *welcome news* won't be part of his reaction.

Granted, this would play as a much cleaner scenario if I were no more than a stranger knocking on Theo's door. As it is, I've managed to muck up that option, wholly removing it from the table. I decide to give myself time to mentally craft a plan of action. How do I spring this on Theo and come away with his cooperation? How will I convey, in one conversation, urgency, duplicity, and the necessary result?

I do not go to Braemore on Monday or Tuesday. I don't even call. I tick off hours like a death-row prisoner: the solitude of a last meal, which I don't eat, and what awaits me in the afterlife as a result of the chaos I created in this one. Final tasks, like gathering my nerve and introspection, are interrupted when the brownstone doorbell rings Tuesday night. I open it, finding a stern-faced Sasha on the other side. She does not wait for an invitation but ploughs her tiny frame, dressed in an all-business camel-colored coat, past mine and into the music room. Unlike other brownstone rooms, this is my space. It's also our communal spot to share secrets, laugh, and just be. It's the sanctuary into which you invite your friends. Sasha is the only person I have ever asked to be a part of this room.

"Excellent," she says, staking a claim in the center. "You're not dead." The energy pulsing off of her plays like Pettersson's Symphony no. 6—nerve-rackingly raw and violent. I stand to the side, near the secretary desk. Sasha tosses the evidentiary hobo bag onto the sofa; she plucks brown leather gloves from her hand, one finger at a time, an authoritative *you'll wait* gesture. Focused on the gloves, she avoids eye contact. "Forget my number?"

"No."

"I didn't think so." Her steely honey-gold gaze moves to mine. "What was your plan, Liv, to avoid me forever?" I open my mouth; she stabs a finger in my direction. "It was rhetorical. Anything personal can wait. I'm here in an official capacity."

"That being?"

"You've now missed two classes at Braemore. When you didn't bother to call in today, Principal Giroux reported you. That's not the deal, Liv. Absences from court-ordered community service require a doctor's note or some other viable excuse—like you've been incarcerated on a different charge, robbing a packy or grand theft auto. Did you rob a packy, Liv?" I shake my head. She sniffs. "Not surprising—there's not enough booze in Boston to drown your sorry ass." She tilts her head at me. "Nice bruise. Sorry. But drunken clumsiness doesn't count either. Are you physically ill?"

"No."

"So you're suffering from what? Acute embarrassment? That's rich. I can't imagine a scenario bad enough to keep *you* from going about your business. Seriously, you bashed your husband's Porsche in with a baseball bat in the middle of Newbury Street and never blinked. You told a judge to go fuck himself and spent the weekend in jail, still managing not to miss symphony practice. Or has embarrassment evolved out of a deeper faux pas? The one where you vanish and scare the shit out of everyone, then admit to being a stumbling drunk and spending the night with your ex—which, oh by the way, thanks for sharing with me."

"So you know Sam Nash is in town."

"I know a lot of things, Liv. Like the fact that your ex-husband's sudden appearance is nothing compared to accusing *me*—the one person who has always had your back—of having an affair with *your* husband!"

"I, um . . . The two of you did—"

"Don't even try it," she spits. "Fucking Rob all those years ago . . . It was about as emotionally moving as your annual pap smear." I swallow this down. Whether it was moving or not, a mental visual of them together stings—oddly so for a marriage that is supposedly over. "It was one wrong choice before he ever met you, and a long-ago lie devised to protect a budding romance. How the hell was I supposed to know you'd end up marrying the guy? If I recall, you did try to toss him to the curb after three or four dates."

"I can see how you couldn't have predicted the future."

"And I did think about telling you—more than once. It just never . . . Well, it never seemed to serve a purpose other than clearing my conscience."

"I can relate to that." But Sasha isn't listening; she's on a roll.

"I can't speak for Rob—he's not my business. But *me*? The fact that you'd think that about me?"

"Things added up, Sasha. Things that still don't make sense."

She takes a fuming turn around the room, her small fists squeezed tight. "Think of it like any court case, Olivia. It's not up to me to defend my innocence. It's up to you to prove my guilt."

"Maybe so, but you have to agree . . ."

"No, Liv. I don't have to agree. You prove it. Prove that your conclusion is based on anything but circumstantial evidence." She waits, as if this is a courtroom and the judge has just demanded that the prosecution present its hardcore evidence.

I point to her hobo bag. "At dinner. You dumped a bunch of stuff on the table. There was a boarding pass, a claim check from The Bed. Out of all the hotels in New York, Rob was staying at The Bed. Same window of time from what I can deduce. You didn't tell me about your trip. You never said a word."

Sasha folds her arms and huffs at me—as if she is the seasoned trial attorney and I am the idiot client who has chosen to defend myself. "It does not prove I was there to sleep with your husband. If that's all you have to sell to the jury . . ." She folds her arms, her expression humorless.

"But it certainly appeared—"

She holds up a hand. "You're not getting how this works. Let me help you out. I admit it; I was there."

I blink, surprised. "Okay, so would you care to explain it, other than the most obvious conclusion? I called your office that day. Carly told me you were in court."

"I was. *In New York*. I was deposing a witness we were having trouble pinning down. I went to the source."

"And you just happened to stay at the same romantic hole-in-the-wall hotel as Rob?"

"Being as I highly recommended the hotel when we recently had lunch here, it's not that incredible of a coincidence."

"Okay, but why wouldn't you tell me you'd been to New York? The night we had dinner, you were distracted, on edge."

"I believe I did tell you it was a long day with a witness—I just didn't say where."

"But why?" I stride past, flailing a hand in her direction. "Add to that you and Rob. You've been oddly chummy lately, whispery phone calls, the picnic lunch in my kitchen." I motion in that direction. "I don't know much about the law, Sasha, but in everyday life, those sound like pretty damning facts."

The energy around Sasha stops moving, and her lawyerly façade deflates. My eyes widen as her small chin begins to quiver. I back up. Have I made too good of a case? She can't get out of it. She can't do anything but confess to circumstantial evidence. "I didn't tell you because of what I was doing in New York—besides deposing a witness. I was with Zowz."

"Zowz? From your office?"

"No. Zowz from the Southie. Yes, him."

"So?"

"You're right about Rob and I having more than a few whispery conversations lately. I ended up confiding something to him that I couldn't confide to you."

"Which is?"

"Zowz." She sighs softly. "We've been . . . sleep—" She stops, looking sheepishly between my music stand and me. "You're right about the affair, Liv. You've just got the wrong guy. Zowz. I've been having an affair with Nick Zowzer. There. Are you happy?"

"That's the lamest excuse I've ever heard." I shake my head. "It's impossible. You've never said one pleasant word about Nick Zowzer, let alone expressed a desire to sleep with him." My head shakes harder. "And forget him. You'd never have an affair with anybody!"

She splays her hands wide into the space in front of her.

My hands thrust to my hips. Fabulous. I've just proven her case. I take a conciliatory step back. I suppose it is fabulous. "Oh," I murmur. The larger ramification hits home. "Then I guess that would explain how I . . . Or that you and Rob aren't . . ."

"Yeah. We're not, and now you know."

"I don't get it. You confided this to Rob, but not to me. You live with Jeremy. You hate Nick Zowzer. He's your biggest rival." I stand dumbfounded, the facts still sinking in. "You're having an affair with Zowz? Oh my God . . ." My stark gaze is glued to the brownstone's front window. Life moves along Commonwealth Ave. There isn't a passerby who could trump this tawdry tidbit. I look back at Sasha. "Geez. You're going to have to give me a few minutes . . . maybe days to absorb that one."

"Okay, so based on that statement, would you have jumped to tell you?" She sinks onto the sofa, her hands knotting. "Rob was an easier dumping ground. Maybe because we already shared one dirty little secret." We trade a dubious glance. "And I admit . . ." Her voice shakes.

"Part of the reason I didn't tell you was because I didn't want you to see me in that light."

A snicker seeps out of me. "Because I'm a total screwup and you're beyond reproach."

"No!" Sasha glances from her clasped hands to my face. "Maybe. On some days." She looks at me. "I'm sorry, Liv. I shouldn't have told Rob over you. But a person can only keep a secret like that for so long before they have to confess it. He was in the right place at the right time. And it wasn't even on purpose."

"Lunch in my kitchen."

"Between the pastrami on rye and a mini carrot cake." I sink onto the sofa next to her. "I know you love carrot cake, so I brought you one."

"So I guess Rob got my carrot cake and the earful," I say. "Can you back up, fill in some Zowz blanks? You claim to all but loathe the 'slick, smooth-talking bastard.' The butt of Viagra jokes. How did you and Zowz ever . . ."

Sasha's hand thumps dejectedly into her lap. "No matter how I explain it, it'll sound like nothing but a seedy office romance—pull the blinds, after-hours sex on the leather Steelcase sofa . . ." A swallow bobs through her delicate throat. She doesn't look at me. "Jesus, Liv, we've all but had sex on the copy machine. I couldn't tell you that."

"And for how long has this been . . . Have the two of you . . ."

"About two months."

"Two . . . ?" My mouth gapes—at the timeframe, the visuals. The fact that almost-infallible Sasha is having an affair—with *Nick Zowzer*.

"Nick, we . . ."

My attention turns to Sasha as she employs Nick's first name. When Sasha introduced us a couple of years ago, I had to ask his first name—she'd never said.

"Nick lost a case. Interestingly, his client was a kid who used to go to Braemore. Zowz said the system totally screwed the kid over—serious grown-up jail time. And not because of his crime, but because the kid had turned eighteen between the alleged crime and initial court proceedings," she says. "For once, instead of feeling rivalry, I felt bad for him. He had a bottle of Glenlivet. I helped him drown his sorrows for a while, then . . ."

"Then what?"

"The first time we had sex, it was in *his* office." She finally looks at me. "After that I went home to my fragile, forever-needy significant other. Someone who is only ever affected by his personal wins and losses. Everything about Zowz, including sex, was the polar opposite. So how's that for timing?"

"Sounds like maybe I've been rubbing off on you after all."

"I swore it wouldn't happen again—ever. But it did. I liked it . . ." Sasha says this as if Zowz could be purchased in dime bags. "I liked being with someone who I didn't have to constantly reassure. I mean, yes, he'd lost a case. All it managed to do was humanize him. Suddenly, the crasser, louder parts of Zowz felt more like a champion for the cause, not a loudmouth, brash attorney."

"I know you said things with Jeremy weren't good. But I thought maybe you'd show him the door before you . . ."

"So that's part of my guilt. Jeremy doesn't know. I can't tell him. The state he's in. It'd crush him." Sasha clamps a hand over her mouth. She jerks up off the sofa and takes a wide turn around the small room. "And I'm an awful person."

"Sasha," I say firmly. "You are not an awful person. Just stop. Yes. Sex on the sly with Zowz . . . *Nick* isn't exactly commendable or typical Sasha behavior, but if he's what you want . . ." I stop, still trying to get my head around Sasha and the man she most commonly refers to as the office pit bull—*rabid* office pit bull. "Is he? I mean, do . . . are you in love with him?"

"I don't know," she says. "Add that to my motivation for secrecy. I'm not sure what it is. The trip to New York, it was the first time we spent the night together." She glances at me. "Rob never saw us at The Bed . . . But I saw him in the lobby. I ducked out of sight; facing him would have been too surreal. I mean, what would he have said, 'So how's the affair going, Sash?' But when you accused Rob of having an affair with me . . ."

"Oh my God, he was confused beyond belief. And probably doubly pissed off. But why didn't he just tell me about you and Nick?"

"Because I all but begged him not to. I wanted to tell you when I was ready. Says something about Rob's trustworthiness, doesn't it?"

"Underneath my fast-talking, high-stakes husband . . . Well, that appears to be a lot of loyalty. I, um . . . Seems I owe him, both of you, an apology."

"To be honest, when Rob told me about the *evidence* from The Bed, the shoe shine cloth, the claim check . . . After rolling it to your interpretation of something I definitely was keeping from you . . . I can see how you got there." She sighs. "It's not that far off from how people end up doing life for a murder they didn't commit. On the other hand, knowing the truth, Rob was angry and hurt . . . So was I." Sasha's eyes are teary, as are mine. I believe the only thing we've never done in this room together is cry. "So aside from all that shitty stuff between you, me, and Rob—an ongoing affair with Nick Zowzer is my current problem."

I don't speak. I don't know what to say. Sasha doesn't require sage advice, she gives it. Her delicate hand wipes at a bead of sweat that has formed on her upper lip. The only time I've seen Sasha sweat is during her cycling class. "Sasha, you'll work it out. Whether Nick Zowzer turns out to be the love of your life, or just the exit door you needed to prove Jeremy isn't."

"Even so . . . It's an affair. I'm lying to the man I live with. What does that say about me?"

"Sash." She looks at me. "You have no idea what a real lie sounds like. The unforgivable kind that can really cost you . . . a friend, a husband . . . a son."

"A . . . ?" Her face perplexes. "What do sons have to do with this?"

"You came here to ask why I haven't been to Braemore for the past two days, right?"

Sasha wipes a hand across the tears on her face, nodding. "Partly," she says. "Mostly I think I wanted to tell you everything I just did. I couldn't put that on Rob anymore. But yes. I need an answer for your absence. I wasn't kidding, Liv. Judge Nicholson isn't going to give you much of a leash."

"Okay. I'll explain—everything." A breath shudders out of me. "But prepare yourself. What I'm about to tell you will make sex with Zowz seem like a swan boat ride in the Public Garden."

CHAPTER THIRTY-THREE

Olivia

Which thread to pull first? While I mull it over, Sasha digs into the culprit hobo bag and comes up with a package of tissues. Jumping inside, vanishing amid the eyeliner and lipsticks, is an appealing option. "Like I said, this will clear things up, including why I didn't tell you Sam Nash was in town. It will explain why I hate New Year's Eve, and what seems like a sudden fascination with a young music teacher from Braemore."

"All of those things in one explanation?"

I've piqued Sasha's interest. "Really, they're just one thing."

"Go on, I'm listening." She is listening, though it's Rob's voice that enters the music room.

"I think I'd like to hear this too."

Sasha turns and I look toward the pocket doors. "I didn't hear you come in."

"I was quiet. I caught the tail end of what Sasha said. I know it took a lot for her to do that. Can't say I was comfortable knowing what you didn't, so I didn't interrupt." His travel bag lands with a thud on the foyer floor.

Discomfort rises like a July sun; each ray is tied to the accusations and realizations of recent days. Burning through all of them is my uneasiness. "I, um . . . I'm glad you're here, Rob."

"Are you?" He makes a skeptical face. "Surprising. I thought for sure you'd be at Mass General, doing some hand holding." I don't reply. "I assume he's still with us."

"If you're asking if Sam is still alive—yes."

"I meant he didn't go back to California."

I sigh at my ill-fated assumption. "No. He'll stay here for now. He's too ill to travel. He, um . . . Sam also doesn't know his best option for treatment is right here. That's, uh, in part, why I'm glad you're home." I wring my hands vainly, as if this will keep my confession knotted tight inside. "I won't have to tell this story twice. And let me start by saying you won't think any more of me when I'm done." Sasha and Rob exchange curious glances. "More to the point," I say, ramping up my nerve, "you both deserve to know." I've backed up, standing alongside the secretary. "In some regards this will blow you away. In others . . ." I exhale hard. "It'll be another *go figure* Liv moment." The wringing stops. "Maybe the *mother* of all Liv moments."

"Liv, what is going on?" Rob presses.

Their frames are both pulled pole straight, folded arms mirroring—body language saying neither have much wiggle room left for Olivia Klein antics. "Sasha wants to know why I skipped out on Braemore." I pause. I'm about to annihilate what's left of . . . *my family*. The one I came within a razor's edge of destroying this past week. This should finish them off nicely. "I didn't go because I wasn't ready to face Theo."

"Why?" Sasha shakes her head. "What does Theo McAdams have to do with any of this?"

"Great question," Rob says. "But I don't find Olivia's statement that odd. Despite the sudden resurrection of Sam Nash, something's been off, or up, with this kid since she started doing time in Theo's classroom."

I smile at him. "Bravo for knowing your wife better than I would have imagined." I hold up my hand, holding off Rob's next sentence. "The truth is I've been lying about Theo McAdams since the day I met him, which wasn't in his classroom at Braemore."

"You knew Theo McAdams before that?" Sasha looks curiously at Rob. "Liv, is there more to yours and Theo's relationship? Like maybe what I asked you at Neptune Oyster?"

"What did you ask her?" Rob's fair eyes dart between Sasha and me, as if he's trying to decode girl talk.

"I asked if she was sleeping with him."

"Excuse me?" Rob says, his neck craning forward.

"No. I'm not!" I insist. "But . . ." I sigh, reaching for the key to the drawer. I open it and place the *Ledger* clippings onto the desktop, all of them. Then I back away so Rob and Sasha can peruse the stack.

"I don't understand," Sasha says, flipping through. "I saw the clipping from this year, the one that gave you the Braemore idea." She turns toward me. "But I don't get this . . . *collection*." Rob picks up a few of the stories. It takes him a moment longer; he doesn't have Sasha's head start.

"Why are you stalking these . . . *kids*?" He makes his way to the bottom of the pile. "Since 2002."

"Not the kids," I clarify. "Just Theo McAdams.

"Liv told me she's been following the stories." Sasha looks at the yellowed stack, then me. "But I didn't know about the scrapbook collection. After needing a project to fulfil her community service hours, Liv noted the musical link between Theo and herself. See." She points to years of Theo updates, the ones mentioning his musical prowess. "That's how she ended up in his classroom. That's how it started."

"It's not quite how it started," I say.

"Go on." I hear Sash's lawyerly tone. I sense Rob's wary concern, like he's sitting on a bomb that's about to explode.

"You both know about my past with Sam Nash." They nod. "You also know that I told you I got pregnant—somewhere between a dorm room and a marriage that lasted .08 seconds."

"I know you said that *not* being pregnant was for the best," Rob notes. "That because of it, Sam went on with his baseball career and you went—"

"To New Zealand. I went to Phillip's, where I spent the next year." I let the rest break like a dam—or as my water did all those years ago.

"Liv, what, exactly, are you confessing?" Rob says.

"I lied to Sam and to my parents about the miscarriage. While I was there, in New Zealand, I had a baby. A boy . . . on New Year's Eve. Eleven fifty-nine p.m., December thirty-first—a date and time that would be easier to navigate if it were April third or October twelfth. Those dates, they slip by without extra fanfare. But New Year's Eve, one minute to midnight . . ." I smile and swipe at a tear. "The world is waiting and ready, every year, complete with horns, confetti, and an annual poke at the most implausible moment of my life. The thing I got most wrong." I point to the news stories. "Or ridiculously right . . . Since reading those stories, since knowing Theo . . . My perception has gone from living with what happened all those years ago to being amazed at what I've missed out on."

I blink furiously. I have never cried openly in front of Sasha, and Rob ever so sparingly—the night my father died being the single scene in my head. I have never cried for Theo. "I gave him away when he was a day old—to people who could love him like I couldn't, because that's not who I am. It's not what I do, right, Rob?" I want him to agree. I want him to say, *"Yes, Liv, you would have made the world's worst mother. We decided as much together."* But all I can really recall him saying on the subject is, "I don't know that fatherhood is on my to-do list. I'd probably be better off with a dog—so would a kid."

Tears drip from my chin; I run my hand across my snotty nose. "Of course I was sneaky about the adoption because that *is* classic Olivia

Klein. I purposely chose parents from the States. And not ones from Ohio or Texas but around the corner. In my twenty-one-year-old head, it somehow made it an easier thing to do. I mean, a kid. What in the world would I do with a kid? I'd already proven I couldn't get anything right—please my parents or keep a marriage together. Sam's last words on the pregnancy were to end it. Once he thought the baby was gone . . . After the accident, it wasn't such a leap, from being pregnant to *not* being pregnant—"

"Whoa! So Sam Nash . . ." Rob says. "He doesn't know about Theo?"

"Nobody knows, except Phillip . . . and Scott. Of course Theo knows he's adopted, but he has no idea . . ."

An odd expression fills Sasha's face. This must be her reaction when a client she's judged as innocent and misunderstood suddenly confesses to bludgeoning the body. Her wide eyes move between the news stories and me. She looks at Rob and takes a step back from this particular disaster.

I keep talking. "From the time Theo was a baby, I've known that his parents lived within a short drive of the Wellesley house. And for years, it was enough. Unbeknownst to him, we coexisted under those rules. Then September 11th happened. Theo's adoptive father, David McAdams, died that day. Because Theo was mine . . ." My gaze moves around the music room: the Guarneri, the other things that qualify as mine. I try to match the feelings. They have nothing in common. Possessions, whether it's a coveted musical instrument or the gift to play it, neither compares to the disavowed feelings for an infant, or the ones I've been made aware of now. "That's how it felt . . . even if I did give him away. And what happened to David McAdams, I'd managed to fuck up Theo's fate, just like I did everything else. If I'd chosen a family in New Zealand or one in Texas . . . Theo wouldn't have had to grow up without a father."

"Yes," Sasha says, "but it's not like you could have predicted—" I hold up a hand. I refuse counsel.

"When Shep Stewart started writing those stories, I couldn't believe it. Tragedy gave me a window; an annual report on a life I'd produced but couldn't be part of."

"Oh, Liv . . ." Sasha takes another turn around the tiny room. I want to ask if she'd prefer to step into the living room, it's much larger. "Liv, I . . ." She stares; it's gaping and appalled. "How could you keep something like this from me . . . *from us*? You let me arrange your community service hours and you said nothing, you never even hinted . . ."

Irony is a strange mistress. My confession would have leverage if Sasha and Rob *were* having an affair. "I . . . By the time I met you both, it was years later . . . decades. I was comfortable with the truth my parents knew; I was more comfortable with you both not knowing." The news clippings seem to glare at me; Rob and Sasha look as if they are doing the same. "It never felt like a secret. Not until I turned it into one by suggesting I serve time in Theo's classroom." I move my hands in a vague gesture. "Well," I say more softly, "not until we all ended up here."

"So why now?" she asks. "In the middle of the current dust you've kicked up. Why confess Theo now?"

Rob's expression shifts from surprise to realization. "Because Theo McAdams is, somehow, Sam Nash's last chance." He looks to Sasha. "In between accusing us of having an affair, Liv's ex—excuse me," he says, "current father of her son, indicated a bone marrow transplant was his only hope." Sasha listens to the last of the puzzle pieces. "Although the little I know about bone marrow donors, I don't think offspring is the go-to source for a match."

"They're not," I say. "But there is a treatment option. It's called a haplo, or half match. In some cases, where there isn't a sibling or random donor match, a child can be the donor. From what I've learned, it's a simple blood test to see if Theo's a match."

"You're right . . ." Rob says dully, "*the mother of all Liv moments.* On one hand, I can't believe what you've just told us. Or more to the point, that you never told me. On the other . . ." He scrapes a hand around the back of his neck. "You and I . . . we . . . we share a few secrets, Liv. I don't understand how this isn't one of them."

Rob is right; we do share many secrets, our anonymous support of music education, and a much deeper secret connected to music and my father. "I'm sorry. Like I said, it didn't feel like it was a secret. Not until I turned it into one. Not telling you about Theo, I saw it as . . . *my choice*. If I'd ended the pregnancy all those years ago, I might not have told you that either," I say speaking to both of them. "Although I doubt that late-breaking news would hit you like this. Maybe it feels bigger because . . ."

Sasha finishes my thought. "Because there's a live, grown human being attached to it?"

"A person who is suddenly at the center of your life." Rob blinks wide. "Or should I say lives?"

I have no answer. The pained look on Rob's face is striking. It takes a lot to get under his skin—the "Teflon man" Sasha advertised years ago. Clearly, I have found a way. "So now what, Liv?"

"I . . . Well, I suppose I tell Theo. But I wanted to tell the two of you first."

"Why?" Rob says, shaking his head. "Did you need a practice round?"

"Because not telling the two of you before Theo and Sam seemed like yet one more bad decision." But words about doing the right thing, they sound weak given the moment.

"And then what?" Rob asks. "Maybe Sasha and I offer to go with you, back you up when you tell the kid exactly what he doesn't know about the woman in his classroom. The one he cares enough about to nearly tell me to go to hell when you left the gala. I saw it, Liv. He trusts you. He admires you." Rob rubs his fingertips hard across his forehead.

"Holy shit. I'll go as far as to say he's bonded with you—and he doesn't have the first clue why."

"You're right." I focus on the herringbone hardwoods. "I don't think Theo's going to be too keen on me when he hears the truth." I look back up. "But what else can I do? Sam's life may depend on Theo's."

"Another great point," Rob says. "Sam Nash. Good to know he'll be one up on me when you tell him."

"How's that?"

"He'll already be lying down." Rob turns toward the living room and heads straight for the Macallan bottle.

Sasha opens her mouth and then closes it. It's as if she's not rehearsed this cross-examination. "If this wasn't so totally screwed up, Liv, it might be commendable. But as it is . . ." She flaps her arm in a hopeless gesture. "My gosh, even for you, this is . . ." She stops, her small frame sucking in a huge breath. "You have a son. Jesus . . ."

If nothing else, I suppose I've proven her affair with Nick Zowzer is no more than pedestrian gossip.

Her tone shifts, more incredulous. "A grown son that you used me and the Massachusetts court system to ingratiate yourself to for . . . Why? It's not like he's eight or ten—I'm sure he was curious to know. Why didn't you just show up at his door, introduce yourself? Why such secrecy at this late date?"

It's such a complicated answer. I don't know that having lived the last ten years with me gives Sasha enough insight. You need the lifetime. It was something Phillip understood. I think back to the morning after jail, when my mother showed up right before Sasha. How the sole purpose of her visit was to, once again, highlight my low points. How my existence as a Klein isn't about what I got right, but only the wrongs. Even at twenty-six, I did not want Theo to be subject to that scrutiny. Rob returns with his drink in hand.

I attempt the explanation Sasha wants. "When the idea occurred to me, serving my hours in Theo's classroom . . . In that moment, I only wanted to prove to myself I'd done something good. Something right. I didn't mean for it to be any more than that. I never intended to tell Theo. Nobody was ever supposed to know."

"And manipulating me seemed like the best way to achieve that?" Sasha shakes her head "Not good enough, Liv. Not even close. You told me you wanted to do something positive with your gift—maybe even use Braemore to make you a better person."

"No, Sasha," I say quietly. "You said that. I believe Jeremy suggested it. I only said serving time at Braemore might be a good use of my gift. And while it's no more than a footnote here, that much is true. I've been of service, some value," I say, not necessarily thinking of my hands-on effort, but the boon of instruments now in Braemore's possession.

Sasha stares; she's not buying it. Her attitude remains icy—the client she does not like. She snatches her coat from the sofa. "If I can offer basic courtroom tactics, when you tell Theo, start there. When launching a defense for an obvious offender, it helps to paint the perp in the best light possible." She grabs up her gloves and hobo bag. "I, um . . . I can't do this anymore, not now. I can't do you." She brushes past Rob and leaves.

"Sasha!" But the music room's coffered ceiling rattles as she slams the front door.

I wrap my arms around the sleeves of my sweater. Even the rush of November air can't compete with the coolness in the room.

Rob's humorless face meets mine. He sips from his already half-empty glass. "Congrats, Liv. I've never seen Sasha so distraught—not even sitting in our kitchen, confessing her own transgressions."

"And you?" I ask boldly. "Us?"

He takes a gulp of his drink and frowns. "Seems like we've finally arrived at our knockout round."

CHAPTER THIRTY-FOUR

Olivia

With Theo on my mind, I make one more early-morning visit to Mass General. There's no sense in telling Sam right now, getting his hopes up, not yet. That and maybe I want to savor a last moment with someone who is glad to see me. Sam and I talk about good times from our past and the electric times of his glory days. It grows quiet when he admits they're of little comfort now. My comments are less emotional, prattling on about the upcoming symphony schedule and how busy the holiday season is. He says it's okay if I don't have time to visit again. He's heard an excuse. I hear the things I will tell myself when Sam no longer wants me here.

Once again he tries to get me to accept a check for the Wellesley house. "Come on, Livy, I might as well leave it all to you. No one else has mattered that much." He squeezes my hand. "Or still does." I smile at the trusting sentiment. "Course it would be like Tate to turn up after the fact. I'd hate to think the elusive son of a bitch ends up with my money."

While I want to urge him to leave his estate to a worthy charity, I'm too on edge to pursue the topic. As I sit with Sam, my mind races. I try to craft thoughts that will persuade Theo while keeping his hands from gripping my throat. Sam's moved on, talking about Charlene. He says something that draws my attention.

"I should call her. Thank her. If she hadn't pointed it out, I might have never done the right thing and come to see you. Charlene is persuasive—even after it'd been over between us for ages."

A short time later, I leave Sam looking and sounding like a fortune-teller's ghost. Someone who can persuade Theo, that's what I need. Who would Theo be most inclined to hear? I suspect the woman he's in love with. I drive away from Mass General and head straight for the Cross Sound Ferry. A few hours later, the GPS guides me to middle-class suburbia and announces the conclusion of my trip. The canned computer voice is fitting. It almost says: *"I haven't the slightest clue if here is where you should be, but nevertheless, you've arrived . . ."*

I'm parked outside a boxy blue house with dark shutters and cement steps where a lone pumpkin sits—the kind you might buy even though your children are grown. I glance once in the rearview mirror; the bruise on my face has faded enough to vanish behind a layer of cover-up. I'm also wearing a long dark coat, the one I wear on symphony performance nights. It works with orchestra garb and offers the illusion of invisibility. Just like the symphony, I suppose I want to be heard and not seen.

Measures of Oistrakh's Violin Concerto no. 1 wind through my head as my heels click toward the front door of India Church's house. It's a mournful melody that I played while my father lingered. The last piece my father heard before Rob stepped in, conducting music and fate. I ring the bell, which I don't think is working, and then knock. Helen answers. Oistrakh is replaced by Flagler's "Turmoil"—an even darker piece of music. She is less appealing than at the gala, with her bony frame and makeup-less, drawn face, pajama pants, and a T-shirt advertising a rock band I do not know. I shouldn't judge. Yet it's hard not to—her troubles show at a glance. Her arm is extended, holding open the storm door. On it are obvious track marks. Whether they are old or new I don't know. "Is your sister home?"

Her face contorts. At first I think she's going to slam the door, having pegged me for a social worker, perhaps a narcotics detective. "I know you from somewhere."

"We met at the Boston Public Library. I arranged for the string ensemble."

She shakes her head. "No. That's not why . . ." She points a chipped, black-painted fingernail in my face. "You're Theo's friend . . . classroom person," she says. "The one doing time."

I suppose this has to begin somewhere. "Yes . . . Well, no, actually. I'm not here because of that. Is India home?"

"But this has to do with Theo."

"Yes," I say firmly. "But it's not about Theo and India. I need to speak with her about something else that involves him." She studies me; she's going to tell me to go to hell. I grab the storm door that is oddly firm in her grip. "It's important. Very important, or I wouldn't have come."

By sheer will or Helen's weakness, a few moments later I find myself in the Churches' kitchen. The tidy outside was misleading. The modest, not particularly modern kitchen is brimming with dirty pots and pans, open canisters of flour and sugar, a myriad of smells—roasted meats and pastries. Helen catches my ricocheting gaze.

"My mother experiments a lot with food. She's brilliant at coming up with recipes that sell, not so much at cleaning up . . . or anything else." I suppose Helen relates to the disarray. I recall Shep's remark about Daisy Church, a woman who's fought her own demons. On the table are magazine clippings, *New York Times* food articles, scads of notes jotted in erratic handwriting: ingredients, recipes, names, and phone numbers for what I assume are potential clients. It strikes me that nothing here is finished and what's here is in a permanent state of bedlam.

Heading toward the stairs, Helen turns back. "My mom is the creative food genius. My dad handles the particulars. Otherwise . . ." Her gaze rolls over the mess.

"Otherwise it would all be nothing but chaos?"

"I doubt it would even be that."

It's a wonder Take Me to Church Catering has accomplished as much as it has. Perhaps India's presence is responsible for some of it. "Are they here, your parents?" I hadn't given any thought to negotiating parental units. I want India's help. They may only want to protect her. It's a concept I've stood on the edge of for twenty-six years.

"No, they went into the city early this morning. Potential gig at some swanky hotel. Would be a huge deal if they got it. The Boston event went well. I assume Mother McAdams was pleased; she passed our name along." Helen's words are plainly acerbic. "I'll get India." She moves toward the stairs. "Claire is nothing, if not good on her word."

In the fleeting moments of solitude, I imagine how appalled Theo would be if he knew where I was. Why I've come. I close my eyes and swallow it down. Gut instinct insists this is still my best shot. When I open my eyes, the girl Theo loves stands in front of me. Helen stands behind her, which only accentuates the difference. India is striking, though not traditionally pretty—her red hair and freckles keep pedestrian beauty at a distance. Unlike her sister, she is dressed for the day, an Ivy League–looking blue sweater and jeans. A hint of makeup barely masks the freckles, and her wavy tresses look as if she's just finished drying them. She is clearly confused by my presence. "You know Theo?"

"I do. I've been serving community service hours in his classroom since September. My name is Olivia Klein."

"You play with the New England Symphony." Her knowledge surprises me. "I spoke with Theo a while back. He mentioned you. You're a musician, like him."

"A violinist, yes. I, um . . ." I point to the nearby living room, a slightly less topsy-turvy setting than the Churches' kitchen. "Theo and

I, we have a few things in common—some more obvious than others." I've piqued her interest. "Could we talk in there?"

"About Theo?" she asks, walking in that direction.

"Yes. About Theo."

She abruptly turns. "Is he all right? He's not sick, is he?"

For a girl I do not know, the panic in her voice is palpable. "No, Theo is fine. Healthy as a horse last I checked." I can't help myself; I need to see her reaction. "Unless, of course, you count a broken heart as ill."

It's no more than a brief glimpse before India turns away. Yet I swear her hazel eyes have gone glassy. Once in the living room, India and I sit. Helen hovers like a skeleton chaperone. While I'd like to ask her to leave, India apparently doesn't feel the urge. I wait a moment too long, and her take-charge personality, the one Theo described, darts in.

"So why are you here, Olivia? I can't imagine any circumstance that would bring you from Theo's classroom to my living room."

The next half hour passes. I become the preacher in the Church house. No one speaks but me. Not after India's initial assumption that I've come on Theo's behalf—a third-party attempt to mend things between them. She doesn't look me in the eye as she insists repairing their relationship is impossible. I admit to feeling sorry for Theo and his heartbreak. But I quickly assure her it's not the purpose of my visit. India is rightfully perplexed. What else could this be, other than a busybody acquaintance looking to be a bridge? A few sentences later and India is rendered silent; Helen sinks into a wing chair in a corner behind India. I've heard that drug addicts will lie to anyone as a means to their end. From the way Helen's ass hits the chair, I suspect the revelation of my lie has outdone her.

As my story unravels, it's India's hands that react. They start out folded politely in her lap. As I speak, one hand rises to cover her heart.

It slides upward with each sentence, gripping her swan-like throat and pressing firm against her cheek as I say I am Theo's birth mother. Her other hand remains in her lap, curled in a fist as I explain Sam Nash and our past. I do not spin anything; there's no time for gracious prologues. I tell her all of it: the fateful car wreck and New Zealand decision, my deliberate choice of nearby, stateside parents. There's a brief overview of how I went on with my life and how that changed on September 11th. How it changed even more when I took a baseball bat to my husband's Porsche and manipulated community service hours in her ex-fiancé's classroom.

I do take a brief moment to assure her that it was more than a drunken fit, that Rob's costly error has put my own charitable effort in jeopardy. (I save the Shep Stewart update; it's too much at once.) Finally I tell her about Sam's reemergence and his illness. When I get to the part about Sam's relapse and the possible cure running through Theo's bone marrow, India's hand clamps over her mouth. "I know it's a lot to take in, India, but time is critical and—"

"Why?" she says, interrupting. "Why are you here telling me all this?"

I blink, glancing around a well-lived-in room. I thought this much would be obvious. "Because I'm worried about what Theo's reaction will be."

"An excellent question since you've done nothing but lie to him from the second you met him."

I sit up taller. "Not exactly since the moment I met him—just in this century."

The clarification flashes a bit of perspective in India's face. She glances over her shoulder at Helen. In reply, she offers her sister a dumbfounded look. India turns back to me. "What do you want me to do, tell him for you?"

"No, I'll tell Theo myself. I have a return ferry this afternoon. With or without you, I'm going straight to his apartment. I thought if you were there it would lend credibility, keep Theo from—"

"Keep him from telling you exactly where you can go?" India makes serious eye contact. She stands.

I clear my throat, recalling Theo's no-nonsense description of India's iron will and loyalty—which apparently extends to former fiancés. "Look, I'm fully prepared for Theo to hate me, never want to lay eyes on me again. I get it. You, my husband, my best friend . . . I'm good on the hole I've dug for myself, the mistakes I've made. What I can't have happen is to allow Sam Nash to die. Not when I hold possibility in my hand. But you're right. Theo will be angry. I don't want him to take it out on Sam; he hasn't the time or strength. Theo will listen to you. That's why I'm here."

Most people might ask why they should do anything on behalf of a person they've never laid eyes on—give a kidney to a stranger or go diving headlong into their own past, one they so ardently erased. India twists again toward Helen. Helen, who I assume will tell her sister that she is nuts if she considers helping me. That volunteering to be my personal envoy is nothing short of idiotic. She will remind India that reentering Theo's life on any level is a bad idea. Not if she truly wants to move on. Helen, who's pulled on a sweater, covering the track marks on her arms, draws a tremulous breath. She's curled in the chair like a fragile bird in a nest. Yet India waits for her advice. "Seems to me you've done more for lesser people. It's up to you, India, if you think you can handle it."

A few moments later I am in the Churches' tiny foyer, buttoning my coat. India has gone to get hers. Helen continues to hover near the edge of the steps. I get to the last button and make fierce eye contact with her. "Is there something you want to say?" I brace for another tongue-lashing.

"I couldn't give a shit about your ex . . . *whatever*." I cock my head, hearing a bluntness that most often comes out of my own mouth. "But you should know, aside from me, there are . . . other people responsible for India's unhappiness . . ."

"Is she unhappy?"

"India's a *glass half full* kind of girl. But yes, she is. I'm not blameless; I get it. If there's turmoil, it's probably attached to me." She glances around her disorderly, somewhat dirty house. "Genes are what brought you here today, right, Olivia?" I focus on her lucid observation. "My mom and I, we share some really crappy ones. Every day is a struggle. Her manic tendencies could decide tomorrow that nothing is worth more than that next drink—or maybe it'd be better if she didn't exist at all. Sometimes I see her point." It draws a well-earned look of surprise from me. "I'm not suicidal. Just your run-of-the-mill heroin addict. India and my dad, for sure they got the short end of the deal. No matter how it appears on the outside . . ." Helen points to the neat front lawn and cheery pumpkin. "The inside," she says, pointing to herself, the house, "looks pretty much like this."

I smooth the front of my coat, simpering at her candidness. "While I can't relate to your precise demons, Helen, I know what it is to be at the crux of mayhem. What's your point when it comes to your sister?"

"Just know that India is going with you for more reasons than she's willing to admit. Reasons that, in her mind, don't outweigh our fucked-up family." Helen glides a step in my direction. We are nearly nose to nose in the tiny space. Her breath smells of toothpaste and cigarettes. "India needs to forget about us. Move on. But mostly she needs to forgive herself." Helen draws a breath. "While you're busy trying to save that guy's life, maybe give some thought to hers."

CHAPTER THIRTY-FIVE

Olivia

India and I speak very little during the car ride to the ferry. While I can think of plenty to say, I'm fearful of further alienating her. She may change her mind and demand I turn the car around. She only converses to point out a shortcut to the ferry dock. Once on board, India announces that she'll go up to the top deck and sit in the sun. It's turned into an unusually warm late-fall day. But her choice of seat is not about warmth. It's a clear indication that I should sit somewhere else. I claim a stool at the ferry's bar and sit with a glass of cheap white wine for the duration of the sail.

Back inside the car, silence resumes. I turn on some music—a collection Rob once put together for me: Strauss, Mendelssohn, Pachelbel, and a few others. He called it the calming classicals. At the time, I thought it was a sweet gesture—now I'm struck by his effort to assemble intricate scores he only knows because I exist. I'm surprised by how much I'm hoping music will underscore this day. We're well into our journey up Interstate 95 and Pachelbel's Canon in D when India finally asks a question. Do I like playing in the symphony? I offer a canned response the New England Symphony PR folks would like to hear. "Yes. Of course. It's an honor to play for them."

"I don't know much about music, but I think Theo has that kind of gift." She points to the car stereo as we listen to a distinctive section of solo violins. I feel her sideways glance. "The ability to play like that, he gets it from you." I nod. "And his father . . . *Sam*," she says tentatively, as if in reverence to David McAdams. "You said he played baseball professionally."

"That's right. I don't follow sports, but I know Sam is quite celebrated, a pitcher for the California Angels."

"My dad might have heard of him. He's a baseball fan."

"I'm sure that's possible. Inherent things like music or athleticism . . . If Theo had to inherit something, I'd say he got the two best parts."

"He went to Cornell on a lacrosse scholarship. Did you know that?" I nod again.

India is quiet; her fingers trail along the leather stitching on the Audi's door. Her gaze inches toward me. "I saw it before you told me."

"Saw what?"

"Your smile." I look in her direction, not producing one. "When I came into the kitchen, you smiled. It was just polite reflex, maybe nerves. But the first thing I noticed was your smile, the shape of your face—it's exactly like Theo's."

"I believe it is."

"You have beautiful blue eyes." My chin tips upward, a fast glance in the rearview mirror—eyes completely different from Theo's. "But I love . . . loved Theo's eyes. Does he have his father's eyes?"

"He does," I say, gripping tight to the steering wheel.

"Theo never talked about it much, his adoption." She grants me a glance. "Not really a guy topic—not even when they're being sensitive . . . introspective." I nod at India's wisdom. "But I know he's wondered, more than he ever said."

"Wondered what exactly?"

"If his biological parents were in love. I think it was on his mind because of what he remembers about Claire and David McAdams."

"Because they were so in love?"

"Something like that. Theo told me he once put the question to Claire, asked if she knew. She told him that of course his biological parents were madly in love. It was exactly how Theo came to be their son."

"But that's not what Theo was really asking," I prod.

"Not really. But he didn't push for more. He'd never . . ." India trails off, a deep sigh seeping out of her. "Theo would never do anything to upset Claire. But yes, he's always wanted to know if . . ."

"If his parents were in love or if he was the product of a one-night stand?" I pause, considering Shep Stewart's rawer conclusion. While the conniving reporter can assume what he wants, I am sickened by the same notion crossing Theo's mind. "Has he wondered something worse, India? Has Theo wondered if he's the result of a heinous crime?"

There's a small nod from India. "Don't get me wrong, it's not like Theo's spent years dwelling on it. But it's one thing I'm sure he'd like to know . . . if his birth parents were in love, or . . ."

I do not smile; I've not earned any reward here. I simply answer India's question. "Then Theo will get one bit of positive closure today."

India sinks back into her seat. "Until his father . . . David McAdams died, Theo did have the perfect childhood."

"Good to know." I hear a snarky Olivia Klein tone. "I mean, having gotten to know Theo, that's apparent. But what about after 9-11, India? I know you weren't there. But you do know Theo. I'm sure he talked about his life after that. It must have been difficult for Claire."

"No one would argue the fact. And she did a brilliant job raising Theo. You'd have to be the most thoughtless, callous human being to find fault with her . . . the things she wants for him."

We entered Boston proper a few miles back. I ease onto an exit ramp. What the hell, it's not like India can change her mind now. "Why do I hear a *but* on the topic of Claire?"

"There's not," she quickly defends. "I mean it's understandable after such a tragedy. Claire McAdams lost the man she loved; she was devastated. It's perfectly logical that her only son would become her whole life." She looks right at me. "Isn't it?"

◆ ◆ ◆

India leads since she knows precisely where Theo's apartment is located. She's grows increasingly quiet as we approach the building. Whatever her thoughts, now is not the time to interrupt them. We wait for the elevator and I take a quick peek at my cell phone. There's a missed call from Rob, the house number; he's left a message. I want to listen to it, a combination of dread and desperation.

But I can't do that right now. Besides, what would I say? *"Hey, don't mind me while I listen to this message. I'm just curious if I have a home to go back to when we're done here. Or Rob may just want to let me know that my personal items have been relocated to a PODS container on Commonwealth Ave . . ."* I smile Theo's smile, which India gulps at, and drop the phone back into my purse.

There's a window at the end of the hall on the sixth floor. Dusk is settling over Boston. Except for overnight news—a delay on the T and the robbery of a local liquor store—the city will wake uninterrupted. The next time I awake, nothing will be the same.

At the door, India looks at me. "You're very clever."

"Meaning?"

"Theo may be so stunned to see me that your bombshell will pale in comparison."

"Right back at you, India. I wouldn't think someone who doesn't love Theo would have bothered to make this trip."

India's eyes fill with panic. I've called her bluff, maybe forced Helen's observations into her path. I rap my knuckles on the door before she can reply or run.

CHAPTER THIRTY-SIX

Theo

Theo is in front of a music stand, playing *Sad Romance*, a melancholy but soothing classical piece. After long days he sometimes listens to popular music, but he's more often drawn to works like this. It's always been this way and something Theo wonders about. It does not feel like a choice but more of a default setting. It's been a difficult day. Braemore was total chaos. Antonio was arrested for selling prescription drugs. Later, a fistfight—the kind with knives—broke out in the cafeteria. By the end of the day, Theo wondered if he should have taken a job as a prison guard. He is not feeling particularly useful. He's not helping anyone. He questions more things than before he accepted the position at Braemore. He ponders Olivia Klein. She's been absent for three days now. But Olivia did insist she's prone to bad choices; perhaps this is proof. She's also not returned his calls, which Theo finds worrisome and rude.

His playing is disrupted by a knock at the door. Approaching the spy hole, Theo reverts to thoughts of Antonio. He wonders how far his good intentions would take him if a student were to show up at his apartment. Would he be welcoming or worried that they were high or carrying a weapon, maybe both? His address isn't hard to find. With the violin in hand, Theo glances through the tiny hole. He sees a distorted dream; it looks like India. He blinks and looks again.

A few moments later, India and Olivia Klein are standing in the small living room. Theo is so stunned he can't sort the thoughts in his head—what he should say or how he should act. He attempts to place the violin on the bar bordering the galley kitchen. He misses.

Olivia steps forward and catches the instrument. "Guess you weren't expecting . . . *us*."

Theo glances at her, but he's mesmerized by India. "What . . . what are you doing here?" He doesn't mean to be abrupt. But aside from one accidental FaceTime chat, India's been resolute about her feelings. To his surprise, Theo doesn't jump to the conclusion that India's come to reconcile their relationship. Turning up at his door, unannounced, wouldn't be India's style. Secondly, why would she bring Olivia Klein with her?

"Theo," India says, "we're here to talk to you, tell you something."

"Is my mother all right?" The assumption comes all too easily, and an old dread clamps down on Theo's gut.

"Yes," Olivia says. "I'm sure your mother's fine. This doesn't have anything to do with her. Not directly." His darting glance moves between the odd pairing of women. "Could we sit?"

He looks at the leather sofa—the one where he and India had sex more times than he can recall. He catches India's gaze, which is also pinned to the weathered piece of furniture. They all sit, though his ex-fiancée chooses a modern, deeply curved chair across from the sofa. Theo knows it's deliberate because India hates the chair, having complained that it is ugly and uncomfortable since the day he brought it home. She sits tall with her hands pinched between her knees. He wonders if they are trembling. The feeling of dread doesn't ease.

"Theo, I'm going to be blunt . . . Honest," Olivia says. "Something I haven't been since walking into your classroom in September." She tucks a piece of hair behind her ear and fidgets. These are habits Theo's noticed, mostly when he plays the violin, once when a common allergy to strawberries came up in conversation. Olivia fidgeted then, scraping at her head like she'd eaten a bowlful. It was right after Theo said, "Strawberries do that to me too, an unbelievably prickly rash."

"I've asked India to come here with me for a lot of reasons," she says. "Mostly because you're going to be angry with me. More importantly because I need your help. If I'd come alone . . . Well, I don't know how cooperative you're going to be feeling in a few minutes."

"I don't understand. How do you even know India?"

"I'm nothing if not resourceful, Theo." Olivia smiles, then doesn't. There's that tickle of familiarity he cannot place. "Maybe that's the first *honest* thing you should know about me. I'm good at ploughing through most anything if it's a means to my end." Theo's glance moves to India. He has no clue what Olivia is talking about. "When I first came to your classroom, I told you I followed Shep Stewart's 9-11 stories, right?" Theo nods. "That part is true. But I didn't follow them for the reasons I said. I didn't read them because I was interested in Andrea Wakefield, Tara DeMarco, or even tuned in to the tragic life of Joaquin Perez. I was only interested in your story, Theo. Your life."

Theo stares, wondering if, along with quirky, impulsive, and musically gifted, Olivia Klein is mentally unstable. Perhaps she's brought India here against her will. "I . . . I don't understand. Why would you be interested in me?" Olivia looks nervous, an expression she wore on the first day of class but not since.

"Theo, just listen to what Olivia has to say. While it's not what I'd call . . . *honorable* . . ." India shoots a look at Olivia. Theo can read it like the most familiar diatonic scale—she does not approve of Olivia, but she is not completely unsympathetic. "What she's going to tell you is true. And it's important."

Olivia sits up taller; she grips her hands in her lap like a prayer. "Theo, do you remember a brief conversation we once had about birthdays? You were surprised that I knew yours, right? December thirty-first." Theo nods, thinking back to his first in-depth talk with Olivia. "I made some excuse about your mother having mentioned it in one of Shep's stories, or suggested that you'd said it, though you couldn't recall anything of the kind."

"We were in the café, near Braemore. We, um . . ." He looks at India once more. "We ended up talking about relationships, how sometimes they don't work out."

"That's right. And you were correct about your birthdate. You never told me; your mother's never mentioned it. Another time we talked, you said you walk when things are bothering you. I told you I did the same thing." Theo nods and shrugs at the disconnected information. "Of course, a lot of people could say something like that. It's not such a peculiar habit. Certainly not something that could be described as . . . inherent." Theo nods again, though an urge to inch away from Olivia is now present. "And, um . . . And we . . . the two of us, we could take a walk like that to the Boston Conservatory right now. Once there, we'd find a dozen violinists, all gifted musicians. Couldn't we?"

"I guess. But I don't see—"

"Theo, how many of those violinists would have a gift precisely like ours? The way we perceive music, understand it, feel it—regardless of my lack of passion or your intensity? How many?"

Theo thinks for a moment, though clearly this is not an odds calculation. And it's true. It's nearly inexplicable, the way he and Olivia interpret music. "It's abstract . . . singular. We seem to share . . . Funny, right before you got here, I was thinking about things we have in—" Theo dead stops. But his heart gallops off in a pounding rhythm, his brain rushing to catch up. He shuffles farther down the sofa. But for the first time since they arrived, Theo is more focused on Olivia than India. In fact, he's suddenly hyper-focused on her face—the shape of it and her smile. Of course, she is not smiling right now, she looks more like she's about to face a firing squad. "Jesus," he gasps. Olivia is nodding. "Tell me you're not saying . . ." Theo's head moves in the opposite gesture.

"I know your birthday, Theo, because I was most decidedly there the day you were born."

"You don't have any children," Theo counters. "You told me a story about being pregnant once. You said that you lost the baby—a miscarriage after a car accident."

"You're right. I did tell you that story. But it wasn't true, not the miscarriage part. The baby survived, Theo. *You* survived."

He continues to shake his head. "That can't be. For one . . . for one my biological parents were from New Zealand. That's where I was born."

"You were born in New Zealand because that's where my brother lives. He has for almost thirty years. The miscarriage is a lie I've been peddling since it all happened. I . . . It seemed like the right decision at the time. I told the lie to my parents. Eventually I told it to my husband and best friend. Worst of all, I told it to Sam Nash."

"Sam . . . *Nash.*" Theo instantly recognizes the name. Like a weirdly wired science experiment, he connects to the other half of his missing DNA. He recalls Olivia's description of the man she was briefly married to, the one who played baseball. Theo thinks of his six-year-old self, a boy who stormed a soccer field with the inbred agility of a pro athlete. He remembers thinking, *I'm just like my dad, because my dad was a football player!* Theo rakes a hand through his wavy brown hair, remembering eleven. It was the age it occurred to Theo that superior athleticism was encouraged by David McAdams, even admired, but not inherited. He feels a thwack of realization, the origins of his talents. He wants to stand, but Theo is unsure if his athletic legs will hold him up. He looks at India.

"It's true, Theo. Olivia came to my house this morning. She told me the same things she just told you. I, um . . . I just couldn't imagine you hearing this alone. That's why I'm here."

"Why? Why didn't you tell me?" he says to Olivia. "Why did you come into my classroom and pretend to be nothing but a stranger?"

"Theo, I didn't plan it. Nothing I've done is as calculated as it looks." She grimaces. "But then and again, it never is. Ending up in your classroom . . ." Olivia pauses, perhaps rethinking her elucidation. "Oh my God, Theo, there's no single reason that will make sense. It just happened—because Sasha was standing in my music room telling me I had to choose something in the way of community service. Because I'd spent the weekend in jail, the direct result of doing nothing more than being Olivia Klein. Because my mother showed up at my door, reminding me of the same thing she always does—how everything I touch turns into a disaster. That even as a grown woman, an adult, I hadn't escaped the disappointment of my youth. I . . . I felt so completely awful. I wanted to grab onto something good. In the moment . . . with that day's Shep Stewart stories staring up at me . . ." Her fervent pace slows. "Instinct said *you* were that something good."

Olivia pulls in a tremulous breath. Her clear blue eyes pool and she blinks furiously. "I needed to see if I'd managed to do anything right. The *Ledger* stories, they made you sound so accomplished, so . . . *perfect*. The moment I met you, Theo, I knew that lying my way into your life was worse than the things I'd done to get me there. Classic Olivia Klein impulsiveness." She says this as if it's a viable excuse for what he's hearing. "My mother . . . *your grandmother* . . ." Her mouth, *his mouth*, curves to a deep frown. "She wasn't without a point."

"I don't . . ." Theo takes a breath. "Days went by. Now months." Theo's eyes are so wide he thinks they may pop from his head. "You could have told me after the first day of class or the tenth. You might have said something during any number of conversations, over coffee, at my mother's charity event. You confided in me, Olivia. You trusted me enough to tell me your husband was having an affair. And yet . . . yet you kept right on lying about who you were. I don't understand. What kind of person does something like that?"

For a moment Olivia doesn't speak. Her gaze bounces around the small room. "Someone like me," she says. "Theo, listen to everything I'm saying. It was never my intention to tell you. We weren't supposed to have this . . ." Her arm circles the empty air. "Conversation. The friendlier we got, the more deceptive my presence became. I promised myself I'd walk away when my community service hours were over. That getting to know you was a gift I didn't deserve. In turn, I never wanted you to suffer . . . well, exactly what you're feeling right now—betrayed, and not thinking very much of the woman who gave birth to you. Vanishing as suddenly as I appeared . . . What is it they say? Never rob a bank without an exit strategy. I had an exit strategy." Theo hangs on to his composure, though barely. "It's just at the door, I got caught on a trip wire."

Theo looks to India. "I was surprised when she told me. Not as shocked as you are, I'm sure, but surprised. And everything you're feeling . . ." India's chin quivers. She smiles small. "Like I said, despite what's happened between us, I didn't want you to hear that alone."

Theo closes his eyes. He wants time to turn back, to before Olivia Klein invaded his life, to before the day India left him. Really? A part of Theo wants to go back to before September 11 and ask David McAdams what he should do if his birth mother were ever to show up masquerading as a human being. When Theo opens his eyes, Olivia is looking into his. "So if *not* telling me was your grand plan, what earth-moving thing—other than honesty or my right to know—drove you to this?"

"A few weeks ago, Sam Nash came to town. He wanted to apologize for things that happened before you were born, things that led to our breakup."

Theo listens, trying to get his head around the idea that while his father was a college football hero, his birth father is one of baseball's all-time greatest closers. Theo thinks about a box of boyhood belongings; inside, he is almost sure, is a Sam Nash baseball card. He desperately tries to recall the man's face; he's more likely to recall his stats. Theo's stomach clenches as a more specific memory surfaces.

Theo and his father once went to a Red Sox–Angels game at Fenway. Sam Nash pitched a shutout ninth inning. The Sox lost. Theo was angry and upset that day too. He remembers his father saying, "Give him credit, son—the guy is responsible for a lot of spot-on pitches." Apparently, David McAdams was more accurate than he knew. But the facts are too much to grasp. "So when Sam Nash showed up, what? You finally confessed everything to him. And now he wants to meet me or something?"

"No," Olivia says, her gaze dropping away. "Not quite. When Sam showed up I didn't tell him either. He still doesn't know you exist."

"Theo," India says, drawing his attention. "Sam Nash is very ill. He has leukemia."

"Acute myeloid leukemia, which has relapsed," Olivia clarifies. "He actually came here, to Boston, after beating the disease once. Six or seven months ago, Sam got a solid medical report from his doctors in California—that's where he lives. It was as close to a clean bill of health someone can get with this disease. When he showed up here, the fact that I was doing time in your classroom . . . Suffice it to say his sudden reappearance felt like curious karma. Even so, with the rest of my life, my marriage to Rob, in such a chaotic state, I didn't tell Sam about you. Since then, Sam and I have seen each other. We've talked. We made peace with much of what came between us. And I did consider telling him . . ." Olivia pauses, perhaps wrestling with the odd fit of honesty. "But I didn't do it."

Theo connects precarious dots; he sees the one that's a bull's-eye on Olivia Klein. "You didn't do it because telling Sam Nash meant you'd have to confess—not only to me, but to your husband and everyone else you've lied to for twenty-six years. Am I close, Olivia?"

She swallows hard. "You're not completely off. Although I truly believed it was in everyone's best interest to leave it alone." Olivia presses her prayerful hands to her mouth for a moment. "When you told me . . . When you said you were adopted, Theo, you never said you'd been dying to meet your birth parents. In fact, you seemed ridiculously pleased with the ones you had. I didn't see an aching need from you to alter that reality."

Theo is taken aback by her bluntness. Yet, he cannot argue this point. On occasion, Theo has fantasized about his birth parents. What adopted child doesn't? At the age of eleven, shiny images of strangers are a quick fix when your mother is angry because you knocked over the fish tank. Flawless birth parents are easily conjured up when you make a C in AP chemistry. You're positive your hyper-perfect biological parents would never go on, like your adoptive mother, about how a C may ruin your Ivy League chances. On the other end of the spectrum, in a few darker moments, Theo has wondered about the unknown. Who is he and how did he come to be? But Olivia is right. Theo's never seriously considered seeking out his birth parents. Not when he ended up with the best parents a child could ask for.

Yet Olivia's next words, they smack of twisted mother-son telepathy. "When I saw the relationship you have with Claire, when I listened to the way you talked about David McAdams, why in the world—especially considering my questionable presence—would I want to introduce myself as your birth mother? Sure, if I'd been honest from the start . . . But even then, I had no desire to be compared to what you view as perfection."

Theo is quick to pounce on what is clearly inherent brusqueness. "Don't be ridiculous, Olivia. Claire and David McAdams weren't perfect. They just didn't lie to my face."

Olivia looks at India, who seems to shrink from Theo's declaration about his parents' honesty. She glances away from both of them.

"Nevertheless," Olivia says quietly. "No matter what you think of me, the reason I've come here, told you all this, is because Sam needs your help. It's possible, Theo, that you're the best chance he has to achieve another remission."

Olivia goes on to detail Sam's illness, personal medical particulars that hit his ears like a complex math equation. It is difficult to absorb on top of everything else she's dropped in his path. She uses a phrase called *haploidentical transplantation*, or a half match. Theo gets the gist of it—an offspring or parent of the ill person is the go-to source for this treatment. It's not a sure thing, but it's a possibility.

Olivia says that no random bone marrow donor has been found, and that Sam Nash's brother cannot be located. Theo processes this, forcing the term *uncle* onto his brain. Uncle Kevin, he's his uncle—a man with a son who looks just like David McAdams. Uncle Martin, Claire's brother. He's also his uncle. Not some oil-rig loser who can't even be located to help save his own sibling's life. Theo sinks deeper into the sofa. Father. All this talk is about saving *his father's* life.

It can't be. Theo has spent sixteen years accepting his father's death. He cannot get his head around a live version, particularly one who may die all over again.

Olivia goes on to say that when Sam Nash was first diagnosed, she didn't know he was ill. But this time, not only does she know he's sick, she also knows he has a son. A son who is a potential, life-saving half match.

Right before Olivia arrived, Theo was questioning his usefulness, whether or not he was making a difference in the lives of his Braemore students. And here, in his own living room, Theo is presented with an opportunity to literally save a man's life. Theo has always thought of himself as the sort of person who would do the right thing, run into a burning building instead of out. He's positive that on September 11 David McAdams did everything he could to save others in a building that was already burning. Since then, Theo perceives this as the marker he wants to emulate, the man he wants to be. He listens as Olivia winds down and the three of them sit in eerie silence. Theo considers, thoughtfully, the things he's learned. Finally, he formulates a response.

"Can I ask you a question?"

"Of course," Olivia says. "Anything."

He wants to laugh at her willingness to suddenly share. He keeps his composure. "Sam Nash. This is the guy you told me about—the one who wanted you to get an abortion instead of having the baby? The one who wanted a baseball career more than he wanted a child."

Olivia nods vaguely. "Yes, but when I told you that . . ."

Her words fade and Theo nods back harder. He finds he's not feeling any of the things David McAdams taught him—whether by influence or actions. Theo is unmoved by compassion for another human being. Instead, he realizes something else: he is very much like his mother. His mouth twitches as impulsive anger rips through him. "So if all that's true," Theo says, "why should I do a damn thing to save the life of a man who wanted to end mine? A man who went happily on his way the moment he thought I didn't exist."

CHAPTER THIRTY-SEVEN

Olivia

Instead of taking India back to the ferry, she asks me to drop her at a girlfriend's apartment. I imagine India doesn't want to sit in a car with me for that long. The friend also lives on the outskirts of Boston proper, a short drive from Theo's apartment. After his declaration of disgust, Theo asked me to leave. He looked pensively to India. For a moment, I thought some good might come of it. I thought India might choose to stay. She did not; in fact, she moved faster out the apartment door than I did. It doesn't add up. She thought enough, felt enough, to come in the first place. The motivation for India's behavior grows increasingly muddled. A glimmer of an idea broadens—one where India's breakup with Theo centers on something other than her lack of feelings for Theo.

"Here, turn here," she says, pointing at the upcoming corner. Her hand trembles like her drug-addict sister in need of a fix.

It's a disparaging thought. *I should talk* . . . "I'm sorry, India. Sorry that you went through all that for nothing."

"It wasn't for nothing. It was for Theo. It was exactly what I said. I couldn't imagine him hearing about his birth mother, not like that, without anyone there." India swipes at dripping tears. "Just pull up here."

Her fingers are wrapped around the door handle, and before the fair, flaming-haired India can escape, I say, "One last thing . . . please."

India's whips her head around. "I won't beg him for you. I'm sorry that man will die without Theo's help. But really . . ." She narrows her watery eyes. "You have no one to blame but yourself."

I hear truth but focus on a finer point. "I wasn't going to ask you that," I say. "I'm not surprised by Theo's reaction. But I had to try."

She sniffs. "I guess even you would do anything for the man you love."

I don't respond. I'm not sure that's what I did. When India doesn't bolt from the vehicle, I keep going. "What I want to know is why you agreed to come with me in the first place? I appreciate not wanting Theo to be alone . . . Well, alone with me. But why didn't you call Claire, ask her to be the buffer?"

"Why didn't you?" she snaps.

I hear a mutual ping of animosity.

"I could have. It would have been easier on Theo, rather than dangling you in front of him, reminding him of what he's lost. Of course, that's easy for me to explain—why further humiliate myself in front of Theo's adoptive mother? The hole I dug . . . It's already pit-like. What's less obvious is why you didn't turn to Claire. Why come with me, when a preemptive call to her would have given him something soft to land on while spearing me nicely?"

"I don't know. I didn't think that fast." She shoots me a look. "I'm not a conniver."

"No, you're not. But you are quick and clever, India. So why didn't you want Claire on hand to provide a shining example of motherhood while I confessed my sins, old and new?"

"Maybe I should have." Surprisingly, India laughs. "Of course if Claire were there her *shining example of motherhood* would have shredded you into bite-size pieces."

"She would have been angry, India . . . surprised. But would she really have gone off the deep end?" India doesn't reply. She only looks toward the street lamp and triple-decker house where her friend lives. "What happened tonight wasn't about Claire."

"It happened to Theo. It happened to Claire." India twists toward me. "You caused Theo pain. Claire won't stand for that. She hasn't since his father died. How do you fault her for that mind-set?" She reaches for the door handle again. "I have to go."

I grab her arm. I've nothing to lose. "India, tell me something. I heard Claire caught you kissing your old boyfriend. Is that true?"

Her tone hardens like an ex-con. "It is. And how do you know that?" But the tone doesn't last and she doesn't wait for an answer. Her voice trembles and her story spills out. "I'm not good at hard liquor—martinis in particular. I'm also not making excuses. It shouldn't have happened. Two martinis and Tom talking about old memories—how marriage is such a big step. Did I think about the fact that I'd known Tom longer than the man I was going to marry? Did it matter that Tom was still in love with me? It was scary and flattering and confusing all at once. As I got up to leave, he caught me off guard. Tom kissed me, and my future mother-in-law called out my name." India shakes her red head and swipes at tears. "You want to talk about humiliated? It . . . it was so unbelievably . . . awful."

I hang on to her arm. "Trust me, India. The judgment error you made doesn't put you within a mile of my league. That and I'm not sure why one fleeting bad moment had to change your entire future."

"Well, you're not me." She aims a steely gaze in my direction. "I'd imagine they're different thresholds. I don't deserve someone like Theo."

"Oh, I'm sorry," I say, homing in on discrepancies. "I was under the impression you left Theo because you were unsure about the two of you, because you doubted how much you loved him after kissing the old boyfriend."

"Would you please stop saying that," she snaps. "And what's the difference? None of it matters."

"I think it matters a great deal. Tell me something. What's she got on you other than a kiss? How did Claire convince you to break up with her son?"

"What? She didn't."

India opens the car door. My grip around her other arm tightens. "Not so fast, sweetie. I spoke with your sister at the gala. She hinted at Tiger Mom's protective instincts. Her buddy, Shep Stewart, he sweetened the pot by telling me that Claire wasn't too keen on the idea of Theo marrying into the Church family. Tell me the rest. My guess is there's a part Theo doesn't know." It's visual standoff. "I swear, India, I'll turn this car around and go right back to his apartment. I'll tell him my suspicions. It will only add to the wonderful day he's had."

"He'll hate you."

"He already does."

India yanks her arm from my grip. "Isn't it enough? Claire saw me that day. I even knew about the stupid Booktini bar because she'd suggested it. But never in a million years . . . in a city the size of New York did I imagine . . ."

"Running headlong into her? Interesting timing," I muse about something I have no hope of proving.

"Saying I hate that it happened doesn't begin to cover it. Claire walking in on . . ." India stops long enough to catch her hiccupping breaths. "Even so, at first I thought Theo and I could work it out. Telling him wasn't easy. I still can't believe I hurt him like that. And he didn't say, *'No biggie, India. Kiss whoever you like . . .'* But he did tell me . . ."

"Tell you what?"

"Theo told me he had lunch with an old girlfriend a while back. Just weeks before he asked me to marry him. He never kissed the girl or anything. He said he didn't make the lunch date out of doubt—but he still did it. Later, he realized he'd done it because . . . Well, he wanted one last glance back."

"So not a kiss, but a good-bye," I clarify.

"A glance," she insists. India focuses on her wringing hands. "Hearing Theo admit to something so small . . . It stung. So if anything, it only made me feel worse about the kiss with Tom. Theo went on to say he didn't tell me because he knew how meaningless the lunch date was. Then he asked me if I was still sure that I wanted to marry him."

"And at that point?"

"Of course I wanted to marry him. I still—" India purses her lips and stares out a rain-dappled window. "Like I said, Theo was hurt and upset that I'd kissed Tom. But he believed we'd work through it."

I pause, reflecting on outcomes. "You know, chances at happily ever after . . . If you get one you're lucky. A second is even rarer. If Theo was so willing, why didn't it happen?"

"Because it kept snowballing. I didn't tell Theo about Claire showing up. I was too mortified, too ashamed. I figured I'd confess to that part when I got back to Boston."

"Claire beat you to it."

India shakes her head. "Claire never told him either. He still doesn't know his mother was at Booktini that day. A couple days passed. I thought maybe it was for the best—give Theo time to cool off. Give me time to feel something less than horrible.

"But in the meantime, Claire spoke to Theo," India says. "He didn't tell her what had happened between me and Tom. I was surprised Claire didn't bring it up to him. Theo's mother and I got along. But I'd seen it—her protectiveness. It startled me more than once. I couldn't believe she was going to let me off the hook that easy."

"She didn't. Did she, India?"

And through her tears, India smiles. "A tongue lashing—like the one you should have gotten tonight. That wasn't Claire's plan."

"Her plan was to erase you from her son's life."

"How do you know—"

"Because I understand how someone like Claire thinks. Her past is nobler than mine and her street credit earned. But tragedy doesn't make her a good person. It just gives her a wide berth."

"Lucky Theo." She gives me a long once-over. "To have ended up with two such similar maternal creatures under sheep's wool."

"Not exactly," I say. Whatever my shortcomings, I see what Claire and I don't have in common. "With me," I tell her, "and the exception of this Theo mess—you get what you see."

"Meaning?"

"Meaning if I had seen you kiss an old boyfriend, I would have kicked your ass in public. But I would have let you and Theo work out the particulars. Claire didn't do that, did she?"

India averts eye contact. "I had two more days at the catering convention in New York. On the last day, Claire showed up. She asked if we could have coffee, talk. She was very direct. Blunt."

"What did she say to you?"

"A lot of things. Starting with the fact that I should be so ashamed, she didn't know how I'd ever face her son again, never mind forgive myself. I explained that I'd already told him. That while Theo was upset, he was willing to forgive me. She said I was taking advantage of his generous nature. In the moment, that's exactly what it felt like. Claire said I didn't deserve him."

"You kissed an old boyfriend, India. You didn't commit murder and ask Theo to help you hide the body."

"I think Claire would have had an easier time with that." She runs a sleeve across her nose. I dig in my purse and come up with a package of Kleenex. India accepts this much from me. "Claire did a lot of talking that afternoon—including talk about my family's shortcomings. I wasn't in much of a position to defend myself."

"No doubt Claire is expert at pouncing on vulnerability."

"Even so . . ." India sucks in a tremulous breath. "She wasn't wrong. Theo, he should be with someone . . ."

India doesn't finish. She wants to describe the woman her ex-fiancé should be with. I suspect the idea is more than India can stomach.

"Eventually," she says, "Claire got around to Helen and her point. She's aware of my sister's drug problems. She even knew about Helen's most recent overdose. Claire had an envelope of information with her—the details and a room waiting in one of the best treatment centers in the country. Nothing like what my family could ever afford."

"Oh my God, she blackmailed you into leaving Theo."

India crinkles her brow. "She called it an even trade. She was quick to ask if I thought it was a matter of time until Helen overdosed again." She offers the tiniest smile. "It was something we agreed on without question."

"What a bitch," I mutter.

India looks at me as if no one has ever thought this about Claire McAdams, let alone said it out loud. "From there, Claire went on to note lifelong family issues—my mother's history isn't too different from Helen's, plus a suicide attempt years ago. A variety of unworthy, susceptible behaviors. Helen's slips . . . I slipped, even if it wasn't drug related."

"So by the end of your conversation, Claire had you convinced that Helen could greatly benefit from her generosity and Theo would be better off without you."

"Helen is doing so much better." India's knuckles tap against the rain-soaked window. I imagine it doesn't come close to the tears she has cried. "And I've spent these past months reminding myself that, like it or not, Claire wasn't wrong. Theo does deserve someone better than me."

India has no respect for me. Nothing I say will convince her otherwise. I sink back into the Audi's leather seat, thinking Theo deserves better than all of us.

CHAPTER THIRTY-EIGHT

Olivia

When I return to the brownstone late that night Rob isn't home. There's no note, not even the kind meant for the cleaning lady. I'd listened to his message after leaving India—it was only empty air, as if he'd dialed and then changed his mind. My thoughts waffle between a business trip and Rob simply exiting my life, the ways I pushed him toward the door. My own mother's forewarning.

I wake in the middle of the night with my arm gripped around Rob's pillow. I breathe him in. Instead of betrayal, it occurs to me how smitten Rob was all those years ago, to plot with Sasha after a single date with me. To call and ask her to make a pact, expunging their one-night stand for smoother courting ground. I think of the disastrous dinner I made for Rob in my Bay Village apartment, how that same night ended in unparalleled passion and the more concrete beginning of us. I am reminded of our trip to Italy, before we took the turn toward *this*, and Rob's better financial victories—many investment deals that went his way. His first reaction, always, was to reward us—well-spent time together and tangible things, like a remodeled master bath. While Rob's not much for common gestures that define husbands and wives, and he only brings roses when his error is flagrant, he's made other, more meaningful statements. I bury my nose in Rob's pillow until I can't breathe at all. I think of Rob's most remarkable act—something like a cat bringing you a bird. It's valor that some might define as murder.

On the day my father wouldn't die, Rob sat silently in an upholstered chair in my parents' bedroom. It was three a.m., the light was dim, the musical demands endless—a stunning feat from any other dying man. I'd played so long my fingers bled and my body achieved the point of dutifulness for which my father had always hoped. I listened to Asa Klein's faint corrections about rushed measures and *less than clean* staccato beats. I played Mozart and Strauss and Tchaikovsky and a dozen others to the point where I knew death was the only way out. I was fine if it was mine. The hospice nurse came in, saying that my father's breaths had shallowed and she didn't think it would be long. She said the same thing the hour before. Then she left the room. My mother, in her exhausted grief, had finally gone to lie down in my old bedroom. It was Rob who convinced her to go by assuring her that he'd oversee my father's care.

Another request passed from my father's pale lips. That's when Rob said, "Enough." I didn't say anything. I watched in a hazy fatigue as my father's mangled hand drew upward, grasping vainly at Rob's wrist. Rob, who coolly placed enough fentanyl patches on my father's chest to ensure that his musical requests and heart stopped. At his funeral, in front of the plain pine box, I gripped Rob's hand with my battered fingers and whispered, not *"good-bye,"* but "thank you" to my husband.

Today I continue toward another deathwatch. An hour later, I park in a garage near Mass General, knowing that I'll have to produce more than music, aware that Rob is not coming to my rescue. It would be so much easier to call Sam, engage in a cheery, *"Hi, how are you feeling . . . I'm sure you'll rally . . ."* conversation than it will be to face him. I didn't think ahead—well, beyond telling the truth and letting Theo take it from there.

What is the right recourse after your biological son says he won't lift a finger—or expose a vein—to save the life of his biological father? I suppose that's the rub of science; biology comes with no emotional bond. Sitting in the car, a wave of nausea hits me. I home in on my options. Here's the thing: Is it kinder to allow Sam to die in peace? Am I only inflicting torture on top of a sad fate by telling him now? Or am I merely using this as an excuse to avoid furthering my own well-earned fate—for Sam's anger to be my last memory of him. I reach for the Audi's ignition button. By late this afternoon, I can be in Aruba or Cozumel—fate will play out no differently based on my location.

"Damn it!" Instead of hitting start, I smack the steering wheel. Then I reach for the door handle. "I'm so not the right person to make decisions involving life and death."

Sam is sleeping when I arrive in his room. His color is as ghostly as the sheet wrapped around him. The only personal item is his cell phone, which sits on the bedside table. I didn't answer the last two calls he made to me. There's an uneaten lunch; the smell makes my stomach roll. I discard the tray outside the door as if I'm in the Mass General hospitality suite. Settling my weight onto the edge of the bed doesn't disturb Sam; low, assuring breaths move steadily. Sam asleep in the middle of the day. It's the first clue of a deteriorating man. If he could muster it, Sam would spend his last months or weeks in a Vegas casino, maybe a cruise ship—destination, the end of time.

I study his placid face; time whirls backward. The features are all there, but it's mischievousness I see, maybe the thing I loved most. Something his illness has not yet stolen. I brush my fingertips over his forehead. He doesn't react. We all make choices and I play the *what if* game. What if I hadn't lied all those years ago? What if I'd gotten up the courage to get on a plane to Iowa instead of New Zealand? Did my impulsive choices steal, not just Sam's life, but our entire lives? The trickle-down effect might have reached as far as Rob, never putting him on this path. Maybe my husband missed out on the person who would have made him happy.

Before long, I'm speaking—quietly. For many reasons, I don't want to wake Sam. I talk about years ago, repeating history he knows. Saying it aloud, it sounds surreal—the explosiveness, youthful passion, a moment in time as opposed to the things that result in a lifetime. My gaze drifts from his sleeping, breathing body to the hospital room window. I get to the part that breaks from the story he believes to be true. "I have no idea what to do here, Sam. There's no one left to point out right or wrong. Certainly not Rob—even if he was speaking to me." I shrug. "Although, I have to admit, Rob knows a thing or two about when to pull a trigger." I look back at Sam, sighing. "And forget Sasha. That's even more ironic," I say, drifting deeper into self-analysis. "You'd think after all this time I could predict what she'd tell me to do. But I guess it doesn't work that way. You can't borrow scruples."

Words fall to barely a whisper, and through the smudged hospital window I converse with marshmallow clouds and Canada geese on a flyby. "I lied, Sam. All those years ago, I lied to you about the car accident causing a miscarriage. I let you think the baby was gone." Absently, I reach into my sweater pocket and pull out a crumpled Kleenex. "I was angry . . . hurt that you'd suggested we end the pregnancy. So I let you walk away. I couldn't stand the thought of forcing you into something you so clearly didn't want. I was too willful, stubborn. Too pissed off," I admit. "I wasn't going to let you or my parents decide what happened to my son." I twist toward him. "You have a son."

My heart nearly stops. Sam's eyes are full-moon round, not sleeping; his wide-awake face fills with astonishment.

"What the hell did you just say?"

While *nothing . . . you were dreaming* screams through my head, body language won't cover for me. My back pulls erect and my eyes go wider than his. "A son," I say with a gulp. "He's twenty-six. He lives here in Boston. I only met him a few months ago. He went to Cornell on a lacrosse scholarship, but he became a music teacher. I don't know if he's a better athlete than you, but he's a better fiddler than me. I'm not sure why he's so smart." I rush through the brief bio as if these tidbits are appropriate facts for Sam's gaping blanks.

He draws a huge breath and color flushes through his cheeks. "But you told me . . ."

"I know. I told you the baby didn't survive the car wreck—he shouldn't have. That's what the hospital ob-gyn told me. It's what gave me the idea. You, my parents . . . everyone seemed to take it so well. Hell, my parents were openly elated. It took the pressure off me. I didn't have them berating me for further ruining my life. I suddenly wasn't the rock anchored to your dreams. So I left it that way and I let you go to Iowa while I went to New Zealand, to Phillip's."

Sam fumbles for the control to the hospital bed. The mattress rises. As it does, I brace for the anger, maybe the slap I have coming. "This is a joke, right, Liv? I have—"

"A son." But instead of fury, Sam's solitary reaction is a stark blink. Perhaps he's too weak to offer much more. "I gave him up for adoption—a cleverly arranged adoption. It's, um . . . that's a longer part of the story. And before you say anything else, or think another thought, I have to tell you the part that matters most right now. I'm not sharing this now because the cavalry has arrived." I keep going. "I'm telling you because it's the right thing to do. I deceived him . . . and I lied to you. Because of that, when I told him who I was, who you are . . ." I purse my lips. My soul quakes at the idea of the man I'd once so thoroughly loved possibly dying because of what I set in motion.

"Liv . . ." He reaches out and clasps my arm. "Jesus, calm down. Whatever you did, I—"

"No, Sam, not 'whatever I did.' Don't downplay this. For twenty-six years it was a secret. Never in a million years did I imagine I'd be telling you under these circumstances. Nothing can make it right."

"Wait. Just slow down . . . Back it up a little and start—"

There's a tap at the door of Sam's room, though it opens simultaneously. I stiffen, prepared for this raw moment of emotion to be on display for medical staff, perhaps the janitor. A man strides through on a step of courage. There's immediate facial recognition, almost identical frames. The man in the bed and the one at the door are both caught off guard. Sucking up snot in my near hysterical state, I jerk up off the bed. "Oh my God." I clamp a hand over my mouth. Theo does not look at me but stares at Sam. It's the eyes. While brown may be the world's most common color, there's something extraordinary in seeing your once-lover's eyes on your own son, both of them in the same room.

Theo finally looks in my direction. For a moment I think he's going to say he has the wrong room; he's only there to visit a friend. But his glare grows more defined. "Maybe I'm not so much like you after all." He looks to Sam. "I assume she's told you . . . about me?" Sam offers a vague nod. "I spoke with the bone marrow transplant people—not your doctors, but people who could give me information. I understand that finding this . . . *half match* requires no more than a blood test. I've done that part. If it matches . . . fine." A pause fills the air. "If that's the case, Olivia has my number." He turns to leave.

"Wait," Sam says. The similar tone of their voices is enough to shock Theo into holding still. Then he pivots. "Can . . . Could I at least ask your name?"

Theo shoots a searing look in my direction. "Why? I was offered up as nothing more than a possible cure, a human Petri dish, right?"

"That's not fair," I say. "I was just explaining everything to Sam when you came in—"

He holds up a hand and focuses on Sam. "Theo. My name is Theo McAdams. I'm named after my father—Theodore David McAdams. He was a great man, an exceptional human being. My mother's name is Claire. If I'm here right now, you have them to thank." He snickers, glancing between us. "Quite obviously not yourselves."

Sam shimmies up taller in the bed. "Hold on a second." He glances at me. "I'm processing this as fast as I can—until five minutes ago I didn't know you existed."

"Which I understand is the way you wanted it."

Sam looks to me and I try to pick up where I was before Theo arrived. "It's, um . . . Through circumstance nobody could have predicted, I ended up telling Theo about the night of the car accident—what you suggested, the *possible* solution to me being pregnant."

Sam eases back into the cushion of the mattress and scrubs a hand over his face. He laughs, which surprises us both. "I get it." He looks at Theo. "You're pissed off because a scared, twenty-one-year-old kid—being me—was quick to suggest the easy way out." He looks Theo up and down. "And here you are now, living color irony. I gotta tell you . . ." I'm sure Sam was about to say *son.* It would only be Southern vernacular, but Theo would take it as a northern insult. "I'd be pissed off too."

Theo nods, but there's nothing bonding about it. He merely looks sorry that I ever turned up in his classroom. "Good. So we all agree on that much."

"But it doesn't sound like Olivia told you the whole story. I came to Boston to find her, to apologize for the choices I made back then." He and Theo trade a look. "Hell, kid, what did you just say? Your father was a great man, an exceptional human being." Theo nods. "I doubt he and I had the same starting point in life. Livy tell you that part?" Theo doesn't respond. "Where I came from . . . It was exceptional too. A different kind of exceptional: a leather belt with your name on it, your body used like an ashtray. That's the kid who found out he was going to be a father."

A scar is visible on Sam's arm; from the dip of his hospital gown, another peeks out, burned to his chest. I know Theo sees them.

"From what you said, sounds like you ended up with two mothers. I never had one. You've known Livy, what? A few months? Also know you have more information about your birth mother than I'll ever have about mine. And Liv's past, it's not physically violent . . . But torment is hardly limited to physical acts. Sorry your biological parents didn't come perfectly wired. But it seems to me—given us—she tried to do right by you."

"Doesn't excuse what she's done recently," Theo says dryly.

"See the part about not being perfectly wired." Sam goes on with his point. "All of my past put me at a disadvantage when it came to conversations about you." He points to me. "I know what she wanted back then—she wanted me to swoop in and say it would all work out. In the end, Liv knew better. She made the best choice . . . for me . . . and for you. I won't let you think otherwise." He smiles at me. "She plays a mean fiddle. But there's a hell of a lot more to be said for the number-one fan of the man from Tennessee."

"Why do you both keep saying that?"

"One of the things I came to tell Livy was that—regardless of any baby we did or didn't have—I made mistakes. Can't do a damn thing about it now. Clearly, by coming here, you've made your decision. You're a good man—no thanks to me. I appreciate that," Sam says solemnly. "If that's all it turns out to be, if you can't get past the rest . . . I understand."

Theo nods. He turns to leave. At the door, he turns back. "Will one of you let me know—either way?"

"I'll let you know," I say, having edged back to the side of the bed where Sam's hand links with mine. Theo stares for a moment, focused on the tangled fingers and lives in the room.

I spend a little more time with Sam, filling in the rest of the story. I do not avoid any blame on my part, and I give Theo all the credit for doing the right thing. Sam's exhausted, but adamant about convincing me otherwise. "Livy, you need to know, you did the right thing all those years ago. Think it through—if you told me about Theo back then . . . I like to think I would have tried to live up to expectations. But had that happened, we wouldn't have survived it, not in the long run. For whatever it's worth, Sam Nash—pitching legend—that would have never happened either. You saw it; take the credit. And truth be told . . ." His words slur, Sam succumbing to the meds a nurse administered. "I'm glad I didn't have to choose. Might have left me a little bitter, instead of the fun-loving guy I am." A gurgle of laughter precedes sleep. "A son. I'll be damned."

Once home, I am misguided by the dimly lit brownstone. I assume either Rob is not here or he's sequestered in his basement fortress. Inside the foyer, my name ripples through; I hear my mother. It's nearly ten o'clock. I find her seated in the living room, poised in a high-back chair, her foot swinging rhythmically as she sips a mixed drink that I know she did not prepare. Rob is standing at the wet bar. He cheers a drink in my direction.

"Based on a long conversation with Rob," she announces, "I've decided a few things about the future."

I look between her Elizabeth Arden–painted face and Rob's, who smiles crookedly at her. "Like what?" I wonder if Rob has outed me; I brace for her to lay claim to her grown grandson and surely lace into me for—after the fact—having the audacity to give away a Klein. "Isn't it rather late for you, Mom?"

"Once Rob and I talked things through, I decided to stay until you came back from wherever it is you've been." My mother looks me over like I've just rolled out of a hotel room bed, not a hospital room. "I'm going to winter early in the Boca condo. I'm leaving day after tomorrow. Of course, I don't normally go until after the holidays. But considering the circumstances . . . Well, I agreed with Asa's notion that an early change of scenery wouldn't be the worst thing."

I glance fast between her and Rob, but make no correction. "And if the Wellesley house is gone come spring?"

She sips her drink and her chin tips upward. "If it's gone, that's something I'll have to come to terms with. Rob says he'll make certain everything goes to storage. I won't lie to you, Olivia. Just like your father, I had every intention of dying in my own time, on my own terms, in that house." Rob stands a bit taller and clears his throat. "So that will be . . . *different.*" She places her drink on the coffee table and rises. "I'll be busy packing. I won't have time to see you again before I go. So I waited." She looks toward Rob, as if looking for an assurance that she's done her part. He is busy texting someone. More quietly, she says, "Whether it was a violin or your life, Olivia, it's always been rather unstrung. I suspect your marriage will just be another casualty." She says good-bye to Rob with a warm hug and a passing peck on the cheek to me. Even the cursory show of affection is odd. She pauses, speaking to both of us. "Just a last word on the Wellesley, as clearly it's causing distress between the two of you . . ."

"That and a few other things," I murmur.

"To lose the house means giving up a coveted possession." She frowns and draws a blunt conclusion. "I'd burn it to the ground if it meant having your father back, even for a day. A house is far from the most important thing at stake here."

I follow to the foyer as she exits. When the door shuts, I press my forehead against the cold glass. "You didn't tell her."

"About Theo?" I nod, still not moving my head from the glass. "No. It was your secret to keep. It's yours to tell—or not, Liv." There is something different in his tone, detached. I turn, never moving away from the door, my back now pinned to it. Tucked around the corner of the music room are two suitcases—the kind he wouldn't take on a business trip. Rob has moved closer to the foyer, nearer the exit. His hands are stuffed in his front pockets, his face drawn. "Really. Regardless of

Theo, how much longer could we do this? I told you years ago, I don't do vicious circles."

"I . . . It's been a little chaotic, Rob. I really haven't had time to sort out—"

"Our marriage? Yeah. Well, there's a surprise. I guess hidden sons and ex-lovers will keep your calendar full." He puts on his coat, which is hanging over the banister.

"Wait." My heart flutters in an erratic rhythm. "Where . . . where are you going?"

He smiles—a Cheshire Rob grin if I ever saw one. "Does it matter?" He approaches the door, then answers. "I'll be bunking in my office for now." For a moment, I take a dramatic stance, Rob physically having to remove me to get past me. I'm rushed by the notion of how much I don't want him to go. My teeth sink into my bottom lip, tears well. I've done nothing to make him want to stay. I slide away from the door. He opens it and gathers his luggage. He doesn't look back, but he does seem to waver. "If it makes you feel any better, Liv, you didn't fail at us alone."

CHAPTER THIRTY-NINE

Theo

It's not his house keys, nor his iPhone. It is Theo himself that feels misplaced. He's taken the day off from Braemore. It doesn't matter, class let out over an hour ago. He's spent his day playing the violin and staring at the fire escape on the brick building adjacent to his. He wishes escape were so easy, the flames slightly less caustic. When he called Principal Giroux to report his absence, Braemore's first in command told him he received a call from the Suffolk County DA's office. Olivia Klein wouldn't be back. She arranged to complete her remaining community service hours elsewhere.

Principal Giroux wanted to know if Theo thought the environment proved too overwhelming for the symphony violinist. Theo replied, "She did okay with the kids. She did her part in other ways. I think it was me that she had issues with." Principal Giroux made an interesting remark, "Whatever the woman's shortcomings, she knows herself. Behind-the-scenes support is more in Ms. Klein's wheelhouse than up-close encounters."

It's been several days since Theo's trip to Mass General. He's not heard from anyone about Sam or his blood test. Theo is antsier about the result than he might have imagined. Claire has called, wanting to have lunch this Saturday. But the idea of lunch strikes him as incredibly frivolous. He is more confounded about what he might tell Claire about Olivia or Sam Nash. If all this happened in high school, even college, she would have handled the fallout. Theo corrects the conclusion: Claire would have run interference, made certain he stayed grounded. He can only imagine how far she would have gone to keep news from Theo that she deemed distressing.

Theo's just about to reach for his violin when there is a knock at the door. So lost in the hazy craziness of recent days, Theo doesn't take the precaution of peering through the spy hole. He opens the door. And twice now Theo is confronted by a dream. India stands across from him. He steps back. "He's dead. Isn't he?"

"What?"

"Sam Nash. Did you come here to tell me he's dead?"

India shakes her head. "No. I mean, I don't know how he is aside from when I left Olivia the other night. Wasn't it a match, your bone marrow?" She asks this while coming inside the apartment, and Theo closes the door.

"How do you know I went for the blood test? When you left here . . ."

She turns. Her red hair and fair complexion, her steadiness, it contrasts and complements everything in his life. "I know you, Theo. You were angry. But no matter the circumstance, you're not going to let a man die, not if you can help it."

This would be the easiest of conclusions for India to draw. She knows him better than anyone. In fact, it's India he's wanted to talk to about the whole Sam Nash, Olivia Klein situation—not his mother. And not because the news would upset Claire, but because India can grasp things about Theo from the proper perspective. He's a grown man. He doesn't need protection from the truth about his biological parents. He perhaps needed time to absorb the erratic way in which he learned the story. But it's hardly cause for warm cocoa on the couch of his childhood home and his favorite meal being prepared, all of which would have been Claire's response.

"I went for the test. I haven't heard any results." He walks to the violin and plucks at a few strings. And instead of asking India why she's come, he grabs onto the thing he wants most—the right person to confide in. "I went there, to Mass General. I met him."

"Did you?" India says, shrugging off her coat as if her presence is as natural as when she lived there. "And what was that like?"

"Weird. Uncomfortable." Theo snickers. "I didn't think of it until just this second, but in any other circumstance I would have been meeting a baseball legend. That part never crossed my mind."

India smiles. "So do you want to go back, ask for his autograph?"

"No. But I can't say having another conversation with him sounds as horrible as I would have thought." Theo stares into India's eyes. "I wonder if that will happen."

"Do you want it to?" Theo doesn't reply. "Olivia didn't seem to know an exact timeline if there's no match. But if it's what you want, I would think there's a window to talk—get to know one another a little."

Theo lets go of the violin. "Guess I shouldn't take too much time to think it over."

"He's not David McAdams, Theo. He won't ever be that. But not too many people get a second chance at having a father." India's arms are folded. "And one who's a baseball legend, of all things. I have to admit; it's fascinating—seeing where all your gifts come from."

Theo crosses to a Power Rangers Megazord tin box. From inside, he withdraws a Sam Nash baseball card. "I knew I had this card. Lifetime ERA, 2.35." India crosses to stand beside him.

"Is that good?"

Theo smiles. "Uh, yeah. The word *elite* comes to mind." He stares at the card. "No wonder I could thread a lacrosse ball between two tight midfielders, past the goalie, and right into a net." They both look at the card, and he hears India's breath catch. He sees it; she sees it—Theo's eyes. "It's, um . . . it's interesting. To live a quarter of your life before seeing someone who looks like you."

"Kind of like my hair," she ponders. They trade a glance. "Haven't you ever noticed? I'm the only redhead in my family. At least the only one I've ever seen."

"I never thought of it. I just saw it as one more thing that made you special." Theo places the card back in the tin box. It's quiet for a moment. They both speak at once before India quiets. "India, what are you doing here?"

A tremulous breath rises from her chest. "Olivia, for all the turmoil she's caused . . . She and I had a long conversation the other night. She gave me some good advice."

"There's a surprise."

"Mmm . . . I can't totally disagree. I won't go into all the details. I'm not sure that matters, not right now. What matters . . . The reason I've come, is you and me." Her sweet face turns grave. "I kissed someone else, Theo."

A hurt that had faded rises like a blister, although it's not nearly as painful as India having left him. "Old news, don't you think?"

"And you also know how sorry I am that it happened—however it happened."

"I knew that too, the same night you called to tell me."

"You forgave me, Theo. But I couldn't forgive myself. And because I couldn't do that, I let myself be manipu—" She stops, examining the wooden flooring beneath their shoes. "I convinced myself that the only fair way out was to let you go. Olivia pointed out that you don't get too many turns at happiness. In fact, you might only get one. So I'm here . . ." Theo inches closer and listens harder. "If you're still offering me a second chance, I'm taking it."

Seconds later Theo is kissing India. The two of them are moving toward the leather sofa. The bedroom is too far away. His hands don't know where to move first—winding through her hair, touching her face, reaching for the buttons on the shirt she is wearing. Throaty little hums vibrate from India. Her body is trembling. Thoughts of the first time they had sex skip through Theo's head. He'd like to say he remembers all the times, but it would be like saying he recalls every beautiful sunset he's ever seen. Yet this does remind him of the first time. Confident India was nervous then, admitting that wanting something and having it were often two very different things. Months later, she told him the reason she was so nervous was because she kept thinking, *"What if it ends . . . What if he goes away . . . ?"*

Back then, Theo dismissed any such idea, but now he shudders too knowing how close the thought came to pass. "Theo, are you all right?" He pauses, poised over India on the sofa. He looks down into her hazel eyes, the lashes tinged red like her hair. They are wet—so are his.

"Promise me that no matter what else, these past months . . . Promise me nothing like that will ever happen again. The *you leaving me* part, I mean. I don't think I could survive it twice, India."

"I promise." She says this as if it is the simplest assurance, like saying she will meet him for coffee or reminding him of an appointment. "I . . . do you have any idea how much I love you?" And Theo believes her, not because India's current declaration is so amazing, but because it's the past seven months that have felt like a lie.

Soon there is nothing but India's bare skin on leather, the old sofa playing its part and joining in the rhythm of their reunion. The sofa makes sounds Theo hasn't heard in a long time, the crunch of the cushion as their weight sinks into it. There is the more humorous second as the legs of the sofa eek along the hardwood floor. Theo drowns in the scent of India—ginger tea body wash. It soaks into his brain, which grabs at it—the sense of belonging for which he has been searching. There is the taste of all of her as Theo makes a rapid but thoughtful descent from her mouth and beyond her stomach. India shifts and Theo catches a glimpse of her fingers, reaching and finding the plusher throw pillow. Theo indulges in a level of intimacy that his dreams have begged for night after night. The vibrating hum from her throat heightens, crashing into a lovely lingering gasp. India's entire body trembles in a very different way.

Moments later he hears, "Theo, please . . ." India speaks in an urgent whisper, reaching for his pants, which are the only remaining item of clothing between them. The rest plays out not so differently from all the other sunsets experienced on this leather sofa—Theo seeing brilliant hues, fiery oranges and reds. Some are India's hair; others are attached to the feelings that rush him during a heated and well-executed act of emotion. In the end, Theo is breathless and happily lost, happier still for India to tell him what comes next.

An hour later they are dressed, having talked a bit about the everyday things they missed. India's applied to several different graduate programs. She wants to be a school psychologist. Theo says this is wonderful. He always knew she would decide on a career perfectly suited to her ability and agility for guidance. At one point, Theo casually remarks that his mother will be surprised by their reunion. To his amazement, India says she already knows. She went to see Claire that morning—just to keep her in the loop of her son's life. India smiles. "She adores you, Theo. I only thought it fair to let her know how I will *never* let anything come between us again."

Just as India asks what Theo thinks of his position at Braemore, his cell rings. It's the hospital and the woman from the blood and bone marrow donor center. With no more fanfare than telling him that his blood type is B positive, she informs Theo that he's not a match—not even good enough for a half match. Theo imagined he might feel bad if he wasn't a match, but he doesn't expect such a punch of disappointment. India is right there, her arms bracing around him, telling him how sorry she is. Without Theo saying a word, she understands the angles of awfulness the news brings.

"Should I go see him?" Theo asks, his glance trained on the Power Rangers Megazord box. Like David McAdams's driver's license, Theo senses the baseball card will become an odd treasure. "What if he's angry? What if he only really wanted to know me because I could have saved his life?"

India considers this for a moment. "I don't think that will happen, Theo. Remember, you were as much of a surprise to him as he was to you. And Sam Nash knew the odds of you being a match were small. Things being what they are, I'd think a chance to get to know his son would be a silver lining inside a pretty dark cloud."

CHAPTER FORTY

Olivia

I'm sitting in a small waiting area outside Sam's room. I am supposed to be at symphony rehearsal. I've missed four in recent weeks, finally telling conductor Manuel Gutierrez I have a family emergency. Manuel is unsympathetic, telling me what I already know: symphonies suffer when even one violinist is not on par with the other musicians. People pay good money to hear a finely tuned orchestra, not one with a violinist that has come unstrung.

He asks if there is any possibility I will miss our upcoming performances. We have several this weekend. I've seen other orchestra mates miss practices and performances—births, deaths, even miserable breakups. Aloofness, which best describes my New England Symphony persona, is at the root of his cold reaction. Manuel can be empathetic—he's just not going to do it for me. He likely believes Olivia Klein is impenetrable, whether by music or emotion. I sniff at the assumption and purse my lips. It keeps my chin from quivering. Yet I stand my ground. I honestly cannot answer him about practice or this weekend's dates. He presses for details: Is my mother ill? (No, she's fled to Florida, thrilled to learn her favorite masseuse is available year round.) Is my husband injured? (No, he's fled my life, thrilled to be rid of the mayhem I bring to his.)

Nevertheless, I insist it's a grave family matter that will keep me from my orchestral obligations. We end the call on an unpleasant note, with me wondering how rusty my dog-walking skills are. If I lose the chair I will never get it back. My career, at least in Boston, will be over. I imagine how disgusted my father would be. On the other hand, I'm aware of a new threshold of not giving a damn—one where the response is not to run away or act out. It's about fulfilling obligations that I perceive as more critical than the expectations of others. There's a lot to be said for deciding what's most important to you. I glance at my phone. The doctor's been in with Sam for some time, nurses coming and going.

The elevator continues to ding. This time the one-note noise lands on my last nerve. I reach for my purse and iPod. If I can't practice *The Planets*, I can listen to the fifty-minute orchestral piece. I'll do what I can to meet the professional commitment I've made to a talented ensemble of musicians. I pop in earbuds and skip over movement one, "Mars, The Bringer of War." There has been enough of that. I also scroll past "Uranus, The Magician"—a section dedicated to deception. Ditto on that. "Neptune" doesn't work either, morose and unsettling. Absently, my thumb connects with "Jupiter"—the most popular movement in Holst's *Planets*. It is the happiest part of the entire work, a joyous piece of music.

As the measures rise, notes build and the elevator doors open again. It's the lack of a one-note ding that makes me focus on the flood of occupants getting off. Upon seeing Theo, I lurch so forcefully from my seat that the earbuds tear from my ears. India's with him. They are holding hands. The sight evokes a smile from me. "Theo. You came back. You, um . . . you both did."

"I'm not a match."

"I know." I glance at their hands, clamped so firmly it is as if they are made from one mold. "Does, um . . . I guess this means the two of you have worked things out."

India answers. "You made some good points the other night, about the rationale of what things cost and the price that should be paid. You were right."

"That's, um . . . Won't Theo's mother be surprised?" I say, smiling curiously at India.

"Very," India says. "She was the first person I told." She glances at Theo, whose face grows questioning at the odd exchange. "I know how *despondent* Claire was over our breakup, so I stopped on by her house on my way into the city and shared the good news."

"And Claire was . . ."

"Speechless," India quickly says. "Thoroughly speechless."

I assume India's beaming smile says she's given Claire notice, let her know it is no longer Claire and Theo's life, but India's and his.

"I . . . I'm very glad to hear all that."

"How is he?" Theo asks.

"Uh, puking his brains out last I checked."

A nurse approaches, interrupting. "Dr. Chang says you can visit for a few minutes if you like." Dr. Chang is the oncologist who's taken over Sam's care, working in tandem with Dr. Bogart in California. She points to what, in my mind, looks like a hospital butler's pantry. Every time someone goes into Sam's room they visit this station first, gowning-up from head to toe.

Theo crunches his forehead. "Did they start another round of chemo? The people I spoke with said that in a case like Sam's, a trial chemo treatment would be the next option, something he'd have to qualify for. Did that happen?"

"Uh, no. This is the conditioning phase for a stem cell transplant. Sam has a donor."

Theo's eyes go wide. "But I thought I wasn't—"

"You're not. A PI Sam hired ages ago found his brother, Tate. He was in Wyoming working on a cattle ranch. He was agreeable. He had the blood drawn there. It was a match. They say this phase takes about week. Then they'll do the actual transplant. They're harvesting the stem cells right in Wyoming, shipping them here. The doctor can explain the medical particulars better than me, but—"

"They have a match and you didn't call to tell me?"

"Sam asked me not to. He said if you knew there was a chance he'd live it'd be so much easier to come back. But knowing you weren't a match . . . he thought it would tell you more about how you felt. Seeing Sam under those circumstances, it'd have to be something you really wanted to do."

For a moment, he doesn't reply. "Huh. He's right," Theo finally says. "It was harder to come here knowing that I wasn't a match. But it also made me think about exactly what it would mean if I did."

Theo exchanges a glance with India, who asks the waiting nurse, "Can he have another visitor?"

"It's really only supposed to be family."

Theo is quick to reply, "I'm his son."

CHAPTER FORTY-ONE

Four Weeks Later

Olivia

It's late at Mass General, too late for visitors. But since when have rules stopped me? It's shortly before midnight on New Year's Eve. I'm here at Sam's request. He grows a bit stronger every day. His initial test results are promising, white cell counts are up. According to Dr. Chang, the bone marrow transplant appears to have triggered another remission. It is not a cure—it's an optimistic extension, at least that's how a cautious Sam describes it.

Sam appeared more amazed that, once located, his brother was agreeable. I suggested that people change; sometimes they're not the same as they were in their hotheaded youth. I don't know if I'm right or wrong about this when it comes to Tate. He's only called once, and that was to bitch about the procedure involved in the harvesting of his stem cells. I shrugged at Sam. "How much of a miracle did you anticipate?"

I have snuck a split of champagne into his room. In twenty-seven years I have never celebrated this date, not really. We've seen Theo sparingly. This may be because he is busy with India, replanning the wedding they canceled. I like to tell myself it's the reason. In truth, I don't know that Theo is entirely comfortable with the two of us. Or maybe I'm too impatient, looking for the bond I denied, the one I cut but could not sever so long ago. I place two paper cups on the tray. "Goes better with the screw cap," I say.

"Hell, Livy, you're talking to a boy who'd drink moonshine out of his pitching glove." He smiles at a classic Sam remark. "Guess that's not terribly romantic."

Pouring the champagne, I pause and tip my head at him. "Is that what this is, romantic?" Only recently have we upgraded to taking the future from one hour at a time to one day at a time. I haven't thought beyond those parameters or put labels on my relationship with Sam. Seeing him through this was simply the right thing to do. The bubbles fizz and I go back to pouring.

"Doc says in another few days, maybe a week, I can go back to California. Dr. Bogart will take over." He sips the champagne. I don't say anything. "It, um . . . The offer I made in my hotel room stands, Liv. I'd love it if you came home with me."

Before I can formulate a reaction, there's a knock at the door. It pushes open a bit and Theo pops his head through. "Hi."

"Theo," I say breathlessly. I'm not stunned by his presence or his forgiving heart. That, I have learned, is simply Theo. It's something I no longer attribute to biology or nurturing. It's Theo's wiring. What gets me every time is the fact that this circumstance exists. I would have imagined traveling to all Holst's *Planets* and back before ever believing Theo would know who we are.

"I took a chance, guessed maybe you'd both be here."

"Don't you have some great party to be at, a girl lookin' to kiss you at midnight?" Sam asks.

"I'm not much for parties."

"Go figure that," Sam says, looking rather confined inside four tight walls. I've noticed this in recent days—he's starting to get antsy, more like the Sam I know. "I'd give anything for a loud room."

Theo laughs. It's one thing that does not mirror between father and son. "India's back at the apartment. Helen's visiting."

"Oh, how is she?" I ask cautiously.

"Doing it day by day. I think that last treatment program may have been key for her. Even so, India was fine with staying in. A friend was having a party, but she doesn't like to put temptation in Helen's path."

"Probably a smart idea," I say, remaining neutral and positive on the subject. "And you were out walking—alone on your birthday?"

"I told India I wanted to go for a walk. She handed me my scarf . . . the one glove I haven't been able to find for days, and said, 'Why don't you walk to where you really want to go?'" I reach for a third paper cup and hold it out to Theo. "Sure," he says, coming farther into the room. I divide the split into thirds. "A New Year's Eve toast."

I shake my head. "I never toast New Year's Eve." The wall clock reads 11:58. "I drink at one minute to midnight." Then I say the words I have harbored in my head for twenty-seven years. "Family tradition."

Theo nods gently, as if he too is trying on this unlikely concept. He and Sam drift into small talk, and I listen.

"Yeah, Sharks look pretty good this season, but if I've got to watch winter sports, I prefer the Kings. 'Course growing up here I guess you're a Bruins fan."

"Definitely. Seems like they're having a better season than last year."

"Time will tell," Sam says. "They stole themselves a hell of a center from the Blues in the off season."

"They did."

I absorb the moment as the two of them talk basketball or lacrosse, some game involving a ball. The conversation goes back and forth for a short time. Then Theo says he has to go. The visit is brief. For now, it's what works. But I do find myself encouraging Theo to take a cab. There are plenty of sensible reasons: the late hour, drunk drivers and pedestrian objects, icy patches of sidewalk. But I keep quiet as he leaves. Then I stare out the window into the blustery New Year, acknowledging a gust of protectiveness that has kicked up like swirling snow. On the dark street below, Theo exits the building and darts across Fruit Street. He disappears into the night.

"He'll get home fine, Livy."

I whirl around. "Of course he will."

"You'll get used to it."

"What's that?"

"Being his mother."

I arch a brow. "Hmm, I highly doubt Claire will be on board with that idea, even an eighty-twenty split." On Theo's last hospital visit, I got up the nerve to ask if he'd told Claire about me, about Sam. At the very least, I thought I should be prepared if she showed up at the brownstone door with a bribe, asking me to leave town. But Theo said he hadn't. He wanted time to get used to the idea first, saying he would tell her when he was ready. At the moment, he didn't want Claire's input. Despite an inability to keep track of winter gloves and a need to walk aimlessly, Theo may be a wise man.

I do wonder what he would make of Claire's interference in his life. As far as I know, India hasn't told Theo. It's left me quietly outraged; Claire comes away smelling like a rose while I know what my actions have cost me. She will remain the mother Theo admires.

Theo and his mother . . . I am still tinkering with how to tell Theo about Shep Stewart's book plan. Perhaps, once again, India can lend a hand. Over the past few weeks, I've come to admire, maybe recognize, how perfectly India suits Theo, and vice versa. They are well matched. Whatever Claire's misgivings, about this much I'm certain she is wrong.

On his last visit, Theo did tell us that he plans to finish out his year at Braemore and move on. He's applied for a position at the Boston

Conservatory because more than anything else, Theo loves to teach. He's presented an idea to the Conservatory. Pro bono, he will also take on a handful of select students from Braemore, those whose lives could be changed by music. I think like that fermata mark, Theo has found his long-term place in music.

"Liv?" Sam says.

"Sorry," I say, turning. "I was just thinking."

"There's a lot to think about—and maybe I wasn't doing that before Theo showed up. California, it's too far from here. The Brandeis gig is long gone, but if I hung around . . . Hell, it's not like I need a real job. The docs here are great, post treatment is ongoing. I just thought if I was going to have a life, I might as well do something that counts past my last out."

"I agree. You're too young. And you'd be great at something. Besides, I think a third chance may be a charm."

He smiles. I sit on the side of the bed, absorbing a face that makes time turn back. "So that's a plan then?"

"Sam . . ." He tangles his fingers with mine. "I'll always be the number-one fan of the man from Tennessee. But your life is in California. And mine . . ." I blink, looking toward the window. "Well, it's time I figured out one for myself. We can't go back." I let go of his hand. "It's dreamy and it's tempting, but it's not . . . real. I'm not sure it ever was."

He snickers. "Real enough to produce one good thing."

"Yes. Like you said, it's probably lucky we weren't around to muck it up."

He's quiet for a moment. "Yeah," Sam says, brushing his fingertips through a fine layer of my bangs. "I suppose. Even so . . ."

I grasp his hand, drawing it away from my face. "Even so, I think it's important to realize what you feel for someone at twenty or twenty-one, it's so powerful, so intense. It looks magical compared to what comes along at thirty . . . or even thirty-nine." I pause, staring into his brown eyes. "It's a turn youth allows. Everybody gets one. But I don't know that it's sustainable—at least not for me."

"And a relationship couldn't take on a whole new meaning, whatever that is at our age."

"I did that."

"With someone else."

"I haven't taken very good care of it. The things I've done, it's likely cost me a real marriage."

He pauses. "Regardless of what we produced, ours wasn't a real marriage . . ."

"Not the kind that lasts a lifetime. You said that finding me felt like fate, so you wouldn't have to go through this alone." I swallow hard, smiling at him. "Sam, by coming here, you also gave me much-needed perspective: 'Know what to keep and what to walk away from.' Life's not that long, right?"

"But I got it backward, what you're going to keep."

"I honestly don't know if I have anything left to keep. But I won't substitute it. You shouldn't either. You deserve better than that. We both do."

CHAPTER FORTY-TWO

Two Weeks Later

Olivia

Last night's concert was one of our best. The New England Symphony was awarded a staggering standing ovation after a special performance attended by the governor and several dignitaries. We were supposed to hang around for a private meet and greet. I can only comply with so many rules of order, and slipped out the fire exit before someone started making a speech. Before escaping, Mary Alice Porter threw me a look as if I were making an assassination attempt. No doubt I'll hear about it from Manuel. But my personal performance was near flawless, and for what he does put up with, our conductor knows he is fortunate to have Olivia Klein in his orchestra.

However, I was not completely satisfied with a tricky section in movement three of Holst's *Planets*. For the past hour I have been in my music room, working and reworking the measures. While "Mercury" is the shortest movement, "The Messenger" is a swarm of awkward shifts.

I'm determined to make it more legato and better in tune. I have literally played myself into a sweat. I don't hear the doorbell, which now rings in a consistent buzz.

A visitor would be odd. Theo and India were here last Friday for dinner, which I had catered from Sorellina. It was friendly, though I don't believe we've reached a "just stopped by" point in our relationship. Sam returned to California last week. I haven't heard from him since. I imagine like all things attached to Sam Nash, whatever is sparkling in his line of vision has his attention. My mother remains in Boca Raton. I've grown concerned with her past few phone calls—she was vague, not at all her usual cutting self. As we hung up last time she said, "I love you, Olivia." I honestly have no recollection of my mother ever saying these words aloud to me. I was caught so off guard I didn't reply in kind, but hung up the phone, staring like it was an unrecognizable, foreign object.

"Coming," I say now, brushing a sweater sleeve over a damp brow, shuffling in my socks across the glassy herringbone hardwoods. I furrow the same damp brow as a dainty outline comes into view. I open the door. Sasha is on the other side, holding a tray of coffee.

"Should I assume it's poisoned?"

"Oh, that's smart, Liv. Start with an insult. It's, like, ten below out here. Would you get the fuck out of my way?" I skirt back as she ploughs past and into the music room. She sets down the coffee, and her leather satchel slips onto the sofa. Several legal-looking envelopes are peeking out. "I'm handling the transfer of the Wellesley house deed."

Standing in the drafty foyer, I don't know whether the coffee is a peace offering, or just what she happened to be holding on her way over. Arms folded, I focus on the floor as I pad back into the music room. "Since when did you take up real estate law, contract foreclosure . . . whatever the hell you'd call it?"

"I defend accused murderers, Liv. I think I can handle a simple deed transfer. The deal Rob agreed to is straightforward. In lieu of the necessary funds for his share of the golf course deal, the Wellesley property is to be surrendered for nonpayment to . . ." She withdraws one envelope from several in her bag and pulls out a blue-backed document. "The Finch Group."

I swallow down the name of a meaningless, nondescript, on-paper entity. I think of the Klein family, who built the Wellesley house. No one has ever lived there but Kleins. While I might not think of my father, I do think of my grandfather. A man whose gift saved his life, a life he went on to make the most of, living it in that house. It was one thing to plan on eventually selling the house for a greater good—something my grandfather would have applauded, I'm sure. It's quite another to have it yanked out from under you to satisfy a golf course deal gone bad. I imagine the Finch Group will sell promptly to new money, transferring in from the West Coast or, worse, Utah.

Sasha's still rambling. "Being as the deed is in yours and Rob's names, you both have to sign."

"I'm aware of whose names are on the deed." I'm annoyed by her continued dig at my wedding gift gesture, which started as a rock-solid commitment to our marriage, and has since turned into a rolling boulder. "Rob's asked you to do this, handle the particulars?" I have not seen or spoken to Rob since the night he left.

"No," Sasha says. "I volunteered."

"Seeing a lot of him, are you?"

"Here and there." My stomach does a free fall, though my brain doesn't follow. I just don't like the implied imagery. But Sasha knows me well enough to smell weakness. She goes for it. "Over our last candlelit dinner, Rob was distracted by the details of the Wellesley house situation. I said I'd deal with it. That way I could get him home, so I could fuck him faster."

Sarcasm hits with the sear of a branding iron. "Shut up, Sasha! Just shut the hell up."

"Why?" she says as I take a damp-eyed turn around the music room, facing the street view. "What do you care? Sure. Maybe it stings a little more if it's me . . . But know that eventually it will be somebody." I spin back around but don't reply. "Someone will come along, Liv. She'll lure Rob out of his funk—he'll follow because he's lost. Bizarre as it sounds, he's lost without *you*. You make him pay attention—to you, to life. And so we're crystal clear, we met up in a dirty Dunks. There were no candles, boutique hotels, or booty calls involved."

"How sad it has to be qualified. And so I'm being crystal clear, he's the one who left, Sash. He walked out on me."

"Like he had much of a choice? He does have a little dignity left—you keep a huge secret from him—from all of us. In the meantime, you did admit to spending the night at Sam's hotel."

"I did *not* have sex with Sam!" My tone is adamant, but I am, at best, repeating Sam's assurance.

"Fine. Moving on . . . You also rushed to his side at the hospital, kept a steady vigil."

"Without overdramatizing, the man was on his deathbed, Sash."

She holds up a hand. "I'm not saying that's untrue. I'm just pointing out how it looked to Rob. He saw it as where you wanted to be, who you wanted to be with. And if Sam Nash was what you wanted, Rob wasn't about to be second choice *after* he expired."

"Sam is fine. Or as fine as he can be given his circumstance. His brother turned up in the eleventh hour. He was a match and the stem cell transplant worked. He flew home to California a week ago."

"And you didn't go with him."

"Rekindling a romance with Sam was Rob's assumption, apparently yours. Sam was never my choice."

"All right," she says coolly. "An unexpected but promising plot twist. Aside from any Sam Nash complications, Rob feels incredibly guilty about the Wellesley house. Having his name on the deed was your doing, but he knows the risky business was all his."

I fold my arms. "Well. Aren't we both disgustingly imperfect."

"Yes," she says, her head nodding furiously. "You are. And to be honest, Liv . . ." She points to the legal document. "I should be done instead of continuing to put myself in the middle of the chaos that is your life or Rob's."

"Then why the hell did you bring coffee?"

The counselor's mouth gapes. She's been asked a question for which she has no answer. "Because . . ." Her fine features contort and her gold-brown eyes pulse with a fiery flash. "Because you're not the only one who did impulsive things, or jumped to conclusions. When you told us about Theo, I was already angry because of your accusation about Rob and me. What took time, and a cooler head to process, is the bravery of what you did all those years ago."

"Bravery?"

"Yes. It's not something I could have pulled off given the circumstance. A lot of women would have chosen to end a pregnancy that no one around her supported . . . her then-husband or her parents. You also didn't put what you wanted first. Am I at all right here, Liv?"

"What difference could it possibly make at this point? Theo's a grown man."

"I think it makes a great deal of difference, acknowledging something you've denied since you told that lie in a hospital room. So I'm asking, Liv, in case no one else ever has: Did you want to be Theo's mother—all those years ago?"

I brush at a telltale tear, a sentiment that I have never done anything with but deny. I open my mouth, then close it. "More than you could imagine," I finally whisper.

And sometimes, a best friend knows you better than you know yourself.

A shaky sigh seeps from Sasha. "Yet you did what was right for Theo and even Sam Nash." Sasha pauses. "That's bravery, Liv, if no one has ever pointed it out."

I don't validate her conclusion; it only evokes feelings that after a lifetime of harsh judgments I find ill-fitting and uncomfortable. "Right," I finally say, so if anything Sasha will stop talking.

She doesn't.

"After the pissed-off part passed, I realized how you should be applauded for what you did all those years ago—even if there was some serious present-day fallout." We are quiet for a moment. "So don't make the same mistake twice. What do you want when it comes to Rob? For him to be gone from your life?"

I am quiet, trying to separate what I've earned from what I deserve from what I want. "I think maybe too much has happened for there to be any alternative. And even if we could fix it . . . Am I so different from the woman Rob had to *handle* for years? How long until we end up right back here, firing insults and barware at each other?"

"Did you really ever throw glasses at one another?"

While it sounds like a request for a clarification on exaggeration, I believe the counselor is asking a direct question. "No . . . Never really *at* one another, not that I recall."

"That said, you may be right about you and Rob. It may be unfixable." I feel deflated by the obvious. "But as for being the same woman Rob's *handled* . . . I don't think so. Erratic, volatile Liv . . . It's what you want people to see. What's sadder is you still want them to see it."

"I don't know what you're talking about."

A hum rings from her throat. "I hear there's an anonymously funded city-wide orchestra that's made it all the way to a state competition." My gaze darts to hers. Sasha smiles. "Rob let that one slip on purpose. Which 'Liv' do you want people to see, my friend? More importantly . . . Why?"

I ignore the mind-boggling part of her question. "Friend?" Sasha holds out a coffee cup. I accept. I pop open the lid and sip perfectly brewed coffee—black, two hits of artificial sweetener. Not a hint of poison. Friends it is. "I, um . . . I'm sorry, Sash. I'm sorry I thought you and Rob . . . My recent behavior, it's not exactly what the dating service promised all those years ago, is it?"

"They also didn't say there wouldn't be bumps. It'll make for a grand story on our fiftieth anniversary. Other than that, I don't know how to respond."

"Because you don't want to hear it?"

"Because as much as I appreciate it, conciliatory and contrite isn't your best look."

I glance at the legal documents that served as her ruse. "Do you want me to sign those?"

"Maybe you can sign them over dinner tonight."

"Like a date?"

"If you like." She pauses. "Though understand makeup sex is *not* going to happen."

"Right. It'd probably be the last complication you need between Jeremy and Zowz."

"Actually, I'm a free woman on that front. Jeremy was offered a stipend and six-month stay at some writers' colony in Florida. Key West—though I've no idea what that has to do with writing."

"Hemingway—never mind," I say. "Did he accept?"

"He was orgasmic about it. He left last Monday."

"And Zowz?"

She shifts her slim shoulders. "Not quite the same result. Burned itself out about a week before Christmas. I think the idea of us exchanging gifts was too much reality. But it ended on a friendly enough note. So, dinner?"

"You seem oddly anxious."

"If I seriously have to wait one more day to hear everything there is to know about the whole Theo McAdams story, I will burst."

"So this is no more than a desire to hear tawdry details, the high of salacious gossip?"

She widens her eyes. "Is there any other kind worth hearing?"

CHAPTER FORTY-THREE

Olivia

For such a rambling place this house has packed up quickly. Movers have been here for two days straight. Three days ago, while clearing out the back of a bedroom closet, I came across a violin case. The instrument inside belonged to my grandfather—the one he played during his Nazi imprisonment. I hadn't forgotten it; I could just never make peace with how it fit into my life. It sits now balanced on a cardboard box—one of dozens. In fact, the whole place is permeated with the odor of corrugated wood. I open the case, running my fingers over the dinged, crude, life-saving instrument. The gap between my grandfather's gift, his love of music, my father's perpetual disappointment, and mine—there's such discrepancy.

Finally, this seems to be changing. Theo made it change; I made it change. It's my plan to give the violin to Theo. No matter any right things I have done, it feels more earned for Theo and for David McAdams. I will tell Theo the story. How the simple violin saved his great-grandfather's life—and mine, ultimately his. How if you peer high enough into the branches of our family tree, it allowed Theo to be David McAdams's son. I think it's the kind of story he'll appreciate.

I hold the violin with far more reverence than I do the Guarneri. Picking up the tattered bow, I draw it across rigid strings. It's a fairly woeful noise. I keep playing anyway. From behind me there's a rush of cold air, then a voice. "Jesus, tell me your skill set hasn't deteriorated to a point where even I can't recognize it?"

I spin around. Rob is in the doorway of the brownstone. "You're here." Yesterday, I left a message on his cell, asking if he'd come by. He didn't return the call. I didn't know if he'd come.

Rob doesn't respond. His attention is fixed on the boxes, the obvious state of moving. "Liv? What have you done now?"

For a second, I can't speak. My heart thumps as inexplicable and jubilant as "The Mystic," Holst's last movement in *The Planets*. It's exquisitely hypnotic and impossible to explain. You simply have to listen, allow yourself to be taken in by the lure of the beautiful thing being offered to you. I take a deep breath and reach for bold courage. "I sold the brownstone."

"You . . ."

"Sold the brownstone. It was on the market for four hours—three bidders. Selling it took all of twenty-four hours. Sasha's working with the realtor to finalize it. I, um . . ." I stop and think, having attempted to employ good business strategy. Time is of the essence. "I didn't take the highest offer. I took the one that was a guaranteed cash offer."

"But you love the brownstone."

"I do. Oddly enough, I also took my mother's advice, though burning it to the ground seemed counterintuitive."

He peels his gaze off wall-to-wall cardboard. His blue-eyed stare lands on mine. "Eugenia," he says. "She said she'd burn the Wellesley house to the ground if it meant one more day with your father."

"She did. I . . . I'm hoping for more of a long-term plan. As for the brownstone," I say, glancing around. "It will repay your debt and then some. The Wellesley house is spared."

"So you sold it for me, to settle the golf course deal."

I shake my head. "I sold it for us."

"That's quite something, Liv. Generous to say the least." He draws a deep breath. "But let me guess. We're to never speak of it, no one is to know. Is that why you called, what you wanted to tell me?"

"Uh, no. Not exactly. Not at all really." The other things I have to tell Rob, they're proving harder than I anticipated, and I am quiet, tears welling.

"Us?" he says. It's as if my explanation is just hitting his ears. In reply, at least he's not turning for the door; instead, his face softens. *"Us . . ."* he repeats.

"Us," I say back. "Last time you left here you were angry, very angry." He doesn't disagree. A fear I've never felt shivers up my spine. "Are you still that angry? Are you still in the same place emotionally as the last time you left here? I need to know, and not just because I'd like a forwarding address."

"I had a lot of things to be angry about. Things you're not even aware of, Liv; things I've been doing my best to make peace with these past few weeks." I nod small, prepared for Rob to leave, to let him go if that's what will truly make him happy. He draws a deep breath. "But the fact that I'm here . . . It tells me a few things. Maybe things I couldn't even admit to myself until now."

"You . . . you want to be here?"

"Yes." His gaze bumps over the plethora of boxes. "It's not the homecoming setting I anticipated, but less the small stuff . . . like, I don't know, somewhere to sleep or put my rowing machine . . ." He looks back to me. "I want to be *here*."

"Could we . . ." I motion to the stairs. "Do you want to sit? I have some things to tell you." We settle in, hip to hip on the riser of one narrow stair and for a moment let the quiet settle in. "The first thing is about me. The second," I say, raising a brow, "is all about us."

"Sounds cryptic." He smiles nervously; I don't smile at all.

"These, uh . . . these last few months, for whatever has happened, it's also led me to a realization. No matter . . ." I breathe deep in the face of raw honesty. "No matter who a person is, it's almost impossible to see past . . . get past what they've been told their entire life. That their cumulative worth is based upon the success or failure of one thing. It's amazing how a person can end up despising that 'one thing.'"

"That being a violin?"

"That being the person with the gift to play it." From the corner of my eye, I see Rob nod. "A lifetime of living like that . . . It costs. It's enough to make that someone want to hide, shun anything that can be construed as *good*."

"Like a huge charitable effort or the infant she gave away . . . Maybe even the grown person that infant turned into."

"Or a man who sees what the woman refuses to acknowledge. She might be most careless and reckless with him, because she doesn't feel she deserves him." Rob remains quiet. He continues to sit with elbows on his knees, hands clasped. He's still wearing his wedding ring, and my breath catches as he spins it around his finger. I brace for some sort of ceremonial removal.

"I can't disagree," he finally says. "I would just say it's rather amazing that you've realized it. I . . ." He stops spinning the ring. "Even so, even if we had a home to go back to . . ." He shakes his head at the packed-up surroundings. "We can't go back to what we were, Liv. On the other hand, changing who we are together isn't necessarily what I'm after. I like that we're not the ordinary definition of a marriage . . . or even a relationship. It's more about you making peace with yourself—with your gifts and your imperfections. Believing that it's all good."

"Because you were able to make peace with all of me long ago."

He frowns, shaking his head. "No. Because I liked you and your imperfections from the start. You need to catch up."

"Why?"

"Why what?" he asks.

"Why me? I mean, I get the attraction." My knee bumps against his. "I get how our everyday lives complement each other. But why . . . *me*?"

"Because the bigger the risk the more I want it." Rob smiles. "You should know that." His smile, it's the kind of thing you'd miss terribly if it were to vanish permanently. It could be that I had this earmarked as future punishment for myself. "You make adrenaline pump in a way that has nothing to do with business, and everything to do with how a life should be lived. At least my life. That, um . . . that never happened to me before you." He waits a moment. "And you?"

This is the part where I retreat, to a violin, to anywhere that isn't associated with reward. "Secretly, you're the thing I've always wanted . . . *needed* most—somebody who appreciates my gift, but isn't fixated on it. Someone whose damage isn't greater than mine. Somebody . . ." I pull in a deeper breath. "Who I can I have this conversation with."

He clears his throat. "That's a pretty big compliment coming from you."

"Can we do that?"

"Do what exactly?"

"Have more conversations like this?"

In the tight hold of the stairs, in a house that is no longer ours, Rob curls his arm around my shoulder and pulls me closer. "We can try, Liv. We can definitely try."

"That's . . ." I vacillate for a moment, contemplating the thing Rob doesn't yet know. "That's good to hear. It will make the rest . . ." I shift, antsy and unsure. "It will make the big part of what I have to tell you a little easier."

"Bigger than this?" He points to our cardboard-crated possessions.

"Yes. Significantly bigger. Something you'll be surprised, but I hope glad, to hear."

"What's that?"

I twist toward him in the narrow grip of the steps, holding his gaze. "I'm pregnant."

"You're—"

"Pregnant." Rob's jaw slacks, but at least he doesn't pass out, which was on my short list of plausible reactions. "I know, right? Talk about coming from left field." Unlike twenty-seven years ago, I find I am not fearful but joyful over the prospect. "At first I thought it was more like the *change of life* thing. It is—just not quite *that* change. It took a while for me to even consider the possibility; I mean, who would have thought . . . And I haven't been paying particular attention to anything like that, I certainly wasn't anticipating—"

"Liv," he says abruptly, leaning back in the tight hold of the space. "How long . . . I mean, when do you think this, um, happened? You and I . . . we haven't slept together since . . . what? Sometime in November?"

"About then, but we definitely did. Right before you went to New York and everything kind of came apart."

He continues to stare. "Right before the library gala."

"Well, yes. I mean, I can't give you an exact date, but around then."

"Around the same time you spent the night at Sam's hotel."

"I suppose. But I told you . . . Sam even said we never . . ." I stop. "Rob?"

"Oh my God." He says it in staccato beats, as if a period follows each word. Letting go of my arm, he scrubs his hand over his face. "It would be impossible." He blinks into my eyes, his usual confident look downright dazed. "No. Actually, with you, Liv . . . I think it's perfectly plausible."

I smile crookedly, thinking I should have asked the movers to leave his Macallan unpacked. "What, exactly, are you rambling about?"

He takes the kind of breath I've been living on since he walked in, off balance and unsure. "Liv, I, um . . . I hate to trump your big news, but you need to know something. Something Sam Nash confessed to me the day I went with him to the ER."

EPILOGUE

Eight Months Later

Wellesley, Massachusetts

Olivia

I am in the kitchen of the Wellesley house—the architect has just left. I'm not looking forward to the demo, but the kitchen screams 1997, the last time it was renovated. It's a lot to take on in the whirlwind of changes that have come our way.

A woman dressed in kitty-covered scrubs comes through a hallway door. The door leads to a cluster of first-floor rooms dedicated to my mother. She moved into them last spring, when Rob and I moved into the house. Amelia is her companion caregiver. Memory slips attributed to a shoulder-shrug of age spiraled quickly, most noticeably after my mother attempted to board a flight to Bogota instead of Boston on her return home from Florida. Her dementia diagnosis has presented a stranger end of life scenario than my father's.

"She's napping," Amelia says. "I'm going to run to the drugstore while I can. Her meds need refilling."

I thank Amelia, who goes on her way. No matter my relationship with my mother, it's difficult to watch a woman, once so prideful and self-assured, succumb to something far worse than a trip to Vegas. It's one of many reasons we hired Amelia. Eugenia Klein has gone from random forgetfulness to a steady decline of the woman we knew. In the past month, she's taken to mistaking Rob for my father more often than not. More disturbing, she often hugs me, telling me how much she loves me—a piece of her brain desperate to mend our entire lives. I feel sympathy, though sadly my memories are too vivid, scars that cannot be erased at this late hour. The most I can hope to get out of this parent-child relationship is to learn from the mistakes—as noted, catharsis isn't always the answer.

Phillip's recent visit seemed to land my mother in a time warp, continually asking if he knew when his father would be home. While we don't know when, one day Southern-born Eugenia will slip beyond her cagey grasp on this life, like a spent magnolia flower falling silently from a tree of glossy leaves. But more likely she will be restored, reunited with my father on the other side, wherever married Jews and Christians go when they die, whatever the destination of two impeccably matched imperfect souls.

But Phillip's visit was not entirely odd and unhappy. He came to meet his nephews—or remeet the one he said hello and good-bye to on a sweltering January day, and the one born on an equally scorching day last August. By the time I gave birth to Robert James Van Doren the third, Rob and I shared many of those deeper husband and wife conversations. They were necessary and telling. Rob has amazed me by stepping up and stepping in, his grandest moments coming after an amniocentesis test. It was a routine procedure for a pregnant woman of my age, though this particular test was anything but. Among the many things it revealed, it told us that the baby was in perfect health and that it was a boy.

Days before the test, Sam had called. He'd relapsed again; he wanted to know if we would tell Theo. He was still trying to come to terms with what was likely a terminal diagnosis. While it was hard to hear, it gave Rob and me the perspective we were searching for, along with a roadmap as to how to proceed with our lives, Sam's life, and the baby's. A week after the test and Sam's call, Rob traveled to California to see him. I wasn't there—both Rob and I deciding the trip and stress was an unwise choice. I find it hard to fathom the conversation between Sam and Rob, even after my husband relayed the details. I suppose Rob's cool MO and ability to navigate tight spots was a plus that day.

Sam reiterated what he confessed to Rob in the emergency room on that late-fall Sunday afternoon: He lied to me about what happened between us in his hotel room, telling Rob that I wasn't to blame. He lied, he said, because it was the kindest thing he could think to do in the moment. Sam insisted that night was the actions of a lonely man, who knew his fate was inevitable. He desperately longed for a connection that mattered, more so than memorabilia and being idolized by strangers—something Sam said he didn't figure out until it was simply too late. It was that, and maybe a fortuitous feeling Sam had about what that night would produce. When Rob got to his point, telling Sam about the amniocentesis, he was stunned—by the result, by one last possible note of hope in his waning life. The baby was Sam's, and, yes, this son was the half match that Theo was not.

Sadly, it was hope that did not survive to fruition.

Theo flew to California later in the spring to spend time with Sam. He was at his bedside when he passed away on a rainy May morning. I believe both men were grateful for the time together. Sam did not die alone, and while Theo did lose another father, he found solace in simply being there, in the quiet setting of Sam's bedroom, able to hold his hand and offer comfort in this father's last moments. It was so very different, perhaps even *cathartic*, allowing Theo an alternative memory to David McAdams's death.

As for myself, there is of course loss, but Sam had been more absent than present in my life, and like all the memories connected to him, I have given it proper context. What you feel for someone at twenty-one is often so incredibly different from what you know and what you need decades later. Sam was a critical component of my past; he shaped my future. I will always be indebted to him for this.

The Angels happened to be in Boston the day Sam died. Rob and I went to the game in his honor. "So," I said, the two of us sitting in box seats, the price of which made my eyes bug, "this is Fenway Park?" He laughed and fans around us playfully (I think) jeered as we rooted for the other team—Sam's team. Miraculously, I made it through all nine innings. Through glassy tears, I observed the Angels closing pitcher, Rob explaining that this would have been Sam's job. "The game's almost over," I said. "They seriously paid him millions of dollars to play for ten minutes?" No wonder the arts are so highly undervalued. But I watched, mesmerized, the pitcher's frame similar to Sam's and, at enough of a distance, I could see him. I swear I heard him whisper in my ear: *"Watch this pitch, Livy . . . This is what it's all about . . . Mounting tension and the fate of the game . . . Everything's in your hands . . . Stare down the batter . . . Steal a glance toward first . . . Check your signs . . . And . . ."* From the moans around us and the jubilation of the Angels pitcher, I like to believe Sam had something to say in that win.

In the Wellesley kitchen, I look at the baby now, who does not stir, not even when a dog barks. A baby gate that we don't yet need for the baby keeps Harmony—a rescued King Charles spaniel mix—sequestered in the laundry room. I open the gate and he sprints through. The doorbell chimes and Harmony barks again. I shush him—a habit we've been working on.

Amazingly, the baby remains asleep. He is tight-fisted and beautiful, perched in his carrier on the soon-to-be-demolished kitchen counter. The bell rings again, and Harmony and I hurry to the front door; the architect must have forgotten something. I smile at the unexpected presence of Theo, who immediately bends down to greet the dog. We are at the point where a drop-in visit is not surprising. We make our way to the kitchen, where I offer him hot tea. On his ring finger is a shiny wedding band, he and India having just returned from a honeymoon trip to Italy. Rob and I had so many good things to say about our trip, they decided they wanted to experience it for themselves.

In the kitchen, Theo accepts the tea. As always, he's awestruck by the baby. We all are—no one more so than Rob. It could have gone a lot of ways, but not unlike my father's death, Rob has chosen to remain my champion in life. He's embraced fatherhood with the utmost grace, at Sam's earnest request, and with my deepest gratitude. Rob has even extended his breadth of responsibility by taking a State Street job with a financial firm, giving up the fast lane of more volatile investments. It appears to be a reliable mix of risk and reward, and mostly with other people's money.

Theo and I talk for a bit about his trip, and he says that he and India will bring pictures when they come for dinner on Saturday. He forgot them at Claire's last Sunday. As for her comeuppance, sometimes it's best to let nature take its course. Eventually, Theo told her about my existence and Sam's. Since then, I have watched Claire struggle with the delicate balance of sharing her son. No moment was sweeter than when the groom made a toast at his wedding reception, to both his mothers. Honestly? If Claire's gritted smile had been any tighter, she would have chipped a perfectly aligned tooth. Living a faultless life is a high bar, and one Claire can gladly keep.

Theo updates me on India's master's program and segues to talk about his Boston Conservatory students. Bo-Co welcomed Theo's proposal, particularly after he secured his own funding for Braemore students. Sam found the right person to leave his money to, and Theo has worked closely with Rob in determining secure and worthy endowments. In addition to this, Theo oversees a trust, set aside for Jamie's future. I watch Rob and Theo together, and sometimes I think my son has found a third father. In these instances, my heart flutters, hoping for all our sakes Rob lives to a spry one hundred and five. However far I make it, honoring what Rob has done for me—well, I will never lose sight of it again. As for Theo's inheritance, his first official contribution was to our charitable orchestra effort, the details of which I proudly shared with him late last winter.

In turn, Sam and Theo's generosity allows the Wellesley house to stay in the Klein family, now and in the future. It's no longer necessary that its value be earmarked as a future asset. My mother will remain here too, just as my father willed years ago. It's the right thing to do. Theo has no formal relationship with my mother, her illness too far gone to allow her to grasp the complex sudden appearance of a grandson she did not want. When in a room together, she will smile at Theo and he will smile back. Once she said, "You smile just like my daughter." As only Theo would, he replied, "Is that right? I hear she's smiling a lot more these days."

He is right.

Sipping his tea, Theo asks if I miss the symphony, which I left months before Jamie was born. Not yet, but maybe one day—when he is older. If I ever do desire a chair again, it won't be out of demand or spite. It will be because it's what I want. We both smile at baby Jamie. Rob and I took a cue from David McAdams when it came to names. Rob was adamant about not wanting inherent things to have too much effect on his son's life. I know he's right about this.

Finally the baby stirs. He doesn't cry but blinks widely into the bright room. Theo draws closer, letting the baby clutch his index finger. He's too young to produce a smile of recognition, but soon he will smile when he opens his eyes to Theo, to all of us. Theo glances between me and the baby. "He's grown a lot in two weeks."

"Has he?" I say. "I guess you don't see it when you're looking at him twenty-four seven."

"Probably not." Theo's quiet. His face grows contemplative, though he smiles, looking between Jamie and me. "You know, it's funny. His eyes were so blue when India and I left on our trip."

I am cued to the thing I have not yet shared with Jamie's brother. It's something Rob and I needed to find our way with first. "Babies' eye color often changes," I say. "That's what all the books indicate anyway." I walk around to where Theo stands and admire my sons. He's right. The baby's eyes are clearly brown—it seems to have happened almost overnight.

"Liv?"

"What?"

"You and Rob, you both have blue eyes."

I smile at Theo, who offers a hesitant look. "Interesting," I say cautiously, "isn't it?"

Theo's brown irises meet the blue of mine. "I'd say so. It, um . . . it kind of makes me think back to an old biology class. The dark color," he says, looking into eyes that look very much like his. "Two blue-eyed parents can't produce a brown-eyed child."

"Of course they can. It's just perspective, Theo. Rob agrees—in fact, he insists." I begin a conversation that will lead to the best-fitting conclusion, something he is sure to understand. "Tell me something, Theo?" I say, scooping the baby from his carrier. "Did David McAdams love you any less because your eyes were brown?"

ACKNOWLEDGMENTS

Readers might be surprised to know how many people it takes to "write" a book. While the words are mine, the Montlake effort goes pages deep, starting with editor Alison Dasho. She's not only lovely to work with and book smart, but she is always willing to have a conversation and has a wonderful sense of humor—never underestimate a sense of humor in publishing. Quite simply, she rocks. My sincere thanks to Charlotte Herscher, my developmental editor. She has an incredible gift for interpreting all facets of a story, big and small, and conveying her thoughts and ideas in a way that truly resonates with the author.

The Montlake team goes on with a huge thank-you to marketing and publicity, especially Jessica Poore, Author Relations—insightful and quick with a reply to any question. Many thanks to copyeditor, Hannah Buehler; she did an exceptional job but was particularly adept at keeping track of my musical references and ultimately doing my math for me. Overall, thank you to everyone at Montlake who plucked a string in *Unstrung*.

As always, much appreciation to my literary agent, Susan Ginsburg. It continues to be my privilege to be a part of the esteemed literary agency that is Writers House; thank you to Stacy Testa as well.

Research for *Unstrung* took me in many directions, including a tour of the Boston Public Library, Massachusetts General Hospital, and an icy winter trip to the Boston Symphony Orchestra. Sincere thanks goes to Rictor Noren, Chamber Music Faculty at the Boston Conservatory, renowned violinist, and strings educator. His insights were key to shaping Olivia's talent and bringing into focus the inner workings of an orchestral setting. Gratitude as well to YouTube sensation Jeremy Green. This Berklee College of Music rising star was generous and thoughtful with his musical knowledge and talents. Go watch his videos; you'll be amazed!

The professional list continues with Amir Fathi, MD, hematologist-oncologist, practicing in Boston. He graciously allowed me to invade his busy schedule, helping me understand the complexities of myeloid leukemia. Thanks also to Maura Blaney, administrative assistant to Dr. Fathi; she was instrumental in facilitating our communication.

Unstrung meant another round of calls and e-mails to Jennifer Lehman, Senior Deputy District Attorney, Schuylkill County, Pennsylvania. I'm not sure if she cringes or laughs when messages start out "I need to know what the charge would be for . . ." But I'm grateful that she always makes herself available to assist with my characters' legal woes.

Much love and appreciation to Melisa Holmes; it made me extremely happy to dedicate this book to her, someone who has always understood all the things that make me a little "unstrung." Friends and first readers continue with my critique partner, Karin Gillespie—a brilliant writer, who has an exceptional reader's eye. Her input makes an arduous process not only manageable but hopeful. Special thanks to authors Barbara Davis, Laura Drake, Liz Fenton, Kerry Lonsdale, Ellyn Oaksmith, Holly Robinson, Lori Nelson Spielman and Lisa Steinke. Double special thanks to author Barbara Claypole White for her heartfelt quote of praise and for helping to craft *Unstrung*'s cover blurb before she read the book—that's creativity! Steve Bennett, Dan Gusovsky, Laura Essex, members of the Girlfriends Book Club, and the Wednesday night critique group—they all lent a positive vibe during the writing of *Unstrung*.

Readers and bloggers! I want to thank readers who have supported my books starting with *Beautiful Disaster*, and those who are new to my novels since *Ghost Gifts*. I've come to count on so many thoughtful people, who don't just read my books, but cheer me on during the writing process and go on to make recommendations to friends and book clubs, or tag me in one of those Facebook posts that asks: "What are you reading this weekend?" It'd be too difficult to single anyone out, but please know how much your book enthusiasm and friendship means to me. Bloggers are equally important to every author, and I have benefited greatly from their reviews and reader reach over the years.

My father did not get to see this book to print; but he left knowing precisely how I arrived at any ability to tell a story—thanks, Daddy. The people at home are always last on this page, but really they're first. If not for the grounded family I live with—Matt, Megan, Jamie, and Grant—I would never be afforded the opportunity to spend so much time with my imagination.

BOOK CLUB QUESTIONS

1. Clearly, Olivia was greatly affected by her parents, and their expectations for her. Do you think this made her a truly difficult person, or someone who was easily misunderstood by others?
2. Who is the most selfish character in the novel? Who is the most selfless and why?
3. Who is the most honest character in the novel? Who is the least honest and why?
4. Throughout the novel, who or what has the greatest influence over Olivia: Rob, Sasha, Sam, her parents, Olivia's own emotions, Olivia's talent, or something else?
5. Is there a hero in *Unstrung*? Would you categorize the novel as a romance?
6. Olivia is clearly drawn to different personality traits in Rob and Sam. How does Rob differ from Sam, and was he ultimately the right choice for Olivia?
7. Was Olivia justified in her secrecy about Theo? Did you see her actions as deliberate or the unintentional fallout of her chaotic life?
8. Do you think that overall Claire was a good mother to Theo? Would he have been a whole different person if Olivia and Sam had raised him?

9. Did you agree or disagree with Sasha's conclusion that what Olivia did years ago regarding baby Theo was brave? If anything, what should she have done differently?
10. Later in the novel, Olivia makes this observation, "Even so, I think it's important to realize what you feel for someone at twenty or twenty-one, it's so powerful, so intense. It looks magical compared to what comes along at thirty . . . or even thirty-nine." . . . "It's a turn youth allows. Everybody gets one. But I don't know that it's sustainable—at least not for me." Do you agree or disagree with the protagonist's thoughts?
11. To what degree is music a metaphor throughout this book? Did the author's use of Holst's *The Planets* help or hinder your understanding of Olivia's emotions?
12. Did you have sympathy for Sam's confession to Rob about what really happened in the hotel room?
13. Did the ending surprise you? Considering the collision of circumstances that take place toward the end of the novel, did Rob and Olivia make the right choices?
14. What will happen to baby Jamie in the future? Did Olivia and Rob grow enough as characters to provide a happy and healthy environment for him?

ABOUT THE AUTHOR

Laura Spinella is the author of the #1 Kindle bestseller *Ghost Gifts*, soon to be a trilogy. Book two is coming in 2017! In addition to her latest work, *Unstrung*, she's penned the award-winning novels *Beautiful Disaster* and *Perfect Timing*. She also writes romantic suspense, featuring the Clairmont Series Novels, under the pen name L. J. Wilson. Spinella currently lives in the Boston area with her family, where she can always be found writing her next novel. She loves to hear from readers; visit her at www.lauraspinella.net and www.ljwilson.com.